A Date with Desire

Heather McGovern

LYRICAL SHINE
Kensington Publishing Corp.
www.kensingtonbooks.com

LYRICAL SHINE BOOKS are published by

Kensington Publishing Corp.
119 West 40th Street
New York, NY 10018

First Electronic Edition: December 2016
eISBN-13: 978-1-60183-838-4
eISBN-10: 1-60183-838-7

First Print Edition: December 2016
ISBN-13: 978-1-60183-839-1
ISBN-10: 1-60183-839-5

Printed in the United States of America

To Jim, for being the kind of father everyone needs and deserves.

ACKNOWLEDGMENTS

Many thanks to the following people:

My critique partners and executive committee; Jeanette Grey, Elizabeth Michels, and Laura Trentham, for making this story what it is and for being the most eclectic pep squad ever.

The Bad Girlz at *Bad Girlz Write,* for saving my sanity and accepting me for me.

My editor, John Scognamiglio, for believing in my stories.

My agent, Nicole Resciniti, for the guidance, support, and enthusiasm.

My family, for their love and laughter.

And Sebastian, for his face.

ICE CREAM ... AND KISSES

Holding up his spoon, Dev circled a delicious-looking mound of blueberry ice cream under her nose. "I'll let you try mine if you let me have more of yours."

She lowered her lashes, a slow glance at his offering. "You're on."

As he lifted the ice cream she touched his hand, wrapping her lips around the spoon.

The cheesecake was rich and sweet, the blueberries slightly tart, and it tasted like absolute heaven. Anna closed her eyes and moaned over the bite.

"Told you."

"You did." She spoke with her mouth full. "What can I say? I'm hardheaded."

He shook his head. "You know what you want. Nothing wrong with that."

She had no clue what she wanted out of life anymore, but she was sure of one thing. She wanted Devlin to kiss her again . . .

Books by Heather McGovern

A MOMENT OF BLISS

A DATE WITH DESIRE

Published by Kensington Publishing Corporation

Chapter 1

Looking at the Bradley brothers was like staring into the sun. A beautiful, blue-eyed sun, so big and bright the sight hurt a little, but Anna still studied them with a sharp eye as they buzzed around the check-in area.

They were all tall, hair the color of rich coffee, and in the kind of rugged shape that came from working in the mountains. The family photo on the resort's website didn't do them justice, especially not the rakish-looking one in the corner.

He was more like a sun god.

A sun god, sent to whisk a weary traveler like her away from the ever-tightening grip of big-city reality. Pamper her with luxury and cater to her every whim and wish.

Good Lord, she was word-vomiting in ad copy.

Her brain whirred on high-speed work mode when she was supposed to be checking into the Honeywilde Inn and Resort to relax and recover.

Her therapist was right. The time had come. She either took a break or had another breakdown. The choice was hers.

"You'll be in Cabin Five," one of the other Bradley brothers said. His shiny name badge announced him as Roark Bradley, General Manager. "Trevor will show you the way up. Cabin Five sits at the highest point on the property." He turned to who she guessed was the youngest of the three. "Trev, take my truck and have Ms. Martel follow you. Five can be tricky to find until you know your way around."

While he murmured to Trevor about offering to help with her luggage and watching the steep bend in the last turn, the third brother stepped out of his corner.

Devlin Bradley, Hospitality Manager, his name badge read.

Devil Bradley might be more fitting.

The slow, sly drag of his gaze up her body, from the tips of her toes to the sunglasses stuck on her head, would be lewd if he didn't look so adorable trying to hide it.

Arms crossed over his body, he leaned against the reception desk and scratched along his temple, checking her out around the side of his hand and in between his fingers.

Smooth.

All of this, she noticed from the corner of her eyes because she was *not* checking him out too. But, if she were checking him out, she'd say he was easily the handsomest of the three.

No, handsome wasn't right. His brother, the manager, was handsome.

Devlin was sexy.

Tall and filled out, he was still a little leaner than his brothers. His dark hair was too long on top to be considered professional, eyes hooded like he'd recently woken from a post-sex nap, and a jawline that'd make any model jealous. Broody, in a classic James Dean sense, but with a hint of boyish charm.

He was the type they hired to advertise trendy clothing lines, and she was half tempted to call her office and let them know.

But she was not working right now. She was supposed to be on vacation.

Just a woman, on vacation, admiring a good-looking guy as he proceeded to fake cough so she'd look in his direction.

Anna pinched her lips together to keep from smiling.

Devlin was tempting, no doubt a handful, and she couldn't deal with any of that at the moment.

Taking a break from her burgeoning career, leaving her job in the lurch, that was enough to handle. Following her therapist's advice of rest, recovery, and "participating in the process of grief" would likely prove too much.

She had no room in her vacation for blue-eyed devils, she sucked at relaxing, and the process of grief could take a flying leap off this mountain.

"Are you all set, ma'am?" The youngest Bradley straight up ma'am-ed her as he walked by.

Fantastic.

With a smile that weighed more than her luggage, she nodded. "I'm ready if you are."

Trevor Bradley, his name badge stated, bounded toward the front door and she turned to follow. But her gaze snagged with Devlin's.

She meant to look away. Follow the harmless Bradley who would lead the way to her cabin.

If she had, she would've avoided the sensuous curl of Devlin's lips, the flicker of interest. She returned his smile, unwittingly, and that got all of his attention.

His smile spread wider, revealing perfect white teeth, and an all-too-knowing look in his eyes.

Heat rushed up the back of her neck, pinpricks dancing across her skin.

Encouraging him was a horrible idea, but her physical reaction was even worse. Whether she admitted it or not, her body knew what was up.

Devlin Bradley was all kinds of hot, and his being the last thing she needed to tangle with right now only made him hotter.

If his lingering looks were any indication, he didn't think she was too shabby either.

Anna turned on the heels of her wedge sandals and got the heck out of there.

By the time she left the lobby of the Honeywilde inn, the back of her neck was on fire. Hopefully her hair hid everything, because once it flared up, her skin would be cherry-red back there.

Trevor led the way to Cabin Five in a big black pickup truck, the wheels of her Lexus spinning a couple of times as she tried to keep up on the curvy incline.

Her car wasn't made for off-road mountain driving. *She* wasn't made for off-road mountain driving, but she'd been told to choose a vacation at a legitimate resort *or* one of those "retreats." The ones where she'd be in therapy and meditation all day because she couldn't cope with what life dealt her.

No, thanks.

She'd opted for the first appealing vacation spot that'd popped up on her Google search for "upscale North Carolina mountain get-aways."

If she was going to take time away from work, it had to be the mountains. Maybe then she would stop putting off her responsibility.

But "upscale" meant she wouldn't wind up in a pup tent or a cabin with no running water.

Honeywilde boasted peace and quiet, lovely strolls around the lake, hiking, delicious dining, legendary sunsets, and a warm, luxurious atmosphere.

Sold, she'd booked into one of their private cabins immediately, for two-and-a-half weeks.

Take my money, she'd thought. *Just please don't let me fall apart.*

The black pickup stopped in front of a sturdy log cabin; a covered porch stretched across the front with two Adirondack chairs and two rockers.

A little sign post at the bottom of the stairs read: *Cabin Five: Highpoint Escape.*

Escape. "Perfect." She popped the trunk of her car.

Before she could get out, Trevor was at the back, unloading both of her suitcases.

"I've got it." He pulled out the shoulder bag as well, but Anna took the bag from his hands. That one was precious. "I'll get this." She played it off. "I know my two suitcases aren't light."

Had she over-packed? Probably. But did she have any idea what a person needed to pack for a vacation in the mountains? Absolutely not.

The weather could be hot or cold, dry or damp. Was dinner at Honeywilde dressy or casual? Did she need hiking boots *and* sneakers? Until yesterday, she didn't own hiking boots.

Now she did.

Along with something called a rope bag and a pair of god-awful shoes one was supposed to wear in the river. As if she had plans to walk in the river.

The salesman at the outdoor store swore she'd need all of it. He'd known a sucker as soon as he saw her.

All that remained in the trunk was her train case, full of cosmetics, toiletries, and a bottle of Xanax she'd refused to crack open—so far. Anna grabbed the case and her purse and hurried after Trevor.

Once he'd off-loaded her things, he wished her an awesome stay, and took off, leaving her all alone, in her Highpoint Escape.

"Well. Here we are," she said, doing a slow three-sixty in the middle of the cabin's den, her announcement met with silence.

A two-foot-tall bear, carved out of wood, stared back from beside the fireplace.

He was cute, but fat chance of him responding.

When she was six or seven, her father brought her to North Carolina to see the bears. She'd been terrified, but he'd assured her everything was safe. The bear cubs were cute, the momma bear not so much.

Anna grabbed her phone to take a picture. Her dad would get such a kick out of the bear statue.

The phone suddenly turned to a block of cement in her hand, the picture on the lock screen shaking before she tossed it back in her purse.

Her father was gone. She could no longer send him anything. No funny picture, no one-line comments that only he would appreciate.

She sank to the arm of the sofa, the wave of sadness like gravity.

She'd asked her therapist, Susan, about inviting a friend or boyfriend to join her on her break, phrasing the question as though she had a boyfriend or knew anyone willing to put their life on hold to go away to the mountains with her.

In her mind, she'd figured a traveling companion would make the time more enjoyable. Distract her from loss and the ripple effect that was ruining her life.

Susan's answer was a hard-and-fast no.

The point of her time off was to focus on herself, not others, no distractions, so she could overcome her denial of grief, reflect, and yadda-yadda-something about actualization. Anna was supposed to be taking the time to think about what she wanted out of life and how she'd function in this "new normal."

God, if she never heard that term again it'd be wonderful.

She carefully set her shoulder bag on the coffee table and made herself get up and look around. Missing her father was not going to dissolve into wallowing again.

She'd already tried that, and it didn't help.

The one-bedroom, one-bath cabin turned out to be as lovely as the pictures on the website. Everything was on one level except the loft-style bedroom; the floors were rich hardwoods, the windows big, and no over-the-top moose- or bear-themed décor. Minus the one cute bear guarding the fireplace.

Tastefully decorated in neutrals and warm apricot accents, exactly how she would've set up a log cabin—if she happened to own one.

Except—

She peered into the bathroom.

If Cabin Five were her place, she probably would've remembered one *very* important detail.

Nice Jacuzzi tub, a porcelain pedestal sink, and the toilet looked shiny and clean.

And completely without a seat.

"That is not going to work," she announced to the cabin.

How the heck did you forget a toilet seat?

Then again, if three brothers ran the place, toilet seats probably didn't top their priorities.

Normally she'd unpack first and worry about it later, but later might be too late, and she was here to visit the mountains in style, not cop a squat in the woods.

Flipping through the handy binder by the phone, she found the number for guest services. It rang only once before somebody answered.

"Thank you for calling Honeywilde. How may I be of service?"

Good Lord, the voice on him.

Deep and warm, raspy as if recently overused, with a Southern accent slightly thicker than the ones she heard in Atlanta. The way the words dripped from his lips made the question sound pornographic.

She'd bet anything, with nothing more to go on than a voice, she was talking to Devlin.

"Hello. May I help you?" His voice filled her ear, making goose bumps ripple down her arms.

"Yes. Hi. This is Cabin Five."

"Ms. Martel," he said, before she could get any further. "Are you settling in okay?"

"Um . . ." No. She wasn't settled at all, now that he'd purred in her ear, thank you very much. "Yes, everything is great, but there's one tiny problem. In the bathroom, there's no toilet seat."

Silence ruled for a few beats, then, "You're kidding." His voice remained phone sex material, but the dry note of wit made her smile.

"No. I wish I was."

"I am so sorry." Embarrassment and urgency replaced the drawl. "We'll have someone over there immediately."

"Thank you." Hanging up, she realized she was still smiling. Smiling about a missing toilet seat.

When she opened the door to the cabin a few minutes later, the reason why was confirmed.

"Sorry again about the missing seat, but I'm here to take care of it." Devlin's eyes crinkled at the outer edges. In one hand, he held a boxed and wrapped toilet seat, in the other dangled a tool belt. "At the start of the summer season we replace a lot of things and, unfortunately, your toilet seat was overlooked."

"I understand. Come on in." Lord help her, what if he put on that tool belt?

She stepped aside to let him in, and he headed straight through the den and past the kitchen.

As he reached the short hall, he jerked to a stop as if catching himself. "I'm Devlin, by the way. I didn't get to introduce myself earlier."

No, but he'd made quite the impression anyway.

"I'm Anna. Nice to meet you. Officially." For lack of knowing what else to do, and since his hands were full of tool belt and toilet seat, she gave him a slow, wide wave.

Because sometimes she was a giant goober.

"You too." The impish smile on his full lips made her breath catch.

Then he was gone, ducked into the bathroom.

Heat skittered up her neck again, and it wouldn't do. If she let her nervous reaction get out of control, she'd be all blotchy and itchy.

A super-attractive look.

Once a stranger had asked if she was allergic to peanuts or shellfish or something. Nope. Just her body hated her.

She hung back in the hall, furiously fanning her neck.

"My brother, Trev, was supposed to check the cabins for final inspection. We don't use them during the winter, and early spring they're rarely booked, so . . ." The clank of tools drifted down the hall. He was definitely putting on the tool belt.

She fanned faster.

"You might be our first guest up here this year."

Carefully, she moved closer to the bathroom door. On the one hand, she did not need to see him being handy and stuff, doing things with wrenches and whatever. But on the other hand, she couldn't go the entire rest of her life having not checked out the tool-belt situation.

"This shouldn't take but a minute. Is everything else okay with the cabin? Or have you even had a chance to check?" The rough edge in his voice soothed her senses, like someone gently scratching her back.

Before she bothered to look inside, she leaned against the wall outside the bathroom to listen to him talk. "Everything else is fine. The cabin is great, you know, besides the toilet. I can't wait to take a walk and have a look around. See what else is here." She rolled out the idea, hoping he'd offer suggestions, elaborate. Anything. As long as he kept talking.

"You checked in at a great time. The sun should set after a while, perfect for catching the colors during a stroll. You have a good view from your front porch, but the best view is at the main inn on the veranda, and you'd still have enough time to make it back here before dark."

Her toes curled in her wedges. A long walk near sunset sounded ideal, or maybe it was the way he said it.

Finally ready, she leaned in the doorway to find Devlin, tool belt on, squatted down and leaned over, jeans pulled tight around thick thighs, messing with something on the wall behind the toilet.

Wrong. She wasn't ready at all.

Who had legs like that? Long and solid looking, like he could hold a girl's weight if he had her up against the—oh good gosh, she was being a perv.

"The supply line is loose. Tightening it up while I'm down here."

"Uh-huh."

"Oh. Hey." He jerked up, probably not expecting her to be all up in the doorway while he worked on a toilet.

She should say something. Quick. Before this got weird.

"So . . ." *What to say, what to say?*

Her line of sight, and therefore thought, was full of Devlin and blue jeans and *Wow*, and toilets. None of it made for appropriate small talk.

"Food," the word fell out of her mouth.

Of course she came up with food. Now she was smooth too. "I have my own kitchen in the cabin, but I doubt I'll have time to make it to a grocery store today. Doesn't the main inn have a restaurant?" She knew the inn had a restaurant; she'd already picked out the first thing she wanted to order from looking at the menu online. And possibly the second and third.

"We have an outstanding restaurant. Hold that thought." He leaned over again, doing something with a wrench that did delicious things to the muscles in his shoulders and back. Masking nothing, the thin gray T-shirt he wore clung to him, highlighting the dip of his spine, making her fingers itch to touch.

They were supposed to be talking about food. Her neck burned and she fanned it, quickly, while he was distracted.

As bleak as her sex life already was, for over half a year now her desire for anything had gone ice-cold. With no interest, she hadn't even looked twice at a guy. She hadn't read a book past page two, gone shopping except for this trip, or done anything other than work.

Nothing sent that zip of excitement through her body; nothing held her attention for longer than five minutes, so she'd buried herself in her job, more so than before.

Then that had fallen apart too. Her creativity, the flair that made her one of the top execs at the agency—gone.

But now, awareness danced across her skin. Her limbs tingled with anticipation, like coming up with the perfect pitch for a sales campaign—or seeing a gorgeous guy, in well-fitting blue jeans, bent over and doing some plumbing.

"There." Once he shoved the wrench in its spot on the belt, he stood with a groan.

Mercy, he shouldn't have though.

The belt sat low on his hips, accentuating a narrow waist and flat stomach.

Maybe her desire wasn't as cold as she'd thought. Maybe she'd merely lacked the proper stimulus. Because right now, every part of her body was on high alert.

Normally, the first twinge of enjoying life was followed immediately by a pang of regret. A knot of guilt in the center of her chest. Her therapist said the reaction was normal when dealing with loss.

Normal didn't make it any more bearable.

Anna waited on the pang, but nothing yet.

"Do you mind?" Devlin asked.

He'd caught her gawking. Of course he had. She was being so obvious, Pluto would notice. Her sophistication and manners had gone right out the window, and all it took was blue eyes and blue jeans.

Wasn't there a song about that? She'd have to look it up later. Except she didn't have her laptop and her phone was restricted use only. Dear god, she was word-vomiting in her head again.

His rumbling chuckle brought her back. "Is it okay?" he asked again.

When she looked up, he was indicating toward the sink. As in, did she mind if he washed his hands.

"*Oh*. No, no. Go ahead."

He washed up, and she tried to look away, she really did. Yet, she didn't.

"I highly recommend you try the restaurant," he finally said, turning to her, thumbs hooked into the tool belt.

He had to be doing it on purpose. No way was anyone this attractive, this potent, without actually working their butt off to be so.

"Not only tonight though. You need to eat there for breakfast, without question, and lunch too. As a matter of fact, I can recommend a grocery store for quick food on hand, but you'll want to dine with us at Bradley's pretty much any opportunity you get. You won't regret it." Another smile, the corners of his mouth curling up like a promise.

Anna found herself leaning against the frame of the door for support. "You make a convincing case."

"I try." He moved to get past her, and he was inches away before she realized she blocked his path.

"Sorry." She backed into the hall until the heel of her shoes hit the baseboard.

"Don't be." He followed, stopping so he stood right in front of her.

Silence lingered, filling the cabin with a quiet tension. Electric.

Something was happening, though she was lost as to what exactly.

When she was ten years old, her father took her to Caesars Head, and they'd gone way out on the big rock. They didn't go to the very edge, but Anna had still felt the pull of vertigo. The downdraft of the mountain winds. The call of the edge, luring her to go over.

The exact same sensation blew over her, standing in the small hallway with Devlin.

He didn't hide his slow study of her. His gaze, like a lover's touch, brushed her face, down her neck, pausing in the vee of her shirt. Heat spread out from the point of his focus, slipping down, between her legs, making her squeeze them together.

She knew that look. It had to be identical to the one she'd given him while he was crouched on the bathroom floor. The difference being, he hadn't been aware of her hungry stare, but boy, was she ever aware of his.

Too much time had gone by since a man had looked at her like that. The needle-toed dancers were back at her neck, twirling and tapping in tiny hot steps, her whole body lighting up.

If, with one look, Devlin had this effect on her, what would happen if he touched her?

Chapter 2

He ought to get the hell out of that cabin. Too bad he had no interest in leaving.

The toilet was fixed and his presence was no longer required at Cabin Five, but his feet refused to carry him to the door.

His feet, along with every other part of him—except maybe his better judgment—wanted to stay right here, inches away from Anna Martel, with her rosy sweet smile and wicked brown eyes. Luscious curves and whatever was happening with her neck.

Flirting with her was an absolute no, according to Honeywilde policy, but he couldn't resist lingering. What would it hurt to pursue the interest a little? She was checking him out too, and while the splotches of pink on her neck made her appear bashful, the greedy way she eyed him told a totally different story.

Besides, a little mutual acknowledgment of attraction never hurt anybody. Chemistry is good for morale.

"Do you do all the handiwork around the resort?" Anna reached up, touching the tips of her fingers to her neck.

Her nails were a shiny crimson and the color had him instantly envisioning those red-tipped hands all over his body.

"Some." Heat and need spread through his body, and he could *not* be thinking thoughts like that and manage to remain a proper gentleman. He was lousy at the whole proper thing anyway. "When my younger brother forgets to do his job. I can fix pretty much anything, so I get roped in because I'm good with my hands."

Her dark gaze flitted away.

Seeing Anna in the lobby of Honeywilde had been like seeing a silver-screen siren in the middle of the toolshed. Way beyond unexpected, it'd been a shock to his system.

They had beautiful women in the mountains. Plenty of them. He'd taken about half of them out on dates, but they weren't like Anna.

Casual and laid-back reigned supreme up here. A natural vibe, without a lot of fuss.

Here he'd thought Roark's girlfriend, Madison, was fancy, in her suits and pulled-up hair, but Anna was altogether different and not only in appearance. She was a big-city girl, no question.

Her words were perfectly pronounced, with not a whiff of an accent. Expensive luggage sat in the cabin's den, and the sleek black car outside screamed sales or attorney or some other high-and-mighty job. With dark hair that fell to her shoulders and a pair of designer sunglasses still stuck on top of her head, she covered her generous curves in fitted black pants, black top, and black shoes to match. With all that black, she ought to radiate urban cynicism and acidity.

But she didn't.

She looked as worked up and flustered as he felt. Her eyes held as much unmasked interest as his surely did. She studied him, then looked away. Staring, then away.

He'd have to say something, or they'd likely stand in the hallway until sundown.

"Where are you from?" Devlin went with a safe-option icebreaker.

Anna was a guest after all and, regardless of the roving his eyes were doing and how much he didn't want to leave, he had to stay between the lines. That meant polite topics and keeping his hands close to himself.

"Atlanta."

Ding, ding, ding. Big city. He knew it. "Anna from Atlanta."

A smile tugged at her pink lips. "But I'm originally from outside of Charlotte. Fort Mill."

That's—not what he'd expected. "Fort Mill isn't far from here. Couple of hours or so?"

"Almost exactly. That's home, I guess."

"You could go by while you're up here, if you have the time."

"I know." Her mouth pulled down at the corners, a fog of sadness surrounding her as she glanced away again. "I probably should."

Devlin scowled at the downer that came out of nowhere. All because of her hometown? "Or not. You're on vacation. You get to do whatever you want."

"Yeah." A line formed between her arched brows, plush mouth pulled down. Her focus wasn't on him; it wasn't on the cream-colored walls. She'd gone a million miles away in two seconds, and not anywhere fun.

His pulse stuttered, his hands suddenly sweaty. He knew nothing about her situation or why she was unexpectedly sad. The pressure to say the right thing during moments like this made him shift on his feet.

He could fix anything material, but all he'd ever done with bad moments was make them worse.

When she finally looked up at him again, her smile was a wisp of a thing, her gaze distant. "I'll probably go. Maybe. I'm supposed to be getting away from it all, but . . . I don't know. We'll see. Anyway . . ." She shook her head and waved off the decision for now.

"Well, your toilet is all fixed. I should probably get out of your hair and let you settle in. You'll be at dinner tonight, right?"

"You're leaving?" She looked at him like he'd said they were kicking her out of the cabin.

He didn't want to go, but he didn't know what to say in these situations. If she needed someone to talk to, it shouldn't be him. Nobody wanted Dev Bradley to be privy to their problems, and they sure as hell didn't want his advice. A how-to on handling life? Most folks would simply do the opposite of everything he'd ever done, and they'd turn out fine.

"I guess. Unless there's something else around here that needs fixing."

"No. Not that I'm aware."

"Good. Better not be, but if so, just give us a call. Sorry again about the seat."

"It's fine, really." Any blame was dismissed with a flick of her hand.

He turned to go and she followed. As they neared the den and the open-beam, vaulted ceiling, he heard the problem before he saw it.

Then he laid eyes on a disaster waiting to happen.

One noisy-as-hell ceiling fan wobbled hard enough to spin off its base. Devlin stared up, narrowing his eyes at the offense.

Hell.

Trevor had one job. One job, but here he was, about to haul out the ladder because his baby brother couldn't follow directions.

And people called Dev the irresponsible one.

How did he not notice the fan when he first got here? The unreachable chain banged against the light fixture as though trying to break through. Clinking and clunking, the whole thing looked ready to fly across the room and out the window.

"Wow." Anna stopped right beside him, chin up to stare at the fan. The delicate stretch of her neck was once again creamy smooth and, he bet, sensitive. "You know, I'm no expert, but I feel like ceiling fans aren't supposed to do that."

She turned to meet his gaze, a flutter of lashes as she smiled. Anna from Atlanta was back, the fog of sadness burned off by the distraction.

"Guess you aren't quite done fixing things." Something devious flickered in her eyes, reminding him exactly why he hadn't noticed the fan upon arrival.

As she went back to studying the fan, her hair fell back, over her shoulder. Dark brown, wavy and soft, and his fingers itched to touch. Run his hands through it, have it brush against his thighs as she—

Devlin cleared his throat. "Fan's probably out of balance. I've got a ladder in the work truck. I'll be right back."

He hauled ass out of Cabin Five as if he had on a jet pack.

This was bad. Amazing, but bad, and the short jaunt to the truck was the perfect time to remind himself why.

Anna was a guest at the resort. Guests were a no-go, always had been, and always would be. Roark was a stickler for all rules, but this was in his top ten.

And she wasn't only a guest; she was a guest up here alone, for an extended amount of time, obviously dealing with something in her life. Or running from something, or hiding, or whatever the hell kind of reason women isolated themselves in the mountains for weeks at a time.

Regardless of what and why, her troubles were none of his business. He had too much shit in his own life to get tangled up in someone else's issues.

Suggestions on fun things to do on the property, adventure, entertainment in town—for that, he was the go-to guy.

But fixing personal problems? Hell no.

The ability to offer any solid life direction wasn't in his genetic makeup. Roark took all that when he was born, and left Dev and Trevor with scraps.

He was trying to do better, prove he could be responsible and have a clue.

Carousing with Anna from Atlanta wasn't the way to get it.

He could already hear Roark's voice, sniping in his head. *One of the guests, Devlin? Seriously? Can I not trust you with anything?*

Swear to god. He hooked up with one guest when he was twenty, and his brother still treated him like a mountaintop Casanova.

Devlin grabbed the ladder, cursing to himself as he dragged it from the back of the truck. He'd fix this fan and go. Chances were, he'd hardly see Anna around the resort anyway, so it didn't matter. A few hellos here and there. Any temptation would be 100 percent manageable.

Anna waited on him in the den, standing out of the way, hands on her hips, red nails flashing against the black of her pants, and she glared up at the fan like she could stare it into submission.

Dev bit back a groan as he set the ladder up. "Give me a minute and I'll have this thing fixed."

After more than ten minutes, and Anna's assistance with turning the switch off and on, the fan still had a little wobble. Every time he glanced down to ask her to go flip the switch, he saw right down the front of her V-neck shirt.

Being a gentleman, he looked away, but not quick enough that he didn't know Anna had world-class cleavage, and a penchant for black, even in her underwear.

Son of a bitch, he did not need to know that.

"Maybe it needs to be replaced altogether," she suggested.

"No, it's just . . ." He muttered to himself, trying one last thing, tightening the base as much as he could. "I'd rather spend all day fixing it than tell Roark we need a new one. Somehow it'll be my fault it's broken."

"What's that?"

"Nothing. I think you're all set now." He tugged on the chain so it spun at mid-speed, not making a sound.

"Yes." Satisfied, he stepped down a few rungs to hop off the ladder. Then something went horribly wrong. He underestimated the height of the last step and his foot missed the expected landing.

Windmilling backwards, the split-second realization he was going to fall on his ass in front of a gorgeous woman sealed his decision to kick Trevor's ass.

Then, Anna caught him.

Behind him, she stuck her arms firmly under his as he fell, holding on so they both went sprawling on their backs across the sofa.

Devlin lay there, stunned.

That didn't just happen. Shit like that didn't really happen to people who weren't in sitcoms.

"Please tell me you didn't have to catch me," he tried.

Anna didn't answer.

She might be unconscious, knocked out by his flailing limbs. What if she had a black eye?

But then the plush chest at his back rose and fell. "Actually, more like you fell into my arms. Or maybe on me. Either way, I didn't prevent the fall."

Yep. He was definitely kicking Trevor's ass.

Devlin lowered his head with a groan, the smallest sniffing and puffing coming from Anna.

He sat up to make sure she was okay. If she was crying, forget the ass-whooping, he was going to kill Trevor.

But, from the looks of things, Anna was more than okay.

Hands over her mouth and eyes squeezed shut, she rolled onto her side, and began to laugh with her entire body. "I'm sorry." She fanned her face.

"Um." He blinked, trying not to get distracted by the sight of her in the throes of laughing at him. "I'm pretty sure I should be the one apologizing. I knocked you down. In a full-body backward tackle."

That didn't help. She only laughed harder. "I . . . I don't know why it's so funny, but . . . I thought you were going to catch yourself, and then you started . . ." She imitated his windmill imitation.

"Yes, yes." He caught her arms midflight. "I'm sure I looked awesome, falling to my death."

"Then I thought, should I try to catch you? But that didn't work either, and *splat!*" Anna snorted and sniffed, easing herself to sit up.

Chances were good this was how he finally died of embarrassment. Not all the dumb shit he did in college or the time he got busted for streaking at a Halloween party. But because he'd ruined a perfectly great, sexy encounter by falling on his ass.

"I am so sorry," he repeated.

"You mean that isn't how you normally welcome guests?" she teased, swiping the laugh tears from her eyes.

"No."

"Oh good, then I'm special." Anna's unhindered smile was crippling in its beauty, putting her earlier smiles to shame. They were shadows of the real thing.This smile crashed into him harder than the fall.

She dabbed at her cheeks with the back of her hand. "Don't look so embarrassed."

"I *am* embarrassed." He'd knocked down a girl. Since he was three years old he'd been taught that was something you simply did not do.

Roark could *never* find out about this.

With a shake of his head, Dev got up and held out a hand to help her up as well. "Are you sure you're okay?"

She took his hand, letting him lift her to her feet. "I'm fine, I swear. Are you okay?"

"You broke my fall, remember? The only thing hurting is my pride."

One more giggle squeaked out. "Please don't let it hurt your pride. I *needed* that laugh. You have no idea how much."

"Well, anytime you need me to make an ass out of myself, I rarely disappoint. You're guaranteed a laugh. Just let me know."

"I will. Thanks." Anna hadn't stopped smiling since he'd landed, and he was still holding her hand.

Devlin made himself let go, digging his fingers back through his hair. "You're welcome. Anything to please a guest."

Her smile shifted as she bit at her lips.

"So, I'm going to go," he announced. "Before I accidentally knock you down again or, I don't know, ruin your hair and makeup." He grabbed the ladder and made haste to the door. "Enjoy the rest of your stay."

"I will." She followed him again, opening the door to let him out.

He went directly to the truck, loaded the ladder, and wasn't looking back. Staring at her, at someone he wouldn't be getting, or getting anywhere near, was only torturing himself. Which was why, when he reached the driver's door, he looked back.

Anna gave him a little wave, the late afternoon sun throwing her figure into a dark silhouette, but there was no missing that smile. "See you later."

And wasn't that the rub?

He *would* see her later.

He'd probably see her every day for her entire stay. If he saw her day after day, with run-ins like today, flirty smiles and needy glances, how was he supposed to be this new Dev? The Dev who didn't thumb his nose at rules, the guy who did what he was supposed to and never got out of line.

Once he got the truck backed and turned around, he checked the rearview mirror, on the off chance Anna lingered.

There she stood, watching him leave, before going inside with a spin of thick hair and a whole lot of curves.

Holy hell, he was screwed.

Chapter 3

She should've gone to dinner at the inn last night. Not going hadn't stopped her from thinking about Devlin, going over every little thing about him until she drifted off to sleep. Thick thighs, the way his lips curled when he smiled, his eyes crinkling at the outer edge. Inexplicably boyish *and* rugged. The way he moved, confident—except for when stumbling off a ladder.

A smile took over her face and, even though she was alone in the cabin's little loft bedroom, she pulled a pillow over her face to hide it.

Laughing at him for falling wasn't the best reaction, but she couldn't help it. He'd commanded attention in the hallway, making her off-kilter and weak-kneed. The advantage was his, and she'd found herself titillated but a teensy bit intimidated by how easily he turned her into a tingling, horny mess of a woman.

Devlin falling on his butt put her at ease and made him human. More importantly, it'd made her laugh.

She snorted into the pillow again. He was still hot, even as he took both of them out with his arms flapping about.

Devlin was sexy, funny, and he made her want . . . things.

And that's why she'd skipped dinner.

She wasn't ready for things. The whole point of her being here was to heal and deal, not to lust after a gorgeous mountain man who was good with his hands.

She'd never been a flirt, but yesterday she'd given Devlin the eye; staring at him, smiling and waving and generally acting like a fifteen-year-old in his presence.

Looks of disappointment suddenly crowded her vision, a voice chastising her even when she was alone.

Maybe reverting to a teenager was the sign of another impending breakdown.

She'd batted her eyelashes at him, for crying out loud. How could she possibly trust herself to go to Bradley's for dinner? Now she was hungry enough that the pulverized pack of crackers in the bottom of her purse sounded like a delicacy.

Her stomach growled in agreement.

Sitting up in bed, she was at eye level with the den's ceiling fan.

Devlin was why she'd avoided the restaurant, but she couldn't stay away today. Hunger gnawed and she had zilch on hand, cracker dust not counting as food.

She shoved off the covers and made her way down the narrow stairs to the kitchen.

No food meant no coffee. She opened the front door of her cabin, and stepped out onto the porch in her pajamas and bare feet. The high vantage point gave her all the privacy in the world, and the cool morning air woke her up, a little.

She had reasons to be here. Important reasons and they had nothing to do with Devlin Bradley.

Her therapist was big on purpose and being present in the moment. Her purpose while at Honeywilde was finding a way to let go, learning to relax, and figuring out how to avoid blacking out at work again like she was having some kind of attack.

The part about *how* she was supposed to do all of that remained a mystery. She had weekly calls set up with her therapist and a stack of recommended reading. Beyond that, Susan told her she trusted Anna's ability to heal herself.

Ha!

Clearly Susan didn't understand the levels of inability Anna could reach, or how awesome she was at *not* dealing with a situation. But that was progress, right? Knowing you suck at dealing. Acknowledgment being part of the whole process and everything. Or was that only for AA?

"Good Lord, shut up," she told herself.

Almost three weeks of babbling to herself wasn't going to help her feel better. It'd drive her over the edge.

Her stomach pinched, giving off a sound like whales mating.

She needed food. Now. If Devlin was there, she'd have to keep her stares to herself.

By the time she made it from her cabin to the main inn, it was almost ten in the morning, and most breakfast-goers had already gone.

"Table for one, or will someone be joining you?" The hostess gave her a friendly smile. Anna could've choked on it.

"Just me." Table for one, for the rest of her stay.

"Follow me, please." The hostess led her to a small table by the stretch of windows.

Please don't growl, she prayed to her stomach. *Don't do it, don't do it. I'm feeding you right now.*

A white cloth covered the table, with fresh cut flowers placed in the center. The meal might only be breakfast, but Bradley's exuded charming sophistication and romanticism.

She had to get to a grocery store today.

Dining solo wasn't anything new for her, but here it felt awkward and wrong.

A couple of tables held guests who finished up as her waiter poured her first cup of coffee.

Yay. A whole restaurant alone. That was one way to get away from it all. "It all" being other humans. She didn't even have her cell phone as a distraction.

Technically, she had it, but it remained off and in a drawer back at the cabin. She'd been asked to minimize usage to weekly calls with Susan and emergencies.

Avoid social media and burying your face in a screen. You're going on vacation. Try living in the now.

This, for a woman with a job that was predominantly social media and internet based. Her fingers twitched and she itched to plug in, but she didn't.

She could do this. Live in the present, take in the world around her, find the joy in life. Anything to avoid falling apart again.

"Would you be interested in our pancake special?" The waiter reappeared at her table. "Blueberry pancakes, eggs made to order..."

He kept talking, but all she heard was the word pancakes, then Devlin entered the restaurant.

"Yes. Pancakes. And whatever comes with it." She handed over her menu and looked out the window at the mountains before Devlin could make eye contact.

Yesterday was certainly something, but there couldn't be an encore. Focus should be on herself. She had books to read, walks to take. The resort offered a craft class every week, she'd seen in the cabin's guest services binder.

Crafts sounded good. Much safer than Devlin.

She snuck a glance from the corner of her eyes.

Yep. Still undeniably attractive, all man with a naughty-schoolboy smirk as he spotted her. He strolled over with long strides and a disarming twinkle in his eyes, the kind of guy who'd get her into trouble, *if* she ever got into trouble.

Which she didn't.

"Morning," he said, still several tables away, forcing her to either look at him or pretend she was oblivious.

She glanced up. "Oh. Good morning, Devlin."

He gave her a grin that scrunched the bridge of his nose. "Y'know, I think you can call me Dev. Now that I've landed on you, you've earned the use. How are you doing today? Not too bruised, I hope."

With a quick glance down at her coffee, she fought not to react in any way. "I'm fine, as far as I can tell."

"Good." He didn't join her at the table, but stood behind the chair across from her, leaning his weight against it with his hands anchored across the back. The position made the muscles in his forearms roll and stretch. "You didn't make it to dinner last night."

"No, I—" Her gaze shot to his. "How'd you know?"

"Well, I was trying to be a gentleman." He winked at her. The action was subtle, but the effect was strong enough her insides did a few somersaults. "I told the hostess, if you came in, dinner was on me. You know, to make up for yesterday."

"That's really nice of you."

And flattering. Her body buzzed with the high of his attention, and a familiar pang of guilt began to smother the nugget of joy. "Thank you, but by the time I unpacked, it was too late for dinner."

"That's okay. You're having breakfast this morning. On me." He waved down her waiter, his voice low as he spoke, exuding the same kind of confidence she did when she was working.

As the waiter walked away, their gazes met.

"I'd join you, but I have to meet my brother in a few minutes."

Her heart thumped as she struggled with what to say.

An unhealthy amount of time had been spent thinking about him last night. The levelheaded part of her brain pointed out that all of this nonsense, ogling Devlin and flirting, was a way of avoiding the issues she should be facing.

She could concentrate on Devlin, his smile, intense blue eyes, and great hair. Or she could think about her father's death.

All of her vacation could be spent trying like hell to deal, and likely failing. More than six months had gone by, and she still struggled to accept that he'd been taken way too soon. She had to go through life without the person who loved and supported her. How was she supposed to magically make peace with that?

She could focus fully on the task of grief and coping with a stressful job, squash this interest between her and Devlin—Dev. *Or* she could leave the door open, and simply see what happened. Live in the moment. Find joy in the now.

She opened her mouth, unsure of what to say until the words spilled out. "Maybe you could join me some other time?"

She never did this, opening herself up to a guy. It made no sense to be doing it now, but maybe that's why she was able. Flirting with him was a rush that swept the sadness away.

Dev's eyes flashed, the pale color hypnotic the longer she looked at him. "I'll hold you to that."

"Devlin." The oldest brother, Roark, approached their table, shooting a quick look between them.

"Hey, Roark. You remember Anna, our Cabin Five guest."

"Ms. Martel. Good morning." He nodded, looking nowhere near as happy to see her as Devlin.

As he went to sit a few tables away, Devlin shook his head. "I better go get this over with. Enjoy your breakfast."

Dev joined his brother, and Roark sat with his back to her, his breadth blocking her view of Devlin.

Just as well. She needed to eat her breakfast and find out how to get to the local grocery store.

The waiter topped off her coffee and set an enormous plate of food in front of her.

"What's this?" She nodded to the spread of breakfast food before her.

"The pancake special you ordered. Eggs, bacon, grits, biscuits, and of course, blueberry pancakes." He beamed, and then left her with the buffet.

"Alright then, I got the lumberjack breakfast. Fabulous." She wide-eyed her choice, but started on the pancakes, trying not to listen to the conversation a couple of tables down.

"I may need you to take on more around the resort," Roark said.

"I'd—" Devlin's voice caught. "I want to. You know I do. But the festival is something I can handle as well. On the side."

"A big festival isn't exactly a side project, Dev. And it's a huge expense."

They were not partaking in any pancake specials and their coffees sat on the table between them, untouched.

Devlin leaned forward and Anna found something to look at, outside the nearest window.

"We can sponsor the Blueberry Festival and help out the town, or do nothing and come off like we don't give a damn about anyone but ourselves."

"It's not like that. Of course we give a damn, but I can't risk losing tons of money on a new project right now. We have enough to work on here, tons of stuff still needs updating. All that festival has done is bleed green for the last few years."

"I told you, we won't lose money." Devlin's sharp tone grabbed Anna's full attention. "I'm not clueless, tossing out this suggestion. I looked into things."

"Okay. Relax." Roark took a quick glance around, but right now, she was the only other person in the restaurant.

The two were obviously having some sort of deep family business discussion that she shouldn't be hearing. But their discussion was hard not to hear when she was listening in so carefully.

Anna reached for her purse. She needed something to do while eating alone. Their conversation was none of her business.

Normally she'd work on her phone, play a silly game, something. A book made a decent dining companion, but her To Be Read pile was back at the cabin.

She dug through her bag and only one item qualified as reading material, of sorts. A pamphlet of local activities and shops. She'd grabbed it from the binder in her cabin, hoping a list of grocery stores might be included.

Cracking open the pamphlet, she vowed to focus only on the words in front of her face, not the ones being spoken at the other table.

Devlin muttered something else to his brother, and grabbed his mug to take a long sip of what had to be lukewarm coffee by now. "I don't know why the festival struggled the last couple of years, but we can be the main sponsor and make money. I know it."

"I'd have to look at the numbers first. In black and white. All of them."

"Jesus, Roark." Dev set his mug down with a thud. "Waiting for you to look at numbers 'til you're satisfied could take months. We need to jump on this right now or there won't be a festival at all this year."

His brother leaned in, keeping his voice low, but Anna could still hear. "The town hasn't had one in years anyway. I'm not jumping into anything right now."

"Then you're rejecting my idea flat out. Again."

Anna held the pamphlet, cover folded back, with every intention of reading the first page, but the words blurred in light of the conversation nearby.

"I'm not rejecting your idea flat out. I'm saying I need to know more. Get me the figures so I can make a decision."

"How am I supposed to get you the figures? We haven't been involved in any part of the Blueberry Festival for the past decade."

"That's not my fault and you know it."

"I can't step up to the tourism board and demand to see their books."

Roark scrubbed a hand over the back of his neck and shifted his chair back. "Then let's wait for next year, or the year after. We can participate on a smaller scale and get a feel for things before we swoop in and try to take over. Get to know the board, or better yet get on the board, so we aren't asking out of the blue."

"There won't be a festival to participate in if we don't sponsor it. That's what I'm saying. I'm not asking you to fund the whole damn thing. We take the lead, that's all. Sometimes the risk is worth the reward."

Roark was already shaking his head before Devlin finished speaking.

Anna knew without seeing his face, the eldest Bradley brother—and apparently the one who controlled the purse strings—wasn't going to buy what Dev was selling.

All the evidence was in Roark's body language. The stiff set of his shoulders, how he went so far as to move his chair back from the table. Anna knew how to read people and knew when a sales pitch was working.

Dev's fell on deaf ears.

Roark's answer was never going to be yes. His posture was closed off and defensive from the moment they sat down together. Unless he could be guaranteed no loss, Roark was the kind of buyer who wouldn't take chances.

Devlin, on the other hand, leaned forward, animated, all spirit and no facts, and was totally behind the idea of this festival thing—whatever it was.

But if he needed his older brother's support, he'd have to find a better way to get it than mere enthusiasm.

"I have to go." Roark checked his watch and pushed his chair out all the way.

Still in his seat, Devlin watched him get up, the defiant set of his chin sexier than it had any right to be. "You suggested meeting at the restaurant because you knew you were going to say no. Didn't you? You knew you'd say no, regardless of my idea, and you knew you'd get a hell of an earful if we were behind closed doors."

Roark's shoulders rose and fell, and he pushed his chair back under the table. "I'm sure I'll get an earful regardless."

Devlin cut his eyes at his brother, before looking away like he wasn't even there.

"Dev, if you can give me more to go on than your excitement, I'm happy to help."

He sat stone-faced as Roark walked away.

Their interaction twisted something deep inside her, tightening until it hurt.

Some people would never hear you, no matter how hard you tried. Even when those people were family.

Anna shifted her gaze to the stream of words on the page before her. She stared at the page forever, comprehending nothing.

If Devlin left the restaurant as she read, he did so without a sound, but she was too chicken to look up and check.

Seconds clicked by and she was cross-eyed from trying to read the pamphlet.

The deep rumbling of a cleared throat made her jump. "You're either studying that thing for a pop quiz later, or you're fake reading."

With the most innocent expression she could muster, she met Dev's gaze from two tables away. "I'm not fake reading."

"You haven't turned the page in about ten minutes."

Dang it. "I'm making sure I grasp what the article is about."

"That pamphlet is all ads and discount coupons."

"There's an article," she insisted. *Please let there be an article.* "Right here, about . . ." She scanned the page. "Tube riding."

He lowered his chin, hiding some of his smile. "Are you planning to go tube riding?"

"Maybe."

"Good. It's a lot of fun. The locals call it tubing, though. Tubin', to be precise, but I'm glad you're planning an excursion. For a while there I thought you were just staring at the page, listening to me and my brother bicker."

With the corner of his mouth curled up, he finally sipped at his coffee, immediately setting it back down, making the universal yuck face for unintentionally drinking cold coffee.

"I didn't notice any bickering," she fibbed, holding the pamphlet up a little higher to emphasize how captivated she'd been by an article on tubing. Or tubin'.

At that, Devlin rose from his seat.

It seemed he'd simply walk away, satisfied that she hadn't heard a word. Instead he frowned down at his coffee cup and walked over to Anna's table.

"May I?" Again, he put his hands on the chair across from her.

She nodded, and he sat, bringing with him a woodsy smell and something else, something she couldn't identify. A scent with some bite.

"I'm surprised you didn't hear us. Me at least. I can't keep my voice down when I get worked up."

She could continue the lie and insist she hadn't heard a word, mind her own business, not have an opinion, and not open herself up to involvement. But since when had she ever done that?

Anna laid the pamphlet down next to the basket of untouched biscuits. "Okay, maybe I overheard a little, but I was trying very hard not to."

He laughed as the waiter reappeared, in time to pour them each a fresh cup of coffee.

"You mind if I take one of these?" Devlin pointed to the covered basket.

"Help yourself."

He plucked out one of the biscuits, broke it in half, and spread both sides with butter. "Now that you've admitted you could hear us arguing, I apologize. Meeting in the restaurant wasn't my idea, but I'm the one who raised my voice. Sorry about that."

She waved it off, accustomed to raised voices and bickering.

"When are you planning on going tubing?" Dev asked before biting into one biscuit half.

A dab of butter clung to his top lip. He licked it clean, his gaze not moving from hers.

"What?"

"Tubing." He nodded at the forgotten pamphlet. "The thing you were reading all about. When are you going?"

"Oh. Not anytime soon. Probably. I'm still undecided if I'll go." She didn't have a clue what tubing was or how one did it, and the whole thing sounded suspect.

"You have to. You can't be up here for a few weeks and never go tubing or rafting or something on the water."

He knew how long she'd be at Honeywilde. Made sense, he did work at the resort, but the realization still made her smile.

"We'll see. I was thinking the hikes and paddleboats were a little more my speed."

"Oooh, paddleboats." His voice sang with teasing notes. "Don't get too crazy. First it's paddleboats, next thing you know you're hang gliding off the side of a mountain."

Her stomach pitched at the mere mention. "Not me. Why? Do you hang glide?"

"Hell no. I like to get my thrills on the ground. Or on things touching the ground."

Anna sucked down too much hot coffee, and came up coughing.

Dev's eyes widened minutely. "I was talking about my bike."

She sputtered and reached for her water. He sat there and smiled. Not helpful.

"I should go and let you finish your breakfast."

No. She didn't want him to go. Once he left, she would eat alone, buy groceries, and go back to her cabin to read self-help books.

The other option was Devlin. Finishing her breakfast in his company, finding out what the heck tubing entailed, staring into his swoony eyes.

"You don't have to leave. I'm almost done eating." Her words jumped out like they were ready to chase him if he left. "You can stay if you want."

Dev picked up the other half of the biscuit, his eyes dancing with pleasure. "Thanks. I do want," he said, and took a big bite.

Chapter 4

Hell yes, he was staying.

When a woman like Anna outright invited his company, he wasn't about to say no.

Devlin's phone vibrated in his pocket. He was already wired and lit up like the resort at Christmas; the vibration made him jump.

He ignored it. The call was probably from Roark, and he did not need his brother interrupting this moment.

Conversation over breakfast didn't warrant his reaction to her, but Anna made everything within him hum.

She was beautiful, yes, but the allure wasn't only about her looks.

He knew plenty of beautiful women. They came and went from the resort, in and out of town with the tourist season, and he never gave them a second thought.

Anna made him curious.

She showed up at breakfast in full makeup, her hair pinned back, wearing a nice white T-shirt with some metallic graphic on the front he couldn't make out. By all metrics, she looked like the kind of woman to turn up her nose at him for taking one of the biscuits at her table, but she hadn't.

Anna didn't appear to be the type to laugh her tail off about him falling on her either, but she had.

There was a spark of life in her dark eyes that blinked in and out, inexplicably. She was vibrant one moment, shadowed the next—and he couldn't figure out why.

He'd sat right down as she had breakfast, knowing he shouldn't. He was supposed to be mature enough not to do the things he knew were off-limits. Stop tempting the devil. If Roark saw him insinuating himself into a guest's mealtime, he'd have a fit.

Yet here Dev sat.

His phone went off again and he bit back a curse. "Excuse me." He dug his phone from his pocket. Seeing his sister Sophie's face on the display, he answered right away.

"What's up?" He angled himself away from Anna for privacy. If his little sister called during work hours, it meant something was wrong.

"It's what is not up that's the problem," Sophie answered. "We've got no ferns on the patio level of the inn, and absolutely no greenery out front. We're supposed to have hanging baskets and urns, some of those cute topiaries, and we got zip. It looks like barren stone when it's supposed to be lush and springlike for Mother's Day weekend. Mother's Day, Dev. I'm fixing to freak out."

"Does Ms. Brenda have them ready at her shop or—"

"Yes, and Trevor said he'd go get them for me yesterday, but he didn't and now I can't get in touch with him to find out what's going on."

Of course she couldn't get in touch with Trevor. Money said their baby brother had either left his phone in his room or let it die again, and was on the far reaches of the property or off somewhere, doing god knows what.

"I can't go because we're having new linens delivered this afternoon." Sophie's voice went high and thin, a sure sign she was at her wit's end. In the background, papers were slapped against a surface. "I mean, thank you, Madison, for the rock-star wedding and cash boom that made all of this possible, but I've got a million little upgrades to oversee while we still look tacky as crap outside with no greenery."

Last fall, Roark's girlfriend, Madison, had put Honeywilde back on the map. Her clients had their celebrity wedding at the inn and nothing had been the same since. The change was welcome, but Dev and his family were working their asses off to keep up with demand.

"Calm down, just let me think." Devlin tried to soothe her. If the problem could be solved by going to Brenda's, he could help. Unlike the rest of the folks in town, Brenda liked him.

Then again, he'd never given Brenda a reason not to. Too bad he couldn't say the same about everyone else.

He checked his watch. "I'm free until later this afternoon. I'll call Brenda and if everything is ready, I'll go get the plants for you."

"You will? Oh, thank you." Sophie let out her breath. "You're awesome."

He glanced over to find Anna studying him, intent.

"Yeah, yeah." With the appreciation in her eyes he had to look away.

"And my favorite brother."

"I better be."

As soon as he hung up, he called the florist his family used for everything, and didn't look over at Anna again. He couldn't concentrate on talking to Ms. Brenda *and* make eyes with Anna.

Sure enough, everything was at the greenhouse, ready to go.

"Are you going to have some extra hands?" Brenda asked. "And enough room?"

"Why? How many plants are we talking about?"

"A little over fifty."

"What the—*Fifty?*"

"Mmm-hmm, a little over fifty."

"What are we going to do with fifty plants?"

"Now that, I can't tell you. Your sister said she wanted a lot of greenery, so a lot of greenery she's going to get."

He didn't have enough room for fifty-plus plants. He'd have to take Roark's truck and one of the little trailers. Even then he might end up driving with a fern in his lap.

"You better bring someone with you, hon." Brenda sweet-talked him, as per usual. "I'm at the store alone today, and you know my back won't let me help with all those ferns."

He wouldn't expect her to do their grunt work anyway. "I'll find my brother and get him to help me load them. I should be by in about half an hour or so."

"Okay. See you then."

Devlin ended the call and tossed his phone down, scowling at the black rectangle. When he finally looked up and made eye contact with Anna, he picked up his phone again, schooling his expression as he typed.

"Fifty plants?" Anna rested her elbows on the table. "Sounds like a lot of work."

"Yeah. Sorry about that." Guests didn't need to hear about their operational woes. He texted Trevor, telling him to get his ass back to the inn.

"No need to apologize. You've made my morning a lot more entertaining than eating alone with my pamphlet."

Entertaining. That was one word for it. "You think this is entertaining; you ought to see me trying to wrangle fifty plants."

She tilted her head and hit him with a sparkling smile amid full pink lips. "Did you say you were going to town to get these plants?"

He hit Trevor's number to try calling. "The plants are outside of town, but the florist we always use is in town. I have to go by and say hello or I'll be on her list. You don't want to be on her list." And he wouldn't go into town to say hello for anyone else.

Ms. Brenda was special enough to overrule his aversion to going into town.

Just because he wanted to pull off the Blueberry Festival and do something right for a change, did not mean he wanted to hang out in town, risk seeing that look on people's faces when they saw him.

Thanks, but no thanks.

Trevor didn't answer his phone and Dev ended the call with a muttered curse. Roark couldn't help out because of his meeting, plus he'd still be in a snit about their conversation.

"Can't find anyone to help?" Anna asked.

"Not yet." He'd have to make do alone. Loading and unloading would take longer, but with the trailer, he could manage.

Might not be able to move tomorrow, but he'd manage.

"I need to go into town too." Anna pushed her plate away, carefully placing her napkin beneath the edge. "For groceries and stuff. Sort of learn my way around, but I have no idea where to go, so . . ." Anna let the sentence go with a shrug of her shoulders.

He could not ask her to help him.

Namely, because her helping him broke about five different resort policies, including the insurance policy. On top of that, he simply wouldn't ask her to do something like haul plants and dirt around.

Falling on her wasn't enough; now he was going to make her do manual labor on her vacation? Hell no.

"I'm happy to go along and help you pick up some flowers, if you'll show me the best place to buy some groceries."

Offering to give him a hand was sweet—and it was an offer that meant spending a large part of the day together, away from the resort.

No one around to make a fuss about them hanging out, no prying eyes.

It was a horrible idea with "Best Idea Ever" spray-painted over the top.

"Thank you, but I can't ask you to do that. I'll be picking up a lot more than a few flowers. Fifty ferns, some large arrangements, probably plenty of extras because Ms. Brenda likes to take care of us."

"Oh. Then you'll definitely need help. It's up to you though." Anna let her words dangle there. An open door. The invitation for him to step through and do something.

He *really* shouldn't ask her to help though. Not that he was known for doing what he should, but . . .

No.

Sitting together at breakfast was one thing, but moving a bunch of plants around in the blazing sun and heat? That was no one's idea of a good time.

"I can't ask you to help me. I don't mean that as a pleasantry. I literally cannot ask a guest to do labor. If you got hurt, we could get sued, and Roark would kill me."

Her gaze flitted away, up and around. He could almost see the wheels turning.

"You haven't technically asked me," she finally said. "We've entered into no binding agreement that would hold you liable. And I really do need someone to show me how to get into town and where to find a grocery store. I know nothing. If I happen to be present to lend a hand with some plants, so be it."

He wanted to ask her why she'd do this for him. Helping someone she hardly knew with their hard work went beyond their attraction and flirtation.

Trying to understand a person's true motivations was like trying to catch snowflakes. Maybe she simply wanted to spend some time together, get away from the resort, stretch her legs, who knew?

He wanted to spend some time with her too though, enough so that he'd endure a trip to the grocery store in town.

A small voice, almost too miniscule to hear, told him he knew better than to fraternize with a guest.

The rest of him said to hell with it.

"Okay, but here's the deal." He scooted his chair in and leaned forward. "Loading plants, especially fifty of them, is dirty work."

"I don't mind getting dirty."

He smirked at her choice of wording. "You absolutely cannot lift anything heavy or do anything that might get you hurt. Ferns. That's your zone." There. He'd given her every disclaimer he could think of.

"Ferns only. I might get dirty. Then you're taking me by the store. Got it."

He tossed his hands up. "All right, then. I guess we're going to get some plants. I'll need to get the keys to the truck. If you want to ride with me, you can. That's completely your decision."

"Exactly. You're under no responsibility here, whatsoever."

It was the sort of thing he'd been accused of for years, except this time he didn't mind. "If you'll give me your number, I'll text you when I'm ready out front."

Anna's expression froze. "Actually, I don't have my phone or I would. How about I meet you outside in ten minutes? Since I don't have to worry about waiting on the check, that shouldn't be a problem."

They agreed, and by the time he tossed some bottled waters in a small cooler, swung by the front office to nick Roark's keys while he was in his meeting, and fired off a text to Sophie to let her know he was taking care of the plant problem, Anna was waiting for him in the inn's portico.

Leaning against one of the stacked stoned pillars, in her big, dark sunglasses, she looked more like a celebrity on vacation, dressing down to hide from the paparazzi, than a—whatever she did for a living—on vacation.

He'd guess she was an attorney or in finance, but he'd have to unearth the real answer.

"We'll take Roark's truck." Devlin pointed to the side of the inn where his family always parked.

"Not the work truck from yesterday?" She followed him, climbing up into the passenger seat once he unlocked the doors.

The work truck was a piece of shit. He wasn't taking her anywhere in that thing.

"There's too much stuff in the back of the work truck." Plus Roark's was nicer and more impressive.

The Chevy started with a rumble before settling into a purr, and he backed out of the parking spot.

Roark might be ticked when he found out Dev took his truck without asking, but if he'd asked, it would've led to a ten-minute discussion and runaround, even though this truck was the best option for the job.

Asking also meant Roark would be more likely to catch on that Dev had plant help. Best to leave matters be for now.

"I've still got to hook up the trailer before we go."

The detached garage, where they kept the trailers, tools, Dev's bike, and the '69 Camaro that would run someday, was about a quarter mile down a dirt road that went from the parking lot, around the side of the inn, and headed in the direction of the cabins.

"I didn't even know this was back here." Anna sat forward as they pulled up to the hidden garage.

"That's the point. Roark added this a few years ago and wanted it, and I quote, 'nestled into the environment so it'd blend, seamlessly.'"

He hopped out and attached the trailer, and they were on their way back toward the inn, bouncing down the dirt road.

Normally, his gut would be in a knot about going into town. Whether or not he saw any familiar faces or got any incriminating glances, he'd still get the twist of anxiety, like walking into a room and realizing they were just talking about you.

But today he had a distraction, and a wonderful reason not to think about much but the woman beside him.

The truck leaned, taking a particularly deep turn, and Anna grabbed the "oh shit" bar with one hand, clutching her seat with the other.

"Don't do a lot of off-roading in Atlanta?"

"I try to stay on the road whenever possible."

"That's no fun. This is nothing. If you want real off-roading, there are some insane trails across the back of the mountain."

"In my Lexus? I was lucky I made it up to the cabin."

He meant he'd take her, but he must not be making that part clear. She'd never want to go with him anyway. Anna probably didn't think of off-roading as fun. He didn't know what she did for fun, but he bet it wasn't bouncing around with four-wheel drive, seeing how far you could push a truck without getting stuck.

Testing his skill and trying his luck, finding his way out of a tough situation, made Dev feel alive.

It also ended in him having to be towed a couple of times, but that wasn't the point.

"I can see it now." Anna let go of her seat long enough to sweep her hand in front of her. "I finally take a vacation and go four-wheeling, then career off the side of the road and wreck my car."

Finally taking a vacation. Big-city life must not allow for a lot of time off, so she'd chosen to come alone . . . to the mountains? "I have to ask. What made you decide to come up here by yourself and rough it, when you finally took some vacation time?"

Anna pinched her lips together, her gaze trained on the road.

"You don't have to tell me if you don't want, but I thought people like you went to places like all-inclusive resorts in the Bahamas or something."

"Honeywilde is hardly roughing it. You're a three-star resort according to the website, and you made it into national magazines after hosting a rock-star wedding."

He peered over as they reached the paved road that'd take them down the mountain, but Anna kept staring straight ahead.

"True, we are pretty luxurious where it counts, but the natural setting is still rustic. You agreed to haul landscaping for the better part of your day too, and you were looking at tubing as a way to pass the time. There's at least *some* roughing it involved in all of that."

She shrugged, but didn't look over. "I'm not a fan of hundred degree heat, and sand all over me. Honeywilde is low on both."

He let his query go, but there were obviously other reasons she'd chosen Honeywilde. Reasons she didn't want to get into, and he wasn't one to pry.

"And what do you mean, people like me?"

He glanced over and Anna narrowed her eyes, a challenging look, daring him to answer without putting his foot in his mouth.

With a grin, he focused on the road. "Fancy people."

"I'm not fancy."

"Sure you aren't. Your suitcases alone are worth more than our work truck. You think I don't know what that brown-and-tan design means? I look at magazines, especially when Honeywilde is in them. I know things."

She made a sound like she might laugh, but stopped it. "That doesn't necessarily mean I'm fancy."

He debated with himself for all of about two-point-five seconds, then reached across the center console and peeled her hand away from her choke hold on the seat.

At first, she stiffened at the contact, a tremble making her hand shake, but she didn't pull away. A few seconds blew past and she relaxed in his hold.

Her skin was smoother, her touch warmer, than he'd imagined.

Why did she have to be so soft? He glanced over again. Long fingers, with the red polish perfect and shiny on her nails. "How much did you pay to get your nails done like this?"

"I don't know."

"Plenty, I bet. This paint job is immaculate."

"So?"

"So, your luggage, the expensive car, fancy nails—I'm just saying a log cabin on the side of a mountain, tucked in the woods with the bears? At first glance I wouldn't have guessed roughing it was your scene."

Her grip tightened on his hand, squeezing much harder than she looked capable of. "There are bears near my cabin?"

"Probably not, but—"

"*Probably* not?" She squeezed tighter.

He winced as he maneuvered the mountain turns with one hand. "Not? I'm sure there are no bears near your cabin. That's kind of my point though. You're in the mountains. Bears live in the mountains. The possibility does exist."

She relaxed her grip, and didn't pull away. "As long as they don't live in Cabin Five, the bears and I won't have a problem."

But the two of them might.

His eyes were on the last curve and flattening road, but her hand was still in his. He shouldn't be touching her like this, familiar and lingering. And she shouldn't be letting him.

Somebody needed to be smart here. One of them needed to curtail the touching, yet time ticked by and . . .

Yep. They were holding hands.

When he glanced over, she was watching the passing pines and oaks. "I don't mind seeing bears from afar. I like the mountains and trees, the lack of skyscrapers. And noise."

They went another half mile before she met his gaze again. "I came up here because I wanted to get away from my everyday life. This place is completely different from Atlanta, and I needed that." She wiggled her fingers, the sensation sending a ripple of pleasure up his arm. "But how do you know so much about fingernail polish?"

She was changing the subject, but he didn't mind if the new topic was her sexy red nails.

"I don't know anything about nail polish, but I know paint. Took me three coats and a whole lot of profanity to get my bike the right shade of red, but it still doesn't look as good as your nails." He moved his hand under hers, stretching the fingers out so the sunlight caught the shine. "Red is a pain in the ass when you start, and if you flub the lines, there's no hiding it. Not like silver or white. Someone did a great job with this. I like the color."

"Thank you. It's called Size Matters."

He jerked his gaze to hers. "You're making that up."

A splotch of pink peeked around the side of her neck. "Says so on the bottle."

He glanced down at her hand again before his focus shot to the road. "Ah, shit."

"Excuse me?"

"We're supposed to haul plants."

"I'm aware."

"And I forgot the gloves. Your nails are going to get jacked up without them. I'll find some." He lowered her hand, reluctant to let go, but he needed to focus.

As soon as he did, he realized he'd driven right past the turn for Main Street.

He should've thought about work gloves before they left, and now he couldn't think who sold them. He couldn't even find his way to Main Street.

His brain had gone numb from touching her.

He needed gloves, he needed to go by Brenda's, and he needed to stop touching her, or risk forgetting why the hell they'd come into town in the first place.

Chapter 5

A nna sat with her hand on the seat instead of pulling it into her lap.

Making it easy for Dev to reach for her again wasn't the reason— though she'd gladly let him.

His knuckles beneath her fingers, a little work calloused, the tougher skin against her palm, all the sensations of his touch—these were things she wanted to savor. If she moved, the feeling might fly away. Disappear like their touch never really happened.

Devlin had asked her why the mountains, saying she didn't seem the type.

He was right. She wasn't the type, but she'd done all-inclusive resorts many times, at work conferences or as part of a bonus. Sitting by a pool in Florida would only remind her of the last time she was there and had only a few hours' break between a meeting and the company's cocktail hour. Trying to relax in that setting would only stress her out.

And the mountains were her father's favorite place. This was where he wanted to be.

Ignoring the fact she had a promise to fulfill, a responsibility to find her dad's final resting place, wasn't going to make it go away. That part of her vacation was about him, and her inability to say goodbye.

They'd visited so much when she was young; a drive up for the day to buy honey and apples, stop and see the sights. He'd get on the Blue Ridge Parkway—going nowhere in particular—to see the views.

He said it brought him peace. She could only hope it'd do the same for her, but she wasn't going to go into all of that with Devlin.

She'd known him less than a day. He didn't need to know what a mess she was. If he did, he'd burn out the tires on the truck in a rush to get away from her. And right now, his company was the only thing keeping her from going stir-crazy.

They followed the twists and turns down the mountain, and she stayed quiet, studying the view out the passenger window until they had to U-turn to get into town.

Downtown Windamere, for being a whole five or six blocks total, had an impressive amount going on.

The weather was still cool enough that the stores had their doors propped open, and even midweek, people milled about on the streets, checking out everything from gift shops to hardware, a pet store to a tattoo parlor.

"Oh my god, how adorable is this town?" She twisted in her seat as they passed Miller's Tool and Tackle shop right next to a salon.

Flower baskets lined the outside of shop windows, a couple of cafés had tiny tables set up on the sidewalk.

In her childhood trips to North Carolina, they'd never stopped in Windamere. That made the town the perfect new thing to shake off the sadness of the past.

"Come on. Are you kidding me?" She held her hand out, presenting the town square, with their government offices in the background, and a statue of a colorfully painted goat right next to the statue of some historic figure. "There's a polka-dotted goat in Town Square."

"Hey, those goats are for a good cause."

"*Those* goats? There's more than one?"

"Oh yeah. People pay for a goat statue, decorate it however they want, and stick it somewhere downtown. The goats stay up all year and the money goes to the hospital for cancer research."

"Atlanta did the same thing with dolphins to benefit the aquarium, but these goats are so much cuter."

What she wouldn't do for her phone to take pictures. That's it. She'd have to buy a disposable camera and actually pay to have film developed. Old-school style.

"Please tell me Honeywilde has a goat."

"Not yet. But I do think it's on the list of things to do this summer."

She smiled, picturing it. "You have to get a goat. Paint it using that warm apricot color you use for all the towels and accents and stuff. And somehow incorporate honeysuckle vines or honey and bees on it.

It'd be the perfect kind of promotion for the resort, and all for a good cause."

"That's . . . actually a really good idea. I'll mention it to my family. There's Brenda's." He pointed to a brick building squeezed into a row of about five more stores, but pulled off Main Street and around back to the parking lot.

"It's not as big as I thought it'd be."

"No, it's a small place, but she has a greenhouse a few blocks outside of town to hold the large orders. She's done our family's flowers for years and she doesn't miss a beat. We'll pick up the order at the greenhouse, but if I went straight there and didn't stop by to say hello, I'd be in big trouble."

Dev parked the truck and they walked around the end of the block, past a bakery that smelled divine, and a children's clothing store too adorable to be real.

The bells over the door at Brenda's announced their arrival.

"Devlin!" A petite African-American woman emerged from behind a riot of pink and purple flowers, her arms open wide as she walked toward them.

"Ms. Brenda." Dev enveloped her in a hug.

"I haven't laid eyes on you in weeks. Since y'all got the flowers for Easter. How've you been?" She patted his arm as they broke apart, looking him over like she was checking for damage.

As she fussed over him, Devlin's smile grew, big and embarrassed, melting Anna's heart. "I'm fine. Hanging in there. Same as always."

"Good, good." She gave him another once-over, and then her gaze fell on Anna. "I swear. It's gotten to where every time you boys come to see me, you bring along a pretty girl. First Roark and now you. Do you work up at the resort too, honey?" she asked Anna.

Anna looked from her to Dev and back again, grasping for an appropriate way to respond. "No, ma'am. I'm a guest up there. I'm Anna."

"Anna from Atlanta," Devlin added.

"Mmm-hmm." Brenda made an inquisitive noise as she shook Anna's hand, looking her up and down too, taking everything in. "And how long have you been at the resort?"

"Ah . . . a day?"

"A *day*?" She cut her eyes at Dev. "How long are you staying?"

"A couple of weeks or so."

She turned to Devlin fully. "Does your brother know you have a guest down here with you to pick up plants?"

"No, ma'am. And it'd be best if he never knew."

Brenda tapped the side of her nose. "I bet." Then she turned toward Anna. "Now, are you sure you want to be doing this? It's hot, dirty work."

"I'm happy to help. This was all my idea."

"I bet," Brenda said again. Then she gave Dev a look that'd break glass. "You better behave. Let me go get your receipt."

Once she was out of earshot, heading to the swinging doors of her back room, Devlin leaned closer. "Don't mind her. She loves me, and loves to give me a hard time."

"Now." Brenda burst back through the doors, flapping the receipt in her hands. "I don't know how you managed to con this nice girl into helping you move a bunch of stuff while she's on vacation, but you could at least be a gentleman and buy her a meal or something, when you're done." She gave Dev a quick wink that Anna probably wasn't supposed to see.

He was right. Ms. Brenda didn't miss a beat.

She turned to Anna again. Keeping up with her was like keeping up with a ping-pong match. "Do you have gloves for moving those plants? You'll want to protect your hands and nails."

"No, but Dev said he'd get some for us."

"Oh *Dev* said?" Brenda tilted her chin down, looking at him from over the top of her glasses. "Well, *Dev* better run in the back and see what I have on hand. I have gloves stuck all over in here."

He nodded, giving Anna an apologetic smile. "Just a second."

As soon as he was gone, Ms. Brenda turned to her again. "He's a sweetheart, that one, but sometimes he gets ahead of himself."

She had no idea what to say to that, so she smiled.

"Have you ever been to Honeywilde before?" Brenda asked.

"No, ma'am."

"You're going to love it. How long did you say you were staying again?"

"A little over two weeks."

She glanced toward the back. "Like I said, that one is a sweetheart. Known him his whole life. He might come across to a lot of people like some kind of big, bad trouble, but he isn't. That boy has soft spots. Don't let him fool you."

Anna blinked, once again lost on how to respond. "Okay."

"When he was a kid, he rode his bike all the way down the mountain, in the dead of night, just to get to my house, because he needed a hug."

"Oh god, not that story." Devlin groaned as he returned from the back.

"Yes, *that* story."

Anna stared at the over-six-foot-tall man before her, imagining him short and probably skinny. Him and his knobby knees, on his little bike, in the middle of the night. "Down that road we were on?"

He rubbed a hand over his face. "Yes. Can we not?"

"You could've been killed on that road." Brenda fussed at him like he'd just committed the act.

"I was almost eleven years old. I was not going to be killed."

"You should've heard what he said when he got here."

"No." He groaned again.

"He said he was sick of his know-it-all brother and he didn't like having a girl live with them anymore. So, he needed a hug and he was coming to stay with me."

Anna covered her mouth. "What did you say?"

"I reminded him that I was a girl too. He said I was too old to be a girl. I was a mom."

"Oh no."

"That's probably enough stories for today." Dev crowded her toward the door. "I've got the gloves. We better get started."

He gave Ms. Brenda another quick hug and she and Anna had to say their nice-to-meet-yous on the way out the door.

Once they were back in the truck, Devlin passed over the gloves.

He started the truck but said nothing about the story or their stop. The story was cute, but the way Dev worked his jaw, his sudden, uncharacteristic silence, told her there was a lot more to it than a kid annoyed by his siblings and simply needing a hug.

Chapter 6

"You were pretty fearless to come down that mountain all alone."
Dev shrugged rather than comment.

"All because you were mad at your brother and sister?"

He couldn't be upset with Brenda for bringing up the time he'd run away. From her point of view, the story was fun. Cute. His complaints about his adopted sister, Sophie, were typical bratty-brother nonsense, his irritation with Roark being bossy nothing new.

Brenda knew a lot about him and his siblings, but no one knew the details of the turmoil they grew up in. She'd always thought the reason he showed up at her house on weekends was for the homemade cookies.

Best to let her believe the lie.

"Must've been something pretty big to make you risk riding your bike down a mountain in the dark."

Devlin finally glanced at Anna, the truck's engine the only sound. Her statement was simple enough, but she was ferreting out answers.

He wouldn't let her dig too deep. Nobody ever liked what they found. "I was being stupid."

"Somehow I doubt it."

He focused on the road again.

If she looked into his eyes too long, she might see: Dev took the risk that night because he was desperate.

His parents had been arguing, again, but this time their anger spilled over onto everyone around them. They never laid a hand on each other, that he knew, and they never touched the kids, but there was so much yelling. Yelling and anger that he couldn't understand.

He was the one Bradley kid, either brave enough or stupid enough— he still didn't know which—to demand reasons why.

Why was he in so much trouble for spilling his glass at the table? It was only water; why did his father yell like it was the end of the world?

Roark had ushered him away, shushing him, wanting him to be quiet and stay away.

Now, Dev knew it was Roark's way of trying to keep him out of the line of fire, but at the time it only felt like being silenced.

He'd had every right to ask why he was getting grounded over nothing, constantly in trouble for the tiniest little thing. But, at least when his parents were upset with him, they weren't ignoring him.

He'd told Brenda he'd run away because of his bratty sister and bossy brother. There was some youthful truth in what he'd said, but his story was still mostly a lie.

Yes, adjusting to suddenly having a sister was difficult, but she wasn't so bad, even from the start. And yes, he and Roark butted heads. People thought the rivalry was brothers being brothers, competitive in almost every way, but that wasn't the root of their issues.

Dev didn't feel like he was in competition with Roark. Growing up, he'd felt obligated to obey him. Roark was the one who gave a damn and took care of them as kids. That obligation chafed at almost every turn because it should've never been that way. For either of them.

But the stuff about needing a hug from Brenda was the truth that hurt the most.

Everything about Brenda was maternal, especially back then. Her kids were only a little older than Devlin and his siblings. They all went to the same school, and Brenda's house was everything theirs wasn't.

Affectionate but firm, she made her kids walk the line, she didn't yell, and she hugged often. Her temperament didn't change like the weather on a fall day. She was steadfast and sure, at a time when the Bradley kids had only volatility and a world of roller-coaster emotions.

When he'd gotten sick of his parents' turmoil and arguing, tired of Roark playing the role of family leader, the only option that made any sense was to run to Ms. Brenda's.

Into the silence, Anna sighed. "You know, I ran away from home once."

Devlin kept his eyes on the road, his hands on the wheel. He didn't ask when or why, even as the curiosity poked and pinched.

"I'd made a C in trigonometry. I was fourteen, a freshman in high school, and I was devastated."

That's it? He would've been ecstatic even to be in trig his freshman year. Instead, that year had been mostly made up of sneaking out, trespassing, and trying time and time again to get a fake ID.

"I didn't make Cs. Never had less than a B-plus in my life. Rather than face my parents with my C, I left."

Now that, he understood. "They would've given you hell about your grade."

"No, not really. My mother might've rolled her eyes or sucked her teeth, but that would've been about the extent of it. My father would've been concerned, but not angry."

"Then why run?"

"I didn't want to tell them. I didn't want anyone to know. I was smarter than a C. My failure was embarrassing."

"Where'd you go?"

"My friend Ginny's house. Her parents were really nice about me showing up at their door with my bag. They ordered a pizza and got in touch with my parents, telling them I'd come over for dinner. They left out the part about my backpack full of clothes and makeup."

He could imagine her big, sad, brown eyes. Who could possibly be mean to her or turn her away?

"Eventually they sent me home, but not until I told them what was wrong. I told them about the C, and it helped. I got to practice saying it out loud before telling my parents."

"That was decent of them."

"Yeah, and my dad took it well. He told me to pull up the grade. No TV and stuff until my homework was done. Grades were priority because I had to get into college, preferably with a scholarship. So, I pulled my grade up and got both."

Smart and driven. But he'd kind of already figured as much.

"I've been meaning to ask . . . what do you do in Atlanta? I was going to guess attorney, but now I don't think so."

"Advertising." She smiled. "I work for the biggest ad agency in Atlanta."

Pieces of Anna began to fall into place. The high-end stuff, her put-together appearance. He'd bet his bike that Anna was hot shit at that big ad agency. She was probably flooring folks left and right, kicking ass, and somebody, somewhere, told her to go take it easy for a while. Take a break in the mountains. Enjoy the fruits of her labor.

"Are you *the* best ad exec at your agency or second best?" he teased.

"No." With a quick look away, she touched her neck. "I don't know. I do all right." Pink splotches dotted the side of her neck, and she wouldn't meet his gaze.

If Anna wasn't *the* best, she wasn't far from it, and for whatever reason, that made her very nervous.

They reached the greenhouse, and Brenda's son walked out to greet them, work gloves already on.

"Yes. Will is here." Dev waved through the window.

"Who?"

"Brenda's son, Will. He can help too, and we'll get these plants loaded without killing ourselves."

"Your sister outdid herself with this order," Will called over as they got out of the truck. "Y'all having another celebrity wedding up there or something?"

Devlin threw his hands up. "This is Sophie being seasonal."

"Yeah, with Mother's Day this weekend and all." Will's attention fell on Anna. "Great. You brought some help."

"Will, this is Anna. Anna, Will."

Once introductions were made, they got to work. He and Will got the heavier planters onto the back of the truck, the smaller items going down into the trailer.

He'd have to creep his way back to the inn to make sure none of the plants were blown to death. They'd look good set up though. So-phie was right to go with a large order, especially if her goal was lush.

Anna stuck with moving the ferns, hanging and standing arrange-ments, but only after he had to remind her their agreement was no large items. Not because she couldn't, but because he wouldn't risk her dropping something on herself and getting hurt.

Or, more likely, him dropping something on her.

He'd assumed she was a stranger to dirty work, but the longer they worked, the faster and harder she moved. They got well over half the plants loaded, but Anna kept going at it like there'd be an award for first one finished. Her focus and drive were undeniably hot.

Staying clean was impossible, and soon soil covered his gloves, dotted his arms, even his face where he'd swiped the sweat away.

Anna stopped on her way back to grab another load, gloved hands on her hips as she caught her breath. She hadn't fared much better. Her gloves were filthy and soil smeared her forehead.

"See? Roughing it," he teased as he passed her with a few baskets of begonias. After he got the baskets loaded, he stood next to her, taking a breather too.

"Moving plants is slightly more work than I imagined, but . . . I kind of like it. Is that weird?"

"Not to me." Sweat trickled down his spine, his hair sticking to his temples because he'd let it get long again. His breath came faster, his heart pounded, and his legs were barking from all the squatting down to grab plants.

And he loved it. Hard work felt great. Anna enjoying it too wasn't weird at all.

Whether he was hauling plants, working on his bike, or trying to fix up the old Chevy, Dev preferred working with his hands. All he thought about was the task in front of him, one he knew he could accomplish, and the effort was immediately evident. The hard jobs were the kind he worked on for days, weeks, even months, and all of the effort may or may not ever show.

"All that's left are the two tall planters and the basin." Will paused with them.

"You and I can get those." Devlin pointed to the largest potted plants.

Anna opened her mouth, but before she could offer to help, he stopped her.

"We've got it. Won't take but a few minutes. I put a cooler with water in the backseat of the truck. If you want to grab some shade, we'll join you in a minute."

The last of the load was the heaviest, and they were tired. He wouldn't risk it.

"Fine. I guess." Anna got the small cooler from the truck and picked a shady spot under the large oak, nearest the greenhouse.

Dev and Will each grabbed a tall planter while she cracked opened one of the bottles and took a long sip.

Her shirt stuck to her, damp from working up a sweat. With her head back, she drank, the pale arch of her neck exposed.

She shouldn't be here. If his goal was walking the line and being a good little Bradley, he should've never agreed to her joining him. The problem was he wasn't a good little Bradley. Never had been. He'd known he was screwed yesterday, yet he'd brought her along with him today, setting himself up for failure.

But if he was a dumb ass for bringing her, and trying to get away with it, in that very moment, he was a genius for the exact same reason.

Her shirt molded to her body with the same appeal as her jeans. Swells and dips in proportions that made the blood rush through his body. Exertion making her skin glow in a way that brought to mind only one thing.

Will whistled softly and Dev stopped, a few inches from plowing right over him.

"I know you're otherwise occupied at the moment, but maybe you could manage not running into me with that planter."

"Sorry."

"It's all good. I understand why you're distracted. Think I could get a hand with this beast though?" Will dipped his chin toward a circular planter, about three feet wide and at least two feet deep, filled with soil.

"Yeah." Dev pushed the planters a little farther back on the truck bed, to make room. He tried shaking off the Anna-induced haze. His reactions and thoughts on her aside, he had a damn job to do. He grabbed one end of the basin, with Will on the other. "One, two— Holy shit, this thing weighs a ton."

Will grunted with the effort as they baby-stepped toward the truck. "How are we going to get it up on the truck?"

"Good question." They couldn't see what was beneath them, the width of the basin blocking their view.

Within a few feet of the truck, Dev accepted that he should've planned better, and now they were screwed.

"Here." Anna hurried over, her gloves on. "You should've yelled for help."

"If you can see the tailgate, guide us toward it and we should all be able to get the edge of the basin on and slide it back," Will directed, using his chin again.

They tilted the base to get some leverage on the tailgate, and clumps of soil began to roll off on Anna's side.

"It's fine. Just keep going."

They managed to get the majority of the weight onto the gate, and then slid it all the way in. The basin was loaded, but not before soil spilled all over them.

Anna brushed off her shirt, only managing to smudge it further. Her shirt clingy and dirty, her skin probably salty and slick, and all he could think was *Yes, please.*

"That's a lot of dirt for a pot with no plants," she said.

"Soil," Will said.

"What?"

Dev leaned closer to her, making a show of covering his mouth to whisper. "If you call it dirt, he'll fuss. Dirt is something you find anywhere on the ground. Soil is special."

"I am not going to fuss." Will slammed the tailgate closed. "Stop telling her lies."

"You always fuss at me for calling it dirt."

"Yeah, well, *you* know better." He hit Anna with a bright smile, full of perfect teeth. "Soil is vitamin rich and intentional. Dirt is plain ole dirt. Now, you mind if I steal one of those waters before I get back to work?"

Devlin held his hand out toward the cooler.

"If y'all want to clean up a little, there's a spigot right outside the greenhouse. Help yourself." Will grabbed a bottle of water on his way back inside the greenhouse, leaving the two of them alone, and filthy.

"I guess we could clean up before we get in Roark's truck."

They found the spigot on the far side of the greenhouse, and the water flowed cool and clear.

"Ladies first."

"Oh." Anna stared askance at the steady stream of water splashing down on the pallet they'd put under it as a makeshift grate. "No, you go ahead."

If she was waiting for the water to warm up or miraculously turn into one of those fancy waterfall showerheads, she'd be waiting awhile.

Dev knelt and cupped his hands together under the flow, splashing his face clean.

"Did you ever think you'd be washing off with water from a spigot?"

"Not really. I prefer a hot bath, but this will do."

He collected more water in one hand, dousing the length of his arm, then the other, rubbing and sloughing the spray down his forearms. Once he was clean—or as clean as he was going to get—he stood and tugged his shirt up to the only patch that wasn't dirty, to dry his face. "Your turn."

Chapter 7

Forget taking a bath. Washing off in the spigot was, without a doubt, the best way to get clean.

Dev pulled his shirt up a little higher to scrub at the hair by his temples, revealing his flat stomach again, the ripple of abs, and skin tanner than it had any right to be in early May. "We probably should've worn shorts. I didn't think it'd get this hot today."

His jeans sat low, the dips of his hips peeking out above the waistline.

She didn't wear shorts in public, no matter how high the temperature got. Her tree trunks weren't made for shorts, but Dev . . .

Underneath the denim, she'd bet her favorite bag he had sculpted legs. The thighs she knew were thick and shapely, but he probably had good calves too, from hiking around the resort's property.

Not for the first time, she imagined those legs with hers hooked over them.

She locked her feet in place. If she didn't, she'd certainly lose her footing. Fall into him the way he'd fallen on her the day before, except face-first and smiling.

Carefully, she leaned down, collecting a little water in her hand, giving herself something to do. She patted at her neck and cheeks. Whatever it took to dawdle and watch Dev dry off some more.

"You've still got some dirt right there." He pointed to her cheek.

She swiped at her cheek, her attempt halfhearted at best.

He shook his head and reached for her. With the fingers of one hand, curled under her chin, he held her face still. With the other, he swiped the pad of his thumb across her skin.

Goose bumps rose on her arms, and not because of the cold water.

If he saw, he'd know exactly the effect he had on her, and she couldn't bring herself to mind.

"Do I look like I've face-planted in mud?" she asked as he touched her.

"Far from it."

"Is there a towel or a mirror in your brother's truck, by any chance?"

"You don't need all that." He leaned away, assessing her. Then he reached back and tugged his shirt up over his head.

And she almost swallowed her tongue.

Dev with his shirt hiked up was hard enough to endure without reacting. Shirtless, he made heat flash up her neck. She put a hand on the side of the greenhouse for support.

Smooth, tan skin, a dusting of hair across his chest, the thick roll of muscle across his pecs and shoulders.

"Here." He bent down and ran his shirt under the water. Once he'd wrung it out, he went back to holding her chin, turning it to wipe the dirt from her face.

She counted to ten, she sang the birthday song—anything to keep her mind busy.

None of it worked. Heat radiated off him, not helping her neck situation at all. If he touched her right now, trailed the tips of his fingers down her neck or anything else, she'd end up sighing or moaning, very loud, and embarrass the crap out of both of them.

A shiver ran through her at the thought, and she pinched her eyes closed.

"Cold?" he asked, way too close for her control.

"I—I wouldn't say that. No."

She opened her eyes to find him staring right into them. His pale gaze gleamed as he ran his tongue over his lips. "No?"

He knew exactly what he was doing; he was making sure she did too.

With water collected in his palm, he cleaned one of her arms, then the other, chasing the rivulets with the sweep of his hand.

He was bathing her—in a sense. The warmth of his skin against hers, his work-roughened fingers applying the perfect pressure and friction, his touch amazing. And she was supposed to stand there and not spontaneously combust?

"Better?" His voice was pitched low and rough.

"Uh-huh."

Heck yes, she was.

"Is this okay?" He still touched her. She was clean, but his hands lingered, making a slow descent to her wrists.

He stepped even closer, a gentle tug on her wrists to bring her toward him.

The question hung there, even as the charge between them grew. He wanted to know if she was okay with him touching her, getting closer, possibly sweeping her into his arms and devouring her mouth with his.

And the answer was yes. She was more than okay with all of that. Shocking, really, to think *how* okay she'd be.

The guilt might come, later, but right now she wanted to know what he'd do next. Feel his touch somewhere other than her arms. Taste his kiss.

Anna nodded, taking the final step, slipping her wrists from his grasp to slide her hands over the curve of his bare arms. "Is this?"

Was any of this wise? Advisable when the point of her being here was to focus? No.

Did she care? Absolutely not.

There was a flash of something else in his eyes then. Something dark and carnal and her body reacted to the promise. The heat on her neck flooded her limbs, tingling all the way into her core.

What if he looked like that during sex? All hungry and perfect and predatory. What if he looked at her like that?

Her pulse pounded, her body aching for whatever he could give her.

The crushing rush of need startled her, as unfamiliar as the giddy high of having her interest returned so blatantly.

And she liked it.

She was alive in the moment. Present. Right now.

Dev bent, his lips inches from hers. "A hell of a lot more than okay," he said. Then he kissed her.

A hot, promising press of his lips against hers, sucking gently until she tilted into him.

He swept his tongue against the seam of her lips, heat flickering between her legs. She opened to him and he slanted his mouth against hers with a low, possessive sound.

She had no idea what that noise was she made in response, but the sound certainly wasn't dignified.

Dev's hands were on her then. His fingers gripping her waist, dragging her against him. He kissed like his thirst for her outweighed even his thirst for water.

His bare chest was a hot brand against her, the hard planes molding into her curves, marking her in a way she'd never forget.

Her fingers slipped on his damp skin and she gripped him tighter, making him growl into her mouth.

"Hey, Dev! Where you at? Can I bother you for some help up here real quick?" Will yelled, looking for them.

"Hell." Dev pulled himself away from her, his expression pained.

"Dev?" he shouted again.

"Yeah! I'll help."

His gaze met hers, apologetic, aggravated, and about as sexually frustrated as she felt. "I've got to—"

"I know."

He went to help Will, and she caught her breath.

Once he was gone around the side of the greenhouse, she fanned herself, pulling her hair up off her neck. Decades remained before hot flashes were an issue, but regardless, her body was a furnace at the moment.

She turned the spigot on again, getting her hands wet to flick sprinkles of water on her chest and neck.

The more she thought about Dev's touch, his skilled lips working a moan from hers . . .

Nope. That was not helping the redness of her skin.

She turned her mind to the birthday song again and the obnoxious pop number played every ten minutes on the radio. Gradually, she simmered down to a low boil, safe enough to rejoin society.

By the time she rounded the greenhouse, Dev was finishing up getting camellia bushes loaded onto an elderly couple's truck.

Will flashed her a quick grin, like he knew exactly what the two of them had been up to behind the greenhouse.

Behind the greenhouse, for crying out loud. She ought to be ashamed, but . . . she wasn't.

"All done. Thanks, man." Will shook Dev's hand, plucking at the wet shirt he'd put back on. "Since you helped, I won't ask."

"Good. Don't." Dev turned to her. "We should probably head to the store now."

"Store?" He'd lost her.

"For your groceries. You know, the reason you came with me today?"

"Oh right. Groceries. That would . . . yes, let's do that."

Will shook his head and waved goodbye. Dev opened the truck door for her, but the ride to the grocery store was quiet.

"Thank you for remembering the store. I almost forgot."

"No problem." His eyes were trained on the road.

No joke, no glances, and not a single mention of their kiss.

Had she done something wrong? Somehow between being putty in his hands and him hauling camellias, had she managed to screw things up?

Water from the spigot dried on her skin, and goose bumps rose in the cool air. Had she been *too* forward? She'd been so certain of his mutual interest, but the possibility existed that she was flat-out wrong.

How easily his silence made her question everything.

They pulled up at a small grocery store, and he showed her around, helping her get enough items to keep her stocked over the next week or so. He was polite but distant.

"We can come back whenever you need more. You don't want to buy so much that it goes stale."

"Good point." He was being helpful. That was at least a little promising.

She'd known Devlin exactly one day. Twenty-four hours. In that time she'd flirted with him more than she'd flirted with any man in her entire life, maybe even if she combined them all.

He caused a buzz beneath her skin. The kind of thing her therapist had talked about. Living in the moment. This was definitely a moment, and she'd kick herself if she'd ruined it.

Back in the truck, more silence lurked as they wound their way up the mountain, until Dev cursed and jerked the wheel, pulling off onto a driveway she hadn't even seen.

He threw the truck into park and turned to her. "Look, I'm not one to dance around stuff. The whole strong, silent bullshit works for my brother, but for me all it does is make my eye twitch."

"Okay."

"That kiss was . . ." Instead of a word, he sighed, rough, with a look of pure pleasure dancing across his face.

Thank god he felt it too.

"Amazing?"

"*Yes*. Amazing. But . . ."

"But?"

He dragged a hand through his hair, slicking it back. "You're a guest. I'm not supposed to be attracted to you. Or—no, that's not it. I can be attracted to you, but I'm not supposed to do anything about it."

"Why?"

"I don't know. Because I'm supposed to be celibate?" He threw his hand up. "That's not true, I do know. Resort policy. Family reputation. Keeping things on the professional level. You know, like any other business."

Fair enough. Probably wasn't very professional to be dilly-dallying with the guests, but surely it happened—at resorts and getaways all around the world. And she wasn't going to cause a scene or make trouble.

She could be the exception to the rule.

"I sort of had a fling with a guest once—"

Okay, so scratch being the exception to the rule.

"—when I was about twenty years old and home for the summer."

That was years ago. College age. Sowing college oats didn't count. They were both adults, fully capable of making responsibly ill-advised decisions.

He glanced over. "I was a stupid kid. The rule was unofficial before that, but because of me it's official now. Especially official for me."

Her insides twisted. Was he saying . . . ?

"If my family finds out, or so much as thinks we're doing things like kissing behind greenhouses, I'm screwed. If they find out you were even with me today, I'm screwed."

"But Will knows."

"Will isn't going to say a word. Neither will Brenda, but on resort property, it's different. I can't . . . I can't do what I did today."

But she liked what he did today.

If there was an official policy against fraternizing with guests, that meant no interaction with Devlin except for harmless flirtations. Now that she'd kissed him, she didn't want to go back to flirting with the idea of him. She wanted him.

Her relaxing vacation suddenly stretched out before her, long and lonely and not relaxing in the least.

All etiquette gone after partaking in their spigot bath, she threw out the truth. "Well, that sucks."

"I know." He ran a hand over his hair again, tugging at the ends. "Maybe if we—"

"What?" She jumped on his words.

"Nothing. It's a dumb idea. I'm a jerk for even thinking it."

"In advertising, there are no dumb ideas. Not when brainstorming. They're simply unformed ideas. Let's hear it."

He studied her for a moment, a smile tugging at the corner of those talented lips. "I was thinking . . . if no one knows I'm breaking a policy, is it really broken?"

The idea ran around her brain. Questionable logic, but she liked it. "I don't think so, no."

He tapped the steering wheel, a car passing them on its way up the mountain.

"Maybe it's like me helping you move the plants. I participated of my own free will, we had a mutual understanding, no one was hurt, and no one has to know."

His tapping ceased. "And we're . . . okay with that?"

We meaning *she*. Was *she* okay with them sneaking around and kissing behind greenhouses, the possibility for more pretty evident, yet keeping it quiet? "I am perfectly okay with that kind of arrangement if you are."

Dev didn't answer right away. He twisted his grip on the steering wheel, and put the truck in reverse, pulling back onto the road. As they took the turn for the resort's long driveway, he finally answered. "I'm okay too. I'm not well-behaved enough to follow policy anyway."

He parked the truck and trailer alongside the inn. "I have maybe a minute or two before Sophie starts blowing up my phone about wanting these plants hung and in place. Tomorrow though, I'm free after noon. I want to take you to lunch. As a thank-you for today, like Brenda suggested."

"Doesn't miss a beat, that Brenda."

"Told you."

"Lunch sounds wonderful."

"Somewhere away from the resort and town. I'll meet you around twelve thirty." He glanced around, but no one had walked down this side of the inn since they parked. "You know, even if I'd gotten busted for you working with me today, any trouble I got into would be worth it. Especially the cleanup after. I had a great time."

Heat touched her neck as she fidgeted with her hair to cover it. "I did too."

"Why do you try to hide when your neck flushes?"

Anna gawked. "You've noticed?"

"It's kind of hard not to."

"Oh my god." She leaned forward so her hair fell around her face, hiding her.

"No." He touched her shoulder, trying to make her sit up. "You shouldn't hide. I think it's cute."

"Cute?" she asked from the safety of her hair. "It's horrible. And so embarrassing."

"Shouldn't be. I like it."

As she lifted her chin, her gaze locked with his. How could he ever find an oncoming case of hives-like spots, cute?

Dev jumped, making her jump too.

"Sorry, my phone went off." He dug it out of his pocket. "It's Sophie. I better let her know I'm back. And make her and Trev help me with these plants. Can you manage your groceries okay?"

She had a whopping three bags total. "I think I'll be fine."

"Tomorrow, then?"

Her pulse did a giddy hop-step. "Tomorrow."

Chapter 8

Dev sat outside, a few minutes after noon the next day, chilling on a bench, as his sister ran around the front of the resort like a lunatic. Her fiery red hair flew out behind her as she chased a big, brown mop of a dog toward the portico.

He was to meet Anna in a bit, and defy the family policy on fraternizing with guests. Friendly small talk was fine, but he and Anna had already gone way beyond that.

His concern wasn't so much about anyone finding out. He had a ton of practice at being sneaky, but in doing so, he was falling into an old habit. Years had gone by since he'd kept anything from his family, but he couldn't tell them about Anna.

Roark would pop a vessel, and Sophie would worry while simultaneously giving him hell about it.

Being circumspect was the right thing to do, and Anna was worth it.

She might look like polish and shine on the outside, but beneath all that was a river of depths and details he wanted to chart and understand.

She'd laughed good-naturedly about him falling on her, instead of making him feel like even more of an ass. Rather than expect an expensive date or leave their interaction at frivolous flirtations, she'd jumped at the chance to help him with grunt work, and enjoyed it. She'd told him about the time she ran away from home too, just so he wouldn't feel awkward about Brenda's story.

The only people he knew who'd do that for him were his family. And they were all crazy anyway.

"Damn dog." Sophie stopped, panting to catch her breath.

For a solid five minutes, she'd chased Trevor's dog, Beau. The most futile act imaginable, especially when the air was crisp and cool. The dog was on a canine high. Best to let him wear down.

"You need to stop running after him, and sit down."

Sophie threw her hands up in the air. "How will I catch him if I'm sitting down?"

"Beau runs because you're running. Getting you to act like a lunatic is his favorite thing."

"Beau! Dang it!" She shouted at him as he ran by.

"Would you get over here and sit down?"

Sophie plopped next to him, crossing her arms and legs in a huff.

Dev patted her head, to annoy her, and she jerked away, cutting him a look. "You're the one who let him off his leash."

"Because he doesn't run *from me*. He'll be over in a minute. And if that doesn't work, I've requested the secret weapon."

"What's the secret weapon?"

"If I tell you, how is it a secret?"

Sophie donkey-punched him in the top of the thigh, laughing as he winced and grabbed his leg.

At the ruckus, Beau stopped in front of them, paws planted wide, tail in a frantic wag, and then he took off in a brown blur.

"That dog, I swear to god. He acts like my best buddy inside, but I try to take him out and—" She flung her hands out toward the dog as he ran around the portico twice.

"That's because you are his buddy. He wants to have fun. He thinks you're playing, which is a lot better than obeying."

They sat there another couple of minutes, but Beau never tired or slowed down. Luckily, Dev had texted Wright about the secret weapon as soon as he saw the dog on the loose.

"Here you go." Wright joined them a moment later, a folded paper towel in his hands like he was presenting a crown.

Sophie stood. "Is that the secret weapon?"

"If by secret weapon you mean bacon, then yes, it's a secret weapon."

Dev took the paper towel from his friend, unfolding so Beau would catch a whiff.

"Did you let him off the leash again?" Wright smiled down at Sophie.

"You can both bite me." She snatched a piece of bacon off the paper towel and walked out onto the driveway, dangling the bacon between two fingers, her head on a swivel in search of the dog.

Wright folded his arms across his chest, wide-eyeing Dev.

"Don't pay her any attention. It's not you. She's mad at me because I wouldn't tell her what the secret weapon was. When she gets crabby like this, I like to remind people she's adopted."

She flipped him off without looking back, but she'd harbor no real anger at Dev's remark. He was the only person on earth who could give her a hard time about being the redheaded stepchild, and she knew he meant it with love.

The truth was, Sophie was normally the jovial, levelheaded one. The calming glue that kept the siblings from tearing apart. But every now and again, if something got her riled, she'd live up to the stereotype of the fiery redhead and the whole world better duck and run.

Wright shook his head. "Yeah, I was going to say, she was in a great mood this morning. What happened?"

"I guess Beau happened." Dev held out the other piece of bacon, waiting for an appearance. He lowered his voice and spoke from the side of his mouth. "Plus I think her date for tonight called and ditched her. And she's pissed, but don't tell her I told you."

Concern flickered across Wright's face, gone in an instant. "Then I don't blame her for being pissed. She's been talking about it for a couple of days now. Some guys are such assholes."

The sound of galloping feet came from around the inn. Beau was close.

"Yep. Single life can be rough." Not for him at the moment; but normally, being Devlin Bradley, and half the town would rather die than let their daughter, sister, or niece go out with you, it was tough going. "But you don't have to worry about sweating the single status anymore." He swatted Wright on the arm with the back of his hand.

"You make it sound like I've settled down and gotten married. We've dated a couple of months."

Dev crouched down as Beau took off across the parking lot but then turned, a streak of brown coming down the homestretch. "That is settled down, in my book, but the point being, you aren't out there dating at random anymore. You have a girlfriend. I know you wanted one, so I'm assuming that's a good thing."

"Yeah." Wright didn't sound all that convinced.

Regardless of what he thought, Wright was one of those guys who always seemed to have a girlfriend. He was what most would consider a catch. Good family—even if they were stuck-up—stable and steady, outgoing, and nice looking—Dev guessed. And the guy could flat out cook. He wasn't their gourmet chef for no reason.

Toss in the fact that he was the most loyal friend Dev had, and one hell of a nice guy—Wright was every mother's dream son-in-law.

Why he'd stayed friends with Dev all these years was still a mystery.

Wright unfolded his arms and shifted on his feet. "It is a good thing, but I'm not proposing next week or anything. That's all I'm saying."

Dev frowned. "Why are you acting weird?"

"I'm not."

Beau barked and bolted down the road leading to the cabins, and a female yelp seized Dev's full attention. "Beau!" He took off after the dog, who was headed straight for Anna.

He wouldn't hurt her of course, but she didn't know that, and that was a whole lot of dog barreling toward her.

"Beau!" he yelled again.

"Beau!" both Sophie and Wright called, right behind him.

Anna froze in place, arms out in front of her as the dog swerved at the last second, and ran around her in bouncy counterclockwise circles.

"Oh my god, that dog scared the crap out of me." Anna held her hand over her heart.

As soon as they got close, Beau caught scent of the bacon. Dev had his full attention then, feeding him as Sophie hooked the leash onto his collar.

"Gotcha, you little escape artist."

"Sorry about that." Dev's gaze met Anna's. "He's a little high on dog life today and he loves new people."

"That's okay. I'm awake now at least."

He scratched the top of Beau's head before stepping away. Now was the time to play things cool. Anna was like any other guest, so long as Sophie and Wright were around. His reaction and behavior toward her needed to reflect that.

"We still have fresh coffee in the great room, if you'd like some."

Anna blinked, and then seemed to catch what he was doing, giving him an impartial smile. "Thank you, but I was thinking more along the lines of lunch."

"We're already serving in the restaurant," Wright chimed in.

"Oh. Thank you, but . . . I might go into town or something."

"Speaking of lunch, I better get back to check on the new mac and cheese I'm trying out. Gouda, man. Gouda." Wright swatted Dev twice as hard as he'd done earlier. "Nice meeting you. Hope to see you in the restaurant." He gave Anna a quick wave and barely made eye contact with Sophie.

Wright would not be seeing Anna at lunch. Dev already had the perfect place in mind.

Sophie looked back and forth between Dev and Anna. "So, do you two know each other?" she asked, as soon as Wright was gone.

Dev had to school his expression so his shock didn't show. How the hell did his sister do that? "Not exactly. Anna, this is my sister, Sophie. Soph, Anna. I had to fix the fan in Anna's cabin the other day."

The two shook hands, which only made him more nervous. More time around Soph meant more opportunity for her to sniff out the truth.

"How are you liking Honeywilde?" she asked, seemingly innocent.

"It's wonderful." Anna smiled. "I'm here from Atlanta, and this is exactly the change of scenery I needed."

"Atlanta." Sophie shuddered. "Too big for me."

"Me too. Sometimes. But big cities are great for advertising."

"You're in advertising? That's so—"

"Okay, we better let you get to lunch." Dev hurried his sister up. Otherwise she'd stand there and chitchat for hours.

"Yeah, I should head back." Sophie jerked on Beau's leash. "Time for Trevor to manage his dog. Sorry again if he scared you."

"Just a bit." Anna slowly reached for Beau, receiving nuzzles and a lick in reward. "Mostly startled me. For a second all I could think was bear."

Sophie cackled, then clamped a hand over her mouth. "I guess he could look like a bear. Maybe."

"Better get him back before Trev starts wondering where he is." Dev hurried her along again.

Sophie dragged Beau away, giving him the stink-eye without saying a word.

Once his sister was gone, Dev dropped the act.

"You okay?" He moved closer, touching her elbow.

"Fine. I only screamed because—"

"You didn't seriously think Beau was a bear."

"All I saw was something furry and brown, running toward me."

She scowled and he couldn't help but laugh. "Come on; let's get out of here while we still can."

They got away from the resort and into Newton in record time.

"Why aren't we going into Windamere? There were so many cute little restaurants."

"Too many people know me in town. I don't want gossip getting back to my brother that I was on a date, and then he'd want to know who, and believe me, there would be gossip. Better to avoid all that."

He played off his choice of location like it was all about keeping him from getting busted for being with her, but an even bigger motivator was how many people only saw trouble when they saw him coming.

How he was going to get those very same people to believe he could bring back the Blueberry Festival, he had no idea.

On the side street next to the soda shop, he parked his SUV, and hopped out to help Anna.

She'd worn pants today, not jeans. Still black, and still hugging her curves like a dream, with a cream-colored blouse that scooped low enough to be a constant cause of frustration.

"This is the place?" She smiled at the red and white awning across the front, the white metal bistro tables and chairs on the sidewalk out front.

They were late enough to miss most of the lunch crowd, and the tables and counter inside were empty except for two gray-haired fellows, sipping milkshakes.

"It's a legitimate soda shop?" Anna clapped her hands.

"I thought this might be a change from the trendy Atlanta restaurant. Hand-dipped ice cream, root beer floats, the works. And the best burgers in town. Don't tell Wright I said that. You like burgers?"

"Love them." They chose a table near the windows and Anna grabbed one of the menus tucked in by the napkin dispenser, holding it close, like a cherished book. "This is like something from *Grease*. It's so cute."

A waitress came right over, and they ordered two teas, neither saying much else until she brought over their drinks and disappeared.

"How long do you have until you're missed?" Anna fiddled with the straw in her glass. "Until you have to get back."

"Hour or two. Roark wants me to be on a call with him and our account manager at the bank, but that's not until three this afternoon. Plenty of time for lunch."

"That's good though, right? Him wanting you to participate in calls with the bank."

Dev cocked an eyebrow. Roark including him was a big step in the right direction, compared to a year of menial responsibilities. But she'd only know he was making progress if she'd overheard more than a word or two of their conversation at breakfast yesterday.

"It's a small step in the right direction, but sitting in on a phone call isn't giving me more involvement. Hell might freeze over before he'd trust me to handle something on my own."

"Something like that festival?"

"You heard more than a little of our conversation."

She held her menu a little higher, peeking over the top. "Maybe? I might've heard all of it. I was trying not to, but I heard enough to know you want to sponsor this festival more than he does."

"Gross. Understatement. He hates the idea and refuses. I've tried for weeks now and everything I suggest gets shot down."

And he needed to keep his big mouth shut. As nice as it was to get that off his chest and have a third, unbiased party to listen, Anna was here on vacation. She'd want to relax, not hear him gripe about work.

Anna leaned over her menu, her voice low. "I don't know your brother, obviously, but I've gotten very good at telling whether or not people are going to buy. From what I could tell, your brother doesn't *hate* the idea of the festival, but it will take a lot to get him on board. He needs convincing."

"Yeah. No joke." He stabbed his straw angrily at the innocent ice cubes. "I don't know why I'm bothering. This festival has been a Windamere tradition for decades, but Roark is dead set against doing anything that might cost Honeywilde some money, besides the basic little upgrades."

"Sometimes you have to spend money to make money."

He held his hand out toward her. "Exactly. But try telling Roark that."

Once the waitress came and went again, taking their order for two cheeseburgers all the way, and a large order of sweet potato fries, Dev sat, drumming his fingers on the menu. Stewing.

"Anyway. We don't have to talk about all that." He shoved the menus back in their slots.

Anna studied him, her dark eyes unnervingly aware. "But I think maybe you want to."

He did and he didn't. Talking about himself, his problems, simply wasn't his style. All moping ever did was bring people down.

With Anna, he definitely didn't want to talk about stuff that made him long in the mouth. They went through the trouble of sneaking away to have lunch together. They should be laughing and having fun.

"Have you given up on bringing the festival back for now or . . . ?" Anna sipped her tea, eyebrows raised as she scoped for details again.

He wasn't going to sit there and grumble about not getting his way though. He'd rather hear about her.

"What would you suggest I do?"

She sat up straight, the straw falling from her lips. "What do you mean?"

"Should I give up on trying to bring this festival back, or keep trying? I want to know what you think."

"I don't . . . I don't think anything about it."

"Sure you do." Less than two days may have gone by, but he already knew enough about Anna to know she'd have some thoughts on the matter.

"What would you do, if you were me?" Dev asked. Plain and simple. "Give up now or keep going, see what happens?"

Her gaze drifted out the window, to the empty sidewalk beside them. There wasn't much to see besides the brick wall of the building across from them, but she was focused on something.

"I doubt I'd give up." Her gaze swung back to him. "I can be a little too persistent for that. As you may have noticed."

He had noticed, and he liked it. "Okay, then I keep trying. How do I convince my brother the idea won't be the biggest disaster to ever befall Windamere?"

She laughed, coughing over a sip of tea. "I'm sure Roark doesn't think *that*."

"You don't know him like I know him. In that big brain of his, he's worrying about acts of God and insurance claims. I guarantee it. How do I get a doubting Thomas to take a chance on something new?"

With a shrug, she pinched her lips together.

"Hey, you're the one who said he didn't hate the idea, just needs convincing. And I know you're on vacation, but all I want is your opinion. How do I convince my brother?"

"I can't guarantee my ideas will be the best."

His mouth fell open. "Are you kidding? You can't be top dog at some highfalutin ad agency unless you have the great ideas."

That at least made her smile. "I never said I was top dog."

"You didn't have to. And even if you're low dog, I'm willing to risk that your ideas are better than mine. Now, what've you got? Hit me with them."

After a brief pause, she set her tea away and focused on him. "Fine. Tell me a little about the festival first. Give me some framework."

Anna was in, he could tell by the spark in her eyes.

He leaned forward, ready to talk about something other than how he felt. "For ages, Windamere has had the Blueberry Festival near the end of June. The whole thing takes place over a long weekend, but it's the biggest event for our town, and a huge source of money for the businesses. They block off Main Street, set up vendor tents, there's food and shopping, usually some music. We get tourists from all over. It's awesome. But for the last few years, the town stopped organizing it. They say it costs too much with no return. No organizer, no festival."

"And your brother believes there's no return?"

"Yep. Because that's what the tourism board says."

"But you don't agree."

"I don't see how. Maybe the organizers break even, or lose a little money at most, but think of the publicity, the public relations for making Windamere's favorite event happen again."

"It'd be a feather in Honeywilde's cap."

He held his hand out again. "That's what I'm saying." Anna got it; why couldn't his brother?

Dev leaned back in his chair, satisfied he was at least making sense to someone. He stretched out his leg, the inside of his calf and knee bumping against hers.

She didn't move, didn't pull her leg away, maybe even shifted to press against him more. Awareness still sparkled in her eyes, but of a whole different kind.

Flashes from yesterday flew through his mind. The way she felt in his arms drove him wild. Firm or supple in the perfect places, the softness of her lips, the way she opened so sweetly. And holy hell, the needy noises she'd made.

Dev shifted in the hard chair, careful not to move his leg from where it touched her.

The waitress delivered their food and they ate the first half of their meal that way, neither of them pulling away. Until Anna uncrossed her legs, the movement rubbing her knee along the inside of his thigh.

Dev swallowed a bite of his burger, practically whole.

She went on eating, her knee against him, the friction of her occasionally tapping her foot under the table enough to make it the most enticing lunch he'd ever had.

Finished with his meal, he cocked an eyebrow. "You know, eventually, I've got to get up and walk out of here. Get on back to work."

"So?"

"So. I can't do that with our legs all tangled together."

"You're the one with the long legs. I'm over here on my side of the table."

"Right. Because you're totally innocent here." He slid back, giving himself a little room. Not because he wanted to, but because he was afraid if they kept going this way, he'd be stuck at the table for about an hour while his jets cooled.

When moving didn't help much, he clenched his back teeth, talking through the frustration. "You never did tell me your idea on how to convince my brother."

She pointed at him with the fry she was about to eat. "I think you need to get the financials on the event from the last few years, like Roark asked."

Well, hell, she really had heard it all. "But how? Walk into the tourism board's offices and ask them to give me all of their information?"

"If it's a government office, their books should be public record. It sounded like the money was the biggest hurdle for your brother. Show him that the event is profitable, or at least not a total loss, and

I bet you could sell him on organizing the festival." She popped the fry in her mouth.

Her suggestion was the same as Roark's, and they both made good sense. But their logic wasn't the problem; he was.

Inquiring about financial records meant he, Devlin Bradley, former town delinquent, would have to roll up into the local government offices, and ask some buttoned-up snot in a bow tie to do him a favor.

Windamere was a small town and people didn't leave. Without question, the chair of tourism would know all about Devlin's reputation.

The thought of it churned the lunch in his stomach. Facing judgmental looks and whispers. He'd done enough of that in the first twenty-five years of his life. Currently, his plan was to avoid all potentially negative interactions, until he could offset his reputation with something positive.

A good deed on a big scale.

Getting Roark what he needed couldn't wait. If he wanted the festival to happen, he'd have to ask for the books.

He leaned forward, planting both elbows on the table. "I knew you'd have a brilliant idea, Anna from Atlanta, but what was it you said yesterday? 'Well, this sucks.' "

"Why?"

Good question—seeing as how there was no obvious reason he should be opposed to asking for public records. Regular people could ask for anything.

He wasn't regular people; not in Windamere.

What excuse could he give her, because there was no way he was telling her the truth.

He was shy? She already knew better.

He was scared of authority? Ha! Since he was seven, he hadn't been able to even fake a fear of authority.

He was . . . nervous. Now that held promise. Everyone understood nerves. Anxiety when dealing with something important. Not really a lie at all. He was nervous about going into town, facing people and his past, but not for reasons she might presume.

"I'm worried he'll say no. Nervous about asking. This is a big deal. I don't want to screw it up." His rationale came out in a rush.

Anna tilted her head, a notch of confusion along her brow. Then it smoothed out, and she smiled. "I get nervous too, sometimes. Not about talking to people, but . . . other things. Talking I can handle."

Her? Nervous? He couldn't imagine what would make her nervous. Drinking the last of his tea, he realized he was paddling upriver with a leaky boat. The only question was, how long would it take him to sink?

"I could go with you to the tourism board. I've had to ask the City of Atlanta for transportation stats before, for an event with the Braves. One time I needed information on arena closures for a movie they were filming. Now *that* was impossible. Movie companies won't give you anything. There's no way Windamere's tourism board is as tight-lipped as Hollywood."

Stunned, Dev froze with his tea glass inches from the tabletop. "Why would you want to go with me to talk to some government lackey when you're on vacation?"

Chapter 9

"I..."

Yes, genius. Why would she want to spend her time away from work, *working*?

Because she couldn't seem to stop herself. Because all she had now was her career, and even though she'd been sucking wind at it lately, normally work was her safe zone.

Not to mention, helping Dev yesterday—kissing him—was the best part of her vacation so far. Who was she kidding? Dev kissing her had been the best part of any vacation.

"I'd like to help," she told him. Versus explaining that the time she spent in his presence was the happiest she'd been in seven months.

Yesterday, the sadness over losing her father hadn't dragged her under, she wasn't freaking out about work, and she wasn't obsessing over what to do if she'd lost the magic touch that'd made her successful. If time with Dev meant spending an hour or two in a beige government office on Monday, then so be it. Bring on the beige.

"I think I could be useful in getting your plan for this festival off the ground."

Dev finally set his glass down. "I know you could be, but . . ."

Uh-oh. He might actually say no to her offer. She'd been almost certain of a yes. He'd looked almost panicked about going to talk to these business people alone. Apparently she could sell the crap out of some overpriced boots, but not her ability to be useful.

"The fact remains, you're on vacation. I can't monopolize your time with my project when you're supposed to be having fun."

So his objection was tied to guilt. Taking up her vacation time. Little did he know this was precisely how she wanted to spend her vacation. "Would it be monopolizing though? What are we talking, an hour or two to ask for some records? Maybe an hour or two every other day if you need to brainstorm ideas? Won't we be finding a way to spend time together anyway?"

"Yeah, but work wasn't what I had in mind."

When she smiled he leaned in, closer to her. A very good sign.

"If I say yes, and you help me out with the festival, you have to let me help you too."

"Help me what?"

"Vacation." With the fingertips of both hands, he tapped the table. "You clearly don't know how. There's where you need my help. If we go to the tourism office later in the day on Monday, we can slip away after. Grab some coffee, take in a sight. You know, do something more in line with actual vacation activities. I'm on shift at reception all day tomorrow, but Monday I can come up with an excuse to be gone for a while."

Her pulse jumped. That meant spending almost half a day with him, and another date, this time without the lunch-break time constraint. "Sounds like we have a deal."

Dev's gaze locked with hers, a warm smile on his lips and a flash of heat in his eyes that scorched. He reached for the menus again, and passed one over. "Yes, it does. And it starts right now."

"Are you still hungry?" She glanced down at the menu that'd been thrust into her hands.

"On vacation, you have dessert."

"I couldn't possibly—"

"Yes, you can. Life is short and the best ice cream around is right here. Don't tell Wright I said that."

She was doing it.

She was going to be on vacation and live in the moment. A moment that included two-dozen flavors of ice cream and about half a dozen floats.

"Hold the phone." Dev tugged her menu down. "They have the blueberry."

"Blueberry what?"

Pointing to a sticker at the very bottom, he emphasized each word. "*Homemade Blueberry Ice Cream in a Waffle Bowl.* They never have it this early in the season."

"I can't eat a whole—" One look at his face and she stopped talking. "A waffle bowl sounds reasonable."

Dev drummed his fingers on the table until their waitress returned. "This is going to change your life. Just wait."

Of all the ice cream flavors listed, the chocolate with sea-salted caramel jumped out at her. And kept jumping, up and down, with little sea-salted caramel hands waving.

By the time the waitress reappeared, Anna needed a napkin for her drool. "I think I'm going to try the chocolate with caramel."

Devlin sucked in air and looked at her like she'd said she was going to steal a child's ice cream instead of buying her own. "No."

"No?"

"Choosing chocolate over blueberry will be your biggest regret."

"I never regret chocolate."

"But it's blueberry season." He pointed to the sticker on the menu.

Anna pointed to the description of the chocolate. "But rich, creamy chocolate with ribbons of sea-salted caramel."

"The chocolate is very good." The waitress shared a look with Anna that screamed, *Girl, get the life-changing chocolate and caramel and bury your face in the bowl.*

"Then I'll have the chocolate with caramel."

"Go ahead and ruin your life. But don't come begging me for a taste after you realize your mistake. I don't share." Dev ordered the blueberry.

"That works, because I don't share either."

Dev paid the tab and told the waitress they'd take the ice cream with them. "We can walk and eat. It's nice out. And you're on vacation."

When their ice cream arrived, his looked suspiciously like it included bits of cheesecake, and that was *not* mentioned on the menu.

They took their ice cream and he led her toward the edge of a small green space with a winding path, in the middle of the town.

Not as quaint as Windamere and its goats, but Newton still had charm.

As they started on the path, Anna stuck a spoonful of ice cream into her mouth. The chocolate with the nip of sea salt took over her mouth. "Oh. My. God."

"Right?"

"Oh my god," was all she could manage. The cold, smooth texture was heaven and the distinct flavor of real chocolate—she could die.

Devlin finally dug into his waffle bowl with the extra-long spoon, and he moaned as his eyes rolled back in his head.

"Yours is good too, I take it?" She laughed.

They walked and ate, but every few steps Dev let out a moan filled with physical satisfaction, and it danced across Anna's senses.

"If you're going to keep moaning over that ice cream, you have to share."

"Nuh-uh. I told you, I don't share."

"Then stop making those noises."

"What noises?"

She did her best impression of his deep moaning.

"I . . . am not sure I caught that. Could you do it again?"

She shoved at his arm and kept walking. This lunch together wasn't simply a date; theirs was the best date she'd ever been on. They were strolling through a tiny park *with ice cream*. No one in real life had dates like this.

Eventually they meandered back toward Dev's 4Runner, and he moaned again, probably when he got one of those bits of cheesecake.

Anna turned to him. "Now you're just showing off. Mine happens to be delicious too."

"As delicious as mine?"

"I don't know, I haven't had yours yet."

He caught her wrist as she brought the spoon to her mouth. His hand wrapped completely around it as he pulled her close, and stole her bite of ice cream.

"Hey! You said no sharing." She laughed, trying to hold her bowl out of his reach.

"I know. Now I'm breaking that rule." Holding up his spoon, he circled a delicious-looking mound of blueberry ice cream under her nose. "I'll let you try mine if you let me have more of yours."

She lowered her lashes, a slow glance at his offering. "You're on."

As he lifted the ice cream she touched his hand, wrapping her lips around the spoon.

The cheesecake was rich and sweet, the blueberries slightly tart, and it tasted like absolute heaven.

Anna closed her eyes and moaned over the bite.

"Told you."

"You did." She spoke with her mouth full. "What can I say? I'm hardheaded."

He shook his head. "You know what you want. Nothing wrong with that."

She had no clue what she wanted out of life anymore, but she was sure of one thing. She wanted Devlin to kiss her again.

"Want some more?" With a spoonful of chocolate held in offering, she waited.

The corners of his lips curled, a flicker of mischief in his eyes. He knew she wasn't only talking about the ice cream. Her ability to be bold around Dev surprised her, but he seemed completely comfortable with it. The more flirtatious she became, the bigger his smile.

He caught her wrist again and leaned down. Lips parted, he stilled, waiting for her to feed him.

With a quick glance around, she found they were alone on the side street. It shouldn't matter. They weren't doing anything wrong, but the gesture was undeniably intimate, especially with Dev and his full lips parted, the tip of his tongue ready.

She'd been raised with the notion that public displays of affection and intimacy were . . . unseemly.

Kissing behind a greenhouse, no one could see you. Feeding each other near the center of town meant anyone could see you.

But she was on vacation. If there was ever a time to do something new, the time was now.

She slipped the spoon between Dev's lips and he closed his eyes with an appreciative noise.

He slid his hand farther down her arm as she put her spoon back in the bowl. "The chocolate is very good, but I think I've had enough ice cream."

"Me too." She wanted a different kind of sweetness-with-bite.

He reached behind her, placing his bowl on top of his SUV, and plucked hers from her hands too. With one step, he closed the space between them, and leaned in, capturing her lips with his.

Sweet and cold at first, his mouth moved against hers, his hold on her solid and sure, heat licking at her senses.

The cool, smooth pressure of his lips gave way to warmth, suction, and then the brush of his tongue at the seam of her lips. She opened, and he dipped inside, moaning again as their tongues brushed together.

He kissed her, giving and taking, never letting up as he reached for her waist, moving them closer to his car, until her back pressed against the door.

He moved his hands up her body, threading fingers into her hair, tilting her head, deepening the kiss. Raw and wild, he made love to her mouth until a moan—throatier and needier than any caused by dessert—escaped her. Devlin swallowed it, pushing his hips into hers.

This was beyond a public display. They were making out on a side street. She ought to slow things down, but she didn't want to. Shamelessly, she shifted her stance, letting him closer, brushing her thigh against his.

Her behavior might be out of character, but the need stirring inside her didn't care about behavior.

"God, you taste good," he murmured before kissing her again. "So sweet."

But their kisses held the promise of things down and dirty and the furthest thing from sweet; and she wanted it all.

Anna reached for him, brushing her hands up his arms to hold on to the curve of his biceps as he rained kisses down the side of her neck. He sucked at the tender skin and she dug her fingers into the meat of his arms, desire lighting her up inside.

She pressed her chest into him, wanting the contact, needing the friction, something, and Devlin growled—legitimately *growled* against her neck before planting a hand on the side of the truck for leverage.

He panted. "That kind of thing drives me crazy."

"The good kind of crazy?"

"The best."

She did it again, arching into him. When he kissed her again, he took her bottom lip between his teeth.

Someone at the top of the street wolf-whistled at them, and Anna broke away to see who and where, Devlin not slowing down a bit, merely shifting his attention back to her neck.

"I think someone's caught us." She nudged at his side.

"Screw 'em." He nuzzled her ear, making her smile, but he lifted his head and glared, and the passerby moved on.

Devlin's gaze met hers, his touch gentle as he brushed his fingertips along her neck. "Got a little carried away, but I'm not sorry."

Heat danced across her neck. "Me either." The heat turned into fire as she spoke the words, grasping their truth. She had to touch her neck to see if it felt hot.

"Don't worry." He lifted her hand away. "We weren't *that* obscene, and your neck is fine. Bright red, but fine."

"Great." She rolled her eyes and Dev smiled, his eyes so clear and so pale, she fancied she could see straight through them, right down into the center of what he was thinking, what made him tick.

But she knew better.

People were never that easy, or simple.

She moved her legs back together, shifting against the tingling between them.

"We should go. I think your two-hour lunch break was up half an hour ago."

He laid his forehead on the arm that propped him up. "Ah hell."

Chapter 10

Devlin walked up to Anna's cabin on Monday afternoon, to find her in one of the chairs on the front porch, feet bare and propped on the railing, reading a book.

"Are you actually reading that one?" he called out.

The book fell against her chest as she gave him a narrow-eyed glare. "Yes. I am."

He took the empty chair next to her, propping his feet up as well. Reading on the porch counted as a vacation-type activity at least.

Now that they'd reached an agreement, her help with getting the festival on track in exchange for his help in showing her how to properly vacation, he didn't feel so bad. All the added time together was a bonus too.

The key was to keep it away from his family, at least until he got their full support in reviving the festival.

"Are you still game for going with me to the tourism office today?"

"Of course."

"Then whenever I have a day off, you have to let me take you kayaking or tubing—something. One of the legitimate recreational activities that Honeywilde has to offer."

"That all sounds . . . terrifying, actually. I was thinking more along the lines of a craft class."

He wrinkled his nose. "Craft class? No, no. See, you definitely need my help."

"Fine, but let's start with the tourism office and ramp up slowly. Is this okay to wear?" Anna rose to her feet, arms out as if presenting herself.

She had on a pair of dark red pants, fitted and cut off above her ankle, and yet another black shirt. This one a short-sleeved button-up that accentuated her waist, and all of her other assets.

"Yes, that looks . . ." Like something that ought to be on the floor of his bedroom.

"I didn't bring any suits since I'm on vacation, but I thought this looked nice."

"Suit?" He grinned. "You don't need a suit."

"I wasn't sure, with it being a city office."

"The city of *Windamere*. We're in the mountains of North Carolina. Town with a population of barely five thousand. And when it doubles that, it's all people trying to escape suits and work. Even the mayor doesn't wear a tie unless he's on the news. You look great."

And he had to be around her, all day, handling himself like a business professional, while she wore those pants.

The office administrator was a woman, probably in her midfifties, with perfectly set blond hair and wire-frame glasses. Her nameplate read *Ms. Hendricks*.

He'd bet anything she'd been a Miss Blueberry Festival, back in the day.

"Do you have an appointment with Mr. Crawford?" She looked Dev up and down.

Of course he hadn't made an appointment with the Director of Tourism. If the guy saw Dev's name, there was a good chance he'd blow off the request for a meeting.

"No, but we only need a few minutes." Anna's posture and presence oozed competence with a hint of authority.

The admin looked Anna up and down, then back to Devlin. Her gaze shifted from looking impressed, to looking interested.

"I'll see if he can meet with you. Who may I say is here to see him?"

"Devlin Bradley with—"

"Honeywilde," Ms. Hendricks finished for him, tilting her head, her eyes sparkling. "I thought you looked familiar. I used to go up there every summer."

Wonderful. She knew the resort, and probably him.

"I love that place. I should've known you'd turn out as handsome as your father. Hang on a minute, honey. Let me see if Mr. Crawford can talk to you for a quick little minute."

Anna lifted an eyebrow as the lady went into Crawford's office. "Are you sure you need my help? You seem to do fine on your own."

"She's not the one I'm worried about."

Ms. Hendricks emerged, holding the office door open. "Mr. Crawford said he has a few minutes, that's all."

Anna went with him into the modest office, but hung back after they'd all shaken hands.

Crawford didn't wear a bow tie. The situation was even worse. He had on a sweater vest.

"You want access to what?" He circled around to the other side of his desk as soon as Dev asked him about the financial records for the festival.

He didn't sit, but stood with the desk and a large leather chair between him and Devlin.

Since that's how it was going to be, Dev stepped closer to the desk. "Not every last detail. Just the basic numbers for the overall cost of the event. We're considering taking on the role as the event organizer, but we need an idea of cost first."

"I wasn't aware the city had approached you about doing anything like that."

Dev shot a look at Anna, and she nodded encouragingly. "They haven't. But the festival is a local and tourist favorite, and we've already gone three years without it."

With a nod, Crawford shoved his glasses up his long nose. "I can have someone pull those numbers for you, but it might take a while. You know we run a smaller staff here during the summer."

"A while being . . . ?"

"A few weeks or so."

He didn't have a few weeks. He should've known things wouldn't be easy.

Anna jumped in. "Surely someone knows an estimate, at least. That would be a start, and we could wait on the exact numbers to follow."

Crawford shifted, pushing at his glasses again. "And are you also with Honeywilde?"

Anna cast Dev a glance from the corner of her eyes, then lifted her chin. "Consultant. The resort is very interested in bringing this festival back to life, and they sought my expertise."

"Then you know Windamere made the decision not to have the festival anymore. The event was too much of a financial burden on the town, so whatever numbers we could provide wouldn't be good. I assure you."

"All the same, we'd like to see them." She tilted her head and smiled, but the expression was miles away from the smiles she gave Dev. "Even if it takes a while."

This was work-mode Anna. Don't-patronize-me Anna. Take-none-of-your-horseshit Anna.

And he dug it.

Crawford worked his jaw. "We'll see what we can do."

This guy wasn't going to give them a damn thing. They were wasting their time and, judging from the ropey vein that was starting to pulse in Crawford's neck, only pissing the man off more and more with their presence.

"Thank you." Dev forced out the pleasantry. "Anything you can provide will be a big help."

Crawford's chin ticked up a notch, mouth pinched. "Maybe if you plan a little further ahead next year, my office could be of more help. Now, if you'll excuse me, I have a meeting."

"Sure thing." Devlin walked away from the losing battle, but he'd be damned if he'd lose the war.

They left the building and got back in his SUV. "What was that guy's problem?" Dev slammed the driver's side door closed.

"You won't get anywhere with men like that. You have to go around them."

"But it wasn't just me, right? That guy was kind of a dick."

"Definitely."

Dev imitated the guy. "If you'd planned ahead, maybe I could help, but right now I have to go to a meeting, so you can kiss my ass."

"He didn't exactly say *that*."

"Close enough. He sounded like my brother." Dev revved the engine and spun the tires leaving the parking lot.

Immediately, he let off the gas. He was better than this now; not that hotheaded guy anymore, and Anna was with him.

"Shit. Sorry." He adjusted his grip on the steering wheel, rubbing the palms of his hands against it.

She flicked her wrist, like brushing away air. "Sometimes you have to let off steam."

Rejection at the tourism office left him empty-handed. What now?

Forging ahead with the festival was a stress he'd brought upon himself and he was currently sitting at a dead end.

At the red light, Anna turned to him. "I could be wrong, but Crawford seemed awfully unhelpful. Is that normal for small-town government?"

No, but it was a normal reaction to Dev's presence. Still, he didn't really know Crawford and he got the feeling the man's chilly behavior had more to do with what they wanted than who Dev was.

"What about the look on his face when he thought you were a paid consultant?" Dev shook his head. Crawford looked like he'd been goosed.

The guy was a shifty, sweater vest-wearing roadblock, but that wasn't going to ruin their whole day. "How about some afternoon coffee?"

Anna's smile soothed his edginess. "I never say no to coffee."

They pulled up at what easily passed as a shanty or shack. A building no bigger than ten by ten, with a walk-up window and drive-thru, outdoor seating only.

"I know the place looks like crap, but their coffee is amazing. Sophie orders our coffee from the same roaster."

Opting to park and sit outdoors, they walked up to the order window as a hippy-looking fellow in a man-bun greeted them.

"The coffee is a dollar." Anna poked Dev in the arm. "A dollar?"

They ordered two; one black, one sweet and creamy, and sat alone at one of the wrought iron tables out front.

As soon as they sat down, Anna took a deep breath and, with a serious stare, opened her mouth. "There has to be someone else you can talk to about the numbers for the festival. That guy was stonewalling us. Getting your hands on paperwork shouldn't be that difficult."

"There is no one else. The tourism office handled every aspect of the festival."

"What if we ask around? The businesses that have always participated in years past. They might be able to give you an idea of numbers, while we wait on something official. We could go around and talk to them."

The extent of what he'd gotten himself into struck stronger than the caffeine in his drink. "If my family finds out you're helping me, they'll kill me."

"No, they won't." She brushed him off and sipped her coffee.

"Not literally, but they'll want to. I'm serious. I'll never live this one down. They might even kick me out for good."

"They aren't going to kick you out. Besides, they'll never know. They don't know about me helping with the plants, or coming with you today."

"Not yet. It's Windamere, people talk. Word will get back. I'm an idiot."

She reached across the table, placing her hand over his, red nails catching the sunlight. "We're smart. We can come up with something. If your family asks, I *am* the consultant you sought to help you. And you paid out of pocket because you're that committed to the project."

Dev laughed and turned his hand, his palm against hers. "Normally takes me more than a few days to be such a bad influence on someone."

"Then we're agreed. If your family hears you're asking around with a mysterious woman, I'm a consultant. You know, I've always wanted to be a mysterious woman."

"You're enjoying this way too much."

"I'm on vacation, remember? Now, who else could we go to for any info on the last few festivals?"

He shrugged, racking his brain. "Maybe Wright knows someone who'd help us out."

"Wright, your chef, who was helping you chase the dog?"

"Yeah, but he's been my best friend since elementary school. His family knows everyone, and everything, in this town."

"Then I bet they'd help. You should ask them."

"Eh. They'd have to like me before they'd help me."

"They don't like you?"

"Not hardly. To them, I was the bad influence, the devil on the shoulder of their sweet, innocent baby boy. Or so they thought." Little did they know, Wright had a wild streak a mile wide, he'd just been wiser than Dev, and knew when to lay low.

Back in the day, Dev had no off switch. Wright was the one voice of reason in his circle of friends, but Dev hadn't listened.

"And now he works for you."

"Not me. Roark signs the paychecks; Wright is only somewhat accountable to me. I want no part in being my best friend's boss. Hell no."

"Probably how Roark feels about being his brother's boss."

Dev stopped with his cup halfway to his lips.

"I don't have any brothers or sisters, so I wouldn't know, but . . . I imagine it's not always easy."

They drank their coffee, silent for a moment, Anna's fingers drifting back and forth across his wrist.

Working for and with family was rarely easy, but they managed. Sure, it had to be tough on Roark, being the boss of his siblings, but he didn't seem to mind. Roark took everything in stride and, if anything, he loved being in charge. No way would big brother ever be the one taking orders and not giving them. He asked for their opinions, but the truth was Roark called the shots at the resort and he was the final say on how they spent the income.

Dev had to show him the festival could be profitable, or it'd never happen. And, to show him, he needed the black-and-white proof.

"I'm screwed if I can't get past that Crawford guy. People would participate in the festival, the way they did for years, but without my brother's backing, there is no festival."

Anna tapped at her cup and sipped. Sipped and tapped.

He could almost see the lightbulb go on over her head, eyes lighting up, eyebrows raised as she plopped the cup down. "Maybe not."

"Maybe not, what?"

"You'd probably still need your brother's support, but what if you didn't need any records to get it?"

"You've lost me."

"I have a few clients, nonprofits that keep little money on the books for tax reasons. So, when it comes time to raise all the money, they have a big event, with tons of publicity, and they do it with corporate sponsors. They ask corporations up front for money. Some of it goes to the cost of the event; the rest goes to their cause. Then the corporations keep giving money throughout the year, because they want the publicity of participating. Think large galas and balls. What if you got the businesses of Windamere to register to participate *first*? Then would Roark agree to use the Honeywilde name as organizer?"

He scowled. "How are they going to participate when I've got zilch for them to participate in?"

"If you're so certain the town wants this festival, get them to buy in now. Call a tent-rental place, get a price for setup and takedown.

Get a price from a company that can handle any audio-visual needs, and tack on a few hundred for wiggle room. Then you know what you'll probably need in deposits. Get them, and go to Roark with what you have. It'd be proof that everyone wants the festival to happen, and with that kind of money behind it, he'd probably say yes."

Anna was sharp as a tack, but her idea was nuts.

"And if he says no, I'm forced to go back to all those people and explain the festival isn't happening." That he'd screwed up. Failed. Again.

"Roark won't say no if the festival won't lose money, right? Then what have you got to lose by seeing who's interested enough to pay up?"

A lot. But her idea was a good one. All of her ideas were good. The kink in the chain was him.

If he could bring back the festival, he might earn something more than people's suspicion. Less gossip and sideways glances, more respect and confidence.

He could prove himself capable and restore one of the few things in Windamere that brought him fond memories. Everyone loved the festival, he as much as anyone.

His family had happy memories of those weekends. Hell, one year Roark had even volunteered for the dunking booth. Dev had never laughed so hard in his life as when he saw the look on Roark's face when a five-year-old dunked him.

Anna suggested he approach the fine business people of town, and ask for their cash and confidence, like it was no big deal.

It was all a big deal. Asking for people's trust, the festival. Perhaps he'd bitten off more than he could chew.

He shook his head and finished off his coffee. "I don't know."

Brenda and her son were one thing. They were about the only locals who didn't look down on Dev with derision and doubt.

Everyone else was polite enough, and distantly friendly, but that was due to Roark and Sophie. His family and the Bradley name allowed for a pass when it came to the occasional run-in or quick business dealing.

But to trust Devlin Bradley, the same Devlin Bradley who'd once gotten busted for spray-painting the statue of the town's founder, contributor to the delinquency of about half their kids, to pull off Windamere's Blueberry Festival? To have faith in him?

It'd never happen.

He'd been counting on Roark's support. When people heard Roark was in, they'd be in too.

Oh, Roark is helping put the festival back together? Great. Of course we'll sign up. That Roark is so clever. He can do anything.

They saw Devlin approaching them with his hand out, they'd think he must need bail or was up to something.

Remember that time he got arrested for breaking into the Tool and Tackle shop? Fifteen. The boy was fifteen years old and breaking and entering. I heard he went to jail.

That was the Devlin the people in town knew. The one who barely got into college and then got kicked out. The one who'd probably be on parole right now if it weren't for his big brother taking him in and giving him a job.

They didn't know the Devlin he wanted to be. The man he was trying to become. The one who gave a damn. Who'd tried for almost three years now to get his shit together and be more. To work hard, to deserve the love his family gave him, willingly, for so long. Somehow make up for over a decade's worth of messing up.

But he couldn't tell Anna any of that. She never knew the old Devlin, and by god, she never would.

"I don't see how it'd work, me asking people to commit and give money. That's not really . . . what they expect of me. My ideas are usually crap." He went with a vague explanation instead of blurting there was no way in hell the people of Windamere would give him money.

"I completely disagree."

"Well, don't hold back."

"I mean it. Your ideas are not crap. You can pull this off, but you have to try. I've seen how people react to you. Crawford excluded. Brenda, the admin downtown, even the hippy barista back there. You're charming, but more importantly, genuine. People like genuine. Never, ever underestimate the power of nice people asking nicely."

She thought he was nice.

Proof she didn't really know him.

"I ask people for money all the time," she went on. "And a lot more than a small deposit for a festival. Convince them they need to spend money to make money."

"And they do it. People give you tons of money because you can make them a ton more."

"Basically."

"And would my consultant go around with me and talk to people? Convince them of the genius in this insane plan?"

"It's not insane." She grabbed his hand and shook it. "You have to at least try. Aren't you supposed to be the adventurous one?"

The plan was a *little* insane, and a lot risky, but what other option did he have? Good thing he was accustomed to risk. "We'll have to go around to businesses on Wednesday. I'm working at the inn all day tomorrow."

"So you'll do it?"

"What other choice is there?"

She clapped her hands. "This might work. You'll see."

"You know, when it comes to people letting go of their cash, they like someone fancy and important to be the one taking it. You do fancy and important very well."

She smiled over the lid of her coffee. "You're plenty fancy. For Windamere."

His laugh burst out. "True."

"Of course I'll go with you. That's my part of our agreement, remember?"

With a wink, he shot his empty coffee cup into the garbage can, ten feet away. "What time do you have to get back?"

"Whenever I want. I'm on vacation."

"Perfect. I'm not due back until dinner." He grabbed her hand, pulling her from the table. "So we have all the time in the world for my part."

Chapter 11

The road curved up the mountain in gentle turns, all around her a blanket of green.

Below them, the town hid beneath the canopy of trees. Only the tallest building and a few steeples peeked through. They climbed higher and higher, as though they could rise above the worries of real life.

But Anna knew that was impossible.

Perhaps she could put her troubles on hold, delay dealing with them while indulging in Devlin's company, but they remained. Lying in wait for the time she had no choice but to face them.

This festival obviously mattered a great deal to Dev, even if she wasn't 100 percent sure why. Bringing back a beloved event for the town was a nice gesture. Could that be it? Profit didn't motivate him; he'd hardly mentioned making money. If going to government offices and asking nicely wasn't his usual thing, any more than asking local businesses for money was, then why was he willing to go so far out of his comfort zone?

The stubborn set of his brow, the fiery look of determination in his eyes, they spoke of things more meaningful than festivals and fun.

"We're almost there." Dev glanced over, a glint of excitement in his eyes.

She could come right out and ask him why the festival *really* mattered so much to him, but that was awfully intrusive coming from someone he'd known a few days.

As an outsider, she knew his reasons weren't her business. The agreement was she'd help him make the event happen, and he'd help her vacation. Nothing in there included her poking around in his feelings, asking a bunch of questions about why he cared. Or why he scowled at the prospect of asking business owners to pony up a deposit for something they all supposedly loved.

"Here it is." Dev pulled off the parkway and onto a narrow drive. The road curved around, and on one side was a narrow, almost makeshift parking lot; on the other, the most beautiful view of the mountains she'd ever seen.

A valley yawned off to their right. To the left, and as far as the eye could see, rolling, endless Blue Ridge Mountains.

Dev had barely stopped the car before she yanked her seat belt free. "Oh my—look at that view!"

She jumped from her seat and headed straight for the short stone wall that protected sightseers from plummeting down the side of the mountain.

The air was cool and breezy, and only the occasional car passed on the highway, which was blocked by an island of trees and rocks, breaking the silence. One other car was parked at the far end of the overlook. A pair of ladies took in the view with their binoculars.

Dev finally caught up to where she'd stopped at the stone wall.

"This is gorgeous. Absolutely stunning."

"I think so too. I think we have one of the best views at Honeywilde, but this overlook rivals it."

"I wish I had a phone. I'd take some pictures."

He turned toward her. "You really don't have a phone? The other day I thought you didn't want to give me your number."

At that, she laughed. She had to. On what planet would she not give a guy like Dev her number? "No. I really don't have a phone."

He reached into his back pocket. "You can use mine and email it to yourself. I think there's a panorama doo-hickey on there, but I don't know how to do it."

"Thanks." She knew exactly how. After lining up the camera, she slowly turned in a semicircle.

Dev moved out of the way of the shot, but his gaze remained steady on her. She didn't need to see him to know.

He took the phone from her when she was done, looking at the picture. "I don't think I could function without my phone. And damn, I want to kick my own ass for saying that, but the point is, how can you not have a cell phone?"

How to explain the absence of communication without going into the whole story, sounding pitiful? "I do *own* a phone, generally speaking, but since I'm supposed to be up here relaxing and getting away from the grind . . . it was suggested I vacation sans phone."

Suggested. That sounded nice and normal.

Dev studied her.

Fine, so the weak explanation made no sense. Not in this day and age. "I was working a lot and had to take a break from my job. I wouldn't break if I had my phone with me."

"How much is a lot?"

"I don't know. About eighty hours a week?"

Dev blow out a sharp breath. "Damn. That's nuts."

"How much do you work in a week?"

"I mean, we're always working, sort of, but we get long breaks. I get to do stuff like this, with you. My job doesn't always feel like work. Sometimes it's fun."

Fun.

She used to think her job was fun. How long had it been since anything in her career could be described as fun?

Dev tucked his phone away. "Eighty hours seems . . . extreme."

Extreme was one way to describe it. Soul sucking was another.

"I love what I do. But . . . I don't know. I got so caught up in climbing the ladder, getting higher up in the agency, I didn't stop to realize how much time I put into it. The success can be consuming, and then one day you look around and you're working all hours and haven't taken a vacation in over a year. I was stressed out and, now, here I am."

Beside her, Dev moved minutely closer. She wouldn't have noticed if she weren't painfully aware of everything he did. Each move and lingering gaze.

"You don't have to wait until you're stressed to take a vacation."

Her situation went way beyond something so simple. She could call her time here a vacation all she wanted, but it was so much more.

"You have a hard time relaxing, huh?"

"Yeah, you could say that. I had to drive for five hours and rent a little cabin, and you still have to teach me how to have fun."

"Yeah, while you help me work. I should refuse your part of the agreement right now."

"No." She spun on him. "No, we have a deal." Too much downtime and time alone would truly push her over the edge.

Dev put his hands on her arms, letting them drift down. "Breathe.

I was joking. Mostly. Not like I'll be asking you for eighty hours a week. Hell, probably not even eight. Besides, I'm too desperate to refuse your help."

Thank god.

Her sigh of relief came out shaky.

"You really are tense."

"This helps." She tilted her head toward the view, stretched out before them.

"I might be able to help a little more."

At least she didn't giggle like a schoolgirl in response, but her neck warmed up regardless.

"Not that, you little deviant." He winked at her. "Maybe later, but for now I need you to sit." He patted the stone wall that came right above her knees.

The side of a mountain. She'd be sitting on the side of a mountain; the only thing between her and the miles of forest below was her big bottom on a foot-wide rock wall.

"What if I stand?"

"It's fine. Sit." He patted the wall again.

After the slowest sitting ever known to mankind, he twirled his finger in the air. "Turn around. Facing the view."

"Um." Her voice shook.

"I'm not going to let you fall."

She turned, letting her legs dangle off the side of the stone wall.

His rough laugh rubbed against her edges, soothing them, if only a little. "You're perfectly safe. I promise. Now . . . shhhhhh."

Anna clamped her mouth shut as the weight of his forearms settled on her shoulders.

Now this, she could get into.

"Drop your shoulders." He bounced his arms a couple of times, pressing a little harder each time. "You're tensing up. Drop them."

She tried, but he still had to push down, and maintain the pressure to keep her from drawing them up again.

"Better. Close your eyes and take a slow, deep breath in. Don't exhale until I tell you."

She frowned. This all sounded too similar to the self-help exercises that therapist Susan had given her.

Dev waited a good seven seconds before he let her exhale.

"Slowly," he instructed when her breath came out in a rush. "One more time."

He made her go through the same thing about half a dozen times, but then—then his fingers were in her hair.

Susan didn't have a single self-help exercise that included this.

Strong, deft fingers. Threading through her hair, until he pressed his fingertips against her scalp, and began to massage.

Her eyes rolled back in her head, her lashes fluttering. Because *wow*.

The pressure of his fingertips moved from her scalp, down to her temples, then to the back of her skull. With a firm touch, he rubbed in tiny circles that slowly grew larger. Her hair would look a fright once he was finished, but this? This was worth having bird-nest hair.

Her shoulders drooped further and she let her head fall back, a small moan escaping.

Dev moved his fingers from the back of her head, digging the pads of his thumbs into the back of her neck and dragging them down.

At first, she flinched, because she thought it'd hurt, but in the wake of all that digging and pressure came relief.

He did it again, and again, until her head lolled on the end of her neck, letting him manipulate the muscles there. His touch shifted lower, until he rubbed at a knot between the base of her neck and her shoulder. "Shhhh. Don't tense up. Trust me."

He dug his thumb in and she winced at the sharp throb of pain, seconds away from telling him to stop. Then, the pain eased, the knot giving way.

She must've made a noise of discomfort, because Dev brushed her hair forward, over her shoulder and out of the way. He kept massaging the knot with quiet intensity.

"That's it." His tone softened. "Breathe. You're doing great."

His gentle encouragement, the soothing rumble of his voice, worked at the tension inside her. A resistance, the kind of tension that had nothing to do with the muscles of her neck and back, released.

"I broke down at work. That's why I finally had to take a vacation." The words spilled out, breaking free from confinement. Her refusal to talk about or share the imperfect places inside her couldn't hold in the ugly truth any longer.

Dev's hands stopped moving.

"I'm sorry. I didn't plan on telling you that." Though she wanted to. Deep down where she couldn't lie to herself, she needed him to know.

She was here because she couldn't do her job anymore. At all. Or her laundry, or eat properly, read a book, give a darn about the simplest responsibilities when they'd always been her priority. She'd reached a place in her life where something had to change or she'd forget how to get out of bed in the morning.

Depression.

The word itself hurt, and her therapist kept using it. Insisting that if Anna didn't want to take medication, then she needed to make a change. Or possibly do both. Only time would tell, but first Anna had to deal with her loss, and how it affected every aspect of her life.

Dev stopped rubbing and, for a moment, she doubted everything that said confessing the truth to him was okay. She doubted her judgment, him, the way he'd seemed completely without judgment.

But he started again, his voice low. "It's okay. You can—if you need to talk, I'm here."

"I was going through a lot." Like her father dying, out of nowhere, but she couldn't bring herself to say the words out loud. Saying them made his death real, and she wasn't ready.

"And working eighty-hour weeks," he offered.

"Yes, working every day, all day, but I was failing."

"You?"

"For the first time ever, yes. I'm good at my job, Dev. So good."

"I believe it."

"And then, I wasn't. How do you work that hard, for that long, putting in so much of yourself, and all you end up with is crap?" She lifted her hands and let them fall. "I'd been so successful for years before, but this year it's been account after account, lost. My ideas kept getting rejected. I went from being the golden child to the one you roll your eyes at. I finally went to therapy, hoping it'd help."

He stopped rubbing again, this time pulling away.

Holy crap, she'd told Devlin she was in therapy. *Why* had she done that?

It took repeating that fact over and over, in her head, for it to sink in. Her life was a mess, her head even messier, but on the outside she did a bang-up job of appearing "normal." Together, even—whatever the hell that meant.

But now, he knew. A guy she'd met a few days ago now knew more hard truths about her than anyone else in her life. What if he thought she was crazy? Now he'd wish he never agreed to do anything with her, much less have her help with work.

Dev took his touch away, but climbed over the wall, sitting down with his shoulder pressed to hers.

His gaze was warm, understanding. He wasn't going to judge her for being a mess, any more than he'd judge her for devouring an entire bowl of ice cream or thinking a dog was a bear.

"My job is . . . Advertising is creative. It takes energy, enthusiasm. A zest for the projects at hand, and I had none of that. I'd lost it all. Lost my mojo. I was spinning my wheels as fast as I could, going nowhere, and the walls kept closing in. I knew I'd lose my position if I didn't step up my game, but I couldn't stop being miserable. Overworked, not sleeping, and one day at work, I just . . . I blacked out."

With a heavy breath, he reached for her. His hand on her arm, then her back, offering a connection, though he didn't say a word.

"I came to in the stupid copy room, surrounded by people *staring*. Of course I wanted to cry, but I kept trying to convince everyone I was okay. Instead, I went home and cried until I couldn't breathe, then couldn't even get out of bed the next day. I called in and my boss suggested I take a little time off. Her words. *A little time off.* But I'll never forget the looks on their faces the day I passed out."

She shook her head, swiping at the one tear brave enough to fall. "Sorry."

"Don't apologize. I'm sorry. I had no idea you had all of that going on."

"I hide it well." She'd been taught well, not to wear her troubles on her sleeve. Hell hath no fury like her mother when she thought you were pouting. Or had any feelings beyond being perfectly presentable.

Now she couldn't do anything but sit there and stare at the mountains, more tears brimming but refusing to fall. Devlin pulled her into the curve of his body. He didn't say anything.

No hollow platitudes and no *there, there.* The quiet acceptance made her crumple, her body sagging against his, even as her cheeks remained dry.

With the solid assuredness of his body, he held her up.

At least half an hour went by. They sat until her butt was numb, but inside she was warm. Comforted.

The sun had slipped a little lower in the sky, clouds casting shadows over the rolling green carpet of the mountains.

"Thank you for telling me." Dev finally spoke. "For trusting me enough."

"Thank you for listening." For not saying she was being overdramatic or stupid.

"Yeah, well. I'm bad at giving advice. Makes me one hell of a good listener."

"I'm serious."

"I am too." When she turned to him, he smoothed her hair back, dropping a soft kiss on her lips. "But I do know how to help you relax and have fun while you're here. And that's exactly what I'm going to do."

He didn't push for more information or the details of her meltdown. He simply accepted her story, and the way he looked at her hadn't changed.

Maybe with a little more understanding but still with a gleam of mischief, and a whole lot of want.

Dev kissed her again, this time not so soft. An intense press of his lips against hers, until the muscles of her shoulders melted like they had during his massage.

He threaded his fingers into her hair, the tips brushing past the places he'd massaged earlier, and his kiss stole her breath. Hot and needy, but he gave too. Sucking at her lips, cupping the back of her head, making the world spin around until she tilted, off-balance, until she clung to him.

They sat on the side of a mountain, literally, but she knew she wouldn't fall. Dev held her, his arms solid and sure.

Going from finally speaking of her breakdown to kissing in a parking lot was the kind of thing she'd never do. Anna from Atlanta would never speak of her weaknesses, but right now, admitting her imperfections and him kissing it better, was exactly what she needed.

The soft caress of Dev's lips, the hum of pleasure building inside, and the thrill of anticipating more. All she knew was this moment.Dev brushed the tips of his fingers across her cheek and she leaned into his touch, consumed by the way he made her feel. This had to be what her therapist meant about living in the now. Present. Everything she felt was undeniable.

"You're going to be fine," Devlin whispered against the shell of her ear, raining kisses along the edge, down her neck.

Her unshed tears were long gone, but she sniffed anyway. How was she supposed to respond?

He smoothed her hair back again, holding her face in his hands so she had to look him in the eyes. "You're amazing. And I feel like maybe you don't know that, so I'm telling you."

"Thank you." She might not sound certain, but she believed him.

Dev thought she was exceptional and maybe, if he thought so, she could be. At least in his eyes, for the time she was here at Honeywilde, she could be.

This time, Anna kissed him; tugged him in by the front of his shirt, a fist full of buttons and cotton, tellingly wrinkling the material and not caring.

She kissed him the way he'd kissed her after ice cream. Seeking tongue and greedy lips. Taking over, taking what she wanted.

Dev's response was instantaneous. A rumble went through his chest and into hers, as he leaned into her. When she broke to take a breath, his words were a hot charge against her lips. "Do that again."

This time she kissed him, and let go of his shirt with one hand, to touch that perfect jaw, the soft scrape of his freshly shaved face, before she threaded her fingers through the longest strands of his hair.

He nipped at her bottom lip and smoothed the bite with his tongue. Then his lips were on her neck as he tugged at the top button of her shirt.

Her body was going fluid, all stiffness in her back gone, buzzing with need and the promise of needs met. They were on the side of the Blue Ridge Parkway, and if anyone pulled in to park, they'd see. And she didn't care.

"I want you." She curled her fingers into his shirt even tighter. "I want you to do more than kiss me. I . . . I need you."

With a hand cupping her breast and his lips still on her skin, Dev spoke, his voice a raspy demand.

"Get in the car."

Chapter 12

Of all the days to be unprepared.

But getting lucky wasn't what was on Dev's mind when he left his room this morning and, contrary to popular belief, he was not that guy. He didn't roll around town with a stash of condoms, presuming he might get laid at any moment.

Devlin crawled into the back seat of his 4Runner with Anna. No condoms, no nothing, his options limited. He would not make this mistake again, but right now he was more concerned with making something happen, regardless.

Necessity being the mother of invention and all that.

Anna wanted more and was as worked up as he'd been since he met her. More was going to happen.

On the one hand, limited space was less than ideal. But how long had it been since he'd made out in the back of a car? A long damn time, and if anyone ever said making out in the car wasn't hot, they were lying.

She slid over, making room, her hair tossed and lips kissed swollen and pink, and Dev was on her, instantly.

Then under her, as he sat and tugged her over to get onto his lap.

She squeaked. "What are you doing? I'm too big."

"No, you're not." He cupped the back of her head and pulled her down for a kiss. Her thick hair, smelling like sweet sin, fell around him. A dark curtain blocking out the rest of the world.

Arching her back, she pressed into him, every bit of his need thrumming through her body, the same.

Twice now they'd been cut short, their moments interrupted.

Not today.

He kissed his way down her neck, where he'd left off the other day. For two nights he'd thought about her smooth skin against his lips. The noises she made when turned on. As he kissed his way across her collarbone, he worked on the buttons of her blouse, pushing and pulling until it no longer blocked his way.

Her shirt gone, she wore nothing but a black lace bra. Breasts filling the cup and spilling over the top.

And damn if the real thing wasn't a million times better than he'd imagined.

Cupping them, he ran his lips over the swell of each, worshipful, but he was helpless not to be.

What could he say; he *was* that guy when it came to the beauty of a woman's body, and Anna was breathtaking.

Above him, Anna threaded her fingers through his too long hair, pressing her breasts against his lips. Desire that overruled any holding back or being bashful, and he loved it.

He reached up her back, until he found the clasp of her bra. Only a second or two for him to unhook, and *yes*.

"Beautiful." The word left him, a greedy sigh that he felt like a gnawing in his chest.

The swell of her breasts, rosy-pink nipples, almost the same color as her lips, the taper of her waist, even the way her dark hair fell over her shoulder to brush over her cleavage—everything about her made him ravenous for more.

In so many ways, he wanted her.

The backseat of his car and in his bed, yes. But he wanted even more. He wanted coffee with her, not only today, but every day this week. Her hand over his, brushing the pressure away with the tips of her fingers.

With all she was dealing with, to want more of her might be the picture of greediness and need, but he did. In exchange, all he could give her was himself. His ability to find ways to laugh, even when life was kicking you in the teeth. And his body.

That he'd gladly give. He knew how to bring her pleasure and she deserved all the earthly delights she could stand.

She reached for the buttons of Dev's shirt, and he had absolutely no shame about his eagerness. He had the buttons undone and his shirt off before she could blink twice.

Anna's gaze took him in, her touch even softer, more reverent than his, as she explored the sensitive skin near his collarbone, down his chest, to the line of hair dipping into his pants. Her light touch tickled and he clenched his teeth to keep from jerking or flinching, because he didn't want her to stop.

She did stop, eventually, resting the flat of her hands on his chest. "You're beautiful too."

"C'mere." Dev held her close, guiding her lips to his, kissing her until her breath came in short puffs once more.

When he moved on to one nipple, sucking and flicking his tongue, she clung to his arm. Wriggling in his lap, hints of a keening noise building in her throat.

She rocked her hips into his, seeking friction, even if she didn't realize that's what she was doing.

He moved, putting his hand between them, over the fly of those red pants.

She pushed herself into his touch, back arched, her eyes wide and dark with need.

"You want me to touch you?"

A jerk of her chin. "Yes."

If she wanted to get off, needed it, he'd be damned if they were leaving here until he made that happen.

Tugging at the button, then the zipper, he worked her pants down enough to slip his hand in. He brushed against the cotton of a low-cut thong, and pushed it down, until his fingers touched her trimmed mound.

Lower, she was all heat and slick desire.

Dev bit back a possessive moan. She was so wet. Wet and swollen and holy hell, he wanted his mouth on her. Wanted to give her the release she so desperately craved. He wanted to taste her, see how many times he could fulfill that need.

Damn backseats.

He could manage it if he just . . .

But then Anna began to move.

Shifting in his lap, she rubbed herself against his fingers, and his eyes rolled back into his skull. He was going to die of pleasure.

Rarely happy or satisfied with the state of anything—he was going to die, right now, because of her.

"That . . . that feels so good," she murmured.

She was killing him.

He shifted beneath her, urging her to lean back a little, for the view and some space to work.

The position put her breasts on beautiful display, and he rubbed at the cleft of her sex, dipping his fingers inside, until he found the perfect rhythm and spot. Anna pushed against his fingers, eyes wide, dark circles, creamy skin stained a delicate pink, and the places he'd kissed and sucked standing out in darker pink blotches.

She pinched her bottom lip between her teeth, smooth brow wrinkling in the concentration.

"That's it, beautiful." He pressed against her clit with his thumb, rubbing her with intent. She was close; her hand clamped down on his forearm hard enough to cut off circulation.

He could come from watching her get off, she did it with such wonder and drive.

"I want to put my mouth on you, Anna. Feel you come against my tongue."

"Oh god." She took in a raspy breath. Eyes squeezed shut, her mouth fell open into a perfect O as she tightened and pulsed around his fingers.

He stroked her through it, helping her ride out the orgasm, not wanting to miss a second of it.

When she finally opened her eyes, huge pupils ate up the rich brown color.

"That . . ." She panted for breath, doing great things for the view. "When you said . . ."

He held her steady by the waist. "That I can't wait to taste you?"

With a bubbly laugh, she tucked her head against his shoulder. "Yes. I thought I was going to die."

He caught her chin, bringing his mouth to hers. Their kiss was languid, less desperate than before, but her wandering hands brushed over his zipper, bumping against the raging hard-on he'd sported from the moment she got in his lap.

She leaned back, the flat of her hand over his length.

Before he could respond, she was tugging at the button of his pants, pulling until his erection popped up between them.

"Yeah, I don't—" He was such an idiot. "I don't have a condom."

She studied his face, the flat line of her mouth confirming he wasn't joking.

Dang it.

"Neither do I. But . . ." They could manage.

He'd made her come in a cramped backseat in what felt like a few seconds, and she wasn't completely without ingenuity.

Carefully, she touched him, trailing her fingers down his length. Dev's breath caught in his throat.

"We could, you know." She took a quick glance around. They remained alone in the long narrow parking area. "I want to do the same for you."

"You want to touch me?"

She nodded.

"Say it. Say it like you did before, outside the car."

Anna leaned forward. "I want to touch you. See if you feel as good as I've imagined."

When she sat back, he was grinning like the devil.

With their fingers intertwined, he lowered her hand to touch him. She brushed the head, down his length, wrapped her fingers around him. Dev clenched his eyes shut, mouth open slightly, his body tightening at her touch.

She buzzed with the power and anticipation. The awareness that she had this effect on him was intoxicating.

She wasn't the kind of girl that men went crazy for, never had been. Her whole life, she'd been satisfied with being plump and cute, moderately pretty.

But that's not how Devlin saw her.

Over and over he'd claimed she was beautiful. Amazing. *Her.*

His claims weren't merely words either. The truth was obvious, from the heat in his eyes, to the way his abs went taut, his erection jerking in her hand, more slickness coating her fingers.

She wrapped her fingers around him and slid her hand up.

Dev sucked in a ragged breath and moved his hand away. He braced himself with both hands on the seat, letting her touch and explore, however she wanted.

She'd thought doing this with Dev was only pure fantasy, with a dash of flirtation. Something to think about as she fell asleep, a daydream to pass the time. But this was reality. The two of them, sneaking off so no one would know they were together, hooking up in the back of his 4Runner.

She didn't have to be a grown-up with a hundred responsibilities. She could be carefree and do things that brought her pleasure and joy.

She pondered the feel of him in her hand, smoothness over strength, the width, the way he clamped his mouth closed over a moan when her thumb brushed under the head.

The sad truth was, this was the first time she'd hooked up in a car. Making out in backseats was what other girls did while she was studying and excelling. Pleasing the powers that be, scared to let them down.

She wasn't a virgin, but a fair-to-middling sex life didn't exactly throw open the doors on excitement and ecstasy.

Her life, up until now, was about focus, not exploration. Forward momentum, grabbing the brass ring and accomplishing everything she set out to do, whether or not the goal was something she really wanted.

But Devlin was for her.

She wanted to touch and kiss him, lick him and drive him crazy, until he couldn't bite back the moans any better than she could. Until his limbs quivered like hers.

He let his head fall back against the seat. "*Damn.* I can't watch your hands on me . . . with that . . . red nail polish."

"I thought you liked it." She glanced down, the red standing out against his skin.

"I like it too much. That's the problem. I might've thought about it . . . real hard one night . . . if you know what I mean." His gaze met hers instead, his words sending bubbles of triumph through her body.

He'd jerked off thinking about her. She'd been the subject of fantasy. *Her.* And she was driving him crazy.

When he squeezed his eyes closed again, she leaned down, flicking her tongue over the head.

Dev cursed, his body tense and thrumming, so she did it again. A small, sucking kiss against his flesh as she stroked him, until he grabbed at her free hand, urging her up.

"Anna . . . shit . . . I'm gonna—"

He was going to come, and she was making it happen.

Dev lusted after her, cursing with the need. The muscles of his stomach drew tight and he grabbed on, around her waist, closing his eyes as he called her name.

His body curled in and he came, pulsing in her hand, spilling over.

The thrill of satisfaction, of power, charged her smile. A rush from winning an account was one thing, familiar and something she missed. But this was new.

Dev was as helpless and enthralled by her as she was him.

She was still smiling when he finally opened his eyes again. Her face hurt, but she couldn't stop.

Dev slumped back in the seat. "I . . . I have tissues . . . give me a sec."

He struggled to pull himself together and for some reason it made her feel light. Giddy.

"Where are the tissues?"

"Middle." He pointed behind her. "Middle console."

Holding on to her, he leaned forward and they both fumbled with the console, finally producing some tissues. Dev cleaned them up, and flopped back, pulling Anna toward him, against his chest.

They lay that way until she grew self-conscious enough to get dressed. Then they lay there even longer.

The sun touched the tops of the mountain range when she finally asked, "What time do you need to get back tonight?"

He checked his watch. "Ten minutes ago."

"Dev." Anna sat up, but he still had an arm around her, and wouldn't let her get away.

"It's fine."

"Are you sure?"

He lifted the shoulder she rested against and let it fall. "You really want to leave right now?"

More comfortable and content than she'd been in years, she didn't want to go anywhere. "No."

"Good. Me either."

She lifted her chin and kissed him, her lips sensitive and swollen from earlier.

"A few more minutes and we'll go," he whispered, his hand smoothing over her hip, over the curve of her bottom.

Ten minutes later, they finally left, and Dev was over an hour late for his shift.

Chapter 13

He managed to avoid Roark that night, and went the whole next day without anyone questioning him on almost missing the dinner service entirely.

His tardiness came with a good reason though.

Not a reason he could share, but between Anna, lying in his arms, and putting on a tie to represent management at the restaurant that night, the choice was clear.

Being fashionably late never killed anybody anyway.

Sophie didn't say anything about his tardiness at their meeting Wednesday morning either, but she caught him checking his watch. "Am I boring you? Do you have somewhere to be?"

"Actually, I'm supposed to have the afternoon off."

"It's barely past ten."

"I'm listening. Big reunion sometime this summer, the Butlers. About a hundred people. I got it."

Sophie pursed her lips, looking like she was about to tell him he was full of shit. "I know you've got it. I need you to help me make sure we've got the details covered before we meet with Roark. You know he's going to ask. And I'm going to bring up the dock needing work."

"All at the next meeting? That's a whole lot to throw in the ring at once." Roark would keep them there forever, plotting out the plans.

"Yes, all at the next meeting," she said, her voice going up a notch. "That's why I brought it up. You're hospitality."

"Okay, okay. Give me the contact for the reunion. I'll coordinate and handle all of that. When we have a firm date and an idea of overnight guests, I'll work with you and we'll sort out the logistics."

"Thank you." She smiled. Then she set her papers aside, stuck her elbows on the table and planted her chin in her hands. "Now. Tell me where you're in such a hurry to get to on your afternoon off."

"I'm—I'm not in a hurry."

"Y'know, back in the day, you were a fantastic liar. I remember the time you told everyone you had a school trip, in tenth grade. Wright told his parents the same thing. And then y'all proceeded to hitchhike to Cherokee, to see if you could get in the casinos and drink."

"Correction. We *did* get into the casino, and drank. Wright had that great fake ID, and he won enough money to pay for a cheap motel and a case of beer. Then we got thrown out. Those were good times."

"You never did get caught either."

He sat back, the memory one of the few that still resonated, warm and golden, in his mind. "Nope."

"Point being, you were a top-notch fibber back then, but right now you're horrible at it. Where are you going today, and who are you going with?"

"Damn, you're nosy."

"Is it that pretty brunette who thought Beau was a bear?"

"No—*what?*" How could she possibly be suspicious based on one brief encounter? Regardless, he answered way too quickly, making her grin.

"Well . . ." Sophie grabbed her papers and stacked them, tapping them against the table to get them lined up. "If it did *happen* to be her—even though you said no—and you were doing something with her today, I'd say she's cute and seems very nice, if wildly over-dressed for summer vacation. I would also say you are going to be in so much trouble if Roark finds out."

"Roark isn't going to find out. That's if I *was* going somewhere with her, which I'm not."

She kept grinning and stacking her papers.

"Shut up. I'm out of here." He got up and shoved at her shoulder as he walked by.

Sophie nosed in his business, but it came from a place of fond pestering, not judgment. She'd keep his secret, same as always.

She still owed him for hauling all those plants too, so she'd cover for him, if matters came to that.

And hell, they might. He'd walked the straight and narrow for a while now; his sneaky skills were rusty.

Anna waited on him by the 4Runner, right on time.

As soon as he saw her, his stomach twisted into knots. He was really doing this. He was going into town to face more than the clerks at the grocery store, talk to more than Brenda or the kids who worked at the movie theater.

Today, he'd ask some Windamere lifers to trust him, and hope they didn't laugh in his face.

On the drive to town, Anna kept the worst of his nerves at bay by talking. They decided she'd open up the conversation, he'd fill in details, and then he or she would go in for the close, depending on who the business owner warmed up to more.

Anna gave him a signal for when it was him and when it was her.

They went over a list of five businesses they'd visit that day. He told her what each one did and why they were top picks. If the five anchor stores would support the festival, many of the other businesses would follow suit, and he might actually pull this off.

Unfortunately, the first two took a long, hard look at Dev, and said no.

The third stop was Della's Delights.

"How much money we talking here?" Della looked Anna up and down.

Della was almost his parents' age, and knew them pretty well. She'd quizzed Roark when they separated, wanting to know where they moved, who got the inn, and why things hadn't worked out for the Bradley family.

Basically, she'd wanted to know it all. Roark didn't tell her jack, except that he ran the resort now.

"A deposit of two hundred."

Della crossed her arms. "That's not so bad."

Anna angled herself toward Dev with a smile. His cue.

"Not much at all, considering." Dev stepped forward. "We want to keep costs low for the local business owners, so after the deposit, you'd need to give us the final one hundred a couple of weeks before the Blueberry Festival."

"That's it?"

"That's it. I've looked at the cost and that fee will cover your vendor tent, cleanup, and setup. After that, we're only asking for a small percentage of net earnings."

"Lord, I thought you were fixing to tell me the price was a thousand or something, like last time. I can't swing that kind of money this year. Couldn't swing it back then either."

Dev blinked. "A thousand . . . dollars?"

"That was the cost the last few years of the festival. Made it so the whole thing darn near wasn't worth it. Even if I sold all the cakes and cupcakes in the world, I couldn't turn a good profit after paying all that overhead."

He and Anna shared a look. They'd gone over the costs, and nothing should create that kind of price tag. If Crawford's office was charging that kind of money to participate, what the hell were they spending it on?

"We won't need a thousand dollars," he assured her.

"Are you in charge of this thing, or your brother?"

That was it. The real crux of the matter. Who'd be running this show—the responsible, respectable Bradley, or that other one who almost went to jail?

After a quick glance in Anna's direction, Dev stood a little straighter and nodded. "I am. I'm handling the Blueberry Festival."

Not moving a muscle, Della waited. Then, "When abouts are you having the festival?"

"Third weekend in June. Same as it used to be."

Dell uncrossed her arms, dusting some of the flour off her apron. From the way she shook her head, the answer looked like a no. He wasn't surprised. Della knew almost everything about everyone; she definitely knew about his past.

The fact that Dev had been a manager at Honeywilde for two years now, that he helped Roark keep the place on its feet and thriving, that he fixed problems now instead of causing them—none of that mattered. All that mattered was he'd spent over a decade trying to wreck his life, and no one would forget it.

"Third weekend in June," Della repeated. "That doesn't give you much time, now does it?"

"No, ma'am. But I work best under pressure."

"I've heard tell about the fancy wedding you-all threw at the resort last fall. Pulled it off in what? A month? Think having the resort and town in the papers and all those big magazines will get more people to the festival?"

"It certainly couldn't hurt."

"But in order to get the tourists and shoppers to the festival, we have to have it." Anna went in for the close. "That's where Della's Delights comes in. You're one of the most successful businesses in Windamere. If you support the Blueberry Festival, it's sure to be a success."

Della considered both of them for what had to be a solid minute before she nodded. "Did you know I used to sell out of every baked good I'd make for the Blueberry Festival? Every single festival. Christmas is still my top time, but I made as much in those two or three days as I would the whole off-season."

"That's the reason we want to do it," he told her. "If enough people are interested, and willing to put down money to help with the overhead, we can get some advertising out. We can drum up enough visitors that everyone benefits and—"

Della flapped her hands at him, stopping him mid-speech. "Hang on a minute."

He wide-eyed Anna as Della tromped toward her office.

Anna mouthed to him with a smile, "I told you so."

Della returned a second later, the full three hundred in her hand, in cash. "I'm not expecting a huge return this year, mind. What with it only about six weeks away and all, but if pitching in means we can have the festival back, I'll do it."

He gaped as she held out the handful of twenties.

Three hundred dollars shouldn't break her bank, but she was giving it to him. Trusting him to take that money and use it for their mutual benefit.

In the end, Anna had to reach for the cash, putting it in the little zipper bag he'd nabbed from Sophie.

Devlin wrote out a receipt for Della, his fingers trembling.

Della moved closer, watching him write. "You know, Viv told me how you got her that job up at the inn."

"Who?"

"My daughter, Vivian. She got a part-time job working the front desk."

"Right." Dev nodded. He knew exactly who Vivian was. "Don't thank me. She got herself the job."

Della quirked an eyebrow. "She said you were the one who told her about the opening and got her the interview with your sister. Sounds to me like *some* thanks are in order."

He handed over the receipt. "Well, she was always polite and professional when she helped me at the grocery store. I thought she deserved the chance if she wanted it."

He shook Della's hand and turned to give Anna the signal that it was time to go.

"Thank you." Anna shook Della's hand and followed him out, but the whole time her gaze burned a hole in the back of his head.

"That was nice of you to get someone a job," she said once they reached the sidewalk.

He shrugged, not meeting her gaze. "What about that thousand-dollar price tag?" He changed the subject instead.

"Oh my gosh, I was going to say. That's insane! Is that really what the town was asking the businesses to pay?"

"Evidently."

He risked a glance and Anna shook her head. "No wonder people stopped wanting to participate."

With the next two businesses, they had varying degrees of success, but a win was a win. They were both willing to put down a deposit by the end of the week, and the family who owned the clothing boutique said they'd throw in a gift certificate if other businesses wanted to go in together and have a festival-wide raffle or silent auction.

The idea was brilliant, and he typed it in his phone to discuss later.

They headed back to his car, the positive results putting a small smile on his face.

"Going better than you expected?" Anna asked.

"Much." The majority of the people were friendly or, at least, indifferent. Only a couple of them scowled as soon as they saw him.

Anna stopped at the bottom of a small set of stairs. "Then let's do one more."

"I don't want to press our luck."

"Come on. We're on a roll. One more." She nodded toward the stairs.

His stomach clenched, pressure instantly squeezing his chest. The stairs led up to Miller's Tool and Tackle. Even if he called on one more, it sure as hell wouldn't be that one.

"That's not on the list."

"I know, but look at the size of the place. It's one of the biggest shops in town. Surely they'd be interested, and we're doing so well."

He didn't want to set foot in that place, never mind approach them for money.

"I'll come back some other day." A total lie. He'd go to every business in town and still not go there. He hoped they'd join the festival once they found out everyone else was participating, but if they didn't, he totally understood.

Anna glanced at her dainty watch. "You said you had the rest of the day off."

"So?"

"So, it's not even two o'clock. Those last three businesses agreed like *that*." She snapped her fingers. "I think we should take our good karma and keep going."

"And I think we should quit while we're ahead."

Anna planted both her hands on her hips. "Okay, what's going on?"

"Nothing." He dug his fingers through his hair. "Why?"

"You've made it very clear how important pulling off this festival is, and you've been killing it today. People are responding to us. You can sell one more person on the event."

Not at the Tool and Tackle, he couldn't.

He shrugged her off again, afraid to speak in his defense.

"Every other day, you can be late for this or that at the resort, but today you want to get back. I'm sorry, but that makes no sense."

Anna had gotten a taste of success too, selling people on an idea like she probably did before she'd hit a wall at work. And now he was getting a taste of what she was like in fifth gear.

Ready to go. No hesitancy, like when she faced a drop-off on the side of a mountain, or kissed in public for the first time.

Anna was wide open, and he was pretty sure he couldn't rein her in.

But he was sure as hell going to try.

"They wouldn't be interested in participating in the Blueberry Festival anyway. What are they going to sell, fishing hooks and screwdrivers?"

"Why not?"

"I promise, we'll come back to them later. If you want to keep going, let's ask the guy who owns the popcorn and peanut shop."

As he turned to go, a steady resolve settled into Anna's gaze and she didn't budge. "No. I don't think so."

"Excuse me?"

"First, you don't want to talk to the business owners because you say it's not your skill. Then today you turn on the charm and three of them say yes. I should've known because you had no problem charming me too. You drive to the next town for lunch and ice cream and coffee, and now you won't go talk to this guy. You try to act like it's nothing, but I've never seen you this tense. What's going on? I know when I'm being left in the dark on a deal, and right now, it's pitch-black."

He wouldn't tell her the whole long, drawn-out story. One story led to the next, and if Anna knew everything about him, there'd be no way she'd still look at him with the same unguarded interest and desire in her gaze.

She thought he was fun and carefree. All she knew of him was the guy he was today, working hard to do something for his family and town, and playing hard in order to spend time with her. Why should she have to know that other Devlin? He didn't exist anymore. "Mr. Miller, the owner of the Tool and Tackle, he doesn't like me."

The truth; in its simplest form.

"You thought the people in the last three stores didn't like you either, and they all gave you a deposit, or more."

"This is different. I *know* he doesn't like me."

"How?"

"I just do, okay? Let's drop it." He looked away, in case she could see how rattled this made him.

"Fine. Then I'll go talk to him and I'll get the sale." A hard line thinned her perfect lips. A look that said he could stand out here on the sidewalk, but she wasn't letting this go. That same determination was probably what made her so great at her job. "Are you going to tell me what's really going on here?"

"No."

She narrowed her eyes with a flash of hurt and anger, then turned and marched up the stairs.

Why the hell was she so pissed? It was one business, and what did it matter that he wouldn't say why Miller didn't like him? The reasons were personal. An uncomfortable truth he didn't want to share.

He dragged a hand through his hair again.

A truth as personal and uncomfortable as, say, blacking out at work and being so stressed out you couldn't do your job, so your boss and therapist basically *made* you take a vacation.

"Ah hell." He took the steps two at a time, his gut like lead.

Anytime he thought about this place, he was thirteen and being threatened with juvenile detention or jail again, and now here he was, strolling in.

They'd never put a thirteen-year-old in jail, but *he* hadn't known that. He'd been scared shitless, though with his big show of teenage defiance and anger, no one would've guessed.

Anna startled when he caught the door behind her, but her gaze softened.

At least he'd entered the building, and the Tool and Tackle was as woody and dark as fifteen years ago. Still smelled as old too.

"Can I help y'all with something?" A feminine coo came from somewhere behind the counter.

The woman who popped up had to be Miller's youngest daughter. A few years younger than Dev, with light blond hair, fair skin and freckles, she looked directly at him, and in her huge green eyes was instant recognition.

Wonderful.

She didn't offer any further hospitality, simply stared them down where they stood.

Anna went still, probably caught off guard by the sudden chill in the air. Rather than give her cheery opener, she glanced at Dev.

He'd made it inside the shop, might as well let the axe swing down.

"Is your father around?" Dev asked, cracking the ice. "I was hoping we could talk with him."

"You sure you want to talk to my daddy?"

"No, but I'm here. And that's farther than I've ever gotten before, so . . ."

"Mmm." Miller's daughter pursed her lips, the contempt oozing off of her. She turned and yelled, "Daddy!"

After some banging around in the back, Mr. Miller appeared, and stopped right in the doorway. "Well, I'll be damned."

Yep, the old man recognized him too. Maybe he should grow his hair even longer, try out a beard.

"I wondered if you'd ever have the brass ones to walk in this store again."

Dev had plenty of brass, but that's not what made him come in here.

The reason, like most good reasons, was a woman—a woman who'd shaken and shed a tear, telling Dev the truth about an ugly part of her life.

Dev's life was much uglier, but Anna hadn't known that when she opened up. She trusted Dev enough to show him who she really was. And the betrayal in her eyes, when he'd refused to do the same, wasn't a look he ever wanted to see again.

The truth was, this was a visit he should've made a long time ago, but denial kept him away.

Karmic, really. Facing one of his biggest screwups with one of the people he wanted to impress most.

There were things he needed to say to Mr. Miller, but he didn't have the right words. He'd replayed the possibility over and over in his head dozens of times and confronting his past had to happen someday.

He just didn't know it'd be today.

"I, uh . . . I know it's past time I came in here. But here I am. And I owe you an apology for what I did."

Miller stared, unblinking.

Dev stuffed his hands in his pockets and studied the scuff on his shoes. "I know it's been a long time, but . . . I'm sorry I stole from you and wrecked your store."

Beside him, Anna's gaze jerked toward him, the intensity burning like a bonfire. But he couldn't look at her. Not yet. Not until he got this out and over with.

Facing Miller meant facing his past, and if he stopped too long to think about it, he'd freeze up. "I was young and stupid and angry. But that's no excuse."

In eighth grade, he'd broken in, stolen a fishing rod, lines, and hooks. The full gear. Refusing to show up at a youth fishing tournament without the gear required to enter, he'd committed a crime.

At first he got into the store to get what he needed. Miller's son, Jacob, was a buddy of Dev's. In some twisted way, he'd figured he might not get in as much trouble for stealing. Jacob's parents wouldn't mind, and Dev's father had promised him for months they would participate.

Then Dev's dad bailed on him. As usual.

His folks weren't going to spend rare extra time and money on him; they never had. But like an idiot, he'd gotten his hopes up.

He should've known his father was bluffing when he promised the tournament, but he was still young, and still believed. Dev told all the boys at school he was fishing too, and his dad would be there and everything would be wonderful again.

Then his father looked him right in the eyes and told him to forget the tournament. Who had time for that kind of thing anyway?

Dev had been furious. And hurt. Not only about that, but everything.

The constant arguing, the tension, the long, icy silences and being ignored. At school there were always jabs and accusations. His family owned a big inn, why was he so poor? Why was he upset? What was wrong with him?

He should be at the top of his class, well behaved, like his brother Roark.

Since he was thirteen, he'd owed the Millers an apology, and he'd avoided it like a hanging.

Like so many other things, he'd dodged what he needed to do in lieu of what he wanted to do.

Now, wanting to help grow and shape Honeywilde into the success his family deserved, wanting to do something for the town he'd run roughshod over back in the day, he couldn't ignore his past anymore.

"I should've come here years ago to face you, but I'm here now. And I'm sorry."

Anna shifted on her feet and Dev finally lifted his chin enough to look at her. Her eyes shone as she pinched her lips tight.

"That's . . ." Miller cleared his throat. "That means a lot, actually."

Dev's gaze spun back to him. It did?

"I appreciate you coming in here and finally talking to me."

He took his hands from his pockets and nodded, wishing he knew how to follow up with something more.

Miller scratched the side of his face before settling his hands near his belt. "You know, I got some money, a couple of years back. A cashier's check showed up in our post office box. The exact same amount as our insurance claim for the damage you did. Always figured it was your brother, but when I asked him about it, he looked at me like I was crazy."

Dev wanted to run. Possibly vomit. Anything but stand here and do this. Yet he had to. This was what people did when they gave a shit. They didn't drink their problems away, they didn't throw fits. They stood up and faced reality.

"It was you," Miller said.

He wasn't asking, and Dev couldn't answer. It'd taken him almost a year to save up the money, but he had. And he didn't want to talk about it.

"You were a kid back then, I realize that. We all mess up, every single one of us, and sometimes it takes a long time to grow up. But I think you have, and . . . I accept your apology."

He studied Miller, but there was no anger or bitterness. Just a man who looked satisfied, a trace of hope lighting his face. Dev fought not to slump under the weight of relief.

"There is something you can do though, to make up for breaking into my place all those years ago."

"Of course. Name it. I'd be happy to."

"Pull off bringing the Blueberry Festival back, like I heard you're trying to do."

Anna's mouth fell open, but she quickly closed it. "How did—" She looked at Dev, then Mr. Miller. "How did you know we were trying to bring back the festival?"

Miller laughed, because to locals like the two of them, the *how* was obvious.

"I got a call about an hour ago from Della Maldonado. She told me you two were going around, seeing who'd be interested in the festival starting up again, because she knows I always loved that festival. I've done some of my best business then, because summer is prime fishing and tourist time. I never did understand why they canceled the thing."

Dev didn't either, especially now that he saw how excited the locals were at the prospect of its return, and all the promising income.

Given Crawford's less than enthusiastic response to Honeywilde's offer to help, and what the businesses said they were being charged, he got the feeling that canceling the festival had nothing to do with good business sense and everything to do with covering the tourism office's ass.

"I'm going to do everything I can to bring it back," he promised, and some of the pressure left his chest.

"Good. See that you do."

Miller left and reappeared with his checkbook, his daughter studying them all.

"Jake always said that you guys getting busted in that church was what scared him straight." Miller glanced up from his writing.

Dev cringed. One bomb of truth from his past was enough. Anna didn't need to get hit with another one.

"Good. Tell him I said hello." Dev tried changing the direction of the conversation.

Mr. Miller stopped writing. "He finally fessed up that breaking into that old church was actually his idea. Just you were the one ballsy or crazy enough to go through with it."

Crazy sounded about right. Crazy. Careless. At seventeen, he'd lost most regard for his well-being. If his own parents didn't give a damn, why should he?

He remembered thinking *to hell with it.* Not like he was going to get in much trouble back home. Maybe if he got sent to juvie, his parents would pull their heads out of their asses. Realize they had four kids who needed them.

He wouldn't justify his actions as a cry for help. There'd been no crying because by then he was furious.

Mad that Trevor was always so quiet. Angry that Sophie still tried to please their folks by trying to be perfect. Pissed off beyond reason that Roark up and left them and went to college.

The knot was back in his chest.

He'd made his apologies, and now he wanted to get the hell out of there. He shot a glance at Anna, finding her wide-eyed again. Shell-shocked.

Who wouldn't be?

"Did you know they fixed that place up last year? Some contemporary church meets there."

Dev did know, but he did his best not to think about that place or how he'd trashed it.

Miller went back to writing his check, and Dev silently willed him to stop talking—thank god.

"Anything else I can do to help, just yell." He passed over the check.

"I will. Thank you." Dev shook the man's hand and got the hell out of Miller's store, the weight of their past a little lighter, but the weight of Anna's stare twice as heavy.

Chapter 14

She couldn't stop staring.

Dev kept his eyes on the road, but he had to know she watched him.

"What?" he finally asked, after ten minutes of driving in silence.

"You broke into a church?"

He didn't look at her, but the sound he made was pained, gruff. After a few minutes of silence, he pulled to the side of the road again, this time into a gravel parking lot, right outside of town.

"I didn't want you to hear about that. It's—" He scrubbed a hand over his face. "Shit. I screwed up a lot as a kid, okay? That's it."

But that wasn't it.

The set to his jaw as he'd apologized to Miller, the slight tremor in his voice as he'd powered through, the moment was unlike anything Anna ever witnessed.

There was no *that's it*, like their interaction was a simple moment, Dev's past something he could shrug away.

Sure, he attempted to shrug it away all the time. Every time the topic came up.

Obviously he didn't want to talk about his past, no matter how much she itched to know.

She had no right to be so curious. Whatever he'd done, whatever he'd gone through, a woman he'd only know a few days had no business prying. But still, she wanted to know more. She wanted to know Dev.

"Do you . . . do you want to talk about it?"

"No." He stared straight ahead, his answer quick and certain.

"Okay."

"I . . . sorry." His chin fell. "That came across rude. I just don't want to relive it and, trust me, you don't want to hear it."

Wrong. But she wouldn't push. Not today anyway.

"Then what if we talk about all this money sitting in my lap?" She lifted the bag and gave him a smile.

Please make it wipe the heavy frown from his face.

Dev twisted his grip on the steering wheel, working his jaw. "That part *was* pretty good, huh?"

She turned in her seat. "That part is wonderful. We have almost eight hundred dollars in deposits, and you're going to make this festival happen."

Today was a triumph. And, while some of the news was shocking, she'd learned a little more about Dev. If most of his past was shocking, if he was a screwup like he claimed, the man sitting beside her now wasn't.

Dev tried, and he cared; enough to lead this festival, enough to listen to her, and enough to feel bad about whatever he'd done years ago.

"I still have to get my brother to agree, and then I need to figure out the rest of the details." Dev squinted out the window. "All in a little over a month."

"You'll do it. After today, any trace of doubt I had is gone. This is going to be great. For everyone."

He glanced over, eyes wide before he blinked. "Your faith is . . . I appreciate it. I appreciate everything you've done. I mean that."

"You're welcome. We should celebrate." Something to lift the mood. They'd been successful; that deserved smiles and laughs and . . . other things.

"I have the perfect way to celebrate."

She bet he did.

"Tubin'."

That was not the other thing she had in mind.

She flopped her head back on the seat. "Tubing. Are you sure?"

"Never been surer. After all that, I need the fresh air. The rush. It's tubing or white-water rafting."

"What about a candlelit meal?"

"We'll do that too, promise. But right now, I have to get out and away from . . ." He waved his hands, indicating what might be the whole world. "This. And it's your turn to do some vacationing. We can swing by Honeywilde, change, and be gone in ten minutes."

She made a big show of rolling her eyes and groaning, but she was still smiling. "Fine. What does one change into for tubing?"

With a cagey shrug, he put the SUV in drive and pulled out of the lot. "Doesn't matter, really. Old tennis shoes or sandals that strap. Bathing suit or T-shirt with cutoffs. Bathing suit *under* cutoffs."

"Cut offs? I'm afraid I don't own any cut offs."

"Cut. Offs." Devlin mimicked her clipped speech. "What about shorts? You brought some, right? Somewhere in your two suitcases."

This time she rolled her eyes for real. Plenty of wonderful things were packed in her suitcases; things that flattered and complimented her figure.

Shorts were the kind of thing *no one* saw her in. Not with her thighs. She wore them around the cabin and that was it.

"I might have some old jeans."

"You cannot wear jeans tubin'. It's shorts or a bathing suit."

The self-control it took her not to huff and pout ought to be admired by somebody. A bathing suit while tubing was worse. Shorts it'd have to be.

God help her. If the river didn't kill her, the embarrassment would.

Her black one-piece and a pair of black shorts were all she could pull together to go "tubin'."

She supposed the outfit was decent enough for the activity. And if Dev could face Mr. Miller, she could face leaving the house in shorts.

Dev pulled up to her cabin and hopped out, waving at her to hurry into the SUV before anyone saw him there.

With her purse in one hand and sunglasses in the other, she rushed down the stairs, not meeting his gaze.

But when he climbed into the driver side, Dev made a noise that could only be described politely, as a grunt.

"What, uh?" She dared to look over.

Lust. Unabashed and bold, written all over his face. "Damn. You should wear shorts more often."

"My legs are huge." She crossed her arms over her thighs, flames taking over her neck.

"Your legs are hot as hell." He shooed her arms away.

"I'm glad you think so, because you're going to get a whole bunch of them today. Try not to let the whiteness blind you."

His chuckle was dark, naughty. "That won't be what blinds me."

They managed to make their way to the "put in" spot without her neck burning up completely.

"All you need is yourself and sunglasses, and I brought sunscreen in case you don't have any." Dev put her bag in the back and locked it up. "Trevor used to work the river in the summers and he'd come home fried to a crisp. Easy to forget you're baking when the water is cold."

"How cold are we talking?"

"Eh, it's almost June, so not bad right now. Better in August, but still tolerable."

Tolerably cold water did not sound like fun, especially to someone as cold-natured as her. This whole tubing thing in general was extremely questionable—from her big white legs, the backwoods location, gravel parking lot, to the hairy bearded fellows running the little shack that held all the banana-yellow tubes.

Then Dev reached behind his head and tugged his shirt off.

He *kept* doing that, and it kept getting better. Tubing was now the best activity she'd ever participated in.

"I'll spray your back and then you spray mine?" he asked.

"Uh-huh." Her head bobbing in a nonstop nod, she turned around.

The first blast of sunscreen hit her, cold and wet, and she jumped, but his hands were warm and strong, rubbing in the lotion with the same capable touch of his massage.

She let her head fall forward, a little hum of appreciation escaping.

Behind her, Dev snickered. "You better stop that," he whispered, smoothing his hands down her arms. "Noises like that will wind up with us in the backseat again, and here we have an audience."

She peeked through her hair at the bearded trio, already checking them out.

"Here." Dev stuck the can in her hand. "My turn."

He turned and she sprayed, rubbing the layer of sunscreen in, even though the can expressly stated "no rubbing required."

What did that can know about anything?

The smooth skin of Dev's back held the same golden color as the rest of him. The tan of someone who worked outside but took precautions, and probably darkened evenly and beautifully by the lake in the summer.

Meanwhile she was white as a sheet, and would only ever burn, peel, and start again.

Somewhere around his shoulders, she got lost in the fascinating firm roll of muscle, until Dev turned and took the can from her. "I think that's good. Beard-boys over there are starting to stare."

He led the way to said boys, all three of them smiling like salesmen. Salesmen who'd moved to the mountains, lost their razors, and tossed out their scissors.

"Y'all picked a great afternoon for tubing," the tallest one said.

"Counting on it." Dev paid the guy and grabbed two bright yellow tubes. He started toward the stairs that led out to the riverbank, leaving Anna to smile and wave awkwardly as she passed the river guides.

"Don't mind them," Dev said as they neared the water. "They're harmless. Just admiring the view and too young to know how to be smooth about it."

"What view?"

"The view of you."

Her neck warmed, tiny hot feet dancing their way across her skin, but she didn't bother fanning or trying to hide the flush. Dev liked it, and he knew compliments brought the color on. That's probably why he did it.

"Here's the deal. Keep your shoes on, because of river rocks. I'll tether our tubes together, and take them out toward the middle. All you have to do is hop on."

All she had to do? Walk out into a raging river, almost waist deep, and hoist herself up onto a big yellow tube. Without looking a fool.

And okay, maybe the river wasn't raging, but the water was no lazy river either.

Dev stepped into the water, with a little shiver.

Not a good sign.

He kept going until he neared the midpoint, and waved her toward him.

Taking a moment, she said a silent prayer.

Don't fall off the tube, don't drown, don't die, don't accidentally flash a boob at a stranger while falling off the tube and trying not to drown.

Stepping into the river was like stepping into an ice bucket. Anna let go with a yelp and a string of muttered almost-profanity.

Devlin, already in the water up to his calves, laughed.

"Not helpful," she yelled.

"It is not that cold."

"It is exactly that cold."

"If you keep moving around, you'll get used to it."

"Why can't we get on the tubes over here?"

"If you sit in shallow water you won't go anywhere."

Not going anywhere sounded great.

"Your butt will drag the bottom."

That did not sound great.

Dev bounced in the deeper water as though the best things in life were found downriver. He slapped the yellow tubes down, kept them from getting swept away with one hand, and waved her over with the other.

If he was this excited, surely there was good reason. She could have a little faith and give this a try.

Maybe.

Dev was laughing again.

"You're having way too much fun with this."

"You will too if you'll come on."

Doubtful, she gritted her teeth and edged deeper, one millimeter at a time.

"It's going to be August at this rate."

"Shush. You said I'd enjoy this. I'm not enjoying it yet. I will go as slowly as I want."

"You *will* enjoy it when we're actually tubing. All you're doing is torturing yourself with the slowest river entry known to man."

He pretended to nod off as she finally made it to his side. She was tempted to splash him, but she wasn't willing to suffer through any possible retaliation.

Dev opened his eyes. "Oh, you made it. Good for you."

"Smart aleck," she mumbled.

"Move your legs like you're running in place." He demonstrated and she stared at him like the crazy person he was. "If you don't want to be cold, you have to do this."

"Fine." She ran in place, feeling like a doofus, but slowly her limbs went from cool numbness to tingling with energy.

"I tethered our tubes together. Go ahead and hop on," Dev instructed.

She kept running. "Say again."

"I tied our tubes together since this is your first time."

That part, she understood. Hopping was what she had questions about. Girls with hips and butts and thighs her size didn't simply hop up on things. She'd make a show of herself for sure.

"Hop on up. I'll hold the tube, I promise."

Still she hesitated, but Dev looked so sincere. Reflecting a crystal clear need to be relied upon, his eyes alone were enough to make her set pride aside and go for it.

"Okay. Here we go." She announced the launch to herself as much as him. "I'm hopping."

A hand on either side of the tube, she half hopped, half fell onto the tube. "I'm hopping. Oh my god, so much hopping." Wriggling and bouncing around, she got turned over, butt centered in the tube, legs dangling over the side.

The display had to be something akin to a sea lion waddling across the beach and stumbling into an inner tube, but when she looked up, Devlin's smile was not one of humor.

Devilment curled his lips and something hungry flashed in his eyes. "*Damn. You. Shorts.* Every day for the rest of vacation."

Anna used her foot to flick water at him, only managing a tiny spray.

"I mean it." He turned, tossing the words over his shoulder. "If I didn't think you'd try to drown me, I'd ask you to get off and jump back on all over again."

Dev hopped into his tube with a splash and, without his feet to anchor them, they were off. Swept away with the steady flow of the river.

With a jerk, she clamped her hands down on the handles of the tube, words leaving her mouth that sounded like *Ergh*, and *Don't want to die.*

The water leveled out a few yards down, and they moved slower and slower, coasting to the point where they both finally had to paddle.

"This is why they don't put in down here," Dev explained. "Tourists don't want to start a tube ride with a bunch of paddling, but the momentum makes it so you only have to do a bit of work right here before the good stuff."

"What's the good stuff?"

As soon as she asked, they hit a dip and curve in the river.

"This dip comes up on our left, so lean right a bit," he told her.

She white-knuckled her way through the first little splash, but it really wasn't bad at all. She'd been on waterslides rougher than that.

"Next one is a little steeper. Coming up on our right."

That one made more of a splash and was right on par with a wild-water ride.

The water propelled them down more and shallower declines, the occasional steep one, and turns that made them spin 360 degrees. But rather than worry at each new dip and dive, she anticipated it. Dev kept holding her tube periodically, even though they were tethered together, telling her what would come up next.

He wasn't going to let anything catch her so unaware that she'd flip over or fall out. She wasn't worried about the unknown, she was excited. Nearing the end of the cascade, she wanted more.

"Last one's the best one," he called over, his smile bright white in the sun.

Ahead, the river dropped maybe a foot or two. Anna held on tight, while Dev held on to her tube. A couple of feet wasn't much, but the result was a rush of water that shot them downriver, fast enough that her hair blew back, a jolt of adrenaline rocking her system.

She opened her mouth and let out an honest to god, "Whee!"

From there, the river calmed. Not enough that they had to paddle, but there was no intimidating rush of water either.

They bobbed along, Dev maneuvering them around any obstructions, until the river opened up wide, the leaves of the trees fluttering in the breeze, the sky above them a perfect cornflower blue.

The smooth speed of the water and wind in her hair rushed through her senses. The air suddenly smelled cleaner, the midday sun a little bit warmer on her skin. She didn't know why her face hurt, until she realized she was grinning from ear to ear.

She tilted her head back, soaking it in. "Amazing."

"That's what I was thinking," Dev agreed. But when she glanced over, he wasn't looking at the sky.

"This is great. Thank you."

"Didn't I tell you you'd love it?"

"You did. You were right." A wiggle started at her hips and snuck its way down to her toes. She couldn't help it.

She wiggled her feet and giggled. "Let's do it again!"

"What?"

"I'm serious. You were right. I want to go again. Please?"

"What the lady wants on her vacation, the lady gets."

When they reached the let-out spot, she was first in line to get back on the shuttle to ride up and go down the river again. She raced past him and the beard-boys at the put-in spot, splashing through the water and hopping on her tube as soon as he joined her.

In her life, she'd been wrong plenty of times, but thinking she'd hate tubing was right up there with thinking she'd look good with bangs.

Tubing was wild and fun. Only one other thing would be even more wild and fun, and that too included Devlin.

Chapter 15

A nna glowed. Not from the sun that shone on her skin or the wind that touched her cheeks, but from the inside out.

She'd never looked more beautiful, more appealing, more vibrant, and he'd never wanted her more than he did right then.

Considering he'd wanted her every day since he met her, that was saying something.

She shivered, standing next to his SUV, and Dev jumped out of his daydream and into action. "I have a dry shirt. Hang on." He dug in the back and found one of his clean undershirts.

She tugged on his old T-shirt and smoothed it out, looking herself over.

The pieced-together outfit was the sexiest thing imaginable. Shorts wet and clinging, thin white shirt sticking to her curves in that black bathing suit. The perfect combination of seeing everything without really seeing anything drove him mad.

Anna glanced up, still trying to fix the shirt. "What? What's wrong?"

"Nothing." The day, the moment, the woman—all of it was right.

She tugged at her shirt again. Without the perfect outfit, hair, and makeup just so, she was noticeably unsure of herself.

"Stop." He stilled her hands, taking them in his. "There's nothing wrong with you."

"I probably look like a drowned cat."

"You look hot."

A laugh erupted from the back of her throat. "I doubt that very much."

"Do I need to prove it to you?" With her hands still in his grasp, he tugged her forward, slipping one hand beneath the shirt, smoothing it over her stomach to her side, pulling her flush against him.

Her gaze darted about, but the river guides were gone.

"You're thinking drowned cat, but you don't see what I see." His thoughts, when she looked like this, and after he'd spent all afternoon being tempted by wet skin and close contact, were far from sweet and flirtatious.

With the tips of his fingers, he brushed along the side of the suit to the opening in the back. "I see skin. So much fair skin. Even in my white T-shirt, I can still see the black bathing suit underneath. Teasing me. Might as well be black lingerie. And I see shorts. The kind I want to peel down those smooth thighs."

Her throat worked as she tried to swallow.

"Are you going to let me take you somewhere better than my backseat? Get you out of those wet clothes and put my mouth on you, everywhere, like I was dying to the other day?"

She opened her mouth, like she was going to speak, then closed it. And then opened it again. "But I'm all gross and rivery."

He leaned down and pressed his lips to her cheek, kissing his way down her neck, to the wide opening of his shirt. "You're delicious."

"I'm dirty."

He pulled away enough to see the worry line marring the creamy skin of her forehead. Covered in sunscreen and river water, Anna wouldn't feel . . . good enough.

She wouldn't be able to enjoy the moment, and by god, they were due a ton of enjoyment.

With another kiss near her ear, he whispered, "Then I'll bathe you. Strip you down and wash you. Touch and kiss you *everywhere*. Use my tongue on you until you can't form words anymore and—"

She leaned back and clamped her hand over his mouth, eyes wide, her neck bright. "And we should go do that."

"Back to your cabin?" he mumbled behind her hand.

"Right now."

They could not get back to her place fast enough. They hit the porch of Cabin Five at a near run, not even closing the door behind them before he was on her. Her lips cool against his, arms around his neck as he finally managed to kick the door shut.

Spending all day with her, glowing, happy—they were practically frolicking—now he wanted her naked.

Over him, under him, beside him.

"Hang on. I have an idea." Leaving her in the den, he hurried to the bathroom, the raised Jacuzzi tub one of the nicest on the property. He even knew where to find the bubbles.

When he returned, Anna hadn't moved an inch.

"Come here."

Slowly, she moved closer.

"What's your idea?"

He grabbed the belt loop on the damp shorts and tugged her into a kiss. "We are taking a bath in that tub. You haven't even used it yet, have you?"

"No."

"It's a good thing you have me." He worked open the button of the shorts.

"Bubbles too?"

"Of course." With both hands, he shoved at the wet material, wriggling down and down, over smooth thighs.

Something or someone had convinced Anna her round hips and full thighs weren't right, or weren't good enough. Whatever made her think that could go straight to hell.

Anna was everything that turned him on. Sharp mind and a curvy figure. He'd told her as much, but he wanted to show her.

Once he peeled the shorts off of her, he tossed them aside. Before he went to work on her suit, he tugged off his shirt, her focus and her hands immediately on him. He slid the straps of her suit down, revealing one breast, then the other, kissing his way down as he dragged the suit lower. Lower still until the clingy black material moved over her hips, and she wriggled her way out.

And there she was, completely bare to him, pink dotting her neck, her hair wild and unruly, creamy fair skin, her dark pink nipples and a little thatch of black hair between her legs.

Anna was glorious. The kind of woman artists spent centuries rendering.

"I am so naked," she whispered.

"Yes, you are."

"You're not."

In one swift move and a shake of his legs, his swim trunks were kicked aside. "I am now."

The naughty gleam came back in her eyes as she looked him over. Nothing she hadn't seen before, but there was a difference between making out in the backseats of cars, and standing together, naked, no way for either of them to hide.

"We better hurry before the tub gets too full." Taking her hand, he led her to the bathroom, bubbles reaching the top of the tub. He shut the water off and threw a couple of towels down.

"This is—" She ran her hand down his arm to where they held hands. "Thank you."

He stepped in first, holding her steady as she stepped in. As they eased down, some of the water splashed onto the towels, and bubbles rose up to where he could barely see her over the sea of white foam.

Her laughter echoed against the tile as she blew a glob his way. "Did you use half the bottle of bubbles?"

"Why bother with less?"

One smooth leg caressed his under the water, but the contact wasn't enough.

"This won't do. You're too far away." He crossed his legs and scooted closer, grabbing the backs of her knees and draping her legs over his.

"Better?" she teased.

He worked his hands up both calves, massaging until she leaned back, her head right above the bubbles.

"Much. You?"

"Getting there."

"You know you don't have to be perfectly clean and made up for me to want you, right?"

Anna scooped up some bubbles, blew them over his shoulder, and didn't answer.

"Dirty and hauling plants, rinsing off in a spigot, wet and cold in a river, you're still as much of a knockout as the day you checked in."

She was gorgeous with all her hair and makeup done, and she was equally hot like this, with none of that. But Anna didn't seem to know.

"I do like being fixed up." She dropped her hand back into the water. "But I liked it today too. On the river. I felt . . . amazing."

"You were amazing. Once you finally got on the tube."

A glob of bubbles got flung his way, hitting him square in the forehead.

He laughed, swiping them away, and slid his hands lower in the water.

With his thumbs he rubbed small circles up the inside of her calves, rubbing his palms up her shins. "Do you know how much restraint I practiced today, watching you hop around on that tube?"

"In shorts, I probably looked like a beached manatee."

"Stop it. A lot of things came to mind, watching you, and a manatee was not one of them. Seeing you float down the river, with these gorgeous legs spread wide in that tube."

"Oh god." She inched lower in the water, trying to hide, but he leaned forward too, making her giggle.

Then her laughter faded, replaced with something a hint more devious. "You know, I noticed your legs too. That first day I was here."

"Oh yeah?"

She nodded, getting bubbles on her chin. "In this bathroom, when you were bent over, fixing the seat. You had on jeans, and that tool belt."

"You little vixen. Tell me everything."

"And I thought . . ." With a shake of her head, she glanced away.

"What?"

She lifted her chin barely above the bubble line. "Nothing. I can't say it."

"Yes, you can." Because he needed to know about as much as he needed his next breath.

"I remember thinking your legs looked thick and strong enough to hold me up against the wall, and we could have sex that way." She sunk completely under the water, her head disappearing in the bubbles so she could hide.

A moment later, she reemerged and he'd already moved so he'd be leaning over when she popped up. As soon as she swiped at her face to open her eyes, he caught her lips with his, kissing the water away, bubbles slipping down onto his nose.

"You ever had sex up against the wall?" he murmured, and kissed her again.

A quick shake of her head.

"Then we are going to fix that." He kissed her again, slanting his lips over hers until she arched her back, rising up for more. "Mmm, but not first, I don't think. Not right now. When you least expect it,

I'm going to catch you around the waist, and press you back against a wall. Give you everything you imagined that first day, and then some."

Her neck was practically crimson with her admission and his promise, but her expression was pure satisfaction.

Maybe she'd never confessed anything like that out loud before. Knowing her, she might've thought it plenty of times, but to speak of such things would be too forward for a lady.

He liked forward. And, if he got to be the first to satisfy such a desire, maybe she'd confess more.

The last bit of suds slid down her hair, and he swiped it away. Smoothing his hands lower, he brushed over each breast, down her stomach, her hips. "Are you clean enough now?"

With a pinch of her lips, she nodded.

"Good." He dunked his head underwater and popped up. He stood, opening the pop-up drain with the heel of his foot, and grabbed a fluffy towel from the nearby rack. He held the towel open for Anna, wrapping her up before helping her from the tub.

"I'm beginning to think you're a romantic." She tucked the towel a little tighter around her.

"Maybe." He grabbed the other towel, drying off and dropping it on the floor.

"A very brazen romantic. It doesn't faze you in the least, does it? Standing around naked."

He lifted a shoulder. "*You* standing around naked fazes me. For me, it feels nice. Breezy."

Once she dried herself off, Anna let the towel fall to the floor.

As glorious as before, and even a little more relaxed, her eyes were still huge, dark pools. She silently pleaded for assurance, confirmation that what he saw in her, both the physical and the person underneath, was acceptable.

When in truth, Anna was beyond acceptable. She was exceptional.

Dev stepped closer, tilting her chin up so she'd meet his gaze. With a slow sweep of his lips over hers, he brushed her mouth, skimming the seam of her lips with the tip of his tongue. "Let's go upstairs. Let me kiss you until there's no doubt left." He let his hands drift to her waist, lower, brushing the back of his hand against her so she gasped against his mouth. "Then have sex for hours. For as long as it takes for me to hear what you sound like when you come for the third time. Until neither of us can move, let alone worry about anything. Until all we want to do is sleep, so we can wake up and do it all over again."

Chapter 16

Anna leaned into him, mesmerized by his voice, imagining him doing all of those things.

And heaven help her, she wanted it all.

Devlin thought she was sexy, *amazing*, and right now, she felt exactly that way.

His belief made her brave. Gave her the courage to take his hand and, stark naked, lead the way to her bedroom.

As they climbed the stairs, Devlin made an appreciative half hum, half growl behind her. Her butt probably all up in his face.

She turned as they reached the bedroom, her back to the bed, and he pulled her into his arms.

Keeping every word of his promise from earlier, he kissed her until her blood ran molten hot, her limbs loose as he eased her back onto the bed.

With smooth lips, he explored. From her lips to the tips of her fingers, across her breasts with sweet suction, and down her stomach, to nip at the insides of each thigh, all the way to the arch of her feet; a tantalizing tour of every inch, until she writhed on the sheets.

Hungry for him, her body thrummed. She clenched the bed sheets in her fists, desperate for him to kiss the one place he hadn't touched.

He spread her legs, caressed her thighs, and moved forward until he knelt between them. Lust darkened his gaze as he leaned down. "You want me to kiss you here too?"

A jerk of her chin was all she could manage.

Her legs began to tremble and he looked at her like she was something to devour, to worship.

With the tips of two fingers, he barely touched her, a torturous brush against her flesh. And she cried out.

The side of Dev's mouth pulled up, a smug look that only made him look more desirable. Then he touched her again, and the first sweep of his tongue against the top of her slit was like lightning in her blood.

Tugging the sheets on either side, it took every ounce of her control not to jerk them off the bed completely.

Devlin wedged in closer, moaning greedily as he licked at her, touching her with fingers that were just rough enough to rub every nerve the right way, then soothing her stimulated flesh with his tongue.

He kept on and on until, like he'd promised, she was a wriggling mess, helpless beneath him. Switching back and forth, with his touch and his tongue, he kept her orgasm right out of reach. Right on the brink.

It danced there, within her grasp, but he was going to make her say it. Or ask for it.

She arched into his mouth. "I'm so close."

"I know."

A moan stuck in her throat—god, she was *so* close.

"You want me to help you come?" The purr in his voice as satisfied as it was needy. "I want you to. I want you to come with my tongue on you. I want to feel you."

She choked back a cry, the first wave of her orgasm building.

Devlin's dark head between her thighs, he growled against her, working the flat of his tongue at the cleft of her sex, until that wave built. Her muscles tensed, her body sang, and her climax hit her. She squeezed her thighs against Dev's shoulders, trying to hold on.

Moving against his mouth, she soaked up every bit of ecstasy he offered.

Ever since Devlin had given her that innocent-as-the-devil look in the lobby of the inn, she was addicted. Addicted to the blue of his eyes, the line of his jaw, the purr in his voice when he was up to no-good, the touch of his hands, the length of his hair, the way he made her feel—everything.

This feeling, the thrill and relief, she rode the high of it until she lost direction. Until she didn't know up from down.

When she finally opened her eyes, Dev lay beside her. Flopped over onto his back, a grin of pure satisfaction on his face.

His erection stood up, almost brushing his stomach, and she

wanted to touch him again. Feel the smooth skin over the hard length. So she did.

With hands that trembled so slightly only she would know, she skimmed her fingers up the back of his cock.

He sucked in a breath, his body tight beneath her touch as his gaze clashed with hers. She ran her fingers back down and over his sac, and he clenched his thighs, shifting around.

"Anna." Her name was barely a breath, and when she wrapped her fingers around him, leaning down to flick her tongue against the head, he gasped her name again.

She covered the tip with her lips, then took the length of him into her mouth.

"Damn." Devlin grabbed at the sheets too.

She slid back, lifting her gaze to meet his, but his eyes were squeezed shut. She did it again, his breath raspy as he said her name again.

His back arched and she kept going, using her hand to stroke his cock until his hips moved in time with her.

She put her lips back around the tip, kissing him there, and Dev almost came up off the bed.

"That—" He sat up, and dragged her in, taking her mouth in a rough kiss.

He licked his way inside her mouth and she opened to him, needy. Shameless.

"I want to be inside you." He kissed his way to her ear.

"Yes."

"Do you want to be on top?" he asked when he broke away.

"I . . . I don't know." Being on top she was so . . . there.

More than anything though, she wanted this. More, and Devlin, and yes, but she'd never told a lover what she wanted, much less taken control and been on top. She followed, and sometimes even enjoyed, but she never made the call.

Her eyes had to be as wide as the moon, and he licked his lips, completely unashamed. "You can tell me. Tell me how you want me. I guarantee you it's a win-win, no matter what."

"I . . ." The realization stunned her.

She *did* want to be on top. She wanted to set the tempo and remember what she'd felt like being in his lap in the car, her hands on his thick shoulders, fingers splayed across his chest. His hands on her hips, making that possessive sound deep in his throat.

"Because I want you on top," Dev said, somehow knowing what she couldn't put into words. "I want to see you, and touch you. Watch you above me when you come again, and then roll over and pin you down—"

An embarrassing whimper escaped her lips. Holy crap, all of that sounded—*yes*.

"On top." Her voice shook. "I want to be on top."

He grinned, energy coursing through his body. The need in her shaky voice went straight to his cock. "Give me one second."

He leapt off the bed and bolted down the stairs. In seconds flat, he was back, foil square in his hand. "Wallet was still in our pile of clothes."

As soon as he was back on the bed, she kissed his chest, over his shoulder, grazing the skin with her teeth.

"Hell yes." He dragged a finger over his chest and toward his collar bone. "Do that again."

She did, running the tips of her teeth against the tendon, making his blood sing.

He threaded his fingers through her hair, holding her there. "Again?"

After she did, his mouth was on hers, tongues tangling, until he couldn't tell whose kiss was more desperate, or who was closer to losing control.

He managed to get the condom on and leaned back, bringing her with him to straddle his lap.

She eased up, positioning herself, and as she sank down on him, slick and hot and tight, her hair fell into his face. Soft and wet, silky, so similar to how she felt, clenched around him.

He almost came right then.

She slowly eased up and Dev held his breath.

This was her rhythm to set. She was free to do whatever felt good, take her pleasure and give more, however she wanted.

Every bit of them being together was bliss for him. What mattered was Anna. For reasons he wasn't ready to examine, this needed to be extraordinary for her. More than memorable, he wanted it etched into their brains and on their skin. Something they'd always have. Something they'd share.

He steadied her with his hands on her hips. Once she settled, her legs straddling him, he caressed her sides, her breasts.

They'd never made it a secret that they wanted each other. From early on, the mutual desire was clear. Only the situation staved them off. But knowing was nothing like doing something about it. From her greedy looks, to the flick of his tongue against hers, to the place where he throbbed deep inside her, he knew this one time—no matter how extraordinary—would never be enough.

He rocked his hips into her, moving his hand to brush his thumb over her clit.

"You . . ." She caught her breath. "Do that again?"

He did it again, and she moved her hips, until they found the right rhythm.

When they did, he let go, freeing his hands to touch and rub, press and caress, until Anna finally let go too.

She stopped holding back. With both hands planted on his shoulders, she rode him, and the passion in her eyes was the most erotic thing he'd ever seen.

Her face set, that look in her eyes as she chased her pleasure with every ounce of her being. The same persistence with which she did everything else.

Dev pressed his thumb over her clit again, rubbing in circles.

She clenched around him. "Yes."

He kept going, and when her rhythm got lost to her pleasure, he took over, thrusting into her, faster and faster, until Anna squeezed her eyes shut.

She clenched around him again, her mouth falling open as her whole body tensed.

He was about to explode too.

Spending all day with Anna and having her now—he'd ridden the edge of coming for what felt like an hour, but still he wouldn't.

He rolled them over, keeping her legs wrapped around his waist.

He'd teased her earlier, saying he wanted to hear what she sounded like when she came for the third time, but his taunt was the truth. He wanted to make her come again. When she thought she couldn't, but one more orgasm really can be pulled out, with a raspy cry or a moan.

He wanted to swallow that sweet keening sound down with a kiss. Lock it inside where he could keep it forever. Even after she left.

Hair tossed and wavy, eyes glazed and so dark they looked black, Anna gazed up at him. "My legs won't stop shaking," she said, and broke into a grin that thumped at his chest.

Her thighs trembled and he smoothed his hands down the inside, back up the outside. "You're okay though?"

The smile on her face went impossibly bigger. "I'm . . . more than okay. Not . . . not used to that kind of workout."

"Mmm." He leaned over and kissed her knee, then the top of her thigh, a little freckle near her hip that made her flinch, her stomach, in between her breasts, and finally her cheek. "We're not done."

She smiled, her eyes glazed, and he pushed himself inside of her, easy, in case she was oversensitized. But the only sound she made was a soft cry of pleasure. He eased out and did it again, rocking into her until their breathing increased.

Anna lifted one leg, rubbing up the outside of his thigh, before hooking it over his hips to encourage him.

He thrust into her, still not too fast, for her as much as him. There was a tempo to sex, and he'd had enough to know you didn't rush to the finale if you wanted it to be grand.

Once she relaxed, her grip on his arms tight but the tension in her legs loose, he thrust harder, faster. The way he liked it, but wasn't about to attempt until she was ready.

"Oh god, yes," she cried out.

The feeling was like nothing else. Burning attraction and need, and Anna looking better than he dreamed with tossed hair and the flicker of another orgasm making little tension lines between her eyebrows.

"I . . . you . . ." She gasped for breath, her next word barely a whisper. So faint he could've imagined it. "Harder."

He wanted harder. Wanted to feel her everywhere, wanted to be stiff in glorious places tomorrow, wanted to feel the stinging pull in the backs of his legs later and know why. But not everyone was into that.

When he wanted down and dirty, some women took it as an insult, but the exact opposite was true.

He could get off no matter how he got sex, but he enjoyed sex the most when unfiltered, unchecked. Raw-edged, and honest. And he wanted that with Anna.

Something that whenever she thought about it, she'd get that delicious flush to her neck, and he'd have to shift in his seat and adjust himself, because the memory alone was enough to bring it back to life.

"You want it harder?" He whispered against her ear, certain he'd heard her right, but damn if he didn't want to hear the words again anyway.

"Yes." Her answer was a hiss on the air.

And he gave her exactly what she wanted. What they both wanted.

Dev shifted, pushing her farther up the bed. He pressed her thighs a little higher, angling her hips to his, just so. With one hand he held the headboard, the other grasped her hip.

He thrust into her hard, sparks flashing across his closed lids.

Beneath him, she gasped and moaned with pleasure. He didn't let up, mesmerized by the play of pleasure across her face.

His orgasm rushed toward him with the increased speed and friction, and she clenched around him, the fingers of her free hand digging into his side where she held on.

"I . . . I'm going to come," she said, wonder and confusion filling the words.

"Me too. You feel so good."

Her nails bit into his back, and she let out a throaty, desperate noise as she came.

That was his undoing.

He folded over, his spine bowed, and he cried out, the build of waiting and holding off making his orgasm bowl him over. His temple pounded and his body throbbed, a heady rush that tightened his whole body. A high that made the room spin and flip.

And the last thought that flew through his mind, in that perfect euphoria, was he hoped he didn't fall on top of her again.

Chapter 17

By the time she woke up the next morning, the cabin was full of light, the loft bright, her bed warm and rumpled.

Anna rolled over to find an indention in the pillow where Dev had slept, but no Dev.

Some banging and a muffled curse downstairs meant he was either trying to make coffee or make it to the bathroom.

Snuggling further down into the covers, she let the edge of sleep creep over her. She was comfortable and cozy, and for the first time in years, she'd slept through the night.

Rested and content, a soft soreness between her legs reminding her of all the reasons she'd slept well.

Devlin.

His desire for her, his acceptance of who she was, no matter the situation, and his gentle—or not so gentle—nudges forward.

The morning felt fresh. She was somehow . . . different.

She blinked open her eyes, forcing the last of sleep away. Her heart was lighter, the air not so heavy.

Anna sat up, her pulse jumping. Colors were brighter, everything shifted subtly but enough for the truth to reverberate down to her bones.

Happiness.

Still, today, she was happy. A buoyant bubbliness inside, and glowing warmth all over. The emotion chased her all day yesterday, from their success with the businesses in Windamere, down that river, right back to this cabin.

And it'd caught her.

She was happy.

Tears filled her eyes and a few slipped free, sliding down her cheek.

She'd been so certain she'd never know real happiness. Not the kind that came in brief flashes, but the solid strength of the kind of happiness she felt in her bones.

Yet here she was, and she was grateful.

And so very, very unworthy.

The tears began to sting and she pinched her eyes closed, but they kept coming. The waterfall that she'd held back for so long, thinking if she didn't look at her grief, name or acknowledge it, maybe the sadness would dry up and go away.

Her tears rushed forward and she was powerless to stop them.

What right did she have to happiness? Her father was dead and she hadn't been there for him.

She wasn't supposed to be happy. She was supposed to be grieving. This trip was meant for her to grieve, to deal with her life, because she couldn't before, and now she had the nerve to be happy?

Her father had done everything for her. With all that he had, he raised her, trying to create enough love for two parents. Then he was robbed of his life, and she hadn't even been there for him in his last hours.

Guilt clogged her throat.

She really was selfish. Exactly like her mother said.

Her days at Honeywilde were supposed to be spent in reflection and reading all of that crap her therapist had given her, trying to get a handle on life and loss.

For crying out loud, she hadn't even been to see her mother yet, and she had to face her, but instead she was off having a grand time with the most gorgeous man, having bone-melting sex. She'd done none of the things she'd set out to do.

None of it.

Because she was awful. A horrible, awful person.

She drew her knees up, wrapping her arms around them and burying her face in the blanket.

The scent of coffee reached her first, then Devlin's rumbling morning voice. "I made coff—what's wrong?" In an instant, he was right beside her, the clunk of two coffee cups being set on the bedside table before he wrapped his arm around her. "What happened?"

"It's . . ." She choked back a sob, uselessly swiping at her face. "It's not you . . . I'm okay . . ."

He rubbed her back in slow circles. "You're obviously not."

The truth came spilling out of her again, his concern a sledge-hammer that slammed right through every blockade she'd carefully constructed for months. "My father died."

His arm tightened around her. "Oh god. Did someone call you? Anna, I'm so—"

"No, no." He'd misunderstood, which, given the circumstances, made sense. "Not now. Not recently. Almost seven months ago. I should've said something the other day when I told you about my breakdown, but . . ." She shook her head, unsure how to explain.

The plan was never to tell him any of this. This wasn't his burden to carry. He said his lack of good advice made him a good listener, but taking on her grief, shouldering the mess that was her life, was not part of their agreement.

"I'm sorry." She swiped at her face again. "I was so happy when I woke up, and then I felt horrible for being happy. Guilty and self-ish, and I didn't mean to start bawling, but . . ."

"Shhh." More slow circles rubbed into her back, helping her breathe. "It's okay to be upset. Your dad died."

Fresh tears erupted at his words. Tears that should've been shed months ago, but no one else had ever said the words aloud around her. She'd heard *he passed* or *he's no longer with us.* Coded truth that didn't deal with the reality of what happened.

Her dad was dead.

At the funeral, she'd stood stoic next to her mother, who'd been twice as stone-faced as Anna. If Anna had shed one tear, mourned openly, it would've caused holy war later on. Not at the funeral, of course. Never around people, that simply wasn't proper, but at home her mother would've ripped into her for making a scene. For making the funeral all about her.

Anna turned her face into Dev's chest, his T-shirt warm and dry at her cheek, smelling of him. "This might be the first time I've cried."

"Then you're due."

Hadn't she already been here with him? Confessing all the crap about her job. The last thing she wanted was to dump her problems on him, but problems were hard to hide when you got caught blubbering into a blanket.

"Do you want to talk about it?" Dev's deep voice rumbled against her.

Did she? Deep inside, she knew she should. Her therapist's voice echoed in her mind, telling her about the stages, and how accepting the damage and loss in our lives meant talking about it. Ignoring things really didn't make them go away.

"He had a massive stroke, from a blood clot." She sniffed, her nose stopped up, eyes puffy, no doubt looking like hell. "He was going to turn sixty this year. He lived for a little over a week after. I went to see him, but I had to go back to work. I wasn't there when he . . ." With a shake of her head, she bit at her lips. She'd managed to say it once, and that's all she could do. "It's the other reason I came up here. I should've dealt with this better."

"But with the job and everything else, you couldn't."

"I was making it worse." But how could she deal with her father being gone? The one person who cared and let her be, was gone forever. Who had the tools to handle that?

She sure didn't. But she could live in denial like a champ. Her mother taught her that very well. Even at Honeywilde, she'd been adept at denial. Life was easier when you didn't think about it.

"After his funeral, I went right back to work, thinking—I don't know what I was thinking, but buried myself in it, and my work suffered, I suffered. I lost bid after bid, no new accounts, and that caused more stress and more hours. Then, I blacked out in a copy room. Because I'm a mess."

"You're allowed to be a mess."

No, she wasn't. She lifted her face and met his gaze. "I've never been allowed to be a mess. Ever."

Something hard flashed in his eyes as he worked his jaw. "Well, now you can. You've heard how screwed up I am, and you're not even close."

"You don't want me dumping problems on you though. We're supposed to be having fun. Talking about this definitely isn't fun and—"

He cut her off with a quick, firm kiss on the lips. When he pulled away, his face was set. Determined. "It's okay if you need to talk about this. I can be . . . I'm here to listen."

The hesitancy in his voice was obvious, but he looked sure. And with Devlin, maybe she'd be able to say more. Not about her father being gone, but everything else about him. The real him, the parts she wasn't allowed to remember and miss because her mother didn't want to hear it.

"Were you close?" Dev asked. "You and your dad?"

She nodded, wiping her nose. "We understood each other. He was strict and he expected a lot, good grades, behavior, but he loved me. He let me be me."

Moments flashed, making a smile tug at her lips. "He loved the mountains. Loved coming up here to drive on the parkway. We never made it to Windamere, but we'd drive all around here in the fall, pick apples, buy random stuff at little shops. He'd say we needed a break from work and school, and we'd hop in the car."

Her smile hurt, the memory still fresh enough to be yesterday.

"I moved away for college, and stayed away when I started working, but we still talked. I taught him how to text, to keep in touch, and he was one of those one-long-text texters. He'd write an entire letter via text, all about what'd happened that week. My phone would blow up while I was in meetings and there'd be ten texts from his one long story. It was funny because, you know, dads."

Dev's arm tensed around her. "Yeah. I'm not close to my dad, but I think I know what you mean."

Anna eased back, but didn't leave the shelter of Dev's arms.

Devlin wasn't close to his father? This from someone who worked with and was obviously tight with his family?

"I figured your whole family was tight."

This drew a dry laugh from Dev.

"I know you said you and Roark bicker, but that's normal for siblings. I assumed you were all one big happy family, if you run a resort together."

"Hardly." Another puff of laughter. "I mean, we're better now. We had that huge wedding here in the fall, but I wouldn't say we're one big happy family."

That was at least the second time he'd mentioned his family being better *now*. Meaning at some time before, they were worse, but he never went into any detail.

"The other day you seemed to be getting along great, chasing that dog."

"We get along okay now. For the most part. Took time to get here, but we manage." His gaze drifted to her hair, and he smoothed his hand over the messy strands. "We're family."

Dev curled his lips in and nodded, stating these facts as accepted life truths. But his eyes told a different story.

Sadness hovered in the pale blue, strain pulling tight lines in the corners. The vulnerability in his eyes, talking about such things, spilled into that raw place inside her. She wished he'd say more, and tell her why his eyes held sadness. The other day at the tackle shop, Dev's past popped up, but he refused to say more, and she hadn't wanted to pester him.

She shouldn't expect him to open up and spill the truth, simply because she'd done so. There were parts of Dev he kept tucked away, and their time together was finite. One day she'd leave, and that left no grounds for her insisting he tell her more.

It didn't stop her from wishing though. Wishing he'd be completely honest, share more of the imperfect parts from his past, so she'd know she wasn't the only one who was messed up.

"And Roark and I . . . we bicker because we're two different people, with two very different opinions. Sometimes we get along fine. Other times, we . . ." He shook his head. "It's complicated."

"I have one of those too. My mother." Who she needed to go see. She'd been a couple of hours from her mom's house for over a week now, and still hadn't visited.

If she was strong enough to open up and talk about her father's death, surely she was strong enough to handle a visit with her mother.

Putting it off would only make things worse once she got there. She'd already missed Mother's Day, but now she had to face her mom and the loss that hung between them. The two of them seeing eye to eye would never happen, but they were mother and daughter, and they hadn't spoken since the funeral. Seven months ago.

"I need to go to Fort Mill. My mom is there and I haven't spoken to her since right after Dad died."

Dev tucked strands of her messy hair behind her ear. "I'd wondered what made you look so uneasy about going home."

"That would be why. Visiting with her is . . . challenging." *To say the least.* "But I need to go."

"Today?" His eyebrows notched together.

"No. God, no. I need a day to emotionally prepare. I'll go to-morrow."

"Good."

"I doubt very much it will be, but I'm going anyway."

"No, good that you're not going today. I have a little more free time this morning, and I'd like to spend it with you." He leaned forward, skimming his lips over hers.

That sounded ideal.

"And . . . I'm sorry to hear about your dad." The sincerity and softness in his gaze could've brought fresh tears, but he kissed her again.

"I thought we were having coffee."

With a quick glance at the coffee mugs, he frowned. "That was fifteen minutes ago. I don't like cold coffee."

"Me either."

"I know another good way to wake up though." He caressed her neck with the tips of his fingers, brushing them down, over her shoulder. "*And* a great way to make us feel better."

She bet he did, and after cracking open the vault on all she kept locked up, spilling it out into the bright daylight to show him, she needed his touch. The reminder that even if she was messed up, she could still feel, and one day she might be okay.

The day they met, Dev said he could fix anything.

With her whole body, she would show him that if he was damaged too, that was okay. She didn't mind. They might both be a little broken, but neither of them was beyond repair.

Chapter 18

The next morning, Dev had a manila envelope in his mail slot. No return address.

He tore it open and pulled out three pages of what appeared to be a ledger book, printed from accounting software.

The account held no title, no number, no defining features at all except a date of three years ago. Then he reached the middle of the page.

> D. Delights
> Tool & Tackle
> Mtn View Café

Next to the business names were credit amounts. Five hundred, seven hundred, all different, and beside them the notation *BB Festival*.

Their payments to participate in the festival.

But Della had made it clear she was charged a thousand dollars the last few years of the event. If that was true, was this evidence that the board only deposited portions of that money?

Where'd the rest of their payments go? And who'd mailed him this information? The only people who knew he'd been to the tourism office were Anna, Crawford, and Ms. Hendricks. Of the three, only one person was in the position *and* had the disposition to help him.

"Dev, we've got five minutes." Sophie passed him on her way to the front.

He put the papers back in the envelope and folded it into his back pocket. Regardless of what the mail meant, he had to face his family and tell them what he'd done to get the ball rolling on the Blueberry Festival.

He ended up facing his family, and then some.

"Devlin." Madison jumped to her feet as soon as he got to Roark's office.

Since business had picked up at the resort, their meetings moved from the great room. Dev wasn't overly fond of the new location—it lacked a coffee trolley and his favorite spot on the couch, but he picked his battles.

"I haven't seen you in weeks." She gave him a big smile and a brief hug.

Madison had come a long way from her first days at Honeywilde. Always professionally polite, the woman had a hard outer coating that didn't crack until Roark got his shit together and told her he loved her. Since then, every time Dev was around her, she had warmed up a little bit more.

Which was good. Because if she and Roark kept going the way they were going, she'd end up being family too.

God. Married to Roark.

He loved his brother, but Roark could be such a control freak. How Madison stood him was beyond understanding.

Then again, Madison loved Roark and his weird little ways, and she could get through to him like no one else ever could. She made him more tolerable and, from early on, she had a way of making Roark agreeable.

Hell, he'd agreed to host a huge rock-star wedding with less than a month's notice. His overcautious brother, Roark, hosting a rock-star wedding. Hell, if he did that, maybe there was hope for the festival.

If Madison thought something was a good idea, Roark was likely to go along with it.

"I've been busier than usual," he told her, a genius idea taking form.

"Busy is good. That's what you wanted."

During the wedding, Madison saw how much Dev wanted in on making things happen at the resort, and she'd been the one to give Roark the nudge needed to make it happen.

"Exactly what I want, and I'm working on getting the Blueberry Festival back for this summer. In downtown Windamere."

"That's great." She beamed. "How are things going?"

"Good so far. Roark still isn't sold on the idea though."

"He rarely is. Sometimes you're best served to keep moving forward and let him sell himself."

A sound strategy. "But other than getting Roark on board, it's going great."

"Must be, you look better than the last time I saw you."

He scowled, teasing her. "Thanks?"

"Not like that." She scowled back. "Like you've gotten rest or sun or something."

He hadn't been resting. When he wasn't working, he was with Anna. Today was the first day they'd spent apart. Being around her was good for him; he couldn't deny it . . . even if he couldn't admit it.

Madison studied him, her keen green gaze dissecting everything. "There's something else though. Besides the suntan."

He shrugged.

"Maybe it's the lack of snark."

Hell. He hadn't said one snarky thing yet this morning. "I've only had one cup of coffee. I'm working up to it."

"Then let's get some before Roark starts talking."

They walked out to the great room, poured their coffee, and Dev told her a little bit more about the festival, carefully leaving out any mention of his cohort.

"Morning." Roark met them when they got back to his office, looking like he'd been up for hours.

Knowing him, he'd already run ten miles and done a load of laundry.

Sophie, looking crankier than usual, shuffled in with her coffee, grunted, and sat next to Dev.

"What's up with you?" Dev whispered.

"Don't ask."

He wouldn't. He knew better. Sophie had the best disposition of the lot of them, but when she was in a mood, you let her be.

The only problem being, he needed her support on this. He needed her upbeat and positive when he told everyone his plan and what he'd been up to.

A moment later, Trevor joined them, quietly grabbing the empty seat on the other side of Devlin.

"Morning," Dev tried.

Trevor gave him a silent nod.

This was bad. Worse than bad. If everyone's day had already

gone to crap before 8:00 a.m., how the hell was he supposed to get them stoked about the festival and his plan?

Roark gave Madison a quick wink—which he probably thought no one saw, because Roark thought he was smooth like that—and pulled his chair up to his desk. "What's everyone got on their agenda today?"

Dev waited. Surely someone had something on their agenda to break the ice.

The room remained as quiet as a tomb.

"Okay, then there are a few things we need to get done before the weekend."

"I have something." Dev got the words out before he could back out. If he didn't speak up before Roark got on a roll, he'd lose his opportunity.

Anna's words marched through his mind, reminding him why this might work.

Your ideas are not crap. You can pull this off, but you have to try.

"I went by the tourism board's office the other day, to get those numbers you asked for."

Roark leaned forward in his chair. "You did?"

Next to him, Sophie was suddenly a lot more alert.

"You said you wanted to see them, so I tried to get them."

"Okay. And . . . how did it go?"

"About as good as you might think. The guy took one look at me and said they weren't available, but he might be able to find something in a few months. Basically, I could kiss his ass, I wasn't getting any information."

"Why wouldn't he give you anything? That's weird." Sophie scrunched her nose.

"I thought so too."

"The folks in the tourism office *are* weird. I wish I'd known you were going." Roark gave him a look, laden with something Dev couldn't comprehend.

"I was trying to get the ball rolling and surprise you."

"Maybe, if we get the information within the next few months, we can shoot for the festival next year."

Of course that's what Roark would say. Be safe, be patient, and wait on all the T's and I's to be perfect.

Before, Dev would've caved, figuring Roark's way was the right way—and plenty of times his way *was* correct. But sometimes, Dev's way made more sense. Sometimes you had to take a little risk and try, in order to be rewarded.

"Actually, we don't have to wait until next year, and we don't have to wait on the tourism board to get us any numbers."

Roark sighed, his shoulders slumping slightly. The action was subtle, but since Dev expected as much, he couldn't miss it. "I told you, we can't sink money into something that has a reputation for failing. I know the town loves it, I always enjoyed it too, but the city bled money on this event for years, which is why they stopped having it. We can't afford that kind of loss. Not right now, maybe not ever."

"Well, I did a little research of my own, and the town loves the festival because all the businesses make a ton of money, every year. The city claims it's a loser, but the locals don't agree. Until the last couple of years, vendors said they made big profits. The people in town love the festival. Only recently did it become a burden to anyone."

Roark frowned. "That doesn't gee haw."

"I know."

"But until I can see something, some kind of proof, we're not sponsoring the festival. It's a huge responsibility and we aren't in a position to take it on."

"But—"

"No." Roark gave him a hard look, caught somewhere between frustration and a plea to let this go. "Dev, no. We can't."

His insides knotted up at the strain in his brother's eyes. Too familiar, from not so long ago. When Dev wanted to leave the resort altogether, before he got his life on track, and figured they'd all be better off without him.

Dev, no. I'm not letting you walk out of here. I can't. You're my brother. We'll figure this out together.

Roark always had his back, from the time they were little to the time Dev came home with nothing.

You're going to stay here and help me. We'll have to be smarter and more careful than Mom and Dad, but this resort is home. Our home. You're not going anywhere.

But Roark could never see that sometimes his idea of having Dev's back meant holding him back.

"Now." Roark lifted his eyebrows and blinked at the surface of his desk. "I wanted to discuss the stand-alone dock and beach..." He scrubbed at the back of his neck, the storm of emotions gathering around him as close as they did Dev.

The rest of the family looked on, wide-eyed and waiting, because they knew. This was how bad things started between them. From butting heads when they were kids to not even speaking when he got thrown out of college. Sometimes their disagreements were bad, sometimes they were horrible, but they rarely surprised anyone.

All of them suffered through their arguments, not only Dev and Roark.

"Beach rejuvenation," Madison offered.

"Yes. Beach rejuvenation." Roark's face went pink, a sure sign he was aggravated. "Thank you. We need to talk about how much it's going to cost to bring in more sand, fix the dock, and whether we need to spend that kind of money right now."

"Actually, the profit available from an event like the Blueberry Festival is exactly how we could afford to do extra things like renovating the lakefront and getting a brand-new dock, instead of patching things up." Dev sat a little straighter. He wasn't accepting his brother's no. This meant challenging Roark, but he'd done it plenty of times before.

Dev clutched his coffee mug until his fingers hurt. A dense knot settled in the center of his chest. He could do this. And he could do it calmly, without it descending into the yelling and arguing he'd hated so much as a boy. He could talk, civilly, to his brother and make him see the benefits.

Somehow, he could make Roark believe in him.

Roark rubbed at his temple, refusing to meet his gaze.

"As the sponsor of the Blueberry Festival, we could make a few thousand dollars in less than a week."

"Dev." Roark lowered his chin.

The tired look in his eyes added an ache to the ever tightening knot in Dev's chest. "Would you listen? Please? For one second, have an open mind about my ideas and hear me out? I have a plan and it's already working." And if he believed in the plan Anna had helped him develop, he had to stand up for it.

Madison bumped her leg against the back of Roark's chair. The move was subtle, but Dev saw, and appreciated it.

"I know my plan for sponsoring the festival will work out, because I spent a lot of my day off, going around to local businesses, asking them if they'd be willing to make a deposit to participate. Since then, a few more have called me, directly, because they heard from others that I was asking. I have almost a dozen businesses interested and over half have already given me their deposits."

"Oh my gosh." Sophie, still sleepy eyed, leaned toward him. "You went around to all of those people?"

He kept his jaw firm and nodded, refusing to meet her gaze. She knew how he felt about the people in town and she knew how most of them had viewed Dev for years. If he looked at her now and saw even a hint of pride or hope in his little sister's eyes, he'd probably lose it.

For so long he wanted to be deserving of that look, but he wasn't there yet. Too many things could still go wrong.

"That's great, Dev," she said, and left it at that.

Roark sat forward too, arms folded on his desk. "They gave you deposits. What did you do with them?"

"They're in the safe downstairs."

"You gave them receipts, I hope."

"Yes, I gave them receipts. I'm not an idiot."

"I wasn't implying—" Roark cut himself off, tight lines forming around his eyes, working his jaw as he thought.

Devlin could only imagine what Roark might be thinking, because his mind didn't work that way. Roark would be considering a hundred different things that could go wrong with the deposits alone. Then, the hundreds of other things that might blow up on them by planning a festival for the whole town.

Making it happen wouldn't be easy, but where Dev saw opportunity, Roark would see all of the potential pitfalls.

"Did you give them any kind of guarantee you could bring the festival back? Because we aren't in a position to guarantee anything."

"No, I didn't promise or guarantee anything. I told them the festival was a stretch, but a definite possibility." And Anna had told them the same, but he couldn't mention her. Not including her, crediting her, telling his family about this amazing woman who fell into his life—or vice versa, really—gnawed at him like midday hunger.

She deserved recognition, credit, and his family would be dazzled by her.

They'd probably wonder what the hell she was doing with Dev, but he wouldn't blame them.

Roark went from staring at the top of his desk, to staring at Dev. "I can't believe you went out there and did that."

He didn't mean it in the same way that Sophie had meant it. Roark's tone was one he'd heard enough times, he knew it well. He couldn't believe Dev would do something so ill-advised. Risky. Stupid.

"Look, some of the business owners even said they knew it might not happen, but wanted to make deposits in case it might help things along. They want this to happen, same way I do."

"But you can't take people's money if you can't guarantee the event is happening."

"They gave it to me knowing the event was a fifty-fifty shot."

"Fifty-fifty? Dev, seventy-thirty we can't pull this off, and now you've gone and taken people's money."

Madison cleared her throat. "We've pulled off a successful event with worse odds."

Everyone's gaze jerked to Madison, still leaning back on the credenza behind Roark.

"Well, we have," she said, arms crossed.

"I don't want to have these people's money when this plan falls through," Roark argued. "It opens us up to quite a bit of—"

"Risk." Dev finished the sentence for him. And Roark said *when* it falls through, not if.

But his brother's lack of faith didn't deter him. If anything, it charged his resolve, goaded him on. When Anna, a woman who'd known him a week, could believe in him, why couldn't his own brother?

Roark had been there, front row to all of Dev's failings in life, and that was the only explanation. The problem always came back to how much Dev had screwed up in the past, and if his family couldn't get past it, then neither could Dev.

"I get it, okay? I get that you're worried I might screw up because that's all I did for most of my life. You don't want ringside seats to my imminent failure, but you made me the hospitality manager here. Am I a part of this business or not? Because if I am, this is my idea and I have solid reasons to think it will work. If I'm not part of this business, then tell me now so I can take my ideas elsewhere."

The bomb of his words exploded in the middle of Roark's office, and they all sat there and watched it burn.

No one said a word for what felt like time eternal.

Dev wanted to take it back, even though the truth of how he felt needed to be said. He'd held it in for too long. Roark meant well, trying to big-brother the hell out of him, but if Dev was part of this family and resort, then he should have a voice.

He didn't want to take his ideas elsewhere.

His life was here, with the people who'd stood by him, loved him, and held him up for all those years. But he didn't need to be held up anymore.

He needed his family to trust him enough to let go.

"Of course you're a part of this business, that's not—" Roark paused, the battle with himself heightening his color. "That's not what I meant, at all. I want us to be smart about this."

"I am being smart."

"And careful. I'm trying to help."

"Well, you're not."

"Okay." Sophie held her hands out, a lot more alert now. "Let's all take a minute here. Everybody stop, and breathe."

"Yes, please." Trevor remained leaned back in his chair.

After a moment, Madison pushed herself off the credenza, standing up straight. "I happen to think it's an excellent idea, Dev."

Everyone stared at her again, and Roark's mouth fell open a bit.

"I do." She put one hand in the air and began ticking things off on her fingers. "First, some of the businesses were enthusiastic enough to give Dev, a wonderful but admittedly inexperienced handler in such matters, deposits, so if Honeywilde made a show of sponsoring the event, I imagine most, if not all, businesses will follow suit. Two, we put a little money into the event and, as I believe is customary, ask for a percent of sales or charge for space, however it works. Even if we don't make a profit, we break even."

"Advertise the hell out of it," Sophie added. "We don't have much time if we want to have it before the Fourth of July, but we get the word out and bring tourists in."

Devlin watched them go. Both of them brainstorming, both supporting him, both smart as hell.

Anna would get along with them like a house on fire.

If they ever had the chance to meet her.

With a smile, Sophie nudged Dev. "Good for you for getting out there and trying. I know going to all those people, putting yourself out there like that, couldn't have been easy for you."

Roark's gaze shot to his, realization finally dawning all over his face.

Yes, Devlin had stuffed his pride in his pocket and gone to some of the same people who'd talked trash about him for so many years—and asked them for support.

Roark didn't say anything, but a hundred different emotions danced across his face. The protective big brother wondering if he was okay, the business owner concerned for the resort, and the man, who'd stood by Devlin for years, believing in him and berating him in equal measure.

"I—I didn't think about that, Dev. I'm . . ." He nodded, mostly to himself, and reached for his coffee, taking a sip before he spoke again. "Good for you. It's great that you're doing this. I just, I want to be sure we have all our bases covered. I want us to discuss this as a family, so we're all on the same page."

"Yes!" Soph jumped into the positive opening Roark left. The hint of possibility in his tone. "We need to all be on the same page before we move forward with the Blueberry Festival."

Before, not if.

"All in favor?" she rushed to ask.

Everyone's hand shot up, except for Roark, who appeared to be in a mild state of shock.

Trevor kept his hand in the air, even after everyone else's was lowered. "*And* we could each take on a job so it's not too much work on any one person."

A telling hush fell over the room.

"Yes, I'm offering to take on a job. What? I'm here too, right? And the festival sounds like fun. Unlike putting a new roof on Cabin One."

"Dev, how much money do you have in deposits, total?" Sophie asked.

"With what we collected the other day, plus a few businesses that contacted me yesterday, almost fifteen hundred dollars."

Trevor let out a high-pitched whistle as Sophie's smile grew impossibly bigger.

"We'd need a lot more than that to cover costs," Roark pointed out. "I'm not saying no," he quickly added. "I'm not. Merely . . . pointing out facts."

"There are a lot more in deposits to be taken. We only hit six places this week, two called, that leaves more than half of Main Street untapped, not to mention the businesses off Main."

Roark's eyebrows bobbed. "Okay. Just . . . let me talk through the major points and potential issues, and if it's possible . . ." He looked around and Dev followed his gaze. This was the most rapt attention Roark had ever received at one of these meetings. "If it's at all possible, we'll do it. We'll sponsor the Blueberry Festival."

Sophie clapped, and Madison smiled at Roark with no small amount of admiration.

"But—and this is a big but here—if we can't make the festival work and it looks like it'll sink us into a money pit, we simply can't. Every step of the way we need to be sure. Not because I don't want to, but because we have to do what's best for Honeywilde."

They reviewed the logistics, every detail from who would be best suited to cover what aspect of the festival planning, to where to rent the pop-up vendor tents, to how much of a percentage to take from sales. They all agreed that keeping the event small, its first year in revival, was best.

Roark made a quick list of every item he could think of to worry about, and as each one was checked off by those in the room who had a solution, the knot in Devlin's chest loosened. Hope spread in its place.

Maybe he could do this. He'd taken on a huge task, something that he believed in and enjoyed, and maybe he could make it work. If he pulled this off, for once he would be known as the guy who'd revived the town's favorite event, and helped local businesses, and did something positive. Not the guy who wreaked havoc all over town.

The meeting wrapped up, and Madison took Trev's vacated seat, leaning in to talk. "I could use some of my contacts for promotion and advertising too. Some people at a few of the magazines and papers still owe me favors for getting them pictures of the wedding. I might be able to get a last-minute spot for the festival, at no cost. Wouldn't hurt to ask."

"That'd be great." Exposure from a big magazine could make all the difference.

Sophie leaned over the arm of her chair too. The two of them hovering near Dev like bees. "We should come up with something clever for the ad. Something that'd entice a ton of day tourists."

"Yes." Madison chewed at the corner of her lip as she thought.

Lightning struck. Dev knew an advertising genius; all he had to do was ask her. "I might be able to come up with something really catchy."

"You?" Sophie cocked an eyebrow.

"Sure. I mean . . . give me a day to think about it. Brainstorm and stuff, but yes. I can come up with something." Otherwise known as waiting until Anna was back from her visit with her mom so she could help him come up with something.

"When you do, ping me and let me know. I'll see what I can get printed." Madison got up to speak with Roark, and Sophie walked out with Dev, still studying him like he had food stuck on his face.

"What?"

"Since when do you know anything about being catchy?"

"I know stuff," Dev insisted.

She didn't say anything, but her expression disputed plenty.

Dev didn't know shit about being catchy, and they both knew it.

"That girl who was scared of Beau was in advertising though, wasn't she?"

Hellfire. *How?* Sophie met Anna one time, for maybe five minutes. She couldn't possibly pick up on all she did.

"I don't remember. Was she?"

"Dev." His sister stopped walking, lowering her voice and her chin.

"Fine. I'm pretty sure she was, but that's got nothing to do with this."

"When you were talking about going into town, talking to the business owners, you kept on saying *we*. *We* did this and *we* got that."

"No, I did—" *Shit.* Yes, he had.

"Now, nobody else seemed to notice, but nobody else is me. Either you've got an imaginary friend, or someone is helping you. And my money is on the pretty girl."

He didn't say anything, and neither did she. His little sister stared him down, waiting to see who'd crack first.

"Soph, please don't rat me out." Of course he cracked first. "It's not anything bad, I swear."

With her hand up between them, she shook her head. "I'm not going to rat you out. C'mon, this is me we're talking about. Besides, who am I to judge anyone else's dating habits or love life?"

"Did you have another bad date last night? Is that why you were so grumpy this morning?"

"Um, do you want me asking about your dates? Because I sure don't want to talk about mine."

"Good point."

"But you better be careful. The last thing you need is some fun with a guest, flying up and biting you in the ass."

"I know." But he wasn't about to stop seeing her. How could he? He'd debated his attraction and intentions at first; now there was no other option. He liked Anna—a lot—and all he had was another week and a half with her. He wasn't about to throw on the brakes now.

Since when had he ever thrown the brakes on anything? Sure as hell wasn't starting now.

She'd be back from visiting her mom by tomorrow, and he couldn't wait to tell her his family was behind him. He'd have their help and support, and he owed so much of that to Anna. He wanted to celebrate somehow—and then work his ass off to make the festival a reality— but first celebrate, with her.

And prove to her she was as extraordinary as he'd insisted.

Chapter 19

The prospect of spending time with her mother gnawed at her for months, and the longer she'd put it off, the bigger the bites.

Anna tightened her grip on the steering wheel, wishing she was already down the road and back again. Get in, get out, don't pay any attention to what her mother might say and, no matter what happened, *do not* play the game.

That was the plan, and she had to stick to it this time.

Anna pulled up at the two-story colonial in Fort Mill, letting the engine run. The sights and the flood of memories rushed toward her, surrounding the car, filling it until she could drown.

The tree where her father built her a tire swing—the swing was gone now, naturally. The row of azaleas where she'd had her prom picture taken every year, and every year her mother pointed out what was not quite perfect about the dress or her hair or her size, or all three.

"Get in, get out, and don't pay attention. Do not play the game." She repeated the plan out loud, counted to ten, and got out of the car.

After ringing the doorbell twice and knocking, her mother finally answered.

"There you are." Her mother tossed her hands up like she'd been the one waiting at the door. "I was wondering if you were ever going to show."

"I told you I'd be here right around lunch. It's not even one o'clock." *Dang it.* She shouldn't have even argued that much. Any attempt at defending herself would fall on deaf ears.

If her mother believed herself the sufferer, there was no changing her mind.

She pushed open the glass door to let Anna in.

"Well, it's a good thing I didn't lie down for a nap or I would've missed you. You'd have come all this way for nothing."

The bluster was completely for show. She didn't nap. She'd never napped a day in her life. For one, she thought naps in the middle of the day were lazy, or something old people did. Second, and more importantly, it'd mess up her hair and makeup.

Anna followed her mother through the foyer to the sitting room used only for formal company.

The furniture was stiff and ornate, in pale colors that dared you to spill a drop.

Her father hated this room and so did Anna, and she'd never once sat in here, as though she were company to be received. She might as well be a door-to-door salesperson or church deacon.

"I'd offer you some lunch, dear, but seeing how late it is, I'm sure you already ate." She settled on the edge of the stiff-looking sofa, her hands in her lap. "You never were one to skip meals. I can get you some tea though."

She fought not to pinch her lips together at the remark. Her mother wanted a reaction, some drama so she could accuse Anna of being emotional or ask her if she had her period.

Anna kept her expression neutral. She'd get no reaction today. "I'm fine. Maybe some water later."

"Are you on a diet again?"

Anna blinked, reminding herself of the little speech in the car. "No. I simply prefer water over tea."

"Good." Her mother nodded, lips pursed. "I was going to say, drinking water won't do it. I helped out at the church on Wednesday and that awful lady, Mrs. Gregory—do you remember her? Huge woman, always has been. Anyway, she had some god-awful carton of water with lemons in it, talking about her cleanse—like anybody wants to hear about her cleanse—and I'm thinking, lady, it's going to take a lot more than some sips of water to make a dent in that fat."

They spent more than an hour that way. Her mother talking at her, not to her, and Anna gritting her teeth and bearing it. All cutting remarks, disguised as casual conversation. How this person or that person's daughter moved out West to follow her dream, and how devastating it must be.

To her mother, a girl moving across the country to have a life, instead of settling down and joining the local Junior League, was the equivalent of failure. However, the people at the country club had sons and daughters who were getting married, popping out kids, curing illness, becoming saints, running for president.

But not Anna.

No, Anna was a successful executive in Atlanta. Almost thirty, still single, and financially independent. And in her mother's eyes, there was no greater travesty than a woman like Anna.

"So. Are you seeing anyone?" Her mother crossed her ankles, not sitting back, her posture still perfect.

Anna was seeing a lot of someone, but she wasn't about to bring up Devlin. The realization that a guy like Dev would give her mother a conniption, made her smile.

His carefree air and humor, rebellious tendencies, and the brazen things he said, were precisely what attracted her to him. That and his face, and his hair. His thighs . . . Fine—everything, really. But Devlin's everything was exactly what her mother would despise.

He was too casual, too free. His looks too intense, his behavior too bold.

"I'm dating, but nothing serious." As soon as she said it, the depth of the lie became clear.

Without discussing their situation in detail, she and Dev had still somehow agreed they'd be casual. Hadn't they? But claiming they were nothing serious rang so false, it shook her.

Anna stared at the tea-set collection in the corner curio.

Her feelings about Dev weren't casual. She seriously liked him and, after only a week—had it only been a week?—she longed to see him again. To be with him, helping and laughing, and muddling through what to do with her life.

"Can you afford to only be casually dating?" Her mother's sharp tone drew her attention. "We can't always be picky."

Anna wasn't picky, but she wasn't settling and she wasn't looking. Still, she'd found Devlin.

"Once you hit thirty, physically, it's all downhill. You've got your father's large bones to deal with too. I had you at thirty and I've never really recovered. And I was small."

Their time together was as painful as ever. Even more so, now that her father wasn't around to act as mediator.

Her mother had always played nicer when he wasn't out of town with work. She worked hard to be on his good side, like they were both his children, competing for love and attention.

When she finally ran out of backhanded comments, Anna turned the conversation to something productive. "I wanted to ask, have you talked to your financial adviser about the insurance?"

Finances were always a fun family topic, but her mother needed that money if she planned to keep up the house and her lifestyle.

"Why? Are you already chomping at the bit for a cut of your father's policy?"

"No." Anna curled her fingers into her hands, her nails biting into the skin. She would not take the bait. She *would not.* "That has nothing to do with why I'm asking. Dad wanted that policy to provide for you if something happened to him. There's plenty of money, and he wanted it invested well because that's your security."

"I bet he told you all about it, and not me. Did he tell you how much there was?"

Of course he had, because Anna was the responsible one. Her father knew, if anything happened to him, there'd be no one to keep her mother from going off the rails, except Anna.

And if she didn't love him so much, if he hadn't done everything he could for her, been the best father anyone could hope for, she'd probably say goodbye to her mother and never look back.

But she couldn't. Her father had loved her mom, and wanted her safe and secure, left wanting nothing. All of that was now Anna's responsibility, and she'd handle it. Whether her mother wanted her help or not.

"He wanted to make sure your future was secure."

"And yours, I'm sure."

"I'm not worried about me." True, her father named her partial beneficiary, even at her age. Maybe because he knew if anything happened to him, her mother wouldn't help out Anna, should she need it.

"I doubt you are worried." Her mother shifted, uncrossing and re-crossing her ankles, her gaze burning holes into the delicate coffee table between them. "What with the money he gave you for college,

I doubt you have reason to worry about anything, sitting as pretty as you are."

And there it was; the final straw that'd finally broken the back of the pitiful, lame camel that was their mother-daughter relationship.

It didn't matter that they'd never seen eye to eye, not even when Anna was a child, or that her mother did everything to tear down Anna's confidence when she was a teen. What really twisted her mother's pearls was that when Anna graduated magna cum laude, her father gave her enough money to pay off any college debt and make a down payment on a little condo, wherever she wanted to live.

She was lucky, blessed, and probably a bit spoiled, but she appreciated everything her father ever did for her. She'd worked her ass off in high school and college to make him proud, got the best job and topped sales, because she had someone who believed in her and she didn't want to let him down.

And her mother resented the hell out of her for it.

"I want to help you get things settled and make sure you have what you need to live."

"I'm not a moron. I can take care of myself."

"I wasn't implying—"

"I might not be as smart as you, but I manage."

"I know you do."

"Don't forget we paid for the education that made you so smart."

"I know you did. I was only asking."

Tense silence fell between them. They'd reached an impasse, and pushing any further would only end in a knock-down, drag-out fight that Anna couldn't handle right now.

She was ready to go and get on with her vacation. Back to the place where she'd left Devlin and sunshine and mountain air and no one critiquing every single word and move.

Had she fulfilled her duty with the visit at this point? They'd now spoken since the funeral. Gotten nowhere, as usual, but they were speaking again.

Progress.

A twisted, painful progress, but progress nonetheless. Enough so that she wouldn't catch hell the next time she called her mom. She'd covered the check-in, the checking up, and the offer to help. If her mother didn't want her here, why torture them both by dragging out their time together?

"What time do you need to head back to Atlanta?" Her mother gave voice to what they were both thinking.

When can we wrap this up?

Her mother thought Anna had driven the four hours from Atlanta because she knew nothing about her stay at Honeywilde. She didn't know because she wouldn't care, and if she did know that Anna had taken a break to get her life in order, it'd be the perfect ammunition for years to come.

Better to let her think Anna would drive eight hours today for a less-than-two-hour visit.

"No particular time." *As soon as humanly possible.*

"Well, I don't want to keep you. I'm sure you have work tomorrow."

Her mother's way of signaling she was done dealing with Anna.

I'm sure you have homework. Shouldn't you be outside playing? Where are your friends? Julie's mom can take you to the movies.

Everything was fine though. They'd spent almost three whole hours together with only minor bitterness and animosity. For them, that was success.

"You're right. I should hit the road."

She knew better than to stick around for any niceties so often used in other families. There'd be no *drive safe* comments or hugs. Her mother didn't operate that way, which was fine. Really. Anna stopped expecting it years ago.

Her mother followed her through the foyer, seeing her out. As soon as they reached the door, in her most forced casual tone, she spoke. "Oh, I meant to ask you. Did you take care of your father after they burned his body?"

Anna froze, her hand in the air, reaching for the doorknob. She dropped her hand and turned. "It's called cremation, Mother. His wish was to be cremated and his ashes spread. People do it all the time."

They'd already had this heated discussion before the funeral. She didn't want to go through it again.

"No, it's called ridiculous, especially when we have a perfectly good family plot right here in town."

Her father wanted nothing to do with being buried in that plot with her mother's side of the family, or being put in the ground, period, and that was his right. He loved the fresh air and mountains, and that's where he wanted his ashes spread.

As soon as Anna was able to work up the strength to let go. A final goodbye that she was not ready for.

"Well?" Her mother fisted a hand on her hip. "Have you done it? Have you dumped him off the side of some godforsaken mountain?"

"No, but I'm going to." And she meant it. Her father's last wishes were all going to be fulfilled, no matter what her mother had to say about it.

"Disgusting." Her mother scrunched up her nose. "Desecrating a body that way. And you going along with it to appease him."

"I'm not going along to appease him, I happen to agree, and you—" She pulled herself up short.

Do not play the game, don't give in.

Righteous fury burned in her chest in defense of her dad. Her mother had no right, *no right*. No one had that right. And she used words like "desecration" and "disgust" on purpose and—*Damn it!* She wanted to scream.

Did her mother have any idea how difficult this was without her demeaning the decision?

Whether burying her father or scattering his ashes, putting him to rest and finding closure evaded Anna's ability. Finally letting go was the hardest thing Anna would ever do. Clearly. Since seven months had gone by and she hadn't done it yet.

But of course her mother knew. That was exactly why she poked and poked, picking at the vulnerable places inside Anna to keep her in line, reminding her she wasn't good enough, she didn't deserve all she'd been given in this world; anything to keep Anna insecure enough so her mother had the upper hand.

Well, that was too bad. Because Anna *was* good enough, and it wasn't only her father who thought so.

"I'm going to go now." She straightened.

"Yes, you do that." Her mother stood by the door, hand still on her hip.

If Anna wasn't going to take the bait and give her the drama she so desperately needed, she was welcome to leave anytime.

"I'll call you in a few weeks," she promised.

"Do whatever you want, Anna. You always have."

No hugs, not even a pat on the shoulder or a smile, but as Anna stepped out onto the porch, her mother's words followed her. "And you can keep trying to appease your father all you want, but he's dead now. He's not here to tell you how wonderful you are, so don't expect it from me."

She never had.

Anna squeezed her eyes closed and marched to her car, refusing to look back.

Chapter 20

Devlin raced up the road to Cabin Five. This morning, Sophie told him she'd seen the black Lexus pull in late last night.

His heart hammered in his chest with the eagerness to finally share some good news, and he burned with the need to see Anna again. He wanted to check on how her trip went, ask her for a genius slogan to advertise the Blueberry Festival, talk to her, touch her, and kiss her. Have her legs wrapped around him as he pushed her up against the wall, exactly like she'd fantasized, make the fantasy come true, and maybe even one or two of his.

Just the usual.

All his excitement came to a screaming halt when he spotted her on the porch of the cabin.

Dressed up, as usual, this time in a flowy sundress and little denim jacket, hair pulled back and makeup done, but something was wrong.

Over all the beautiful shine, that dark shroud hung once more.

She smiled as he approached, standing and coming toward him with a warm hello, but he saw through the front.

"Hey." He took her into his arms, holding her close, a reminder she was real and not something he'd imagined. Too good to be true.

"Hey." With a deep sigh, she settled against him like someone who was done carrying the weight of their burden alone.

"Are you okay?"

"I'm great." The tone of her response was off, flat enough that he knew she was not great. He'd seen her great, on the river, in the bed with him. This was not Anna feeling great.

He loosened his hold, but didn't let her go. "What's up?"

"The visit with my mother was exhausting, but that was expected." With her hands on his shoulders, she rose up, bringing her lips closer to his. "But this is better."

And hell if he was ever one to miss an opportunity. He kissed her, long and slow, making clear how much he missed her. Trying to let her know he could make things better in so many ways.

Her arms around his neck, she pressed her body against him, knowing full well that drove him wild.

He slid his hands lower, and lower still, until he reached the small of her back and pressed her in even closer.

This was exactly what he wanted. "I kind of missed you," he murmured.

"Kind of missed you too."

"I have good news."

Anna pulled away a little. "I would love to hear some good news."

"You sure?" He kissed her again, coasting his hand over the curve of her ass. "Because it can wait."

With a giggle, she grabbed his hand, but only held him still instead of moving it off her butt completely.

"No, tell me now before I get completely distracted and forget to ask."

"First, I got some of the financials on the last year of the festival."

"No way, from whom?"

"It just showed up in my mail, anonymously, but I figure it has to be Ms. Hendricks. And get this, our numbers for costs are almost exactly in line with the last festival, but the payments from the businesses all range from about five hundred to seven hundred."

Anna scowled. "Della said she had to pay—"

"A thousand. I know. Which means Crawford had to be messing with the money, right?"

"Sounds like it."

"But, either way, it won't stop us from putting on the event. Because I told my family."

Her eyes went wide as she gave him a cautious smile. "About us?"

"About the businesses, their enthusiasm, and how most of them gave us deposits right off."

Her smile wavered, but didn't fall.

"My family loved the idea, and they want to help. We went over everything in our meeting and everyone will have a job. Even Roark is behind this. Shocking, right?"

"That's great," she said, but her face was stiff, her shoulders held too tight.

When she pulled away, he shifted his hands higher, not letting her go that easy. "No. What is it? What's wrong?"

"It's . . ." She studied the front of his shirt, not meeting his gaze. "It's nothing. I'm emotional after yesterday. This really is great news, and exactly what you wanted. I'm thrilled for you."

Then why wouldn't she look at him? Having his family's support meant the full support of the resort. It meant they'd be there to help him carry out the plan he and Anna came up with.

But . . . it also meant Anna could no longer help as well.

"I am such an idiot."

That made her look at him. "You are not."

"Now that they're involved, you can't be, and here I am jumping for joy and didn't even think about that."

Her hair swung as she shook her head. "No, it's a good thing they're helping. From here on out it'd take more than you and me anyway."

She could be involved if he told his family about her. Except, if his brother found out about her now, any trust, and his tentative free rein, would be wrecked.

He lifted her chin, holding on so she wouldn't look away. "I want to tell my family about you, but I can't."

"I know. I knew that days ago, but . . . but you do want to tell them?"

"Hell yes, I do. Why wouldn't I? I'd introduce them to you right now if I didn't think Roark's head would explode, right before he dropped the axe on the whole thing. This is exactly the kind of thing he gets all stressed out about. If he knew, not only that you and I were . . . fraternizing."

A small smile touched her lips. "Fraternizing?"

"Okay, that's putting it lightly. But if they knew what we were doing, and that I had you out there, working with me on Honeywilde business, unauthorized no less, his head would spin around. Five or six times. It'd be unholy. He can't know." No matter how much Dev wanted to tell.

The complication twisted inside him, eating at him, because it wasn't right. A woman like Anna shouldn't be anyone's secret. Least of all his. He was lucky to have a couple of weeks with her in his life, and here he was—hiding.

"But my sister sort of knows," he confessed.

"How? We've been so discreet."

"I know. But Sophie knows all, and that's okay. She's got ESP or something, but can keep a secret like a vault. I don't mind her knowing."

Her small smile grew that much more, and he had to kiss her, the perfect curve of her lips too much to resist.

The kiss was sweet, her lips soft against his, but he couldn't get rid of the gloomy sensation hanging over them.

Never, in all his years, did he think he'd feel this way, but he wanted to know what else was troubling her.

If something was wrong, he wanted in on the issue. The problem was, she didn't want to talk about it.

She'd gone to see her mom to seek some kind of amends or closure. Either that didn't happen or things went down ugly. She didn't have to talk about the visit with her mother if she didn't want to, but there had to be something he could do to help.

"What do you have planned today?"

"I don't know. Nap. Maybe read."

The book sitting on the porch railing had a mile-long title. All he saw were the words "dealing" and "death." Not the sort of tale she needed, to get her out of her head.

"Nope. I don't think so. Let's do something."

"Don't you have work today?"

He had a shit ton of work to do today: a company to call about the wiring for the festival, a call to make to their insurance company, plus whatever Roark would likely text him to take care of. "Yes, but I have all day to do it. I can work on things later. Right now, I want to make sure you're okay."

"Absolutely not. I'm not going to pull you away from work."

"Work can wait."

"And so can I." Her face grew stern. "Do what you need to first, and then come back. If you can. I'm not going anywhere. I'll be here and we'll do something. I've been selfish enough taking up so much of your time. Now that you have the green light on the festival, you need to run with it."

Her insistence sounded neutral enough, but a certain word she used lit up like flares. Anna was not selfish. He knew that kind of talk because he used to use it. The doubt, the self-deprecation.

She was right about him needing to handle work first, and then fun, but she was wrong about the rest.

"All right. I'm going to get my stuff done, then I'm going to come back here, free for the rest of the day, and you and I are going to spend it together. Deal?"

"Deal. But how about something that doesn't involve water?"

He took care of his tasks that day, responsibly but with an added sense of urgency.

Fancy talk for working his ass off as fast as he could without screwing up.

With Anna gone yesterday, they'd already spent a day apart. He wasn't looking to make it two days.

Normally, if he was hanging out with someone, he wanted his alone time. Required it to keep from getting twitchy.

Not with Anna.

They had a little over a week left, less if he got busy with the festival. The more the event became a reality, the more his free time would be eaten into with extra jobs. And now that he couldn't have her along to help, their window of opportunity was shrinking even more.

So hell yes, he had a sense of urgency.

He took care of hiring a wiring tech for the power to the vendor tents, and he got a quote on renting the tents themselves, both well within budget. By the time he ticked off the last item on his list, it was almost five.

He jumped in his SUV and broke a few speed limits rushing back. As he took the turn at the gravel road that led to the cabins, a brilliant idea bit him. He parked the SUV, hidden behind a copse of trees, and dug the garage key out of the glove box.

He never did this. Ever.

The only exception was the time Sophie's little sedan got a flat in a vicious autumn thunderstorm, and he'd spotted her on the way back up the mountain. They'd made it back in one piece, but both of them looked like drowned rats.

Roark had paced a path in front of the fireplace, knowing they were both out in the storm. There were tornado warnings in surrounding counties, and even though tornadoes never made it up the mountain, big brother still worked himself up into a fret.

In all fairness though, he fussed over them that whole night. Had Wright whip up some soup and homemade bread, went and got dry clothes, built a fire. A full-blown mother hen he'd been, and Dev couldn't lie, it'd felt nice.

Sophie had since gotten a better car, and Dev started paying attention to the weather forecast, but they all still recalled that night with fondness.

Dev reached Anna's cabin on foot, and only had to knock once before she jerked the door open.

"You must be ready to go." He laughed.

"I don't know, am I?"

She still had on the sundress and the little denim jacket that went with it. The issue was the shoes. "Do you have any boots?"

"Hiking boots."

"You need to put those on. Sandals won't work."

She scrunched her brow. "With this dress? I think I packed some booties though. Hang on."

What the hell were booties?

Moments later, she reappeared with black boots that looked like they'd been hacked off just above the ankles.

Booties. Made sense now that he saw them, and hell. The shoes were hot.

"Booties, huh?" He followed her down the porch stairs.

"That's what they're called."

He could think of a few places he'd like to see those booties. Around his waist, over his head, under his bed.

Anna stopped walking and he bumped into her, his focus on the swish of her skirt over the booties, not on where he was going.

"Where are we going?"

Damn good question.

"Um. Keep walking."

She put a hand on her hip, doing nothing to cool him down. "But I don't know where I'm supposed to go."

He put his hands on her shoulders and spun her around, facing down the drive to the cabin. "That way. Just keep going in that direction and I'll tell you when to stop."

They walked along for about half a minute before she shot him a look over her shoulder. "What are you doing back there?"

"Walking. What are you doing?"

This time when she stopped, he managed not to run smack into her. "Are you staring at my behind?"

"Maybe. How many pairs of these booties did you pack?"

"Only these." A smile lit her face. The first full, genuine one of the day, and not a hint of gloom. "You're bad. And shameless."

He moved closer, into her personal space. "You like it."

She didn't budge an inch. "Lord help me, I do."

With both hands on her waist, he drew her in, her breasts pressed to his chest. "Today took forever. I thought I'd never get back."

"But you did. And just in time." She laid her hands on his arms, easing her fingers underneath his short sleeves.

He kissed her. None of this was part of the surprise, but screw it. They didn't get a proper kiss this morning and now, waiting almost another full day to have her in his arms again, the surprise could wait.

Anna slanted her mouth over his, opening so sweetly for him, the hesitance and gloom of this morning lifting away.

She was softness and desire pressed against him, and he was going to end up with a hard-on. Riding with a boner was not fun, but he wasn't about to stop.

"Is this the surprise?" Her breath came heavy against his lips. "Sex in the woods."

He had to chuckle, because that was one hell of a good idea for later. "No, but now it's on the to-do list."

Kissing his way down her neck, he reached the spot that made her rise up on her toes, her body humming with need. "Then, what . . . what's the surprise?"

"It's down the road a little ways."

Suddenly, her fingers were in his hair. Threaded through the longer strands, holding him in place yet somehow tugging at the same time. A low, needy sound grew in her throat. "We should go or we're not going to make it."

He wasn't sure they were going to make it anyway.

"Okay." He started walking with her still in his arms.

If they kept this up, they were going to end up falling down again.

He peeled himself away with a groan, trying to adjust against the stiffness in his jeans. "We . . . Jesus. Okay, it's right up here. Don't walk in front of me or we're back to square one."

The road curved, and to the right was the stand-alone garage.

And his 1970 Harley.

The red was a darker shade than her nails, but as shiny, the chrome getting shinier as he worked on it and replaced parts, the new leather seat made for two.

He climbed on the bike and shifted the weight of his stance, adjusting to have someone ride with him. "Do you know how to ride?"

Anna looked at him, her mouth slowly falling open.

Seconds passed and no answer.

"I said, do you know how to ride?"

"Um . . . a bike?"

A blockade couldn't have stopped the wave of smug satisfaction. "Yes. A bike."

"No?"

Anna moved her legs closer together, her neck dotted pink, her breath catching, her eyes almost swallowed whole by her black pupils. Whether she was aware of the looks she was giving him didn't matter. Hunger rolled off her, and she no longer tamed her desire the way she had that first day.

"Do you want a ride?"

She stepped closer, and for a second he thought she would join him. Throw her leg over and set off to the see the sights. Leave their lust on hold for later, like they had earlier.

Instead she grabbed him; both hands curled into his T-shirt and she bent down, her lips crashing into his.

Good god, *she* was shameless.

As bad as Devlin.

No, worse.

Because they were right here on the road to the cabins, where anyone could pass by and see them. They weren't supposed to be seen together and here she was, ready to climb all over him and that motorcycle.

She needed to get herself together. Maintain some level of chill.

But there was no chill.

Devlin on that motorcycle, white T-shirt stretched tight over his sculpted shoulders, jean-clad thighs doing that thing they did when he spread them over the Harley.

A whimper left her lips, and he caught it, kissing the noise back into her mouth, chasing it with his tongue. He snuck one of his hands around behind her, cupping her bottom and pulling her closer.

The hem of her dress hiked up and he took the opportunity to slip both of his hands underneath.

"Oh . . . hell, are those lace?" He kept moving his hands, his fingers dancing around the elastic waist, her dress high enough she could feel a breeze. And all she could think about was Dev and his thighs and her dress hiked even higher.

"Anna." He purred her name against her neck. "Are these lace?"

What was he even talking about? She couldn't hold a thought while he worked his mouth into the V of her dress, stretching the top of it down. "Is . . . is what lace?" Without meaning to, she arched into him, wanting him to kiss more, harder. Needing his hands on her, like before.

Everywhere.

After surviving her mother, the long drives to and from, too much time to think and be alone, she longed for this. For Devlin. He was wild strength, a force of nature, blowing through her life and twisting her all around, and she loved it.

Cupping her jaw, Dev deepened the kiss and in that moment, all she knew was him. All she wanted was this.

She wanted to kiss him out in the open, unashamed, for him to take her, here or anywhere else. She wanted to let go. Not the kind of letting go that meant she felt nothing. The letting go where she was open to feeling *everything*, without a care for whether what they were doing was proper, whether or not she looked okay, because to Dev, she was always more than okay.

When she shifted around to kiss him deeper, his knee slipped between her legs. Instead of slowing down, she moved forward until she straddled his leg.

"Hell yes," he muttered against her lips, slipping his hands down the back of her panties, holding her in place, his fingers splayed wide so the tips brushed against the seam of her bottom.

She squeezed her legs together around his, the cleft of her sex swollen with need. She barely managed not to rub herself against him and dry hump his leg.

Except then she did, the friction making her moan out loud.

"I want more," Dev growled. "We're . . . I've got to get off the bike."

She attempted to move, but her legs were wobbly and uninterested in relocation.

"Here." He leaned forward, getting off the bike, both of them stumbling away but managing to stay upright. "In here. Come on."

"Where—" She squeaked as he took her hand and tugged her toward the side door of the garage.

He got them inside, the door closed, and that was as far as they got.

Dev was on her. Pushed back against the door, his mouth on hers, hands back under her dress, massaging her bottom until he ran one hand down the back of her leg and hoisted it up over his hip.

"God, *yes*." She'd definitely said it out loud this time.

Possessive in his hold, he pressed his hips against her, the hard line of his erection rubbing her the right way.

Her head fell forward, his mouth not an inch from hers. His breath came in short, hot puffs of air as he slipped a hand in the waistband of her panties, the first brush of his fingertips like a shock wave.

"You like that?" He teased her, moving his hand lower, pressing his fingers against her, stroking down enough to tease her opening, then slipping inside.

Her body buzzed with his touch, her desire. Nothing else crowding her mind, only the two of them and ecstasy.

"Will . . ." To say that took more than a bit of courage, but she wanted it, and she knew she could ask him.

He'd want her to. He'd get off on it.

"Will you make me come again? Like this?"

"I've got a better idea."

He tugged at her denim jacket, shucking it off and tossing it on the nearby work table. His lips were a hot brand on her skin, down her neck, across her shoulder. He nudged the straps of her sundress until they fell off her shoulders. With his teeth he gently nipped and teased the sensitive places near her collarbone.

Then he kissed her lower, tugging at the dress and her bra, until one breast was revealed. He laved attention on her, flicking his tongue over her nipple, taking her into his mouth.

She could come, like this, if he touched her, even lightly, in the right spot.

But suddenly, Devlin was gone.

Her leg fell and she made an unattractive noise of protest, but then he was back.

Tugging at her panties, yanking them down her legs, jerking his head in a sharp nod, brooking no argument that she needed to step out of them, right now.

Her panties were tossed aside too, and then he knelt down before her, putting her leg over his shoulder.

Dev put his mouth on her.

No preamble, no warning. Just hot and wet, urgent and seeking, and she cried out.

With his tongue and teeth, he played her. One hand holding her hip against the door, the other working with his mouth, until her legs began to shake.

Shake and tremble, threatening to let her fall.

But she wouldn't. She couldn't. Not caught between Dev and the door.

He growled hungrily against her, the sounds of a man starving for more, and she flew apart like shards of glass.

With her fingers dug into his hair, she came. Her body trembled with the impact, and he held her, waiting until she settled before getting to his feet.

Desperately, he kissed her neck, the curve of her exposed breast, situating himself between her legs. "Is this what you wanted? What you imagined?"

Better.

"I want you, Anna. Right now."

Yes. Now.

Dev had her pinned against the door, his hair disheveled, skin hot. The garage was dim, well-used, and the rich, smoky scent that she'd associated with Dev since that very first day, was here. The building itself—the mechanics and oils, a wood stove for heat—all of it was a part of him, and the smell was one she associated with comfort and need, happiness and sex, now multiplied. Surrounding her.

Still kissing her, Dev tugged at the button of his jeans. Able to stand without wobbling, she helped, moving his hands out of the way to work the zipper, then he shoved his jeans and boxers down. He tore the wrapper of the condom open with his teeth and rolled it on, before pushing her flush against the heavy door, and hooking her leg around him once more.

Bending low, he took himself in hand, and the long, slow slide of him pushing inside her made her eyes roll back in her head. A hint of soreness lingered from the last time they were together, her body unaccustomed to this much action.

God, she loved it.

The dull throb between her legs, aching for his friction, filling her and handling her because he knew what she'd want. He knew because he'd asked, and he'd keep asking. Giving and taking in ways no one else ever had.

Dev's hands were on her hips in an instant, his breath hot on her cheek as he leaned forward, keeping her locked in tight. "Put your arms on my shoulders. Hold on to me."

She did as he instructed, using the hold for leverage. He eased out and slid back in, her bottom bouncing against the door. But after a moment, he filled her and stayed in close, thrusting roughly inside her.

Her body ignited at the hard, fast friction.

She pushed the back of her head against the door, and let out a low, earthy moan. "God, Dev. Yes . . . that's . . . *yes*."

Where had that come from? Her voice didn't sound like her own. Indelicate and needy, and she didn't even care.

With both hands, she clung to him, trying to keep her grip on his shoulders. But then one hand was in his hair. The thick, dark strands like velvet between her fingers.

She pulled him down to kiss her, needing him everywhere. Less a kiss and more a brief sweep of lips and them breathing each other's air.

"I told you . . ." Dev panted for breath. "I told you I'd have you against a wall. Just like you wanted."

This was everything she'd imagined and more. Every part of her was alive and hot, burning like a wildfire, and equally unpredictable.

Another moan fell from her lips as Dev nipped at her neck. She reached out for something, without knowing what, her hand grabbing at empty air until she planted it above her head, against the door behind her.

The world spun. Devlin murmuring praise, his breathing growing choppy as she pushed back against him. The world faded, white noise filling her head, and she felt only the points where they connected.

His lips brushing the shell of her ear as he spoke, his strong thighs beneath her, his hands all over. "I want to go harder. Think you can take it?"

Yes. Her body screamed.

She wanted to come again with him deep inside her. Feel him for days after. Have the print of his fingers on each cheek. Never be able to look at him or a garage again without blushing. All of it. Now.

"Yes. Harder." The words flew from her lips.

He leaned forward, holding her and pressing his head against hers. He thrust into her, harder and faster, stealing the breath from her lungs. Robbing her of words.

But she loved the way he looked at her, as though he couldn't get enough. The way he went after her, like he'd die if he didn't have her, and held her like he never wanted to let her go.

Her climax struck, not a slow crescendo but a crashing cymbal. The air knocked from her lungs. For a brief moment, she knew nothing but the pleasure coursing through her body.

Dev followed, his body tightening beneath her right before he pulsed inside her.

Orgasms racked their bodies and she felt him shiver and shake with her, before she floated off, weightless.

She landed, minutes later, and somehow he'd moved them toward a wooden table with benches. He sat beside her; leaned back with both arms flopped wide on the table, panting for breath.

His jeans were pulled up, sort of, and her panties were . . . somewhere.

Words failed to come out when she opened her mouth, so she leaned back into him, her head on his arm as they stared at the ceiling.

"How . . . ?" Forget it. She wasn't even going to ask how they made it the five feet from the door without her realizing.

She could barely feel her extremities. Anything was possible.

Later, Dev spoke, still staring up at the ceiling. "This was not my surprise. But I like your idea a hell of a lot better."

She giggled.

"My surprise was—"

Before he could finish, she bolted upright and half fell on him to cover his mouth with her hand. "Don't tell me."

He smiled beneath her hand, his question tickling. "Why?"

"Because I still want to be surprised."

"Then we better hurry or we'll miss it."

Her curiosity piqued, she dropped her hand to grab his. "You have to help me find my underwear first. Wherever you flung them."

His chuckle was deep, satisfied, and too smug by half. "Yes, I did fling them."

She stood, trying to pull him up, but he tugged her back down to sit on his lap.

"And I'm not sorry." He grinned up at her, his gaze tracing her features with what she could only call tenderness. Affection.

He brushed her hair to one side. Even when he didn't say much, his connection was there, in his touch. Mesmerizing.

"I'm not sorry either."

Their gazes locked and he didn't try to hide the way he was looking at her.

He leaned up and kissed her. "You're so beautiful."

She fought the sting in her eyes, because she felt beautiful, and he wasn't talking about her looks. Devlin saw the outside and found her desirable, and he knew the knotted, messed up girl inside, and still looked at her this way.

Like she was more than enough. She was perfect.

Chapter 21

They finally made it out of the garage, and he prayed he still had enough wits about him to ride his bike.

Holy hell, he hadn't expected that when he said the word "surprise," but the two of them in that garage was about the best surprise of his life.

The way Anna had rubbed herself against him, hot and wet and—

Nope. If he thought about it too hard, he'd end up . . . too hard. Again.

He couldn't get enough of her, and having her up against the door, experiencing her reaction and need, wanting him faster and harder, the same way he'd wanted her—It all quenched nothing. If anything, he thirsted for more.

Once he grabbed his helmet and got settled on his bike, he patted the seat behind him for Anna to get on.

She tucked the flowy skirt of her dress between her legs—they'd eventually found her underwear, unfortunately—and climbed on.

With his free hand, he reached back, feeling for her bare leg. Hers wasn't the safest riding gear, but they were only going two miles away. He slid his hand over smooth skin. "You on okay?"

She leaned forward, shifting in the seat and pressing her breasts against his back. "Are you?"

"I think so, yeah."

She held him near his waist, palms flattened low, near the pocket of his jeans. Felt great, but her hold would do shit to help her balance in the turns.

"You need to hold on higher up, with your hands clasped together."

She moved her hands higher, clutching at his chest and giving his pecs a squeeze. Effectively copping a feel.

"I have to keep this bike upright and on the road. Are you going to behave?"

Anna placed her chin on his shoulder. "Are you?"

Good point. "Okay, here's the deal. We both have to behave, so long as the bike is running. After that, it's whatever, but bike is moving, we're behaving. Deal?"

With a nod, she put her helmet on and buckled it. "Deal."

They wound around the road at a leisurely pace. He wouldn't open the bike up and risk it, but some other day he would.

He'd get Anna dressed properly for riding and take her somewhere for the day. Away. The two of them. Her arms around him, miles of road before them. Endless possibilities.

Once he got this festival planned and the work done, he'd have plenty of free time to make her vacation the best she'd ever had.

Then he remembered.

She wouldn't be here when that day came.

All vacations had to come to an end. Picturing the resort's calendar in his mind, he tried to remember the exact day of her checkout. She'd booked the cabin for two-and-a-half weeks. She'd been here at least a week and a half, which gave them a week.

That couldn't be right.

The day he kissed her on the street, he remembered thinking she had so much time at Honeywilde. The perfect stretch of days for a fun summer fling, except what they had didn't feel like a fling anymore.

And it never really had.

The issue wasn't the time left in Anna's stay, because no amount of time would be enough. If she stayed another month, and then left, it'd still be too soon.

But what could he say? Don't go? Don't go back to your life in Atlanta? Stay on vacation forever?

Dev tightened his grip on the bike's handlebars, trying to focus on the turn down the dirt service road.

He couldn't ask her to give up the life she'd worked so hard for, the condo, the job that she used to love and would love again now that she'd had a break.

For the last three years, he'd fought for the accomplishments and kind of success Anna had. Independence. Being the best at her job. What kind of guy would suggest she turn her back on all of that to . . . what? Help him finish planning the Blueberry Festival?

No. He wouldn't be that greedy.

But he would make her last week at Honeywilde count. Rides on his bike, and the dozen other things he wanted to show her, couldn't wait. He'd have to squeeze them in amid the festival planning and chaos.

Not one clue how he'd manage, but he would.

If he didn't take joy out of every last minute he had with her, he'd regret it for the rest of his life.

He already had enough regrets, thank you very much. Anna would not be among them.

The dirt road narrowed and washed out, and Dev brought the bike to a stop, kicking out the stand and killing the engine.

Slowly, Anna let go of him, her hands wandering, taking the long way off. "I could stand to ride a lot farther."

So could he. "We will. One day we'll dress for endurance and go for a long ride, but right now we have to move if we're going to make it. We're on foot from here on out, but it's not far."

"I'm intrigued." She put her hand in his and let him lead the way down the crooked path.

"What about your bike?"

"The bike is fine. People don't come all the way up here to steal bikes."

He stepped off the path, following the rough opening of those who'd cut through before.

"People come up here, for this." Dev pushed a tree branch wide, letting Anna through and out onto the rock outcropping.

"What is—Oh my god." She passed him, her feet carrying her forward.

Anna stopped far shy of the edge, staring at the view of the town below and the range of mountains beyond. "Is that Windamere down there?"

"The one and only. We can go on out to the edge."

"No, that's okay. Here is good." She remained rooted to the spot.

He wouldn't press if she was nervous about heights. Instead he stood right beside her, enjoying the view as much as the first time he saw it.

Outlook Rock was hidden, off the official maps and off the trail. Only locals knew about the place, mostly frequented by Honeywilde staff, and guests who heard about the unique vista from the staff.

The rock outcropping was maybe thirty square feet, flat until the very edge, and smooth enough to sit down on for hours without being miserable.

But what made it truly special was the view and the quiet. Glimpses of the town below and mile after mile of mountains beyond, and with the thick forest all around, a peaceful hush, insulated by trees.

"We can sit." Dev took her hand and they eased down to sit on the smooth rock. "Sunset is in fifteen, twenty minutes. I thought we could enjoy it from here."

She bumped her shoulder against his, smiling up. "Told you you're a romantic."

"I like sunsets. That's all."

Minutes floated by on the breeze, the temperature dipping with the sun so that Anna scooted a little closer. Dev wrapped his arm around her, holding her close, reveling in the feel of her body against his, occasionally catching the sweet scent of her perfume.

Maybe he was a little bit romantic.

He'd never really thought about that part of his personality. Now that he did though, he couldn't pinpoint a time when he was ever like this. Anna brought that side out in him. He wanted to do nice things for her, give her moments to remember long after she left Honeywilde, and make their limited time special. Significant.

If that made him a romantic, then sure, he could live with that.

Anna sighed, laying her hand on his knee. "This is it," she said. "This is the place I need to bring my father."

Dev's gaze jumped to hers. But her father was—

"His ashes. I want to bring his ashes here." She pulled her knees into her chest and looked away, her focus somewhere miles and miles away. "In his will, he stated he wanted his ashes scattered in the Blue Ridge Mountains. Nowhere specific. Just somewhere up here."

With her chin on her knees, she closed her eyes. "This is something I've needed to do for months, but . . . I couldn't let go. I wasn't ready before. The place had to be perfect and nowhere was perfect." She turned her face to him, eyes shining as the sunlight dimmed. "Until now. Thank you."

Unaware of the significance she'd find here, he shrugged off her gratitude. He couldn't take credit for something he hadn't intentionally done.

She nudged him again. "Seriously. Thank you." She peered up at him like he was wonderful. Like he was some great guy, considerate and kind.

"You're welcome," he muttered.

Anna stretched her legs out, taking a deep breath, her head held a little higher. "It's so nice to be back here today, and not with my mother. I know that might be horrible to say, but I don't care anymore. It's true. And finding a final place for Dad means she won't have that to hold over me."

Dev scowled. "I was going to ask how your visit went yesterday."

"Not good, but that's nothing new. My mother can't stand to be around me."

"That can't be true."

"Very true, and the feeling is mutual. We don't—" Anna interlocked her fingers. "You know?"

"Unfortunately, I do."

"My mother and I have been that way as long as I can remember too. But I had my dad, and he was enough. I finally realized that when I went to see her. She's never going to change, but I've changed. I've changed a lot, and her words and her actions won't hurt me unless I let them."

So much easier said than done. For years he'd lived with his parents' preoccupation with their problems, the resentment, turmoil, and complete lack of interest in him. Then he lived with the looks and the whispers, telling himself it didn't hurt, he didn't care, but he was never able to make it true.

"I think we can put up with each other and politely coexist, especially since we both grasp our mutual animosity. Kind of like you and Roark."

Dev flinched. "What? No." That was all wrong. His animosity wasn't toward his brother. It was his folks, even himself, but he loved his brother. No matter how much he got under Dev's skin. "Roark and I bicker, but I don't hate him. We're not best buddies or anything, but he's my brother. We're doing better now."

"Oh, sorry. Guess I misunderstood. You don't really say much about your family, so I wasn't sure." Anna glanced away, but not before he caught the pointed look in her eyes. The flash of frustration.

Dev's whole life was his family and their resort, but what she said was true. He rarely discussed them beyond the basic, surface facts.

"You keep mentioning how you're better *now*; how your family is better *now* and . . ." She looked at him expectantly.

He remained silent and Anna stiffened. She didn't physically move an inch, but he felt her pulling away all the same.

The past and the issues with his family were things he played close to the chest, and Anna had noticed.

Of course she had; she was intelligent, attentive. The longer they were around each other, the more time they spent together, the more obvious his silence and the utter lack of sharing this huge part of himself would become.

But he didn't like to talk about his problems, his family's problems, or the past. He would simply change the subject. Or kiss her. Kissing was good.

He leaned in and Anna eased away, her expression fixed. "I've never talked to anyone about my father."

"I know, and it means a lot that you told me."

Irritation mixed with the shadow of loss that still lurked over her. Dark eyebrows pulled down, her gaze hard. "*Do you?* Do you know? I've never spoken to anyone about work or my father or falling apart. No one. Not even my therapist knows everything, but I wanted to tell you."

"Thank you, but—"

"I didn't tell you because I want your thanks. I told you because I trust you."

Her words knocked the air from his lungs.

Dev tried to breathe, but the weight of what she'd said sat on his chest, pressing down. The air around him closed in, forcing her statement through his guarded mind. Anna wasn't the kind of person to say something unless she meant it.

She trusted *him*.

"Why?" He shook his head, trying to understand.

"What do you mean, why? Why wouldn't I? After all you've done for me. Helping me, listening and not judging me. All you've done is show me I can trust you."

Even after what she heard at the tackle shop? Probably because that wasn't the half of it. "People who've known me a lot longer don't trust me."

"Then that's their loss. Your sister trusts you. She called you when she was freaking out about the plants."

"That's different."

"How?"

"It just is." With a useless wave of his hand, he grabbed for a reason why. One that'd make sense.

Sophie was his little sister. She'd stuck by him, even when he was at his worst. Unconditionally, she had his back. She might've been furious with him for months at a time, but through all the bullshit, she still knew the real him. That he'd never wanted to hurt anyone; he was only trying to hurt himself.

"They trust you, so why can't I?" Anna persisted.

"You . . ." Hellfire, this was hard. "You *can* trust me. I just . . . I wasn't expecting you to."

"And you can trust me. You keep bringing up your family, obviously because they matter, but you won't talk about them. Then you shut down when I asked you about the thing with Miller and the church."

At his continued silence, his refusal to talk reflected on Anna's face.

"You can tell me."

If he did, she'd never look at him the same. There'd be no way.

But he was already hurting her by not opening up, not sharing the ugliest parts of him after she'd shared hers. His silence was a form of rejection. As though somehow he was worthy of listening, being there for her, but she wasn't worthy in return.

And he'd sooner trash his bike than hurt Anna. Not when she was the one who had complete faith in him.

He took a deep breath. "I don't like talking about the past and my family because . . . our past, my past, none of it is great."

She edged closer, offering her support. "What happened?"

More like what *didn't* happen. A string of happenings, over the course of years. Like bad-shit dominoes, falling down through the Bradley family's lives. The resort slowly going under, his parents' marriage falling apart, Dev screwing up left, right, and center, because what better way to deal with your family officially falling apart than to go from troublemaker to full-on self-sabotage?

Then, almost getting arrested wasn't enough, so he went for college expulsion and across-the-board disappointment.

Anna wasn't messed up like she thought. She was lost, and not handling it well. *He* had been messed up.

And even though he was trying to make things right now, had kept his nose clean for years now, and was doing his best to make up for lost time, be the brother he should've been for the last decade, nothing changed the fact that he'd screwed up, big-time, for a long time.

He couldn't change his past. All he could do was work on himself, and everyone in town and their brother knew why. He didn't want Anna knowing it too.

"Did it have to do with breaking into that Tool and Tackle shop and the church?"

Shit.

But she already knew some of his past, didn't she? Whether he wanted to talk about it or not, she was there when he'd had to face Mr. Miller.

"Had a little something to do with the tackle shop, yeah. I don't . . ." He clenched his teeth, warring with his desire to share some of himself with her, when for years all he'd done was keep all the broken, ugly parts under lock and key. "I don't know why some of those store owners were so into me getting the festival off the ground."

"Why wouldn't they be? They like you."

"They shouldn't. They probably like the festival and they're doing this *in spite* of me. That's . . ." He dragged a hand through his hair, scrubbing at the base of his skull. "That's why I wanted you to come along. Me, by myself, they'd have laughed me out of the shop. But with you, I have more credibility. I'm not just the Bradley family screwup; I'm the guy who's maybe gotten his act together."

"Why would they think you're the Bradley family screwup?"

"Breaking into the tackle shop and trashing the place wasn't the last time I got into trouble. Matter of fact, I think it was the first."

"Then . . . the church?"

"No." His laugh tasted bitter. He wished it was only two or three instances of trouble he'd gotten into, and not the dozens. "Some trespassing, stealing. Underage drinking. I didn't break into the church until my senior year. A place to go to get away from the resort, away from my bickering family. Made myself a hangout, invited my friends, and we smoked and drank and painted the walls, burned stuff in trash cans to stay warm."

Her mouth went slack at his purge of cold, hard truth.

Bet he didn't look so romantic now. And now that he'd started spilling the truth, he couldn't stop.

"Roark was horrified. Raised hell about me being a bad influence on Sophie and Trevor, and that only made me madder because he was worried about them, and not me. I spent years being a little shit. Getting in fights, drinking. I was pissed off at the world and I wanted everyone to know. I succeeded too, even got blamed for stuff I didn't do. The rare times I was good, I was still bad. The coup de grâce, though? Getting kicked out of college."

There was no point in editing the facts now. She wanted to know about him; then he might as well let her see.

"After my brother pulled a million strings to get me in, and the local sheriff agreed not to arrest me and Wright and Jake for vandalizing a church because it might keep us out of school, I go and get kicked out."

Her eyes wide, Anna swallowed. Her whole life she'd probably never associated with someone who hadn't graduated with honors, never mind getting kicked out. He didn't want to see shock in her eyes.

"Why were you kicked out of college?"

Her struggle to line up the man she knew with the man he used to be, hurt all the more. He was a disappointment, or at least had been, for a long time, and he didn't want her knowing that guy.

Even if she was leaving someday soon, or maybe especially because their time together was finite, he didn't want to see that suspicion in Anna's eyes, the way it lingered in everyone else's.

"I . . . I had alcohol on campus. But mainly it was providing alcohol to my nineteen-year-old girlfriend and her underage friends."

He wrinkled his nose, scratched it, the memory like a bad smell. "I didn't keep an eye on her at the party we threw, and she got obliterated. As in black out, go to the hospital and have your stomach pumped, drunk."

"Oh my god."

Dev swiped at his brow. Years had passed and that night still brought on a cold sweat.

"I was twenty-one, so I bought the booze and I should've been the responsible one, but I wasn't." Talking about that night brought it all back. Panic like he'd never known. He'd been so certain the girl was going to die and it'd be his fault.

Everything that everyone said and thought about him was true. Dev cleared his throat against the knot threatening to choke him.

Anna reached for him, her hand on his leg. Why would she comfort him? He was the villain in this story, not the victim.

"Anyway, I was the older boy with the bad record, and her father was friends with the dean, so forget a probationary period. It was bye-bye college, hello everyone knowing why I'd come back to Honeywilde."

Frustration made his skin crawl. "But I deserved the punishment, and eventually it made me get my shit together."

"You came home and everything was okay?"

His coarse laugh made her jump. "Hell no. Of course not. That'd be too reasonable for me. No, I came back to Windamere and the resort was on the brink of failure, and everyone saw me as the guy who got kicked out of college—especially since my brother was the prince of Honeywilde—so I did my best to live up to their expectations."

Her shoulders slumped.

Anna was the kind of person who'd want this story to have a happy ending, but that's not how real life worked.

"I partied my ass off and did my best to be destructive."

He would never forget the disappointment in Roark's eyes, or the vein popping out in his temple. It'd been a miracle they didn't come to blows the day Dev came home. They'd fought before—dozens of times, over petty stuff—not this time though. Somehow they both knew, if they fought over something as serious as Dev ruining his life, there'd be no coming back.

"What did your parents say? They had to be livid."

Dev shook his head and swallowed again, even harder. The need for their outrage, their disgust, their feeling *some* way about him, was still a fresh, empty hole inside him. He never cried anymore, but his voice trembled as he spoke. "Nothing. They . . . they said nothing."

Anna remained quiet a moment, but her hand on his leg tightened. "Oh."

One tiny word, laden with an understanding he felt wash over him.

"Is that why you were so self-destructive?"

He jerked his chin in a nod and she nodded too.

"And I was *furious*." He spat out the word. "We could've had everything. All of us. When I was little, we were fine and . . . I don't know what happened. No one really knows what happened. My grandfather starts this amazing inn, gives it to my dad, we have a nice home and we were good kids, and then it all went to hell. Money got tight and either Mom wasn't taking her meds or Dad had withdrawn and was shut up somewhere with a drink. It got to where no one was ever happy, our family slowly fell apart, and no one was doing anything about it."

Anna blinked, her eyes glassy as she studied him.

"Roark did his best to keep us together, but he was a kid too, and he's not the kind to stand up and yell bullshit. I am. So one day, I don't know, I think I was thirteen or fourteen, I start yelling at him for trying to hold us all together. I said, 'If Mom and Dad are so miserable, why are they still together? If they hate the inn so much, why are they still here?' Then they separated. Mom left and as soon as Roark finished school, Dad left too, leaving us an inn on the brink of collapse. Thanks, Dad."

Her shoulders rose and fell with a deep breath, and he brushed the pads of his fingers over her nails, the shine as bright as the day she arrived. "When I moved back home, I'd go out all the time, drinking. I'd make a mess of myself at night and sleep all day. Then . . . one night I got pulled."

"For?"

"DUI." He scratched and shook his head. "Guess I hadn't screwed up enough yet."

She bit at her bottom lip.

"Anyway, the cop who pulled me over? It was Jake. Jacob Miller. Mr. Miller's kid. The guy who was right there with me and Wright in that church, drinking and raising hell all over town. He looks me up and down and all I see is pity. That pissed me off. He'd gotten his shit together, so why couldn't I?"

That night could've been last night, he still saw it so clearly.

He'd been in shock. Seeing Jake all cleaned up, police uniform, put together and an actual voice of authority and reason.

Even when Dev had cussed at him, tried his hardest to pick a fight because, deep down, he'd wanted to get his ass kicked, figured he deserved it, Jake had moved out of his way. Nothing but a calm voice and patient understanding.

"He, um . . ." Dev coughed to clear the knot from his throat. "He told me to get in his car. He'd take me home. We pull up at the inn and, I swear to god, I've never seen Roark run so fast. Sophie is right behind him and . . ." He rubbed at his eyes. "She's crying and Roark yells, 'Is it Dev? Is he okay?' and I realize, their first thought isn't that I've gotten my ass arrested or I'm in trouble again. They think I'm dead. Or hurt or . . ."

The panic on his brother's face, the tears in Sophie's eyes, they still hurt. He'd never forget the look on their faces that night.

He felt as though his heart had stopped, his vision tunneling in on them from the back of that patrol car, even as they couldn't see him. "I wanted to hurt myself, but I'd gone numb. I wasn't hurting myself, I was hurting them. My parents might not care, but they cared, and I was breaking their hearts." He shook off the stinging in his eyes. "Right then I swore I'd stop. I'd never drink again, if that's what it took, I'd work my ass off, scrub toilets—whatever I had to do so I'd never see that look on their faces again."

Anna squeezed his hand, her eyes misting up.

"They were working so hard on Honeywilde, to get it back up and running. All hours, they worked and cared. They wanted this place to be joyful again and . . . I did too. I really did, even though I was screwing everything up. Roark told me I had to work if I was going to stay, and he was right. Our folks were gone, and the only people who gave a damn about me were struggling to survive. The thing that pulled me out of the spiral was I didn't want to see my brothers and sister hurt or fail. I'd failed enough for all of us. I wasn't going to let them go down in flames too, so . . . I started getting my shit together."

"How did that work out?"

"Horrible at first, then really rough." He laughed darkly. "*Then*, painfully and slowly, things got better. Roark always had to take care of us growing up, and I should've been there for him and Honeywilde from the start. Part of the resort is mine and I knew that was something. I wanted to be responsible for what little was mine and, in bits and pieces, Roark and Sophie could count on me enough to help out."

Now, simply helping out wasn't enough. He was a different person. He had ideas and he knew how to work hard. The only way to make people see him as something other than who he used to be was to prove to them he could do more. Be more.

"I want to be seen as more than the problem kid for the rest of my life, you know?"

Then maybe he could stop seeing himself that way too.

Anna turned, her fingers curled, holding his. "And this festival is the biggest way to do that?"

Chapter 22

She already knew the answer.

Now she knew why this festival was so important to Dev; the same way he knew her fear about going on in life without her father, the well-hidden, insecure side of her, and the wild and wanton side that wanted to break free.

More than anything, she'd needed the man with the sly smirk and comeback, always on his guard, to confide in her. She'd needed Dev to be defenseless too, and he was.

He'd let her in and through all his destructive behavior, she saw the man who cared so much he kept hurting himself to prove he didn't. Until he realized he was hurting the people who loved him.

Dev laughed, forced and rough. "Hey, they can't all hate you if you save their favorite event of the year, right?"

Her chest ached, her eyes burned. "No. And I don't think anyone hates you. Not nearly as much as you've hated yourself."

Chin lowered, he lifted his gaze to meet hers. The vulnerability in his blue eyes lanced her heart. "But what about you? Hearing all that, I can't possibly look like a romantic. You still want to waste what's left of your vacation on me?"

Anna kissed him.

She could explain how she felt, use a lot of words to make him understand that nothing he did in his past would change the way she saw him today. She could argue that who he was back then actually made him the man he was now, but Dev wasn't a man who needed a lot of words.

After all of that, he'd be sick of words by now. He showed her how he felt with action, not words, and she'd do the same.

She kissed him long and deep, until his fingers found their way to her hair, his lips to her neck.

So many pieces fell into place. The reason Dev was so determined to pull off planning the festival, even when faced with little help from anyone else. He wanted to revive the event for the town, but his motivations weren't about simply helping out the business owners and locals. This was his apology. To the town, to his family, to himself.

Whether he realized it or not, giving this Blueberry Festival back to the people of Windamere, was Devlin's way of saying he was sorry for all he'd done. Proving to everyone he was a decent guy now. He'd changed.

Some of what he'd told her was shocking and maybe he did deserve to get kicked out of college, but he didn't deserve harsh judgment, at least not anymore.

She'd seen Sophie and Wright around him, and got no sense that they saw him as anything other than wonderful. The older brother, Roark—she had no idea how he felt, but her opinion was crystal clear.

Devlin never meant to hurt anyone except himself, and he was doing everything he could to make up for years of destructive behavior. If this festival was to be his redemption, then she'd do everything in her power to make sure the whole thing was the biggest, best festival this town had ever seen.

She leaned away, catching her breath. "Didn't you say you needed my help with the festival? For something behind the scenes?"

"I need you to do an ad for the festival. But we can talk later. No more talking." He ducked his head for another kiss.

She leaned away, smiling. "No, I want to do this for you. This is important and I can help. Whatever you need, I'm here."

He studied her. Seconds dragged by and he merely looked at her. "Why are you so good to me?"

Her turn to shrug off the praise, the attention. "I believe in you. And I believe in what you're doing. I want to make sure this happens."

Bafflement that she was so willing crossed his face, still. "We need a slogan. For the festival. Something catchy that we can put in the papers and Madison can get in the big magazines next month. Something that will make what is basically a three-day craft and food fair so irresistible to day- and weekend-trippers, they come here and spend all their money."

Anna smoothed back her hair, trying to think. "Hmm. Irresistible. Mountains. Food, crafts." The words bounced around her brain like a rock tumbler.

She needed to spit out a gem for Devlin, and she'd been low on inspiration and sparkly ideas for months.

But this was important. More important than any deal she'd made at work.

This was a way to thank Dev for everything he'd done, for taking a rattled, strung-out woman and making her feel human again. Showing her not only how to get away from it all, but how to be brave and deal with the obstacles as they come.

"Get away. Mountains," she murmured to herself. They were in the mountains, up high, great-tasting food, arts and crafts. "Great taste in food . . . in art . . . up high . . ." Luckily he didn't think she was nuts for talking to herself. "Higher elevations . . . I've got it!"

Dev jumped.

"I've got it!" she said again, unsure who was more surprised, her or Dev. "The Windamere Blueberry Festival—Elevate Your Tastes. In the background you have a graphic of the mountains. In the foreground you need a banner, if you don't already have one. Blue lettering, classy font, maybe blueberries on one side, handmade craft image on the other. Nothing too cutesy, though. You want clean lines, classy. Style. You want the buyers to know it's a food and crafts fair of quality items. We live in the times of the rebirth of farmers' markets. People want local and fresh and unique. You need to play into that. Quality, and what's popular right now, will bring in the urbanites, and they spend a lot of money."

Eyes round, Dev stared.

"The people from nearby counties will already be sold. They'll be here and be your bread-and-butter sales; you're going to reach them by word of mouth alone. What you need is something to go beyond that market. Next level. Sell it to the people in Charlotte. Sell it to Greenville, Charleston. Then everyone is selling out of their on-hand supply and taking orders to fill later."

He blinked, still staring. "You . . . you came up with all of that? Right then?"

She blinked too, her heart pounding, eyes starting to mist. "I . . . I did. Oh my god, Dev. I did it! I came up with a slogan." She threw herself into his arms, squeezing him, squeezing her eyes shut.

A few minutes, and she'd brainstormed something that didn't suck. Months of dull, uninspired, crap ideas, and now this. Her dry spell was over. She'd found her spark.

"I'm impressed." Dev's voice brushed against her ear.

"Thanks. I am too. I used to be able to do that all the time, and now . . . maybe it's back."

"I knew you could sell. I heard you with the locals, but not like *that*. That was . . . damn."

"Thanks."

"I'll tell Madison. I'll give her your idea and she'll know how to get the graphics together. Probably take a few days, but I can show you the finished ad when we have it."

Warmth surrounded her. Even sitting out on an overlook, cold rock beneath her, the light of the sun slowly fading, she was warm inside.

"This festival is going to knock people's socks off." Dev smiled, pride making his eyes even brighter.

Seeing him like this, surrounded by all the beauty of the mountains—the view of the sunset, of the valley and ridgeline beyond it—he remained the best sight she'd seen since she got here.

Anna's spirit grew lighter as the sky grew darker, her soul buoyant. Like she could fly right off the side of the mountain and ride on the wind.

Dev was a blast of fresh air that blew through her worries, scattering them to the wind, chasing her reservations away. With him, she could be carefree. She'd been able to find a bit of the peace and calm she was searching for, and the relaxation.

In the least restful way possible, she'd learned how to relax. Working with Dev, real manual labor with him, going on adventures, and having sex—and through it all, she'd been revived.

She was dealing and healing, and he was realizing who he could be. They were helping each other, and nothing had ever felt so right. Or so real.

Chapter 23

"What are the pink Post-its for again?" Dev flicked the edge of one back and forth.

He'd been in Sophie's room, staring at the poster boards with her, for over an hour. They were trying to figure out where to put all the vendors that'd signed up, with more joining every day.

"Stop jiggling them." Sophie slapped her hand over the Post-it. "You'll mess them up and they'll lose all their sticky."

"Someone's been working with Roark for too long." He threw both hands in the air and backed away from the table. Mostly, he was kidding. Sophie was invaluable, working extra hours to get the logistics ironed out.

When he'd asked if she was sure she wanted to add so much to her workload, along with everything else, her answer was the more work the better. That'd set his brotherly radar on alert, but she insisted she merely wanted to help.

With Sophie's help, and a little creativity, he'd managed to still see Anna in between his festival responsibilities.

He'd seen Anna every day since he'd told her the good news about the festival.

Since she'd gotten him to open up about his past.

Something he never thought he'd do, never *wanted* to do, until her. At first, opening up was like the time he had a tooth drilled, but then, everything came pouring out, and she didn't hate him for it. Didn't condemn or judge him. Best of all, she still wanted to be with him, so they could spend every free moment of her vacation together.

But it wasn't enough time. Three days was all she had left of her stay. They'd hiked, ridden his bike. He'd made her paddle-boat out with him to the floating dock to assess the work required to get it back up to code—a lot, it turned out.

And they'd eagerly had sex every time the mood struck them, on every one of their adventures. Except for the paddleboats.

Tomorrow, Anna's ad ran in all the local papers. He wanted to celebrate with her, and he had the perfect idea how.

"Come back here." Sophie waved him over and straightened the boards on her work table. "Don't touch the Post-its, but I need you to look at them."

Dev carefully approached the table, hands behind his back.

"The pink ones are for food vendors, because that makes sense."

"It does?"

Sophie bumped him out of the way and went on explaining. "Blue is for crafts, merchandising, et cetera. And green is for produce, plants, livestock."

"Livestock." He chuckled.

"Hey. The Greenlees will bring some chickens to sell. They always did before."

"I know. I seem to remember a little redheaded girl rolling back up to the resort with a guinea hen and Mom having a fit."

"And I remember my dear brother telling me a hen was a great idea, and giving me money so I could bring Gretel home."

He laughed. Even now, the guinea hen story was funny as hell. Gretel was a diva hen if there was one, and she refused to stay in a roost. Ever.

"But Mom let me keep her."

Of course she had. Their mom had a soft spot for Sophie. Not as rowdy as the boys, at least not when their mom was looking, and orphaned.

Sophie had been their chance to do something right, together, as a family. One of the few times, but they'd done pretty good.

"You're doing a great job with the layout, Soph." He bumped her with his elbow, which resulted in her bumping him back, twice as hard, and this went back and forth until it ended in her knuckle punching him in the arm.

"When are you going to grow up?" Dev rubbed his arm. Sophie punched hard.

"That's not immaturity, that's revenge."

"For what?"

"I don't know, but I'm sure there's something and I'm sure you deserve it."

A knock at her door stopped him from getting her back. "Who the . . . Who is it?" she called out.

"It's Wright."

She spun on Dev. "Why is Wright here?"

"Because I asked him."

"Why?"

"To help us look over the layout."

"I thought that was my job."

"It is, but we've got about two dozen food vendors and not enough space. He's our foodie. I figured he could give some insight on what should go where and who's on what end of Main. How we could consolidate. I don't know."

A furrow formed between her brows.

"Is that . . . okay?" He was almost afraid to ask.

Wright and Sophie had always been friends. Wright was basically part of the family, but judging by the frown putting all of her freckles in a twist, Soph wasn't too pleased with his appearance.

"I'm not giving him your job, Sis. You know I trust you to handle this. It's nothing like that, but I thought he could give us an opinion."

"He's got opinions all right." She rolled her eyes.

The last thing he wanted was for his baby sister to think he was stepping over her, not trusting her or superseding her in any way. He knew all too well how that shit felt, and he'd be damned if he'd do it to someone else. But he got the feeling her issue with Wright's presence wasn't all about treading on her role in planning the festival.

Her scowl disappeared; in its place a smooth, placid calm—that was twice as disturbing as when she looked angry. "It's fine. Wright can be here if he wants. And he can give us his recommendations, but I'm not guaranteeing I'll take them."

"Okay." Dev frowned as he went to answer the door.

She always took Wright's advice. In the past, Dev had actually gotten Wright to suggest things to Sophie, knowing she was more likely to listen to Wright, when she'd flat out told Dev to shove it.

"Hey." Dev opened the door and found a man who looked like he was being led to the slaughter.

"Okay. What's going on? You look scared, and Sophie is in a foul mood. It's messing with the balance of my universe."

Wright waved him closer. Stepping back from the door and keeping his voice low, he scrubbed a hand over his hair.

"Listen." His face was a muted pink. "Now's probably not the best time for me to weigh in on the tent setup and stuff Sophie is handling."

"Okay, but why? First she looks ready to spit nails when I say you're coming over, and now you won't even come inside."

Wright crossed his arms, swiped at his face, dropped his arms and shifted around. "I think I pissed her off."

"Yeah, no shit. What'd you do?"

"Nothing really. I said something stupid. She's not going to listen to a thing I have to say, and I can assure you she doesn't want me here."

Wright was a good guy, and had about the most even-keeled disposition of anyone at Honeywilde. With him, things always seemed to be "okay." The only time he got in a twist was about food—be it really great food, or when things turned out really, really bad. Otherwise, he was at chill level ten.

To see him on the back foot now didn't sit well.

"Well, tough shit. I want you here, and I want to hear your opinions. I also need the both of you to do something for me."

"Something with the festival?"

"No. Later tonight."

"Dev. Now is not the time—"

"Soph owes me one and I'm calling in a favor from you. A small one. Won't take you an hour. Now get in here." He shoved his best friend toward the door.

Wright dragged his feet, but eventually made it inside. Sure enough, Sophie gave him a look that'd kill a lesser man.

But Wright didn't wither. He stared back at her, dead on, like he was ready for battle. "I told Dev I'd give him my opinion, so that's what I'm doing."

Sophie didn't so much as blink, and Wright faltered for a second, but caught himself.

Dev imagined tumbleweeds blowing through the room, saloon music in the background, that's how ridiculous this was. They weren't the type to keep grudges or hold on to their anger, so whatever little spat they'd had, they could both hurry up and get over it.

Wright was the one to break off the stare to look at Dev. "What is it you want to know about the festival and tonight?"

"What's tonight?" That got Soph's attention.

"First"—Dev pointed to the large board on the table between them—"the festival."

He got both of them to focus enough to work on the layout of the tents, and eventually they found a way for the big vendors to all fit on Main Street, but he'd have to get approval from the city to set up on two or three side streets.

"They used those streets when the festival was at its peak."

"They close these down for the Christmas parade too." Wright pointed to the board. "The application for closure is simple, and it's easily approved."

His parents headed up the Christmas parade every year, so he'd know.

"Perfect. I applied the other day. Is there anything else we're not thinking of?"

They glanced back and forth at each other over the table, but no one could come up with anything.

"Great. Then I need you both to do me a favor."

"Wary" wasn't a strong enough word to describe the looks on their faces.

"Soph, I need you to take my shift at the restaurant tonight. Wright, I need you to cook that steak thing I love."

"The flank steak with the field greens and—"

"The crusty bread. Yes. To go."

Wright's forehead wrinkled. "Why?"

"And why should I take your shift at the restaurant? It's *your* shift."

"Because you owe me a favor and I'm calling it in. Fifty-plus ferns and plants, remember?" He turned to Wright. "I need the dinner to-go because I'm going on a picnic."

"Does this have anything to do with—" Sophie caught herself, and asked the rest out of the corner of her mouth. "You know who?"

"Maybe. Are you going to cover my shift or not?"

Her eyes to heaven, she nodded. "I guess. But then we're even. No more owesies."

"Who is you-know-who?" Wright asked.

Sophie turned on him, her arms still crossed. "That's Dev's business. Are you going to make the picnic or not?" Every sharp feature of her face dared Wright to say no. Even her button nose appeared harsh.

He didn't know what Wright had done to gain such ire, but it'd better not be anything too shady. All the usual bickering was fine. Anything more and, friend or not, Wright would catch hell from him.

"I'll make the picnic. Damn." Wright crossed his arms as well.

"Excellent. Thank you. Now, excuse me. I'm going to get ready." Dev backed away from the table.

"I'll go with you." Wright turned and beat Dev to the door.

Rather than wait and, with his perfect manners, hold the door for whoever was behind him, Wright marched through it and headed down the hall as fast as his overlong legs could carry him.

From the open doorway, Dev tossed a glance back at Sophie. "You care to tell me what the hell that was all about?"

"No." She grabbed one of her boards off the table, then seemed to catch herself and held the presentation gently. "It's nothing."

"You sure?" His big brother alarms were going off. Made his hackles rise up, even when it came to Wright.

"Of course I'm sure. I'm just annoyed. Wright's a guy. You're all annoying at some point." With her board in her hands, she turned away, his cue to leave pretty obvious.

Just as well. Dev didn't have a decent rebuttal anyway.

Chapter 24

"This is the dressiest thing I packed." No matter where she went, she always took a little black dress. Because, like now, you never knew when you might need one.

"You look . . ." Devlin stepped back from the door, his gaze wandering up and down. "Amazing."

"You too."

He had on dark blue slacks and a crisp, white button-up shirt. In the weak light of her porch, his eyes shone brighter, his face more intent, serious, and impossibly, even more handsome.

"If you're ready, we can go."

"Since I have no idea where we're going or what we're doing, sure. I'm ready."

A small smile curled his lips. "You'll see." He held out his arm, at the perfect angle for her to place her hand and be escorted.

They made their way down the stairs of her cabin and into his SUV. After that, a short drive, farther along the gravel road, until the road turned to dirt, and then not much of a road at all.

"Are we on a path of any kind here or merely hoping for the best?"

"There's a path, trust me."

Eventually he stopped and put the car into park. "It's right through those trees."

From all she could tell, they were in the middle of the woods, certain to lose the car if they wandered more than a few feet from it.

He grabbed a big basket from the backseat and opened her door, his hand out for her to hold. "Follow me."

"I'll have to."

Dev had brought a flashlight—thank goodness—because the woods were pitch-dark, but they hadn't walked far before she saw light, flickering through the trees.

As they got closer, the dots of light became little solar lamps, stuck in the ground, lighting a path down to the lake's edge. This side of the lake didn't have a beach area, but the forest gave way to a small grassy opening, reeds and willows lining the water.

In the middle of the opening lay a huge plaid blanket with solar lamps at each corner.

"Hang on." Dev set the basket in the middle of the blanket and walked in a wide circle.

For a second she thought he'd dropped something and was searching, but then she saw what he was up to.

With a long barbecue lighter, Dev lit candles all around them.

Anna put her hands to her mouth, but a small squeak escaped. "You did all this?"

Devlin flashed a grin. "A candlelit dinner. You said you wanted one."

"This is so—"

"Don't say it. I know. But the candles are also functional. Citronella. In case any mosquitos think they want to snack on us."

He could say all he wanted about function. Anna saw through to the romance. If he wanted function, he would've taken her for a meal inside. Instead they were outside, by the lake, with candlelight. Between taking her sightseeing, rides on his bike, ice cream and long walks, Dev was clearly a dreamer and a doer, and a lover of passion and sentiment—and she adored that about him.

"Here." He knelt next to the large basket and patted the blanket. "Sit down."

She wanted nothing more.

From the basket he pulled cream-colored china plates, a silver setting, and linen napkins.

"This is—I'm so . . ." Words couldn't do justice to the way she felt.

No one had ever done anything like this for her before. She'd been on plenty of dates, usually one that acted as first and last, and that was the end of that. Never anything special and definitely not a picnic arranged especially for her.

He finished unpacking, a spread of Tupperware between them and two mason jars full of tea over ice. "I wanted to take you on a date. A real date, with a nice meal and dressy location, but lately, by the time I'm done with my day, most places are closed. I can't take you to the restaurant here. This seemed like a good alternative."

"This is better than good. Dev, this is amazing."

"You deserve it. The festival is going to be a hit, thanks to you."

She shook off the credit. The thanks were all due him. He'd helped her find her shiny ideas again. Her inspiration. Brought her back to life. "I only helped. It's thanks to you, and your family."

Rather than argue, he lifted his mason jar. "Okay, then . . . how about *us*? We made this happen."

"Here's to us." She tapped her glass against his.

With a small sip, he went to work unsealing containers and serving two plates of food, as pretty as anything she'd ever seen in a restaurant.

"That's impressive."

"Wright is a nag about presentation. I can't take any credit for the food. He made the meal, along with detailed instructions about how to serve."

Flank steak, some kind of small salad, carrots in a glaze, roasted potatoes, and a loaf of bread that smelled divine.

"I don't know what to say."

"Say you're hungry."

"I'm hungry."

They ate the scrumptious meal, Dev insisting she try his steak because it might be better than her steak.

She wished he'd packed wine, but understood if he wasn't one to drink anymore. Still, wine would dull her confusion, her dilemma and unreasonable wish. But that'd take the whole bottle.

She was leaving in a few days, and the days were passing too fast. Dev worked longer hours, but they still found time. The last couple of weeks had been some of the best of her life; it would soon come to an end, and . . . she wanted to say something.

But what?

Tell Dev he was about the best thing that'd ever happened to her, and *best of luck, have a nice life*?

That wouldn't do.

Tell him he'd saved her from the ditch of depression and made her feel capable of carrying on again, and how about he leave everything and everyone he loved and come to Atlanta to be with her?

212 · Heather McGovern

That wouldn't work either.

What had she done? What had she gotten herself into? This was supposed to be a simple arrangement. A deal they made that she'd help him out with his project, and he'd help her unwind.

But it'd become so much more than that, and she couldn't make what they shared fit back into something easily defined.

Dev set his fork down with a clatter. "I have more good news."

"Do tell." Anna shifted, sitting up straighter. Good news was perfect; anything to make her stop thinking about leaving.

"Madison got your ad in on the fly. It's hitting newspapers tomorrow and she'll have it in June's issues of a couple of bigger regional magazines. Barely under the wire, but the ad will run everywhere we wanted it to."

"That's so great!" She shared a kiss with him, but couldn't help but wonder what Dev told Madison about where the ad came from.

Not because she wanted credit, the ad was her thank-you for the past weeks, but would any of them—Madison, his friend Wright, Roark, Sophie—would any of them ever know of her existence?

Would she come and go from Dev's life, like she'd never been there at all? Seemed impossible, considering his impact on her, but she didn't know and he wasn't one to say either.

She didn't want to be some ghost in his life, someone who'd drifted in and out, never to be spoken of. Yet, what were her options? She had none. His family couldn't know, and she had to go. She'd done this to herself, and that's what twisted her up inside.

In a matter of days, she'd leave, and his family, the closest people in his life, would know nothing about her. They wouldn't even know she existed, or the difference Dev had made in her life.

Over two weeks they'd gone along like this, and the secrecy hadn't bothered her. She paid no mind because hiding made sense. All she'd wanted was time with Dev, and she'd gotten it. But this man knew more about her than anyone. She'd told him about her mother. If she asked, he'd go with her to spread her father's ashes.

The two of them weren't simply a fling anymore. What began as a fun flirtation, then a deal of mutual satisfaction, wasn't staying in the little box anymore.

And she had no idea what to do about it. Wanting to do anything about it at all was selfish. They had a deal. She agreed to this, happily. Willingly.

"So the ad will start running tomorrow." She had to stop thinking and start talking, or she'd work herself up into a fit.

"Yes. I can't believe it. This is really happening."

"What does your family think? Are they excited?" Why had she asked about his family? Hearing more only rubbed salt in the wound.

"Ecstatic. Sophie's helped me a ton. She's been great."

Anna should stop listening. Stop asking. Stop getting closer and closer to him. For days, that's all she'd wanted. It's all she wanted still, but the needs of her heart didn't change the fact she was leaving. She had no choice. Being closer to Dev would only make it hurt more when she left.

In Atlanta she had a home, a successful job and responsibilities. A life.

Honeywilde was vacation and fun and relaxation. And a wonderful man. This getaway had served its purpose, but that's precisely all it could be. A getaway. Not real life. The other option was to come back. Occasionally. Visits. But that'd only reopen the wound, every time, and she wasn't a masochist.

"And get this." Dev touched her hand. "Roark hasn't just been onboard, he's happy about it now. Pleased with something that wasn't his idea and *excited*. I think."

Dev's mouth fell open as he overdramatized his shock, his lips soon curling into a smile showing all his teeth.

He was thrilled, and Anna was thrilled for him.

"I know I shouldn't give my brother such hell. He's a good guy. I can't help it though. This might be the first time ever that I've gotten to lead . . . anything."

"Makes sense. You want to please Roark and do something on your own that he'd be proud of. I was the same way with my dad. I liked him being proud of me."

"Roark isn't my father."

Dev's curt response drew her up short, his defensiveness revealing plenty. Probably more than Dev was ready to accept about his relationship with his brother.

"I mean . . ." He immediately laughed off his serious reaction. "Sure, I've done plenty he doesn't approve of, so it might be nice to have one thing he's okay with. Other times I intentionally irritate the shit out of him, because someone has to. He'd have everyone marking time otherwise. Someone has to shake him up."

A muscle twitched and pulled in his cheek. "He once sent me an email with suit suggestions for an event. The celebrity wedding we held in the fall actually. The whole thing almost goes mushroom cloud, Roark's girlfriend—the event coordinator—runs away, but he gets her back, they get everything pulled together, and Roark still finds time to tell me I should wear my navy suit or the black one to the wedding, but definitely not the gray."

"You're making that up."

"I still have the email. I'll show you."

"He does it because he cares."

"And because he can't turn off the role of raising us. At least Soph and Trevor get some of it too. He went out and bought a suit for poor Trev to wear. But, in all fairness, if he hadn't, Trevor would've shown up in jeans or a brown leisure suit."

"What did you end up wearing to the wedding?"

"Come on now. What do you think? The gray one, of course. And the wedding was still a huge success. Even with me in a gray suit."

Even his smirk hurt. And she was self-centered to let his happiness make her sad, but it did.

In three days, her visit at Honeywilde would end. She'd leave without all the weight she'd dragged here, with less grief and without the stress of being overworked.

But she'd also leave without Devlin.

When she was done here and went back to Atlanta, to see if she could manage her life any better, she'd be going back to a life that didn't include him.

Her days, without Dev's smirk, his wit, his insistence that she try to let go of her doubts, would be long and dull. Lonesome and as sad as when she'd left to come here.

She was better now than the day she checked in, but she'd only solved some of her existing problems, and had created new ones.

With a smile that made her face ache, she squeezed Dev's hand. "You're going to have a huge success with this festival too, I can feel it. I hope you and your family are ready."

"We will be." Dev stuck a piece of bread in his mouth and took a long time to chew.

A success she wouldn't be around to witness.

She could come up to the festival itself, but then she'd have to leave. Again. A long-distance relationship was out of the question. Hundreds of miles away, both of them busy. With her job and insecurities, their time apart would be a recipe for failure. Not that Dev had given any indication he had interest beyond the here and now.

He'd been very honest that day, in their agreement. She'd help him with the festival and he'd show her how to have fun. Anna was his good time, and while she had no doubt he cared about her, that didn't mean he wanted some long-distance relationship.

And Dev would never ask her to give up anything for him. Even if she wanted to, even if she could, he'd never ask.

"Speaking of, I was thinking, what if you . . . what if you didn't leave?"

Or would he?

"Wha . . ." She could only imagine her blank-faced expression. "What do you mean?"

"I mean, what if you stayed here?"

She'd be happy forever.

No. No, she wouldn't. She couldn't stay. That was ludicrous. Staying meant quitting her job and quitting her job meant she'd have nothing. Sinking her career would eventually lead to resenting Dev, and it'd be all her fault.

Besides, stay and do what? Be jobless, penniless, and hidden up in Cabin Five until Dev was ready to tell his family about her? Even if he told them tomorrow, she had nothing here but Devlin. She couldn't survive off writing ads for Honeywilde's once-a-year festival. Her career was who she was.

For years she'd pushed back against her mother's ideal of dropping everything just to have a man; she couldn't do that now.

"I . . ." If she gave up everything to stay with him, it'd mean jumping off a ledge; a ledge over the unknown, where she could plummet to failure, or fly. "I can't."

Dev grabbed his tea and buried his face in a sip. His heart hammered in his chest, the sound thumping in his ears.

Of course she couldn't; the idea was irrational, short-sighted and selfish, but he couldn't help it because having her here was what he wanted. "That's . . . I knew it was a stretch, but—"

"What would I do here? I mean, *if* I stayed. Where would I work? How would I support myself?"

"I don't . . ." He shrugged. He hadn't thought out all of the details.

All he knew was he didn't want to lose her and if she felt the same, maybe they could figure something out. "I don't know."

Anna was leaving in three days. He didn't want her to go, but staying meant giving up her life; giving up everything she'd worked so hard for, just to be with him.

Stupid idea and he cursed himself for even mentioning it.

She had the kind of life people dreamed of, strove for, worked toward for years. Giving that up with no prospect, no guarantee, or even a chance that she could have that kind of life in podunk Windamere, was impossible.

Sure, Madison had come here to be with Roark, but she could do her job anywhere.

And Roark could promise things, and deliver. He could do anything he wanted.

Dev had nothing to offer Anna. A tour guide and a good time, but she deserved someone who provided a million times more than some advice on how to have fun.

He could ask to see Anna again though. For all the good it'd do. Hell, it'd probably only hurt worse. Seeing her again in a few weeks, only to have her leave again for an indefinite amount of time.

"Of course I want to see you again," she finally said, her gaze distant.

He worked his shoulders up and down, that knot twisting in his chest, pressing on his ribs. "Could you come up for the festival?" It wasn't enough, but it'd have to do.

Anna blinked and glanced away again. She blinked some more, her breath slowing. "I could. I should be able to get some time off."

When her gaze met his, exhaustion filled her eyes. He felt it in his bones.

"I'm sorry," she said.

Dev frowned. "It's . . . it's fine. I understand. We had a deal, and I knew you weren't going to be here forever. You can't drop everything just to . . . don't be sorry."

None of this was ideal; he understood that. He wasn't a total idiot. They'd gotten themselves into a no-win situation. He sure as hell didn't have the solution, and Anna's eyes were so sad they shredded his heart.

She sniffed, unable to stop her lips from wobbling. "I'm so sorry."

Immediately, he had her in his arms.

He swept her up, refusing to be the cause of her tears. "It's okay."

"No, it's not," she said into his shirt. "This sucks."

He hid his smile in her hair. It did suck. It sucked big-time. "We'll figure something out. You'll come up for the festival and then, I don't know. I can come see you and . . ." Visiting was a bandage on a broken situation, and they both knew it.

She pulled away enough to look up at him, her eyes glassy.

They didn't have an agreement for the future, no guarantee of what came next, but they had this. They had each other, right now.

Dev brushed his lips against hers, kissing her until everything hurt a little bit less. They kissed until his heart stopped hammering with fear, and began pounding for a different reason.

With a soft sigh, Anna lay back, pulling him with her. She wrapped her arms around his neck, the bottom of her black dress drifting up her thigh.

The future and the answers may lie out of reach, but she was right there in his arms.

The two of them, a big blanket, the lake and a clear night sky— this they knew how to deal with.

He still wanted her, would always want her, no matter how many answers they didn't have.

"I wish we could make time stand still." Her words feathered across his cheek.

"We can try." He kissed her again, deeper, running his hand up her thigh, under her dress. He knew one way to stop the clocks from turning, make them both forget about what lay ahead.

He ventured further, until he brushed his hand over the lace of her panties. Toying with the waistband, he skated his fingers back and forth between the material and her skin. Then he slipped his hand between her legs.

"Yes." She arched against him, lifting her hips.

He kissed his way down her neck and slid her panties off. Even as desperately as they kissed, their touches were slow. Intent.

She reached for the fly of his pants, working the button and unzipping, and then, the woman who was once too bashful to tell him her fantasy, looked him right in the eyes. "I want you on top of me. I want you on top, and I want you to make love to me. Then, I want it harder, so I can still feel you for days."

With fingers threaded through his hair, she pulled him down.

They kissed like she was leaving tonight. And he did exactly what she asked for.

Sweetly and softly at first, he opened her. He made love to her until her heels dug into his lower back, and she moaned, needy. A plea that sounded like his name.

Then he took her.

Her hands under his shirt, those red nails biting into his back, he thrust into her. Over and over, the whole world silent except for her tiny gasps of pleasure. And when she tightened around him, her head thrown back and her dark hair an inky fan across the blanket, he came too.

He came and came, keeping his eyes open, telling himself that only having Anna for the next few days was better than never having her at all.

Chapter 25

Coffee in hand, Dev shuffled around his room, trying to wake up and be ready for the day.

Trying to accept the reality he was losing Anna.

Last night, they'd made love on a blanket, beneath the stars, and he didn't do stuff like that. Ever.

Anna was right; he was a romantic, but only because she'd turned him into one. She made him want things he never wanted, made him do things for no other reason than to see her happy. Next month, Honeywilde would put on the town's biggest event, because of her.

And she was leaving.

She wouldn't be around for the final stages of planning. Hell, she might not be around for the event itself. Maybe she could make it, probably.

Dev plunked his coffee cup down on the table with a curse.

To hell with that.

He had to do something. No idea what. He'd come up with something though. Losing her was unacceptable.

By the time he finally made it upstairs, the lobby and great room were alive with guests. He had to make the rounds, put on a smile, and ensure everyone was happy, all while his mind and soul churned for an answer.

There had to be a solution. A way he could keep Anna without asking her to give up her life.

Once he'd made his appearance, he headed to Roark's office. He passed by the new reception area, where Sophie was training their newest employee, and grabbed the pile of junk stuffed in his mail slot.

Outdoor catalog, several catalogs for business-logoed everything, office supply book—none of which he subscribed to, *Cycle World*, and two envelopes. The invoice from the tent company and an envelope that made him stop walking. The Windamere tourism office.

He turned and shoved the rest of the mail back in his slot and tore into the envelope.

The extra street-closure application went to the city's transportation department. Tourism really had no need to be mailing him anything at this point. Unless they'd finally mailed him the financials.

This could hold the answer he'd been looking for. Proof that Crawford's office had intentionally scuttled the Blueberry Festival to cover Crawford's ass.

In his haste, he tore the top of the letter, but read the important paragraphs below.

Dear Mr. Bradley. "Blah, blah, blah . . ."

> *We regret to inform you that the Windamere Department of Transportation declines your application for street closure on June 17th through the 19th, including Main Street and all adjacent streets.*
>
> *As always, you may appeal the decline of permit through our website at www—*

"What the hell?"

"Shh!" Sophie reprimanded him.

He read the letter again, certain he'd misread.

> *For Main Street and all adjacent streets.*

The pressure began at the base of his skull. As he stomped into Roark's office, the pain only got worse.

"Crawford is pulling the plug on us."

Roark stopped sifting through papers. "What?"

"The weasel at the tourism office. He's trying to shut down the festival because he knows it'll be a success."

"Wha—" His brother shook his head. "Slow down. Who and how can he shut us down?"

Dev tossed the letter on top of the other pile of papers on Roark's desk. "Crawford is the head of the tourism office, the one who wouldn't give me any information on the festival's financials, and he's a little shit."

Roark picked up the letter, reading quietly as his expression turned graver and graver. "Shit."

"That's what I said. And he's causing us a world of it by trying to block the road closures."

"But we already had approval for Main Street. How did this happen?" Roark waved the letter at Dev. "This came from Transportation. Crawford isn't part of that office."

"I know, but they all know each other. They all get in each other's ears. Bastards."

He should've known this would happen. Something somewhere was bound to go wrong. It always did. Since when had anything ever been easy in his life?

"We could work around not having any side streets, but Main Street *has* to be closed. It's where all the vendors set up; all the pedestrian traffic."

"I *know*, Roark. That's why Crawford is blocking it."

"That doesn't make any sense."

"Makes plenty of sense to me. He doesn't want this festival to happen."

"Why wouldn't he—Dev, that doesn't make any sense either."

"Yes, it does. Remember when I went to ask him about the books? The profit and loss numbers for the festival?"

Roark ran a hand over the back of his neck. "I remember."

"He acted suspicious about the whole thing, and basically told us not to hold our breath on getting any help from him. So we move ahead without pressing him, and I hear from the shops in town how much they used to get charged to participate. Thousands of dollars, Roark. It's outrageous. But everyone wants in again, because we aren't charging that much, we're down to the home stretch, and now he's blocking us. Why wouldn't he want this for the town?"

"I don't know."

"Well, I do. The guy skimmed money off the festival for years, and shut it down when he couldn't cover his tracks anymore. He doesn't want the Blueberry Festival to happen, because for years his office claimed the thing was a big loser. We bring it back and it's a raging success, he either looks suspicious as hell or incompetent."

Roark shook his head, mouth open, set to argue.

"No, I mean it. You should've seen him that day, and all we did was ask politely. And as the planning has gone on, we've seen the money people are willing to invest. The vendors all say the festivals were profitable; you've seen yourself the kind of crowds the festival draws. If that many people and that much sales end in a loss, it's got to be because someone is misusing funds."

"Misuse of—Dev, you can't throw around terms like that and not know what you're talking about."

"I *do* know what I'm talking about. I went to business school, same as you, just you got the piece of paper and I didn't. I've been out there, talking to the shop- and store-owners. I know what they went through. I also got this copy of the books, probably from Crawford's admin, and nothing adds up. Vendors were paying a grand, and tourism only tracked two thirds of that. Where's the rest?"

"Dev." Roark threw his hands up. "What are you talking about?"

"Crawford. I know he's up to something and I think his admin sent me proof."

"Why didn't you tell me any of this before?"

"I was handling this myself. And I was going to follow up later, but now he's shutting us down."

He and Anna had talked about it. How, if the festival was a failure, it had to be because of something shady. He hadn't run to his brother, because he didn't want to. He wanted to do this without Roark carrying the load, but if he had to take on the tourism office, he couldn't do it alone.

"You can't insinuate misappropriation of funds and expect anything to happen except for the whole thing blowing up in your face."

"News flash, boss." Dev grabbed the letter and shook it under Roark's nose. "The whole thing has already blown up in my face. Who'd say no to something that draws in people and money and business and helps everyone? No one."

His brother's shoulders slumped as he paced behind his desk. "Maybe we should've . . ."

"What?"

"We moved forward on this event without having all our T's crossed. I never do that, and I shouldn't have this time either. If we didn't have a contracted green light from the city, we never should've moved forward. I should've stuck with my policy and waited, but you were so excited—"

"So now it's my fault you're giving up?"

"I'm not giving up. You said it yourself. Crawford's office is shutting us down."

"But—"

"They said *no*, Dev. We can't force the powers that be in Windamere to go along with this, and I am not going to push back with accusations I can't prove. We can't accuse people of breaking the law without proof."

"Why the hell not? They did it to me. For years." The knot twisted tighter. Filling him until the pressure against his ribs made it hard to breathe. Blood rushed into his ears, making it hard to hear.

This wasn't fair. They couldn't do this to him again. He was doing right by people now, and if this festival fell apart, he'd be that same loser, all over again.

Roark settled a hand on his shoulder, making him look up.

The sympathy in his brother's eyes made him want to lash out even more.

"I know you got blamed for stuff. And I hated it."

But plenty of the stuff he did do. The worst of it was all true. Roark didn't say the words, but they both knew.

"You can't do the same to someone else because the festival didn't work out. The last thing we need is to get on the bad side of the local government. We piss this guy off and he can make it difficult to get anything accomplished for years to come."

"Piss *him* off? What about us? What about everybody else? If he's up to something, he's going to screw everybody over. Maybe you should think about that."

"I have to think about protecting Honeywilde, and our future. This place doesn't keep moving on the positive path we're on, we're all lost. And homeless."

"Dammit, Roark. You don't get it." And he never would.

They had a chance to actually call out the bad guy here and do something right, but it meant stepping out on a ledge and taking that chance. Risking safety because he *knew* something was right or wrong.

And as much as he admired his brother and respected him, they were two totally different people. Roark wasn't going to take that risk.

He saw the world organized in black and white. Things you did, things you didn't do. Authority was usually right, and people were all as stand-up and honest as he was.

But Devlin knew better.

He'd had plenty of people, including those who were supposed to love him, those in authority, do wrong by him, all because it made their lives easier. Most folks weren't as honest, caring, or forthright as Roark.

Hell, no one was as honest and forthright as Roark, but most didn't even come close.

"Are you going to help me or not?" Dev demanded.

Roark dropped his hand, a rough sound of frustration as he turned. "Help you what, Dev?"

"Help me figure out what this guy is up to and go on with the festival. Make this right."

If Roark wouldn't help him, he was screwed.

He'd have to go to all of those businesses, all of those people who'd finally looked at him like he had a clue, like he was somebody, and tell them there'd be no festival.

He'd have to tell them they were right all along. He was a screwup, and he'd failed everyone, again.

Chapter 26

She was halfway packed; the rest remained scattered upstairs in her bedroom or downstairs, all over her kitchen and bathroom.

But those weren't really *hers*, were they?

Anna looked around the cabin. Not her kitchen, not her cabin, and not her sofa that she sat on, denying her checkout date was two days away.

Her sofa was back in Atlanta. Perfect and rarely used, with the accent pillows picked out by someone she'd paid way too much money.

Here, she'd relaxed on the sofa. Napped, watched television. Made out with Devlin. She'd bathed in the tub, made grilled cheese and hot chocolate in the kitchen, and had sex in the bed. And in the kitchen.

How could a tiny log cabin feel more comfortable, more personally a part of her, than her condo of over five years?

And upstairs, on the chest of drawers by the bed, sat her father's ashes.

Before she left, she had to do this for him. She'd found the perfect spot, and still she put off fulfilling his wish, but now she had to say goodbye.

Goodbye to her father and goodbye to Devlin.

She was an idiot for leaving, but she had no choice. This place wasn't real life, and even though they'd talked about her coming back to visit, once she left, nothing would be the same.

She knew how distance worked. Her father was often gone with his job, and while he was there for Anna, she'd seen what it did to her parents' relationship.

You couldn't be close while being miles apart, and that's where she'd be. Hours away, working—maybe not eighty-hour weeks again, but certainly more than forty. With her commute, she'd rise before dawn, work until nightfall, and maybe have a few weekends free. She could come see him some, but it'd rarely happen vice versa.

Dev worked more on the weekends than any other time, and with the festival a month away . . .

"Dammit." Anna put her socked feet on the sofa and pulled her knees up, resting her head on them.

This was real life. And it sucked.

Outside of Honeywilde and her vacation, she had responsibilities, an identity. She was Anna, from Atlanta, advertising genius and youngest executive at the agency.

When she first saw Devlin, she saw the opportunity for fun, distraction. Even when they'd first kissed, her opinion remained the same, but sometime after, between hauling plants and picnics at midnight, everything changed.

How, during the course of learning how to take it easy, had she fallen so hard?

She knew better, she was smarter than this, but the fact remained. Her chest ached with the inevitable loss.

Maybe she could deny that she was leaving, but there was no denying the feeling of desertion already in her heart.

It made no sense. *She* was the one leaving, not him. But Dev had a rich life here.

For all his talk about her having a life and success, he was the one with a family, a future, possibilities, and happiness.

She had a career, a wildly successful one, but the job didn't care about her. It didn't help her through her grief or appreciate her. And she didn't love her job the way she loved Dev.

Because she did. She loved him.

And as scary as they were, her feelings were real, and she knew how much it'd break her heart when he let her walk out of here.

She had to tell him. Whether or not it'd change anything, he deserved to know she loved him. But then . . . she'd only hurt them worse by speaking her heart and then leaving.

"God." Anna scrubbed her hands through her hair, the way she'd watched Dev do a million times, and pulled hard.

She didn't know what to do.

Three rapid thumps on the cabin door made her jump.

"Who is it?" She unfolded herself from the couch.

"Dev." The rough edge to his voice wasn't the good kind.

Before she got the door completely open, he was inside. "That son of a bitch shut us down."

"What? Who?"

"Crawford. He got the transportation department to decline our application for closing Main Street." A white piece of paper was thrust toward her.

She read the letter carefully, and Devlin was right about the declined application. Whether or not it was Crawford's doing, the letter didn't state.

"They've always approved the closure in the past, right?"

"Yes, but it's always been the tourism office applying."

"Is there any way to appeal? Someone you can talk to about reconsidering?"

"In a town the size of Windamere? No. Crawford is probably drinking buddies with the head of transportation. We're screwed. The festival is off."

"No." The word burst out of her with certainty. "It can't be off; people are expecting a festival. They're counting on you."

"You think I don't know that? You think I want to go around to all those people who finally trusted me, look them in the eyes, and tell them I failed?"

"You didn't fail. There has to be something we can do."

"What can *we* do? You're leaving in two days. What can you do from Atlanta?"

The truth was harsh, stealing her breath, but it was still true.

Dev turned his back on her, walking over to the fireplace and the little wooden bear. "Sorry. That was ... sorry."

"It's okay," she muttered. Lying. None of this was okay. "I'm here now. Maybe I can help. What did Roark say?"

"That we're finished. He's not about to accuse Crawford of any wrongdoing, so we're sunk. Roark won't get the resort involved in something that could be a money pit *or* upset the powers that be. Not now that we finally have one foot on solid ground. Not after what my parents went through, almost losing the place."

"But if Roark knew the whole story, if you told him how shady the guy was, he'd listen. You'd have his support, I know it."

"No, you don't. After what he's been through with me?" Dev's laugh was acidic. "Roark is not going to go against Windamere and cause a stink with the town, over me."

Anna marched toward him and stood in front of the bear. "Then *you* do something about it."

"What are you talking about?"

"If you can't confront Crawford or go through him, go around him. You don't need Roark. Go to the business owners in town and tell them everything is set to go, but the permit was denied. And you're still having the festival."

Dev shook his head. "I can't face them and tell them I failed."

"You haven't failed. You can show them the accounting information. See if any of it jibes with their records. If the money doesn't match up, you could threaten Crawford with a formal complaint."

He stared at her, eyes wide. "My word against Crawford's?"

"Why not? You're the honest businessman trying to hold a legitimate event."

"I . . ." He shook his head again.

"You'll have to face the local businesses regardless. Even if threatening Crawford doesn't work fast enough, they still deserve to know. In the meantime, you keep advertising the event exactly as is. Worst case scenario, the festival takes place in their respective shops. They can put things on sale. That kind of thing."

"*Worst* case scenario? Trust me, that isn't the worst case. You're talking about me taking on the city. *Me.* Asking the people in town to trust me over a government board."

Anna moved closer to him. "You know he's guilty."

"Yes, but Roark said he couldn't—"

"I'm not talking about your brother. I'm talking about you. What you can do."

"I told these people I'd get them the Blueberry Festival they used to have. Not that they'd need to redline items and host it in their shops. I'm supposed to have downtown blocked off to cars, open to pedestrians, lots of foot traffic."

"You can still have foot traffic."

"But I told them—"

"I know what you told them. I was there. Even though I'm some big secret and no one is supposed to know I exist, I do. And I was there."

Dev went completely still. "What's that supposed to mean?"

She blinked, realizing what she'd said. "I don't . . . I don't know. But I know those shop owners will believe in you and accept any changes that have to happen. They'll understand. They know the event won't be perfect the first year out. Della even said she wasn't expecting much, but any move in that direction is what matters."

Dev stared through her, his focus on something far beyond her, and beyond her control. "You don't get it."

"I get that you don't want to go to these people, hat in hand, asking for their help and trust. You're afraid to open yourself up to any kind of judgment, but you're not that screwed-up kid anymore. And they won't think you are."

His jaw went rigid.

"I know it won't be easy." She took his hand. If he'd just look at her, she could make him understand. "Those people might think you messed up, but that doesn't mean you're still that same guy. You're not a teenager causing trouble, you're not hurting anyone. You're trying to help, and they know it. They'll understand. You're the one who can't accept it."

Dev pulled his hand away, refusing to look at her.

"You can do this, you know. Plan this whole festival and make everything happen, all by yourself. You could've done everything these past few weeks. You don't need your brother and you don't need me."

Finally his gaze crashed into hers. "You're so wrong. You have no idea."

"Then go to your brother and I'll back you up. I spoke to Crawford too, I saw those ledger entries. I'll support you."

Dev's beautiful eyes went ice-cold. "You can't support me, you're leaving. And you know I can't roll up to Roark and say, 'Here's someone who agrees with me because she worked right alongside me this whole time. By the way, she's a guest, as you know, and we've been having sex this whole time.' "

They'd been doing a lot more than just having sex.

"Dev." She put her hands on her hips, determined not to let him destroy something so clearly within his grasp. "I'm trying to help."

His jaw looked ready to crack, he held it so tight, but she had to say this. If he couldn't face the fear, the real roadblock here, she'd do it for him.

"Either you go to the people in town and ask for their understanding, or you and I go to Roark and ask for his help."

He laughed, humorless and dry. "Because that would really bolster Roark's confidence in me, the fact that I've been screwing around with a guest."

Anna snapped. "We are not just screwing!"

Dev's eyes went wide.

"We're not just screwing around." She said the words again, quieter. Calmer. As much to herself as to him.

This wasn't news to her, but she needed to hear it, out loud, and if he couldn't or wouldn't say it, then she would.

"No, we aren't." Dev dropped his hands, curling his fingers in. "I don't know that we ever *just* do anything. But you don't get to stand there and preach to me about quitting, when you're quitting too. You're the one who's leaving."

She opened her mouth to argue, but no words came out.

"No matter what happens at Honeywilde, or with the festival, or with *me* or Crawford or any of it, you won't be here. You're leaving, Anna."

She faltered on her feet. "I—I have to. I told the agency I'd be back next week."

A fact he'd known since the day she showed up at Honeywilde, but now it meant so much more.

"Then why do you care how or if the festival works out?" She wasn't going to be around to see the festival pulled off, and now it wouldn't be. What difference did it make?

"Because it's you. Of course I care."

As though he were so worthy of her time and support, but in the end, she still wouldn't be around. He'd opened himself up. Something he never did.

And it didn't change a damn thing.

"You care, but you won't be the one facing the shit storm when it hits. I will." He poked his finger in his chest hard enough to hurt. "You want me to take on Crawford alone, and I'll face the fallout again, and you won't be anywhere near here."

"Because I have to go." Anna's voice rose two notches. "You think I wouldn't rather stay? Vacation forever with none of the worries, magically have no concerns or stress? I want to be here for you, but I have a life that I left behind. I have to work, and live, and support myself. I can't stay on permanent vacation. This isn't real life."

"This is my life." He raised his voice too. "And in two days, you'll drive out of here and maybe see me again, maybe not, and then what? That's the end of us?"

"No, I . . . I don't want that to be the end. I haven't thought that far ahead, but I don't—"

"You didn't think about *that*, yet you can stand there and tell me exactly what I need to do with my life. Go to Roark; tell him the truth. Go to the people in town; tell them to go after Crawford. Do the festival on my own. Do this, do that. You have all the answers about what *I* should be doing with the damn festival, but you can't spare a thought for us? And the whole time you're still planning to get the hell out."

"That's not—I'm not doing that. I have wracked my brain about us, and I don't have the answer, but I have to go back. I have responsibilities."

"That is not why you're going back. You're going back because you're too scared to do anything else."

Anna blanched. Not even her neck held any color.

"You left Atlanta because you were miserable. You can't admit it to yourself, but you're not happy. Like I couldn't see it that first day? The black cloud that hung over you, the stress in your eyes. You're going back to the same shit. You can't take a vacation and then everything's okay. Your life will be exactly the same. You'll still work too much and have *no* life and your father will still be gone, and you'll still be alone. All while the person who cares and wants you, is right here."

Anna stumbled away, her hands going to her face, and he should let her go.

But he couldn't. She had a million options for how he could fix his life, but she wouldn't consider or even discuss the options they might have.

Dev followed her toward the kitchen. She put the island between them, but that wasn't going to stop him from saying what needed to be said. "It's a lot easier to tell me what I should be doing, than think about what you should be doing. You keep telling me to believe in myself. But why should I, when you don't believe in me either?"

"That's not true." She dropped her hands, eyes red, but the fight still in them. "I believe in you more than you do."

"Then why are you leaving?"

"How can I stay?" She pounded her fist on the island. "What am I going to do here? Work at the inn?"

"Maybe? I don't know. But you could be happy."

"I . . ." She sniffed, but a tear still escaped, trickling down her cheek. "I know I could, but I can't just . . . I have to have some plan or idea. I can't just give up everything . . ."

The sentence hung there, unfinished. But he knew the rest without her saying any more.

He filled in the rest. "For me."

"No." Anna came around the side of the island, trying to close the distance.

Dev moved too, keeping the space between them. "You know, you talk a big game, but when it comes down to actions, you're just like Roark. And I can't even blame you. Being with me . . . I'm a risk, Anna. I know that. Compared to what you have in Atlanta, I'm not much. I'm not good enough for you, but at least I can admit it."

She flopped her hands at her sides, the fight draining from her eyes. "You are good enough. I don't know what I'd do if I stayed here. Life isn't that simple. I can't just jump."

He backed away from the island. Anna wasn't going to change her mind. She was strong-minded and willful, and she'd made her decision to go.

All he could do was let her.

"No, life is complicated and imperfect. Mine always has been, but you're the one who's scared. You're leaving in two days, and we both know you don't want to. If I'm a coward for not going on with the festival, then you're a coward for running." He turned, walked out her door, and refused to look back.

Chapter 27

One day. For one whole day he hadn't left his room. Blaming a summer cold.

But the next morning, Sophie showed up at his door, hair wild, face panicked, telling him the news.

Anna had left a day early.

Dev knocked on the door of Cabin Five, but he wouldn't get an answer. He knocked again anyway.

No sleek black Lexus sat parked on the gravel, no books stacked by the rockers outside, no empty coffee cup left on the rail.

Dev dug in his pocket for the resort's set of keys, and knocked one last time as he unlocked the door.

Empty.

The little bags of snacks and goodies were cleared from the kitchen counter. He checked the bathroom, and all of her lotions and potions were gone. Upstairs, the bed was unmade, but nothing of her remained.

He was not going to pick up her pillow and sniff it, already toeing the line of creepy by lurking around her vacated cabin. Why was he doing this to himself? A special kind of torture, making notes of how completely Anna had left.

"Hell." He bent his head to get down the narrow stairs from the loft.

A few steps from the bottom, he sat, his ass hitting the wood with a thud. His shoulders barely fit in the narrow space and his knees were almost up to his ears. Uncomfortable and out of place. Exactly what he deserved.

That's what he was. A screwup, ruining everything he touched, and he'd let Anna go, like an idiot.

He hadn't just let her go, he'd run her off, plain and simple. The best thing that'd happened to him, and he'd pushed and pushed until he pushed her away.

He could've been patient, let her figure things out. Given her time and space, not pressured her about staying.

What was wrong with him?

Devlin curled his hands into fists, squeezing them into his temples.

He was what was wrong with him; impatient and expecting her to leap without looking, just like him. Why should she? He was messed up, and spectacular at screwing things up for everyone else too. She had no reason to think a relationship with him would be any different.

His parents' marriage, college, his life—all of it was a mess. He'd hurt his family, Anna, and through everything, he couldn't seem to get enough of hurting himself.

His chest ached with the emptiness around him. The yawning space left by everyone he pushed away in some misguided need to prove himself.

Now he'd pushed Anna away too.

He'd never see the light in her eyes. Never see the pride when he pulled off the Blueberry Festival. But he was never going to see that anyway.

What the two of them had together, it wasn't supposed to be real. He was a distraction to fill her time, help her cope with her father's death and the pressure of being overworked.

But if what they shared wasn't real, why did it hurt so much?

Anna had been there to help him get the festival off the ground, the extra shove of support when he had none. And she'd done exactly that.

Lifting him up when he was bogged down with doubt. She'd believed in him when no one else had, even when he didn't believe in himself.

She'd claimed as much the other day, saying she believed in him more than he did. She'd been certain about the festival, and his ability to pull it off.

She was as sure of him as he was of the two of them.

They should be together. He might not have all the answers, or a solution to how they'd work out the details, but he knew, in his gut, there was no one else for him.

No one else but Anna. And he had to get her back.

Devlin slapped his hands on his thighs and stood. He stomped out of the cabin, slamming the door behind him. A plan would develop on the way. All he knew was he couldn't lose Anna and he couldn't lose this festival.

He was done losing.

His heavy footfalls carried him right into Roark's office, but his brother wasn't there. He checked the lobby, the great room, the restaurant—nothing. Then he saw Roark on the veranda, Madison beside him, their backs to the inn, taking in the best view at Honeywilde.

The two of them were in love, and everybody knew it. They'd known even before Roark and Madison could face their own feelings, and he and Sophie had done what they could to make them both see.

Their feelings were obvious in the way they looked at each other— the appreciative and understanding, if sometimes humoring, glances Madison gave Roark. The admiration and awe in Roark's eyes. They took care of each other, had each other's backs, and where she was weak, he helped her be strong. Where Roark was flawed, she filled in the gaps.

They didn't always agree, but they didn't fight the way his parents had. They respectfully argued and debated, and even if they got mad enough to stop speaking, the sun never went down on their silence.

They loved each other. Because that's what love was.

Not perfect and infallible, but understanding, patient; love made you a better person than you were without it.

Anna did that for him. She understood him, didn't judge him, and accepted him exactly how he was, while helping him be more.

And let her leave Honeywilde and walk right out of his life. He'd done a lot of stupid shit in his life, but losing Anna topped the list. Youthful ignorance couldn't be blamed. Rebellion, seeking attention, misguided fury—none of that was to blame.

Anna leaving was on him, and he had to fix it. He was going to, but that meant asking for help. Roark's help.

Dev threw open the French doors and crossed the veranda like a storm cloud.

They must've felt him coming. Roark and Madison turned, frowning. He was intruding on their moment.

But their moment could wait.

He stopped in front of them and stiffened his spine, his chin high. "I screwed up, but I'm going to fix it. I need to tell you something and I need you to listen and be my brother, not the resort's manager. Can you do that?"

They stole a quick glance at each other.

"I'll try," Roark said, pragmatic as always.

"I met someone. We've been dating for the last three weeks."

Another stolen look.

"Yeah. Surprise. Anyway. She's amazing and you would be amazed by her, but I let her leave here without telling her how I feel. Actually, she probably knows how I feel, but I ran her off anyway. And now I have to get her back."

"What do you mean, you let her leave *here*?" Roark wrinkled his brow.

Leave it to him to catch the one thing in all Dev said that might be telling.

"I let her leave here, as in check out. Because she was a guest."

"Jesus, Dev."

"I need my brother right now, okay? Not Honeywilde's manager. There's a difference."

Madison bumped Roark's arm, making him study the ground and take a deep breath.

"Okay," he said. Chin still down, he snuck a quick look at his girlfriend. "I'll be quiet and listen."

That made her smile; her eyes softened as she leaned a little bit closer.

Dev knew that look. For days he'd been on the receiving end of a look just like it. Different, darker, more demure and—to him—sexier. Dancing brown eyes and a plush pink mouth, but the most beautiful thing was the affection in Anna's gaze when she looked at him.

If he loved her, then she loved him too. But he'd been too scared to say it.

"Her name is Anna." His voice shook. "She was a guest here and . . . I love her."

Roark jerked his chin up.

Yeah. Surprise again.

"I spent the last couple of weeks working with her and getting to know her and showing her that a vacation meant actually having fun. Because I'm pretty sure she didn't know how."

"Working with—"

Madison elbowed Roark again.

"Yes, working with her. And I know it's enough to get me fired or sued or whatever the hell our policy says, but she's not going to sue me or tell on me. I'm telling you because she deserves the credit for what she did. She deserves not to be a secret. She's too good. The ad for the festival? Anna came up with that. She's an ad exec in Atlanta, and she's a hotshot at it too. Big clients. You know the company that makes those trendy boots that everyone is wearing right now? That's her client. The commercials, the magazine ads, that's her."

Madison tilted her head, not saying a word but smiling from ear to ear.

"Yeah, I know. I'm completely see-through."

She nodded. "You've got it bad."

"Bad enough that it made me stupid and I pushed. But I'm going to fix this. And I'm going to fix the festival too. I can't fail. Not again. Anna believed in the idea, and in me. I'm not going to let her or this town down."

The two of them looked at each other.

"Okay," Roark said. "How?"

"I have two options. One, I go to the shops and tell them what happened, that we didn't get the permit to close the streets, but each can host the festival inside their shops. Or, I confront Crawford about what he's been up to."

Roark opened his mouth, but Dev stopped him.

"You have to trust me on this, Roark. I know he's bled the festival dry. And even if I go around him at first, so the festival isn't delayed, I'm still calling him out. Ms. Hendrix, the office administrator, would get me all of the numbers if I asked nicely."

"I'm sure she would." Madison laughed.

His brother scratched at the back of his neck. "And if you're wrong?"

"I'm not wrong. I *know*, and I've got to trust my gut on this one. You're ration and reason, and I love that about you."

Roark flinched, shock covering his face.

"I know I don't say it much, but I do. I love you, but this situation calls for taking a chance, not being cautious. You're my brother, and I am nothing like you. I used to hate it. I wanted to be you. Mature and respected because you always do the right thing. But I'm not you. I know who I am now, and I might be impulsive, and I screw up on my way to figuring out what's right, but that can be good too. Because I make stuff happen. I made this festival happen. With Anna. We're almost there, and I'm not about to quit now."

Madison smiled and patted Roark's arm as he stood there, still looking shocked. "Which option would you rather go with, Dev?"

"I think talking to the shop owners about making it a sidewalk festival. It's the fastest fix, I'll have more luck with them and . . . and they trusted me with this. They believed in me. I owe them an update on what's happening and, if they'll show me their books, I'd know for certain that Crawford mismanaged funds." He turned to his brother. "If I get the proof, from the stores and from Ms. Hendrix, will you help me? You're the best at accounting. Will you look at the numbers and help me?"

Roark swallowed hard enough to make his Adam's apple bob. "I told you I would. If you're certain he's up to something, then I'm sure he is. I trust your judgment."

His heart punched against his chest.

I trust your judgment.

Until he heard them, he hadn't realized how much those words meant.

Dev had outright denied his need for Roark's approval. Told Anna he wasn't doing any of this for his big brother. Even as he'd said the words, he knew he was lying. Anna would've known too, because she understood Dev. Sometimes better than he understood himself.

"Thank you."

Roark cleared his throat, his hand going to Madison's.

"And the girl?" Madison asked. "Anna."

"I have to get her back, but I don't know how."

"Something tells me you'll figure out a way."

"But if we can help," Roark added, "we will."

Dev looked at his brother and for the first time, Roark had his back, without holding him back. He trusted Dev to go forward with his plan, trusted him to do the right thing.

What's more, Dev trusted himself too.

Chapter 28

Anna read the congratulatory email for the fifth time. Her boss's announcement to the department, singing Anna's praises for the account she won yesterday.

Only two weeks at work and she had an up-and-coming health food chain as their new client. All because of her genius slogan.

Her spark was back. Last week she'd come up with at least three other great slogans and helped an associate with her account. She had the magic again and should be flushed with success, reeling with the triumph.

Instead, she felt nothing.

"Sandwich, salad, fruit cup?" Lucy, the girl from the deli downstairs, made her rounds amid the cubicles, selling lunch to the poor souls who wouldn't, or couldn't, leave their desks for lunch.

Poor souls like Anna.

"Sandwich, salad—oh hey!" Lucy stopped outside her glass-walled office. "You want the usual?"

Anna closed her laptop. "Sure."

Weeks of people tiptoeing around her, shooting her glances of concern mixed with wary judgment, but not a single person had asked how she was doing or said how nice it was having her back.

Even if comments like that were empty social norms, it'd be nice. The people here didn't even bother. They cared a lot about her ideas and closing deals, but they couldn't be bothered to care about her.

Lucy shuffled some sandwiches around on her cart, looking for Anna's turkey on wheat.

"Y'know, I've been meaning to ask, I didn't see you around here for a while. Started to wonder if you'd moved on to bigger and better things."

"I went on vacation."

"Good for you. Must've been a nice one."

"It was." Better than nice. Nice didn't begin to describe what she'd experienced over the last few weeks. Life changing. Altering.

And then she'd run away.

Dev was right. Like a coward, she'd sneaked off in the middle of the night because she was scared. Scared to admit how much she wanted to stay, scared because she didn't have the answers, didn't know what would come next if she stayed.

The office she'd prided herself on now felt like a fishbowl, where everyone could stare at her and wonder why she'd been gone so long. What had been wrong with her? Was she lazy or crazy?

Maybe both. Maybe everything her mother ever said about her was true.

Anna blinked hard and sat up a little straighter. She wasn't going down that spiral. Not right now and not here. "It was very nice. Thank you."

"Cool. I have a few days off myself. Thinking I might go to the beach or something."

"You should. Enjoy yourself."

"Thanks." Lucy took Anna's cash and passed over the carefully wrapped sandwich. "You know, I heard what happened right before you left."

Anna groaned and dropped her chin.

"No, not to embarrass you." She stepped farther into Anna's office. "It's just . . . I've been there and I wanted to say I hope you feel better."

"You've been there?" She glanced up.

Lucy huffed with a laugh. "I'm in med school at night and, before I took on this deli gig, I was trying to work forty hours a week at a nursing home, go to school, and have a life." She rolled her eyes. "I don't know what I was trying to prove or who I was trying to prove it to, but I started getting these headaches, and they checked my vitals at the nursing home. I was dehydrated, low iron, underweight. There I am, supposed to be caring for the sick, and I'm letting myself fall apart. The madness had to stop. My priority was finishing school. So, I put in my notice at the facility and I have this deli job until I graduate. Why overcomplicate things when they can be so simple?"

They shared a look.

"When I quit, my supervisor at the facility told me I couldn't have it all. I'd have to start all over again when I graduated. Low nurse on the totem pole. Like I care? I'd rather start over and stop being unhappy. You know?"

Anna did know. For her though, starting again meant . . . exactly that. In her line of work, she'd have to go to a different agency and ask to work remotely, which they hated, but it did happen, rarely.

She'd be back at the bottom, climbing her way to the top. Having to prove herself all over again, but she would have Dev.

Maybe.

Or she could've lost him forever by leaving.

She rested her head on her hand, suddenly too tired to even hold it up.

"Looks like you could use another vacation," Lucy joked, backing out of her office. "Take care of yourself, okay?"

"I will."

The white paper crinkled as Anna unwrapped her lunch and spread it out on her desk. She did more picking at the bread than eating.

If she were back at Honeywilde, she'd probably be finishing up a long walk or trying her luck in the mosaic-tile class, going to get lunch, either downtown or at the restaurant. Either of which would taste one hundred times better than this turkey sandwich.

Life at a resort wasn't reality, but she'd felt useful and productive, and more than anything, appreciated.

In one swipe of her arm, she shoved the sandwich and paper into her trash can.

An aching loneliness yelled at her from inside.

She couldn't ignore it, drown it out by going right back to work. Didn't matter. The truth was an empty nothingness, threatening to swallow her whole.

She was here and successful—and unhappy.

With a longing that hurt in her chest, she missed Devlin.

Pretending otherwise was pointless. She'd snuck out of Honeywilde in the dead of night, not even brave enough to face him. And she'd said *he* was scared. Ha!

She'd been terrified. Too scared to stay and face him again, and scared to leave. She had no idea what she was doing here. She missed the Anna she was while at Honeywilde. The lightness, the joy, and the love of life.

What was she going to do? Go right back to sixteen-hour days, being the queen of advertising, having late dinners alone in the kitchen? The occasional happy hour with coworkers, pretending she had anything more than a superficial connection with them? They didn't know her any more than she knew them.

Or, she could quit. Make it permanent and official. Leave her job, the work she loved, and resent Dev for making her go.

No, that was pathetic. Why should she have to give up a career she loved to have love, and why should she give up love for her career? Who the hell said she couldn't have it all?

That was her mother's way of thinking.

And it was her mother's opinion that Anna wasn't good enough, would never be good enough to have the things she desired.

But she was wrong.

Anna gritted her teeth. If anyone could find a way to have a job she loved and the man she loved, be hardheaded and persistent enough to make the impossible happen, it was her.

All she needed was a plan, and a way to make a deal with Devlin while they worked out the details.

That was, if he'd even consider taking her back. If she hadn't lost him forever.

"Ms. Martel?" The admin she shared with another exec poked his head into her office. He was right out of college, with wide, hopeful eyes, and she both envied and pitied him for the path that lay ahead.

"Yes."

"You have a delivery."

"Okay. You can bring it in."

"It's, um. It's in the lobby. Security said you'd need to come down. There are too many to bring up."

"Too many what?"

"I'm not sure, actually. They said it looked like bushes."

"Bushes?"

He merely shrugged. "I can go with you to help."

They shared confused looks the whole way down the fifteen floors, but when the elevator doors opened with a ding, and Anna saw what was spread out before her on the lobby's tile floor, she knew.

There had to be a dozen of them, surrounding the security desk, both guards baffled and unamused.

"They . . . these aren't just bushes." She ran her fingers over a cluster of the dark blue berries, hidden beneath some leaves. "They're blueberry bushes."

"Like the kind you eat?"

A laugh bubbled up from her chest. "Yes. The kind you eat."

"Ma'am." One of the security guards approached her. "We need you to sign for them before the driver will go."

Tears burned in her eyes, threatening to spill over. "Of course I'll sign."

The line on the paper was a wobbly blur, her vision cloudy, her cheeks wet.

She wanted to believe this meant something, but what if it didn't? She kept her head down, afraid to let security see how bad her lip was trembling.

She scribbled something resembling her name, all the possibilities tumbling through her mind.

Devlin could be opening the door for her to call him, or this might be his way of making amends. She had no way of knowing. A dozen blueberry bushes had to mean something.

But what?

"Anna?"

A weeping sound escaped her throat.

A voice, painfully familiar and perfect, drew her name out in the delicious way only a Southern drawl could.

With a quick blink and a prayer, she looked up, and found Devlin standing on the other side of her gifts. Long and tall in his jeans, his hair tousled. He stood out amid the suits and shorn hair. He was relaxed, a little rebellious, and everything she'd missed since the moment she left Honeywilde.

"Hey," he said.

She sniffed. "You're here?"

His laugh sounded like he might choke on it. "Took some time to find you, but of course I'm here."

The heat of stares made her neck go warm.

A small audience made up of security, her admin, and some random passersby had gathered.

"Why . . ." With a quick glance that made the onlookers uncomfortable enough to look away, she moved toward Dev. A line of blue-berry bushes stood between them. "Why *of course?*"

Dev's blue eyes shone. "Because you're here."

"But—"

"I was wrong for what I said. For the way I pressured you not to leave. I knew you had to go. You have responsibilities here and you're not the kind of person to shirk those. I should've handled things differently, and I'm sorry."

Anna blinked again. "I should've handled things differently too." She could've been braver, stronger, and told him they would find a way.

He eased a little closer. "I was scared, exactly like you said, but not only about the festival. I was scared I'd fail. Fail you, fail the whole town. So scared that I pushed because I knew if I pushed, I could push you away. Then you were gone and . . . I'd failed anyway."

His blue eyes were wide-open and vulnerable as he told her how he felt. This was Dev with no defenses, and if he was brave enough to take down the last walls, she could be brave enough to jump.

"I want to be with you, and if that means me being here or long distance or whatever, I'll do it. I can be patient and we'll figure it out. If I have to leave Honeywilde, I will."

"No!" She would never let him do that. "You love that place."

"I love you more."

Her vision blurred. She'd never let him, but he'd give up Honey-wilde, just like that, for her. Because he believed in them.

She'd known she loved Dev days before she left, but even love couldn't override her fear, until now. "I love you too. I love you and I was wrong. I was scared and you were right about me being miser-able, but I wasn't strong enough to do anything about it."

"I shouldn't have said what I did about your life here."

"You weren't wrong. Under all of your angry words, there was a lot of truth. I'm not happy here. I'm successful, but I'm not happy. I'm happy with you and I . . . I deserve both."

His smile wobbled. "Damn right you do. And whatever it takes, however many times we fail and have to try again, I'm willing. I don't want to be without you, ever again."

"Me either."

"I know it won't be simple or easy—nothing in my life ever is—but we'll figure it out."

"I know we will. We make a really good team."

"I already have enough regrets to haul around. I'm not adding you to that list. I can't live day after day knowing I didn't go all-in on this with you."

She threw her arms around him. "Me too. All-in is exactly what I want."

Dev kissed her, long and deep, pulling her into him until her feet barely touched the ground. If they still had an audience, she didn't care.

Anna laughed, even though she was still crying. "I have one question though."

He leaned back, brushing her hair away from her face. "What is it?"

"What are we going to do with a dozen blueberry bushes?"

His laughter bounced around the lobby, his smile filling the hollow parts of her heart. "I'm not sure. Maybe bring them with us to the Blueberry Festival?"

Chapter 29

Dev stood at the door of the library's largest meeting room, Anna's hand in his.

"I can't believe Ms. Brenda got all these people to come here tonight without knowing all the details." He looked around the room. Mr. Miller, his daughter Elise, and Jake sat near the front. Della was there with Will and the rest of her family. Pretty much every business owner and their families, along with a few more, filled the room to capacity.

"I can." Sophie poked him between the shoulder blades. "Y'all are in the way. Go inside."

He and Anna moved in and over to the side; Sophie, Roark, Madison, and Trevor were right behind them.

"Are you nervous?" Sophie stood on his other side.

"Who, me? I'm terrified."

"Everything is going to be fine." Madison moved to stand on the other side of Anna.

It'd taken the two of them less than a week to become thick as thieves. Dev got the feeling he and his brother ought to be nervous. If Anna and Madison put their minds together, and teamed up with Soph, the Bradley boys would be outmatched.

Anna turned to him, her smile soothing his jitters. "Are you going to tell me what's going on or not?"

"Shhh." He put his finger over her lips. "The meeting is about to start."

He made his way to the front of the room, Roark right behind him. Dev raised his hands to get the crowd's attention. "If I can have everybody settle down and take a seat."

Once the room grew quiet, he cleared his throat, praying his voice didn't shake. "I'm sure you're all wondering why you're here. I have a few announcements about the festival, which takes place in a couple of weeks, and I have some good news and some bad news."

His gaze met Anna's. She still stood in the back, flanked by Madison and Sophie, Trevor's dark head sticking high above Soph's, and Wright ducking in at the last minute with a wave.

"The bad news first. I wanted to thank all of you for being so supportive and understanding. You all signed the petition to pressure the DOT to get that road-closure permit approved, and your commitment to this event is inspiring. Truly. Unfortunately, the official process is very slow."

There were several boos and moans from the crowd.

Dev put his hand up to get the room quiet. "However, with your cooperation and transparency, and the help of one of Windamere's wonderful citizens"—he smiled at Ms. Hendricks—"my brother Roark and I were able to do some digging into the financial . . . struggles with the past festivals. Some things didn't add up, as many of you suspected."

The entire room began to murmur.

"We approached the tourism office with the same questions some of you are probably asking right now, requesting an official investigation. This was on Thursday. We found out that on Monday, the head of tourism, Mr. Crawford, resigned."

The room filled with gasps and murmuring, cross talk, and a million questions.

He had to get the room to focus again. "I know you all have questions and concerns. We do too. I can't promise you all the answers will be unearthed, but I can promise you, my family is going to continue to dig and pursue this issue until we all have every question answered. But now . . . for some good news . . ."

In the back, Anna still smiled at him. Knowing her, she'd already figured out where he was going with all of this. Excitement and pride rolled off of her, strong enough that he even felt a little proud of himself too.

As he dug into his back pocket for the folded piece of paper, he met Roark's gaze.

His brother nodded, his chin low, biting his lip so he wouldn't grin like a loon and spoil the surprise.

Dev held the paper up high. "In light of the tourism office being investigated, transportation decided to side-step their official appeals process. We got the road closures! Windamere is having *the* Blueberry Festival!"

The room erupted.

Cheers and applause.

Della Maldonado kissed Mr. Miller on the cheek. In the back, his family clapped, jumping up and down, Trevor high-fived half the room, and Devlin could barely see he was smiling so big.

"Y'all need to thank Mr. Graham at the transportation office . . ." Dev had to yell above the happy chatter, and talk through Roark clapping him on the shoulder and jostling him. "He helped get our request approved, on a rush."

No one was even listening to him anymore. They were all too excited.

Having downtown dedicated to nothing but the festival for three straight days was huge. At Anna's suggestion, they'd continued to advertise, even in the face of uncertainty. The businesses had all poured their resources and enthusiasm into the event, and in a couple of weeks, Dev could have a success on his hands.

Someone grabbed his hand, and as he turned around, Anna kissed him. "I can't believe you didn't spill the beans and tell me this week."

"It was killing me. But I wanted to surprise you."

She held his face, her fingers dancing across his jaw. "I'm proud of you."

"I'm proud of us." He kissed her back—this woman who'd believed in him when he didn't. The woman who looked at him like he was wonderful, admirable, worthy of her trust and confidence.

Dev pulled her into his arms and made a vow, right then and there. He'd work every day to be exactly the man Anna saw when she looked at him.

Epilogue

"Shut your face up. Blueberry cotton candy. Who knew?" Sophie shoved a puffy, light blue cloud of spun sugar in Dev's face.

"There's—" With a sigh, he took the cotton candy from her, to get it out of the way. "There's blueberry everything else. Why not cotton candy?"

"Yeah, but it's normally blue raspberry or something fake. Not blue*berry*." She pulled off another fluffy bite and stuck it in her mouth. "Where's your girlfriend?" Her taunting grin was of the annoying variety only little sisters could manage.

"You love saying that, don't you?"

"I love that you're probably going to be the first old married man in the family, yes."

Sophie was right. The way he and Anna were going, and the way his patience didn't hold out for long, he'd probably ask Anna by the end of the year.

Why wait years? When he knew, he knew.

"She got a new account in Asheville, so she drove in to meet with them. But she should be here soon."

She'd been working her ass off for two weeks. As soon as she quit the agency in Atlanta, a head hunter called her about a firm in Charlotte. They knew all about her, and her talent. They didn't care if she worked remote or lived in a mud hut. As long as she came into the office once a week and helped them get the largest accounts from the competition, Anna could do what she wanted.

Including working forty-hour weeks.

Right now she was still averaging about fifty-five, but it was an improvement.

And that's who Anna was. She loved what she did, and now that she could do it on her schedule, she loved it even more.

She was driven, and he wouldn't change a thing about her. Same way she wouldn't change him.

He'd probably propose in the fall, if he could wait that long. Some people would call it impulsive, too spontaneous. But that was him. And those were things Anna loved, and she helped him realize there was no reason to change.

He could be reliable and responsible, and still take risks. Still be Devlin.

"Hey." Roark's head stuck out above a crowd of people swarming the Della's Delights tent.

He waved at someone behind him and eventually he, Madison, and Wright made their way through the throng to join Dev and Sophie on the corner.

"Sorry we're late. I had to run by the tourism office and meet the interim director. Make nice-nice with her."

"Yeah, I had to do that yesterday." Dev greeted his brother by handing over the bite of cotton candy.

After he sweet-talked Crawford's admin into giving him the rest of the committee's financials, she made him promise to come back after they had new staff—not Ms. Hendricks though; she'd work there until retirement, no doubt—and say hello.

Dev met the new interim board members, including Della, who'd volunteered, and tried his best not to look shocked when they asked him if he'd ever be interested in serving.

"Not right now," he'd said. "But maybe someday."

Now that he could believe in himself and those around him.

"What's this?" Wright pointed at the cloud of blue cotton candy in Sophie's hand.

She didn't reply, and Dev side-eyed her as he pulled off a bite for his friend. "Blueberry cotton candy. I don't know that it's up to your culinary standards, but it's good."

Wright shrugged and chewed. "Not bad. I like it."

Sophie took one big, intent step away, cutting a look aside, muttering under her breath. "Yeah, but you'll deny it later."

Fine lines formed at the edges of Roark's eyes as he gave Devlin a hard stare.

Not the stare of decades past, when Devlin had screwed up or got caught making out with the preacher's daughter, but a new kind of stare.

The one they shared when they were on the same page.

Sophie had the friendliest disposition of all of them, so when their little sister grew a chip on her shoulder, it was impossible to miss. For the curt attitude to be directed at Wright though, when they'd always been good friends . . . something was amiss.

"There's your girlfriend." Sophie poked Dev and pointed down the crowded center of Main Street.

Anna approached them, still in her gray summer suit and heels, easily the most overdressed person at the festival.

And he loved that about her.

He wanted to spend the rest of his life with her and her inability to dress down—unless tubing. He wanted her from the moment he fell off a ladder and landed on her, and all she did was laugh.

Laughing, planning, debating, loving, and even arguing with Anna—that's what he wanted. Forever.

"You ready?" he asked her.

"I am."

"Where are y'all off to?" Sophie looked back and forth between them.

"Something we have to do."

She cocked her head to the side. "Right now? Can't it wait?"

He hooked his arm around his sister's neck and drew her in so she had to walk with them as he and Anna left the group. "It's waited long enough. Get a couple of those blueberry cobblers. We'll be back after a while. And tonight, you and I are going to talk."

"About what?"

"You know what. You're not the only one around here who pays attention."

Arms tight around his chest, Anna clung to Dev, her face in the wind.

The knot in her chest, the ache in her heart, they were expected. Normal. Saying goodbye was supposed to hurt, but this time saying goodbye was the right thing to do.

Dev navigated the dirt road carefully and parked his bike near the hidden path to the overlook.

Anna climbed off the bike first. He opened the saddle bag and handed her the plain plastic box.

She curled her fingers around the nondescript box. Something so basic, though it held something precious.

Her heart filled, a sad resolve, like contentment, that only those who grieved understood. Those who'd come through the grief, however long it took, to the other side.

This side meant life and finding happiness, where she could say goodbye while keeping the memories.

She could love and laugh without guilt, and she could let go, knowing life moved on and everything was okay. Life was supposed to move on and keep going. Her father would be happy she'd found her way.

"You want me to stay here or . . . ?"

"No. Will you come with me?"

Dev held out his hand, a look on his face like he'd go with her anywhere. They picked their way down the path, where it opened up to stone and sky.

Anna walked right to the edge, unafraid.

She was strong enough to do this. To stand on the edge and handle the hard parts of life, and come back from them.

With a deep breath, she took the top off the box.

Ashes.

All that was left of her father. Except there was really so much more.

He lived on in her. In her determination and sincerity, in her laughter.

He would've liked Devlin. The fire in Dev's spirit, the way he didn't take anyone's crap, and the kindness he refused to accept any credit for.

If her father could meet him, he'd know she was safe, secure, and loved. He'd be happy for her, because she was happy.

Finally.

Anna scooped her hand into the box and held her hand out.

The wind took him. Blew his ashes across the edge of the rocks, over the mountains, into the valley.

Tears trickled down her cheeks as she let go, fulfilling her father's last wish.

Dev put his arm around her, lending his silent support.

Handful after handful, she gave her father rest, peace, until he was gone.

Gone, but not forgotten.

She didn't leave the edge when she was done. With Dev beside her, she stood stronger. Even with the drop and jagged rocks below, she was safe.

In life, she was going to fall. They'd hit rocky places and nothing would be perfect, but they'd survive. She'd make her way because this was her life. The one she'd chosen, with the man she chose to share it with. Forever.

Because she knew Dev was going to ask for forever. He thought he was sly, but not when it came to her.

What he wanted was written all over his face, now that he'd stopped hiding.

Dev would ask her to marry him, and she'd say yes, and they'd face every mountain and valley, every summit and sunrise. Together.

Please turn the page for an exciting sneak peek of
Heather McGovern's next Honeywilde Romance
A TASTE OF TEMPTATION
coming soon!

Chapter 1

"What's that smell? Is something on fire?"

Sophie cut her eyes at Devlin. "Do you mind? I'm mid-order here." She needed Steve the bartender's wish list so she could place a call to the vendor tomorrow. Then at least this one thing would be off her to-do list. "And I don't smell anything."

She went back to leaning on the bar, writing down what Honeywilde's bartender said he wanted. At the end, she added a few extras, just in case.

One could never have enough swizzle sticks.

"You seriously don't smell that?" Her brother got up from his usual spot at a nearby table.

Like her, Dev preferred doing all of his paper work after hours. He claimed it was the only time he could work without interruption. Yet here he was, doing a fantastic job of interrupting her.

He walked past the bar, scowling and sniffing as he went.

She and Steve shared a look.

All summer long, Dev had been slightly left of center. Dev *lived* left of center, but this summer, even more so. In the weeks since he'd met and fallen in love with Anna, he swung back and forth between being completely distracted by love and totally fixated on random things. To the point that nothing could derail him.

Like right now, and his insistence he smelled smoke.

"I'm telling you, something is on fire." Dev headed to the kitchen.

He'd always had a flair for the dramatic, but Sophie eased off her stool to follow him anyway.

Even on her tippy toes, she could barely see through the swinging doors' small windows into the restaurant's kitchen, but there were no flames or smoke that she could tell. Only Devlin being Devlin.

She rolled her eyes as his pushed open the double doors that lead to the back. "You're imagining things. The kitchen is not—holy shit the kitchen is on fire!"

Sophie bolted through the doors. She pushed past her brother to find the stove engulfed in smoke and white clouds, Wright standing in the midst of it as he doused the open oven with a fire extinguisher.

Her heart jack hammered against her ribs. She opened her mouth to say his name, fear choking off any sound.

Steve rushed in and skidded to a stop beside her.

"I'm okay." Wright turned toward them, answering her unasked question. "Kitchen is okay. I saw the flames in time." He cursed and sprayed the oven with the fire extinguisher one more time, though it did appear any fire was completely out. "That damn thing catching my oven on fire is all." He jabbed his finger toward the racks of the oven.

Sophie couldn't make out what damn thing he meant, because the inside of the oven was all foamy white.

Dev moved closer and glanced inside. "What is it?"

Wright took a step back and slammed the extinguisher down on the prep table. "It *was* a pie. Jesus. About gave me a heart attack."

Him?

Her chest aching, Sophie braced her hands on the other side of the prep table, trying to catch her breath. Her mind hadn't had time to fully comprehend the scene before her. All she knew was Wright and fire, deadly flames, thoughts of him being injured, or worse.

She'd had enough loss for one lifetime. She couldn't handle losing anyone else.

With a steadying breath, she loosened her grip on the table.

Now was not the time or the place to crack up. Wright was fine. A little kitchen mishap.

For over a month now, they hadn't spoken more than a few words to each other, and even then, only if it was necessary for their jobs. She'd frozen him out, with good reason, but the idea of him getting hurt . . .

No. Just, *no.*

"Are you all right?" Dev grabbed Wright's shoulder, looking him over.

There was a time Sophie would've done the same. Without a trace of self-consciousness, she would've put her hands on Wright, reassuring herself he was unharmed, still there for her, unwavering and steady. Her Wright.

But those days were gone.

"I'm fine. Adrenaline kicked in, damn heart is racing and I'm pissed off, but fine."

She managed to make her way to the shelves of glassware, plucked a short tumbler from its spot and, with shaking hands, got water straight from the tap. Mouth dry, if she spoke now, her shakiness and concern would be obvious.

Wright couldn't know how rattled she was. Their friendship embargo was her choice and her doing. Falling apart in front of him all because she thought he was hurt, would demolish the walls she'd put up.

Those walls were there to protect her. They had to stay.

But she had to do or say something. Dev had already given her the inquisition about her and Wright not speaking. If she remained silent after a kitchen fire, he'd be all over her again, wanting to know why.

She refilled the glass again. With a nod, she placed it on the prep table, near Wright.

He stared at her as Dev kept talking, but she was not going to make eye contact.

"What were you baking?" Steve asked.

"The goal was a bourbon-soaked cherry pie."

Dev clapped him on the back. "Man, if you're soaking shit in bourbon, you might be asking for a few flames."

Before, Sophie would've given Wright hell about causing a fire too—or taken any chance to tease or pick at him, as he would with her. She'd have done so out of reflex and never thought twice.

Now, she over-thought every interaction, and there'd be no way she could tease him. The loss twisted the empty spot inside her into a knot.

Too much had happened; too many things had been said between them. Hurtful, angry words that couldn't be taken back. They couldn't return to the role of buddies who joked around with nothing heavy, no real weight, between them.

And, instead of saying the sight of his kitchen, thick with smoke, filled her with fear and panic, she said nothing. Her hands on her ribs like her heart might suddenly break through, she simply stood there. Silent.

Wright lightly shoved Dev, muttering a curse. "It wasn't the bourbon. The butter dripped out of the pan and hit the coils. I made one without any issues, so I wasn't hawk-eyeing the second one."

Dev turned to the unsinged pie, cooling on the counter. "I vote you keep trying. I'm willing to be the guinea pig if you need one."

"I'll keep at it. Minus the flambé." Wright glared at the stove, his jaw tight, hands curled into fists.

He was clearly shaken, and more than a little angry at himself, no matter how much he joked about flambés. He always joked more when something bothered him, and right now he was rattled.

Whether she was mad at him or not, it was her unofficial job in the family, and at Honeywilde, to soothe raw nerves. If she didn't calm the waters, no one would.

She clicked into operations manager mode. "Dev. Steve? We don't want to use the good kitchen towels to clean up once everything cools. Why don't you grab some of the housekeeping towels in storage downstairs?" If she could send Steve and her brother on a task, it'd give Wright a few minutes to bounce back.

"Good idea. You sure you're okay?" Dev checked on his best friend one last time.

"Yeah, man. I'm great. Irritated, but great."

With a laugh and another pat, Dev left, with Steve right behind him.

A moment passed before Wright turned to her, yet didn't meet her gaze. "Thanks for that."

Suddenly, the privacy of the moment was unmistakable. She was alone with Wright, in the kitchen.

A million times they'd been in here, chatting or commiserating, nothing new or unnerving – except for the one time it was.

Lifting her gaze, she studied the top of Wright's bent head.

He was turning the fire extinguisher around; probably berating himself for what he believed was some great failure.

Wright took his work very seriously, and no one was a harsher critic.

"It's a pie. No one got hurt." She pointed out the facts that they both needed to hear.

Wright jerked his chin up, their gazes colliding. "I know. But they could've. I'm a better chef than that. I wasn't paying attention be-cause . . ."

Because of things like what'd happened between them in this very kitchen? Or things like breaking up with his girlfriend immedi-ately after?

"So stupid. I've made dozens of pies."

She hated feeling sympathy for Wright, especially after all that'd happened, but she did.

It wasn't stupid for him to have a lot on his mind. After the break up and how much his parents had probably flipped out about it.

Holy wow, they were hard on Wright. She could imagine the hell he'd caught for not making things work with a girl as perfect as Katherine Hurst.

No—woman. Katherine was not a girl. She probably hadn't been a girl since she was ten years old.

Sophie didn't want to ask. *Shouldn't* ask, but the ugliest part of her – the dark place where she carefully hid her jealousy and resent-ment, any bitterness or other unattractive feelings – had to know.

"Were you thinking about her?"

"No." His answer came quick and Wright chuffed, startling her. "I have more important things to worry about besides all that."

More important things?

Wright's break up with Kate had come fast and hard. Not a friendly parting of ways or even a consolatory, *"Let's still be friends."* Their relationship got nuked in one day, and it'd stunned everyone.

The consensus around town, and the inn, was Kate might be *the one* for Wright. Pretty, sweet, wealthy family to keep his parents happy. Then Wright straight up dumped her.

Sophie had heard all of this secondhand of course, from Dev, since she and Wright were technically no longer speaking.

Some tiny, non-envious part of her actually felt bad for Kate.

Wright had his flaws, and he'd been a complete asshole to Sophie last month, but her family excluded, he was still ten times better than every other guy she knew – which might not be saying much now that she thought about it. Most of the guys in Windamere were dicks.

"Kate and I were finished weeks ago." Wright jerked his gaze away before picking up the extinguisher and placing it back on the wall. "You don't need to worry about me."

"I'm not worried about you." She crossed her arms as she lied.

Of course she was worried about him. She worried about everyone under this roof, but this was Wright.

They'd known each other since the Bradleys adopted her. He was one of her closest friends and they hadn't spoken in over a month.

But he was so aggravating. And talking to him again jumbled her nerves, tilting her off balance. The silent treatment had sucked, but not talking at all was still easier than this.

Before, they could talk about anything. Dates, guys, girls, sports, food, her brother Dev. Nothing was off-limits and nothing was uncomfortable.

Until Wright went and ruined it all.

During the planning of the Blueberry Festival, when Dev was completely consumed and distracted by all things Anna, and everyone was busy planning, she and Wright had taken a sharp left turn into terrain neither of them could navigate.

Now here they were. Wandering, lost, and off track. And it was all Wright's fault.

Six weeks earlier...

Sophie swung her feet, her heels bumping the cabinets under the kitchen's side counter. "Matt might win worst date ever. He didn't get my humor, I could tell he wasn't into me, but he still tried to kiss me. *No.*"

Wright hopped up next to her, ready to run color commentary on her ill-fated love life, same as they always did. "This is your third date. He must be a little into you."

"How do you know it's our third date?"

With a pop of his eyebrows, he shrugged. "I . . . I don't know. Probably because you complained about the other two as well."

And there was the tone; the judgment in Wright's voice when it came to her dating life, and the awful track record.

He wasn't wrong. She had a long list of failed second dates and a guy would have to be nuts to want to be with her, but still, Wright could've dialed it back a smidge.

"Matt isn't into me. He's into getting laid. There's a difference."

"Then screw him." Wright bumped his arm against hers. "I mean figuratively, not literally. If he's that big an asshole, you're better off finding that out now."

They sat close enough together that their arms kept bumping, even when Wright didn't do it intentionally. She could easily rest her head on his shoulder if she wanted to.

Which was only every other day.

With a heavy sigh, she admitted the truth. "He wanted me to be someone I'm not."

"Why would he want you to be someone else? That doesn't make sense."

She asked herself the very same question all the time, but digging for the answer would be too painful to bear.

"I don't know." She tried playing it off. "I could just tell. He wanted a certain kind of girl, and I'm not it."

"What kind of girl are you?"

The kind no one really wants.

"I don't know." She bristled at his concern. Wright had his own girl. A perfect paragon of charm and sophistication, who probably had sex with him every night without a single hang up or ounce of neurosis.

Kate was everything she wasn't, but Sophie wasn't jealous. Their happiness gnawed at her insides, but that wasn't jealousy.

"You don't know?" His question dripped with sarcasm.

"Forget I said anything."

"I thought you wanted to talk about it."

"It's just . . . I don't know. I'm burned out. I'm better off alone anyway. I have my family to worry about. That's enough to deal with."

His arm brushed her again. "You're not better off alone. Everybody needs someone."

"I wouldn't mind being alone." Now that her brothers had someones of their own, she might get a little lonely, but she'd survive.

"Hey." Wright leaned in before turning toward her. He waited quietly until she met his gaze. "You won't be alone unless you want to be. You're great. Matt is the one with the problem."

She had no response. Not only because she vehemently disagreed, but because he was so close. Looking at her like he sometimes did, soulful brown eyes, seeing something special in her. She forgot how to speak.

Her brothers loved her, but as far as romantic relationships, she was terminally solo. A few dates followed by long stretches of a singular existence, her solitude was her choice. It never bothered her until this year. The rest of her family was moving on, finding love and happiness.

Sometimes, she wanted someone in her life. She wanted to be with someone. And that's what scared her.

Being with someone meant letting them in. Too often, letting them in meant losing them.

In the silence, Wright eased closer, putting his arm around her, trying to comfort. "Soph. I mean it. You aren't meant to be alone. Don't say that."

"I'm fine. Probably hormones or something. I don't know."

"Maybe because it's summertime? July is coming up."

She turned to him. "How did you—"

"Come on." His gaze was tender, brown eyes soft with sympathy. "We've lived in the same small town our whole lives. I remember when the accident happened. Everyone remembers."

Her parents' car accident. *Her* accident. Except she was still here, and they were long gone.

"Every summer about this time, you're not really yourself. It's understandable."

Except this *was* herself. This was who she was. Beneath the managerial efficiency and enthusiasm, she was full of doubt. She might be able to run an inn and wrangle her family, but when it came to handling a personal life, she hadn't a clue.

"I was so little when they died." When she'd loved and lost them. "I don't know why this time of year still messes with me. It's stupid."

He tightened his arm around her, tucking her close. A comforting hold that soothed her ragged nerves. "No it is not. They were your parents."

She'd pressed in close, refusing to cry. The anniversary of their death was coming up on twenty two years. What the hell was wrong with her that this time of year still made her nuts?

Wright's warmth and closeness were both things she desperately needed, but would never ask for.

With him, she didn't feel alone.

Theirs wasn't the kind of togetherness she had with her brothers. Never had been. There were times she'd dreamt of them being more than friends. When she was a teenager, again in college, then most recently before he started dating Kate.

Then reality would kick in.

They could never be more than friends. Her family would erupt with the shocking development and his family would have a conniption. Toss in that to Wright, she was first and foremost the Bradley brat sister—romance was never going to happen.

Her consolation was Wright *chose* to be her friend; he didn't have to be. He chose to be with her late at night, fixing the world's problems, and she chose him. It was nice to know that somebody, somewhere liked her for her, and they could be together without fear of everything falling apart.

He'd rubbed her shoulder, his touch light against the top of her head as he brushed over her hair. "You're going to be okay. You're having a bad run of dates and it's a shit time of year, that's all. And, you insist on going out with these losers."

A puff of laughter escaped her, jostling both of them. Didn't he see these losers were the only ones interested?

"Sorry, but it's true. You could do so much better." He kept his arm around her, touching her.

"No I can't."

"Hey." He leaned away, making her look up. "Yes you can. I don't want to hear that kind of stuff from you. Got it?"

Then she wouldn't say more. Didn't mean she wasn't still thinking it.

Wright tucked her back against him, his hand warm on her shoulder. "I'll find you someone. I know some decent guys . . . I think. Who aren't your brothers."

As they sat there, Wright trying to think of someone for her to date, the energy between them began to shift.

The change was so slow, so subtle, that she didn't recognize the difference until it was already upon her.

Wright moved his hand to her hair, threading his fingers through the waves to the ends, caressing her back. And she didn't stop him.

His touch was nice. Gentle.

No, it was more than nice. Her skin tingled, warmth spreading from her scalp, down her neck and over her limbs. She craved touch. *His* touch, and their closeness, even as she knew this wasn't what friends did.

She didn't stop him.

As a matter of fact, her thirteen year old self was jumping for joy. *What if?*
What if she and Wright could be more than friends?
As foolhardy as the thought was . . . what if?
But Wright had been dating Kate for months now. In Windamere, that was grounds to be called a potential fiancée. The women who Wright dated were always sophisticated, stylish.
Sophie felt more like a girl than a woman. Half tomboy, half spastic kid sister. For God's sake, she had freckles and owned one pair of heels.
Wright didn't want someone like her. His track record proved it.
She risked a glance up. He was so close, gaze hooded, and his face even more handsome than usual.
She wasn't oblivious to Wright's good looks. Since she'd come home from college, she'd been even more aware of how truly attractive Wright was.
Good natured, even-tempered, always steady, Wright. Capable of being as goofy as always, but he'd grown into a man. With a rough baritone voice and more rugged features to match, the lanky frat boy she once knew was gone.
In the four years she'd been consumed with college, Wright had been consumed with culinary arts—and catching a severe case of hotness.
Yet, he was still Wright. Like a brother to her, and her brother's best friend. Thinking of him in any way other than platonic . . . it knotted her up inside.
But not necessarily in a bad way.
A thrill rippled through her body.
He touched her hair again, weaving his fingers through the thick waves. He cupped the back of her head, his palm warm and wide against her skull. Then, so gently she almost missed it, he scratched his nails near the nape of her neck.
A shiver shot across her skin and she bit down on her bottom lip.
She wanted to lean into the contact, let him touch her that way, everywhere. Softly drag his nails down her back.
Oh god, she *was* leaning into his touch. Leaning into him.
His hand drifted lower, to the small of her back, as he leaned slightly toward her.

She wanted him to kiss her.

For years, she'd wondered about Wright's kiss. How would it feel? How would he taste?

As he leaned in, she was frozen by her longstanding curiosity, held in place by her desire to have a guy, like Wright, as her own, but knowing she could never actually have *him*.

Wright's lips brushed against hers, tentative at first. When she didn't stop him, he covered her mouth with his, and she whimpered.

He was as warm and sweetly solid as she'd dreamed. Her little noise of need spurred him on, and as he deepened the kiss, all she could manage was to hang on.

She opened to him and Wright swept his tongue inside her mouth, brushing against hers. He sucked at her bottom lip before dipping in again, and Sophie was like putty.

Pressed against him, she gave herself over to the kiss.

This was really happening. It wasn't a daydream or something she conjured up. Wright was kissing her.

He touched her face, fingers dancing across her cheek, then down her neck. He brushed past the buttons of her Honeywilde polo and cupped her breast.

Her begrudgingly small breast.

But he moaned against her lips. A greedy, carnal noise of appreciation, and heat coiled between her legs.

Wright wanted her.

He wanted *her*.

Eagerness and need bolted through her, followed quickly by fear. And guilt.

Wright wasn't hers. He was with someone else. He had a girlfriend. A decent girl. And Sophie was the other woman. She was no better than a homewrecker.

Her muscles went stiff as she jerked away. "What—What are you doing?"

Wright flinched, taking his hands off of her like he'd been burned. In a blur of movement, he was off the counter and on the other side of one of the prep tables. "I don't . . . I wanted to make sure you were okay. I didn't—I didn't mean to do that. I don't know what happened."

"You don't know?"

Wright had a girlfriend. He was not that kind of guy, and Sophie wasn't that kind of girl. He was one of the good ones. In her mind, he would *never*.

But he'd kissed her.

Since when did Wright McAdams kiss *her*?

Sophie slid from the counter and followed. "That was . . . what were we *doing*?"

"Nothing." Both of his hands went up. "I wasn't doing anything."

"You were doing something."

His face drained of color, his eyes going wide before he blinked. A lot. "No, I wasn't."

A honker of a lie if she'd ever heard one and her brain zig-zagged between excitement and disgust, elation and devastation.

If Wright wanted to kiss her, she couldn't be a total loss. He dated these perfect women and he was pretty close to perfect himself.

Except . . . if he wanted to kiss her, then really, he was far from perfect. Guys with girlfriends didn't kiss other girls. They especially didn't kiss their best friend's little sister.

There was no winning ticket here, no matter how she looked at it. Either he hadn't planned on kissing her and she did it, and she was slowly losing her mind, or he'd kissed her, and was destroying the pedestal she'd put him on.

Sophie's stomach dropped. "You kissed me. I know you kissed m—"

"No." Wright gave her a hard look. "I would never kiss you."

"I got the towels." Dev hurried back into the kitchen, dragging Sophie into the present, a knot in her throat from the memory.

Same kitchen, a totally different night, but her friendship with Wright was still in tatters.

She *had* to let go of that night and the look he'd given her. Really, she needed to let go of all of it.

The warmth of his arms, the solid caress of his touch. They'd kissed for maybe ten seconds, and even that was a stretch, but everything was different now.

"Thanks, Dev." Wright took some towels and headed to the sink.

For weeks, she'd nurtured the hurt and betrayal, and feeding it had only made the bitterness grow. Since she'd been crystal clear how furious she was with him, Wright barely spoke to her, leaving a gaping hole where his presence should be.

She didn't like living this way. This version of who they were now, stilted and awkward, withdrawn from each other's lives, hurt as much as him saying he would never kiss her.

The solution was simple. She could stop turning that moment over and over in her mind and try to forget. Rehashing did no one any good anyway.

If she forgot about the kiss, then they might be able to move forward.

She could help him clean up the kitchen, fix the mess from his fire, do her best to keep things casual and light from now on, and maybe things would be okay between them again. Somehow.

The two of them would never be more than friends, but they could at least stop being enemies.

ABOUT THE AUTHOR

Heather McGovern writes contemporary romance in swoony Southern settings. While her love of travel and adventure takes her far, there is no place quite like home. She lives in South Carolina with her husband and son, and a collection of Legos that's threatening to take over the house. When she isn't writing, she's working out, or bingeing on books and Netflix.

She is a member of Romance Writers of America, as well as Carolina Romance Writers, and she's represented by Nicole Resciniti of The Seymour Agency.

Connect with Heather on her website, Facebook, Twitter, or her group blog. She'd love to hear from you!

heathermcgovernnovels.com
www.facebook.com/Heather.McGovern.Novels
https://twitter.com/heathermcgovern
https://badgirlzwrite.com

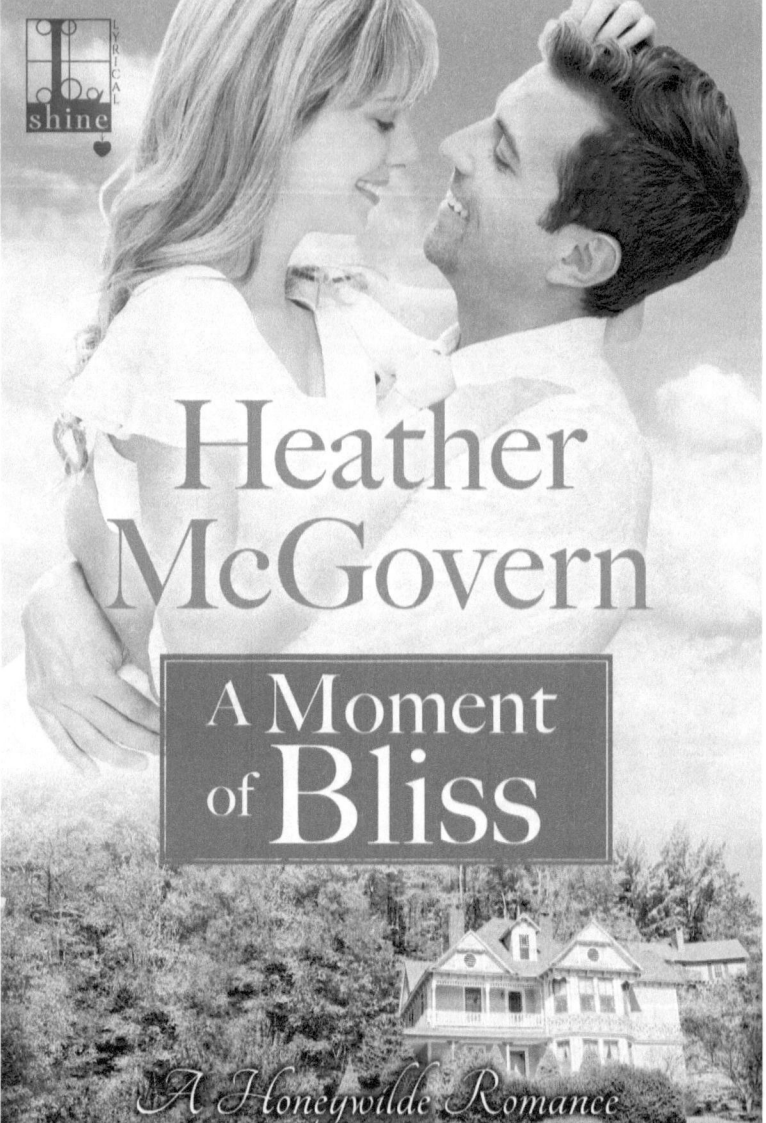

Heather McGovern

A Moment of Bliss

A Honeywilde Romance